SF Books by Vaughn Heppner:

DOOM STAR SERIES
Star Soldier
Bio Weapon
Battle Pod
Cyborg Assault
Planet Wrecker
Star Fortress

EXTINCTION WARS SERIES
Assault Troopers
Planet Strike

INVASION AMERICA SERIES
Invasion: Alaska
Invasion: California
Invasion: Colorado
Invasion: New York

OTHER SF NOVELS
Alien Honor
Accelerated
Strotium-90
I, Weapon

Visit www.Vaughnheppner.com for more
information.

Invasion: California

(Invasion America Series)

by
Vaughn Heppner

ISBN-13: 978-1496124296
ISBN-10: 1496124294
BISAC: Fiction / Science Fiction / Military

"All war is based on deception."

-- From: *The Art of War*, by Sun Tzu (c. 544-496 B.C.)

Preface

Invasion: California is a story about disastrous events. It postulates a world teetering on the brink of starvation due to glacial cooling.

It is a "what if" story. What if the farmable land in the world shrank dramatically, and what if American earth became one of the most precious commodities left? What if other countries—led by Greater China and its Pan-Asian Alliance—decided it was going to conquer U.S. soil? Lastly, what if America no longer dominated world affairs due to a sovereign debt depression and other, mostly self-inflicted, wounds?

Interestingly, there is a historical precedent for continental-sized conquest fought with the latest technology. The Third Reich made the attempt a little over seventy years ago in World War II.

At the start of Operation Barbarossa in 1941, Germany set out to conquer European Russian. In terms of depth, the final objectives were just short of the Ural Mountains. In America, that would be the distance from the East Coast to Kansas City, Missouri.

The Germans' gigantic conquest began along a 1,720-mile front stretching from the Barents Sea in the north to the Black Sea in the south. Again, in American terms, that would be from the northern border of Maine all the way down to the southern tip of Florida.

The Germans invaded with approximately three million soldiers, while the Russians defended in the theater with slightly fewer. By 1943, Germany fielded almost four million

1

troops there, while Russia had put over 6.7 million soldiers in place. Incredible as it may seem, by war's end, the Russians had lost 14.7 million military dead. Some people estimate that their total dead and missing—military and civilian—was 35 million. Those are horrifying numbers, beginning to sound like nuclear war casualties.

What does any of that have to do with *Invasion: California*? In attempting to envision foreign powers invading North America, I used as one of my guides the titanic conflict of World War II, particularly between Germany and Soviet Russia. I suspect that in a future war of such scale, millions of soldiers would march to battle once again.

Invasion: California is fiction about a future I hope none of us ever has to face. Nevertheless, if present trends continue…who knows what will happen by 2039.

Timeline to War

1997: The British return Hong Kong to the People's Republic of China.

2011: China reviews its one-child per family policy begun in 1978 and decides to continue it. This increasingly creates an overabundance of boys as families abort a higher percentage of girls.

2012: China carries much of the U.S. National Debt and continues to sell America a vast surplus of finished goods.

2016: The American banking system and stock market crashes as the Chinese unload their U.S. Bonds. The ripple effect creates the Sovereign Debt Depression throughout the world.

2017: Siberia secedes from a bankrupt Russia.

2018: Scientists detect the beginning of a new glacial period that is similar to the chilly temperatures that occurred during the Black Death period of the Middle Ages.

2019: The Marriage Act is passed. As the Chinese men greatly outnumber the women, special government permits are needed before a man is allowed to marry a woman.

2020: Due to new glaciation, there are repeated low yields and crop failures in China and elsewhere. It brings severe political unrest to an already economically destabilized world.

2021: An expansion-minded Socialist-Nationalist government emerges in China. It demands that Siberia return the Great Northeastern Area stolen during Tsarist times. It also renews calls for reunification with Taiwan.

2022: The Sovereign Debt Depression—and an ongoing civil war in Mexico—create political turmoil in America, particularly in the Southwest. There is an increase in terrorism, secessionist movements and a plummeting Federal budget. All American military forces return home as the U.S. grows isolationist.

2023: The Mukden Incident sparks the Sino-Siberian War. Chinese armies invade. The ailing Russian government ignores Siberian cries for military aid. America's new isolationism prevents any overseas interference.

Modernized equipment and an excessive pool of recruits eager to win marriage permits bring swift victory to Chinese arms over Siberia. It annexes the Great Northeastern Area. Siberia becomes a client state.

2024: Aggressive posturing and long-range aircraft stationed on the Chinese coast cause the aging U.S. Fleet to retreat from Taiwan. China invades and captures Taiwan. Its navy now rivals the shrunken USN.

2026: Newly discovered deep oilfields in Prudhoe Bay, Alaska prove among the world's largest.

2027: The civil war in Mexico worsens. The bulk of America's Homeland Security Forces now stand guard on the Rio Grande.

2028: The continuing modernization of the oil industry in Siberia, the Great Northeastern Area and in the South China

4

Sea turns Greater China into the largest oil-producing nation in the world. China begins to dictate OPEC policies.

2030: The cooling trend worsens, bringing record winter temperatures. New energy sources cannot keep pace with increasing demand. American energy hunger sweeps away the last environmental concerns. All possible energy sources are exploited.

2031: Harsher weather patterns and growing world population causes greater food rationing in more countries. The main grain exporting nations—Canada, America, Argentina and Australia—form a union along similar lines as OPEC. China warns it may cut America off from all oil supplies unless it is given priority status for grain shipments.

2032: China experiences the worst rice harvest of the Twenty-first century. New rationing laws are instituted. Internal unrest rises to dangerous levels as Party officials seek new food sources. *Invasion: Alaska.* The Chinese attack in order to cut off America's main oil source and force the U.S. into favorable food-for-oil trades.

After the armistice, there is growing world furor over the nuclear-tipped torpedoes used in the Alaskan War. Greater China places harsh economic sanctions on the U.S. The German Dominion, the Brazilian-led South American Federation and the Iranian Hegemony soon follow suit.

2033: The Mexican civil war reignites. The SNP—the Socialist-Nationalist Party—seeks Chinese help. Chinese military advisors arrive.

Glacial cooling continues to devastate worldwide crop yields. Led by Brazil and backed by Greater China, the South American Federation declares war on Argentina, a Grain Union member.

2034: Hostilities end with Buenos Aires's capture by Brazilian forces. Argentina leaves the Grain Union and joins the South American Federation.

Continuing sanctions cripple U.S. recovery efforts. Domestic terrorism and secessionist threats increase as political turmoil worsens—the Democrats and Republicans demonize each other, bringing gridlock.

With increasing Chinese military support, the SNP rapidly gains ground in the Mexican Civil War.

2035: Colonel Cesar Valdez seeks American assistance and safe havens for his Free Mexico Army. Mexican President Felipe asks for greater Chinese assistance. China accelerates its troop buildup in Mexico.

Continuing poor crop yields and increasing starvation leads to the creation of the Pan Asian Alliance (PAA). This includes Greater China and most of Southeast Asia. Military preparations are begun for an Australian Invasion.

Hawaii now erupts with racial violence. The Hawaiian Nativist Party seeks independence from "supremacist" America.

2036: China's Thirteen Demands are read in the U.N. Amid the worsening glaciation, they find massive appeal. Demand # 1: America and its Grain Union allies must distribute their abundance equally throughout the world. Demand #2: America must accept third party nutrition inspectors at its granaries and warehouses.

The Hawaiian rebel government seeks foreign help. China sends an invasion fleet. America sends its carriers. The Chinese launch a surprise attack on American satellites and other space assets, combining it with a massive cyber-assault on the U.S. Crippled by the cyber-attack on their datalinks, the American fleet is destroyed in the Battle of Oahu.

General Sims—the former Joint Forces Commander in Alaska during the Chinese invasion—runs as an Independent and wins the Presidency. He signs the Non-Nuclear Use Treaty, pledging that America will never again use nuclear weapons first. He also agrees to begin food shipments through the Chinese-dominated U.N. Some economic sanctions against America are lifted. At the same time, the President declares a state of emergency and begins construction of the Rio Grande Defensive Line due to the 700,000 PAA troops in Mexico.

2037: Seeking to escape forced induction into the South American Federation, the Cuban dictator asks for German Dominion military assistance. The first GD airmobile brigade arrives in Cuba.

Terrorists detonate a low-yield nuclear weapon in Silicon Valley, destroying much of the critical American high-technology center. Evidence points to Chinese involvement.

By the end of the year, the PAA's Mexico-occupation troops number two and a half million. Free Mexico Army assassins kill Mexican President Felipe.

2038: Claiming American provocations, China accelerates its troop buildup. Over four million soldiers occupy Mexico. The first South American Federation troops arrive.

President Sims orders a preemptive satellite assault, using the strategic ABM lasers to knock out all foreign objects that enter American space. He cuts off all grain tribute to the U.N.

The PAA, the SAF and the GD sign a secret accord against America.

2039: Nearly six million PAA troops occupy Mexico, combined with three million SAF troops. The GD moves the bulk of its long-range hovers into Cuba.

-1-
The Stumble

SAN JUAN BASE, MEXICO

The stumble into war began in the bedroom of Colonel Peng of the Fifth Transport Division. He lay naked on top of Donna Cruz, a Mexican teenager with raven-colored hair and the sensual moves of a serpent. The moment of ecstasy quickly arrived and Peng cried out in release.

He rolled off her, yawned and closed his eyes. No wonder soldiers volunteered for duty in Mexico. Yes, war loomed, but the abundance of willing and attractive females in this land was truly staggering. Peng had never won a marriage permit as Chinese law dictated. He wondered if that had been a mistake.

"Colonel?" the girl asked. "Are you asleep?"

He opened his eyes. She sat beside him. What marvelous breasts and such a flat stomach with its outie bellybutton. Oh. The flatness of the stomach was because she seldom had enough to eat.

The rationing in Mexico was strict. The country's painfully-grown crops first fed the "invited" soldiers protecting the Socialist-Nationalist Revolution. That meant nearly ten million mouths, ten million hungry foreigners. Afterward, the Mexican government employees took precedence, the Mexican Home Army and then munitions workers. Every Mexican possessed a ration card. Peng's young temptress had a third class card, no doubt why she supplemented her lifestyle as his girlfriend.

Does she have other "boyfriends?"

"Colonel?" she asked again.

It was atrocious Chinese, but at least she could speak it. Actually, it was much better than most Mexicans achieved.

Peng yawned, idly wondering why he became so sleepy after doing it.

"Do you have a present for me, Colonel?" she asked, smiling as she batted her eyelashes.

"Yes. It's in the third drawer, my dear. I have a package for you. Why don't you get it?"

She scooted off the bed. Peng raised his head to examine her wonderful butt. It swayed seductively as she padded across the floor. Only in Mexico could he have won such a beauty.

She opened the third drawer and squealed with delight, taking out a large package wrapped in red paper.

"It's heavy," she said.

"I have sausages, whiskey for your father and other delicacies for you. There are also several hundred pesos within."

"You are kind to me."

He closed his eyes and lay back. Kindness had nothing to do with it. He was a supply officer and had learned a long time ago that spreading delicacies around solved many problems, including a loveless life. Let the fighters win glory on the battlefield. He would use his position to "buy" what he needed.

"I can return four days from now," she said. It was a long bicycle ride from Mexico City where she lived. He had been thinking about purchasing a room for her nearby. Many officers did that, but Peng had been saving his money, sending it to his aging mother in China.

Peng smiled as he became increasingly sleepy. Four days from now and he would neigh like a stallion as he enjoyed another night with this amazing creature. Yes, four days and— he frowned.

"Is something wrong?" she asked.

9

Through the mattress, he felt her climb back onto the bed. Her warm hands rubbed his chest. She always told him how she loved his smooth skin. It wasn't hairy like a gorilla.

"I'm going to be busy four days from now," Peng told her.

"Oh," she pouted, taking away her hands.

Peng yawned. It was getting hard to stay awake. "I'm going to be very busy moving Blue Swan. Another shipment arrives, from Japan this time."

"Couldn't you get away for just a little while?" she asked. "I really want to see you again, Colonel."

Peng smiled faintly. The girl was amazing in bed but otherwise unimaginative. She never seemed to understand he had tasks to perform.

"No, my dear," he mumbled, beginning to fade away. "I have to oversee everything." She probably couldn't understand that. "Blue Swan is critical," he explained. "It is the can opener that will pry apart American defenses. It would be my death to slip away to see you, delightful as that would be. I…"

Colonel Peng's head tilted until his right cheek sank against the pillow. He drifted to sleep. Thus he never saw Donna Cruz stare at him in amazement.

MEXICO CITY, MEXICO

The next night, Daniel Cruz stared bleary-eyed at his teenaged daughter. She paraded through their tiny living room in a red dress. She was stunning, his daughter. It amazed Daniel that he had ever produced such a pretty girl with such long, raven hair.

"Where did you find the money to buy that?" he asked.

She frowned.

It hurt Daniel's heart to see that. He should have told her how beautiful she looked. It's what he would have told his wife. She had died three years ago. Everything had gone sour afterward: his wife dying and his daughter learning to whore herself out to the Chinese. He knew where she'd "earned" the money to buy a red dress like that.

Daniel picked up a glass, swirling the brown-colored whiskey at the bottom. He sipped, letting the alcohol slide down his throat. A moment later, the pleasant burn and the numbing in his mind began. This was good whiskey, better than he'd had in a long time.

"You're pretty," he muttered.

Donna swirled on her toes. She had such slender legs, perfectly muscled from all the bicycling she did. Wherever she rode, Daniel knew his daughter turned heads.

"Do you sleep with them?" he asked bitterly.

Anger flashed in her eyes. She strode to the nightstand and grabbed the whiskey bottle by the neck. "I brought you this! Drink it and drown your sorrows. But do not ask me what I do as if you're a shocked priest. You work for them, Papa! I work for them! So do not judge me."

Daniel wanted to surge up and slap her across the face. He had bad knees, hobbling like an old man wherever he went. Bicycling to the office every day only made his knees worse. They popped and crackled horribly when he pedaled. He held out his glass to her, deciding silence would be his whip.

She poured, slammed the bottle onto the nightstand and strode across the living room. Before leaving, she whirled around. "You should thank me and you should thank Colonel Peng for his generous gifts."

Daniel sipped whiskey, looking away. He would ignore her. She knew better; thus, he would let her own conscience whip her.

"The colonel is an important man!" she declared.

Daniel snorted. They were always important.

"He's in charge of Blue Swan," Donna said.

"Birds?" asked Daniel, letting his voice drip with mockery.

"No! Blue Swan is the can opener that will pry apart the American defenses."

Daniel's head swung around. With the whiskey in him, it felt like a long journey. He stared at Donna, standing there so fiery, with her fists on her hips.

"What did you say?" he asked.

"They're from Japan," she declared. "He's moving them. He is very important, Papa, and he loves me."

11

Daniel blinked heavy eyelids. He knew this Colonel Peng. His office in the city had dealings with Chinese supply, in charge of traffic control. Daniel worked in the Mexican government, what had become the puppet régime for the foreigners. Once he had believed in the SNP. Now his wife was dead and his daughter slept with the enemy. She had become little more than a whore. Even though he loved her dearly, he recognized the truth. Because he made too little money and drank too much, he couldn't give her what she needed and had to take what she gave.

"Drink your whiskey," she said, interpreting his silence the wrong way.

"Donna," he whispered.

She ran from the living room. Seconds later, the front door slammed as she fled the apartment.

Daniel stared at the glass with the brown-colored whiskey. It was Japanese, too, the alcohol. What his daughter had just told him...if it was true...

He grabbed the bottle from the nightstand and as carefully as possible, he poured the whiskey in his glass back where it belonged. A few drops spilled onto the carpet, but that couldn't be helped. He corked the bottle, set it on the nightstand and went to the fridge. He drew two bottled waters, opening the first and beginning to guzzle. Tomorrow, he needed to be as sober as possible.

Afterward and in a daze, he went to bed. Sleep proved difficult. Five times, he woke up, shuffled to the bathroom and dribbled into the toilet. He hated being old.

In the morning he ate a tasteless burrito, shaved his face with a shaking hand and chose his cleanest uniform.

He pedaled through the city, listening to his knees crackle and pop. He had to ride slowly; otherwise, the pain became too intense. Thousands pedaled with him, hordes on two wheels. At a thirty-story glass tower, Daniel parked his bike in an outer rack, locking it with a chain.

He took an elevator to the twelfth floor. There he worked diligently in his office, only later finding an excuse to head to the fourteenth floor and speak there with Pedro, who was in charge of scheduled routes in the countryside. Pedro was an old friend from elementary school, so many decades ago.

In a storeroom with a single bulb in the ceiling they played checkers. The ivory pieces had an unusual heft to them and were always cool to the touch. The design etched onto the backs showed the ancient Castilian crown from the old country. The ivory pieces came from Daniel's grandfather, inherited at his death. Pedro and Daniel usually played around this time.

After moving a piece, Daniel looked up and told Pedro, "I had forgotten, my friend, that you introduced me to my wife."

"That was long ago," Pedro said as he eyed the board.

"Hmm. It is our anniversary today." That was a lie, but Pedro would never know. "Since my wife is gone, I wanted to celebrate with someone. Would you share this with me?" Daniel asked. He produced the whiskey bottle, which was three-fifths full.

Pedro looked up and his eyes widened. He grinned. He had a silver-colored crown among his yellowed teeth. Pedro was an alcoholic, although he'd never admitted that to anyone, certainly not to himself. "Just a quick sip, si?" Pedro asked.

"Yes, a quick one," Daniel agreed.

A half hour later, the bottle was empty, Pedro having consumed most of it.

"Oh," Daniel said, as he shelved the game in its hiding spot. "I just remembered. Senor Franco is planning a surprise inspection today."

"You lie!" Pedro said.

"I'm only wish it were so."

"He'll smell the whiskey on me."

"I'm sorry, my friend," Daniel said. "If Franco is coming, I must leave for an early lunch."

"Yes, yes, an excellent idea," Pedro said.

The two men departed from the storeroom. Pedro hurried to his office down the hall. Daniel went in the other direction, turned the corner and waited. After ten minutes had passed, Daniel headed for Pedro's office. Upon his entrance the secretary looked up, an old lady whose son, Senor Franco, ran the department.

13

"I forgot my keys in Pedro's office," Daniel said. He meant the keys to his bike-chain and apartment.

Mrs. Franco indicated that he could go in and retrieve his keys.

Daniel entered the office, leaving the door ajar so she wouldn't become suspicious. Despite her inquisitive nature, old Mrs. Franco was absent-minded and would likely forget about him soon. She was playing a computer game and she often spent hours at it, building her internet farm.

After a short wait and taking a deep breath, Daniel sat down at Pedro's desk. The swivel chair creaked and Daniel paused, but Mrs. Franco did not come in to investigate.

As he'd hoped, Pedro's computer was still on. Daniel pressed a key and the screen awoke. For the next twenty minutes, Daniel examined scheduled route shutdowns. Pedro was in charge of them, meaning certain routes and roads were closed to civilian and sometimes to Mexican Home Army usage. During those times the Chinese Army used the roads and routes, often for "secret" convoys.

Daniel searched, and he discovered a route from the main port at Baja Bay to the First Front on the Californian-Mexican border. The route used a code word. From experience, Daniel knew the Chinese often used the main article being ferried as the code. This route word or code was "Blue Swan."

Daniel's heart thudded. According to Donna, this was a secret weapon, one critical to smashing the vaunted American defenses on the border.

With shaking hands, Daniel took out a pencil and paper, copying the route information. Several minutes later, he shut off the computer, said good-bye to Mrs. Franco and headed to his office one floor down.

He would compose a carefully worded report and leave it at a letter-drop near Santa Anna Park. His control was a Swiss national in the ambassador's office. Daniel believed the man was actually a CIA case officer. Whoever he was, the man paid well for good information, which helped Daniel buy cheap whiskey. More importantly, with this he hoped to hurt the Chinese, to strike back at the foreigners who had corrupted his beautiful young daughter.

LANGLEY, VIRGINIA

Anna Chen rubbed her eyes. They were gritty from too much reading and too little sleep. She sat in front of an e-reader in a cubicle in the Central Intelligence Agency, one of the analysts working the night shift.

She had come down a long way in the world since President Clark's reelection defeat after the Alaskan War seven long years ago. From working on the President's staff Anna had fallen into unemployment. This was due to her membership in a new undesirable caste in America: those of half-Chinese ancestry. It had been a rude shock.

Years ago, she had written *the* tome on the Chinese: *Socialist-National China.* It had been a bestseller, had won her a professorship at Harvard and then a spot on President Clark's staff. None of that mattered now. She was half-Chinese. In besieged America that made her suspect. It didn't help that Tanaka—her former bodyguard/lover—had died defending her in Obama Park. Tanaka had killed three muggers, shooting two in the head and breaking the neck of the third. The fourth had stepped out from behind a bush, shot Tanaka in the back and stolen Anna's purse.

Sitting in her CIA cubicle, Anna rubbed her eyes harder, blinked several times and concentrated on the reports. A lamp provided light and several computer scrolls waited for her use. If there was anything in a report she didn't understand, Anna looked it up.

Her life had spiraled from one tragedy to another. After her mother's death, Anna had begun a blog on Chinese affairs, winning syndication on National News Internet (NNI). The mass Chinese cyber-assault three years ago in 2036 had ended that. The nuclear terrorist attack in Silicon Valley had ripened the latent Chinese racism into ugly fruit indeed. The only bright spot had been the election of President Sims. They said he was superstitious, in a baseball sort of way. Keep everything the same, if you could, when you won the big game. She had been in the government during the Alaskan War that Sims had

15

won. Therefore, after gaining an interview with him, Anna had received employment with the CIA, as a lower grade analyst. It was better than unemployment and she was good at analyzing and interpreting data.

Anna sipped tea and leaned back so her chair squealed. She reached up and undid her hair. It was long and dark. She opened a drawer and took out a brush, letting the bristles run through the long strands.

She was seven years older since the Alaskan War. Yet she was still slender, keeping fit primarily because of her sparse diet and her pedal-power plan. In her apartment, she supplemented the energy requirement—provided by a nearby coal station—through stationary cycling. She also practiced the martial arts techniques Tanaka had taught her, which kept her amazingly limber.

She missed Tanaka. It was a hole in her heart. Would there ever be a man like him again for her?

Her brushing hand froze. Anna sat up, removed the brush from her hair and set it on the desk with a soft clunk. She concentrated on the report.

Clicking the e-reader, going back two pages, she noticed it came from Mexico City. From the beginning now, Anna read the report slowly. Was this right? The Chinese were moving a convoy to the front near the Californian border. The convoy carried Blue Swan.

"Blue Swan," Anna whispered. "Where have I seen that before?"

She continued reading and wondered how this person code-named "Spartacus" had known "Blue Swan" was important to the Chinese. There was something missing in the report. She could feel it. It was rated "Yellow." That meant it was considered third class and only slightly reliable.

Anna swiveled her chair and used a computer scroll's touch screen. America was a land of great contrasts these days. Coal fed much of the nation's energy needs and yet some places used the latest technology. Anna put in Spartacus' name and read other reports written by him.

Why is this one coded "yellow?" Spartacus had proven reliable in the past.

16

Anna typed in "Blue Swan," watching the words build on the screen. After typing the "n," a little yellow note-symbol appeared in the left-hand corner. She moved the cursor over the "note" and clicked. Hmm, it was a reference saying "Blue Swan" concerned Chinese R&D. Where had the note originated?

She attempted to find out. Seconds later, her screen flashed red and the words appeared, *sorry, classification exceeds user clearance level.*

Anna sat back, picked up her teacup, sipped and grimaced. The tea had become cool. She liked hers hot.

So, what do I do? Let this go or make waves trying to find out what this "Blue Swan" is?

Anna sat staring at the e-reader. Slowly, she clicked back to the beginning of the report. She wished Spartacus had been more honest and put in exactly how he'd come to suspect Blue Swan.

How important is this?

If it proved to be insignificant, eyes might raise and suspicions become whetted. Why did the half-Chinese woman seek higher clearance? Her position in the CIA was tenuous at best.

"I'm an American," Anna whispered to herself. "This is my country." Each person had to fight his or her personal battles in life. Some had physical ailments, others fought psychological problems and some had to walk uphill against racism or ageism. She had found it better to do and struggle than to accept these limitations.

Standing, blowing out her checks, Anna picked up the e-reader and headed for her boss's office. She passed others in their cubicles, reading reports, typing or eating a snack. A few looked up. Two nodded a greeting.

Anna reached the door, hesitated and let her delicate knuckles rap against wood.

"Enter," a man said. Ed Johnson was the chief analyst of the nightshift. He had gray hair and wore a white shirt and tie, one of the old guard. She had heard others say before that Johnson didn't like her.

"Yes?" Johnson asked, scowling up at her.

Anna hesitated.

Johnson's scowl grew, and he eyed her up and down.

Anna felt soiled by it, remembering how Tanaka's killer had looked her up and down that night in the park. With the smoking gun in his hand—the one that had shot Tanaka in the back—the murderer had stepped up and snatched her purse. His eyes had lingered hungrily. She'd seen his desire to rape. It had frozen her. For months afterward, she had stood before a full-length mirror at home, practicing what she should have done.

At his desk, Ed Johnson scowled, eyeing her as if she was a piece of meat to devour. She wasn't going to accept it.

With a force that surprised her, Anna slapped the e-reader onto Johnson's desk. "I'd like you to read this," she said.

His gray eyebrows lifted. Maybe he hadn't expected such forcefulness. He took the e-reader and went through the report. When he was done, he set the e-reader down, turned it to face her and shoved it across the desk to her.

"Did you see the reporter's grade?" he asked.

"Third, yes," she said. Anna explained about the "Blue Swan" reference to Chinese R&D and that its classification was higher than her clearance.

"What am I supposed to do about it?" Johnson asked.

"Give me higher clearance so I can properly analyze the data."

He folded his thick fingers together, staring at her. He shook his head. "I can't do that, Ms. Chen."

"Then phone someone who can."

"Are you trying to tell me how to do my job?"

"I'm trying to do what's best for my country. I think this could be important. Obviously, Spartacus left out a critical piece of information. It's the R&D information that I need to see in order to make a better-informed judgment on what he is telling us. This is time-sensitive data."

Johnson's scowl intensified, and he nodded now. "You're gambling. You have the guts to back up your gamble, to barge in here and try to face me down. Okay, little girl, I call and raise your stakes. You want to burn yourself, go right ahead."

18

Ed Johnson, Chief CIA Analyst of the nightshift, put a call through to his superior. He told him the pertinent information, nodded, saying "yes, sir," and handed the phone to Anna.

She found herself talking to the Director himself. Anna stared at Johnson. He grinned like a shark.

"I'm hope this is important," the Director said. "Sleep is a precious commodity, and Johnson's call has just stolen some of mine."

"Yes, sir," Anna said. She explained the situation once again.

"Anna Chen," the Director said, "the Anna Chen on Clark's staff, the one who tried to warn him about the Alaskan Invasion?"

"Yes, sir," Anna said.

"I've read your file. You have good instincts. Hand the phone back to Johnson."

Anna did.

Johnson listened, and his eyebrows thundered. "Yes, sir," he said, hanging up afterward.

"Round one goes to you, Ms. Chen," Johnson said. "You have provisional clearance until I say otherwise. I'm adding the condition that you can only look at it here with me."

Soon, in a chair to the side, Anna read the Chinese R&D report. Johnson informed her it came from the Yuan Ring, a spy high in the Chinese military. The informant didn't know what "Blue Swan" was specifically, but it was supposed to be a weapon of special significance against American defenses.

Anna looked up. "Sir, I think you'd better listen to what I have to say."

"Is that so?" Johnson asked.

"If you don't think so," she said, "call up the Director again."

Johnson decided to listen to Anna. Afterward, he told her, "Are you sure you want to raise the stakes again?"

"Aren't you?" she countered.

Johnson shrugged, and he called the Director. The Director listened to Anna and then asked to speak to Johnson. Shortly thereafter, two security officers escorted Anna to a waiting car. They drove to Special Operations Command (SOCOM) so

19

Anna could speak to General Ochoa. All American commandos fell under his orders. That included Green Berets, Rangers, Delta, SEALs, Air Commandos, Psyops, and Marine, Force Recon and Civil Affairs and special aviation units.

Rain struck the windshield of Anna's car. The water distorted the street lights shining into the darkened vehicle as the tires hissed over wet pavement. One of the security officials drove, allowing Anna to read more about the Yuan Spy Ring in Beijing. After speaking with the Director a second time, she'd gained a higher security clearance.

The clock was ticking on Spartacus' data and the Director wanted to make a stab at finding out what made "Blue Swan" so important.

BAJA PENINSULA, MEXICO

In the swelter of an unusually hot Mexican night, Paul Kavanagh's shoulders ached because of his heavy rucksack. His thighs burned as he stormed up a stony hill. With the ruck, special weapons, extra ammo, canteens and equipment, he lugged over eighty-seven pounds. It had been a grueling march since the insertion, sixteen miles of rough terrain and a Chinese patrol they'd had to avoid.

I'm getting too old for this.

The stars shone like hot gems, made more prominent by the moon's absence. The air was raw going down Paul's throat and sweat kept trickling under his night vision goggles. He lifted the device and wiped his stinging eyes.

Because of that, Paul tripped over a hidden rock. He stumbled, his equipment clattering, and he went to one knee at the top of the hill. He sucked air and shifted his rucksack, trying to ease the straps. Putting the goggles back over his eyes, he studied the situation. The twisting ribbon of blacktop down there was empty. The road snaked past boulders and a parallel ditch.

Had the Chinese convoy already come and gone?

This felt too much like Hawaii three years ago, which had been a series of disasters and dead commandos. Paul had the dubious honor of being one of the last Americans to slip away from the islands. He'd fled while under Chinese machine gun fire, tracers slapping the water as he gunned their inflatable over an incoming wave. Lieutenant Diggs had pitched overboard, leaving only two of them to reach the waiting submarine three miles offshore.

As Paul knelt on the Mexican hill, his lips peeled back, revealing a chip in the right-hand upper front tooth. He'd gotten that in Hawaii while banging his face against a rock. With his short blond hair and angular features, it gave him a wolfish cast. Despite his years, he still had broad shoulders and trim hips. In his youth he'd been a terror on the football field, slamming running backs and receivers with bone-crushing force. As he knelt, Paul listened for the enemy, straining, cocking his head.

He heard something in the distance that could have been a big engine. Rocks and boulders littered these hills, with crooked trees and yellow grass. If he could already hear the Chinese convoy—

Paul twisted around. William Lee moved up the hill. He belonged to the 75th Ranger Regiment and was the other American on the mission, although neither Paul nor Lee was in uniform. It meant if captured they could be shot as spies or saboteurs, which Paul figured would never happen. If they survived a firefight, Chinese Intelligence would torture them until they'd extracted every piece of useful information from their brutalized bodies.

Because of that, their CIA officer—who remained safely in the States—had given each of them a cyanide capsule. Lee had asked for a false tooth to hold his, explaining that he might be knocked unconscious during a firefight. The Chinese would confiscate the capsule, therefore, before he could swallow it. Paul had quietly accepted his cyanide, pocketing it and later crushing the capsule with his boot heel on the sidewalk outside the mess hall.

Paul had promised his wife Cheri a long time ago that he would come home to her no matter what happened. It was the only way she had agreed to his reenlistment with the Marines after Alaska. Paul had also vowed after Hawaii that he was going to die in bed of old age. He'd seen too many good men butchered on the battlefield. There was nothing heroic about it, just the ugly mutilation of flesh and the pulverizing of bones. His vows meant he couldn't die here on this mission. He certainly couldn't take his own life.

He snorted bitterly. If only it was that easy. Likely, the vows meant he had cursed himself to a young and violent death. Well, not so young, but brutal, he was certain.

A Mexican woman followed Lee. She was thin like the others and she carried a heavy pack like them too. They were guerillas of Colonel Valdez's Free Mexico Army. The girl, the woman, she was the colonel's daughter, Maria, a legend among the resistance. That she was here showed the importance of the mission. The CIA officer had objected via satellite phone, saying it would be a terrible propaganda blow if she died or was captured. Besides, the mission called for Colonel Valdez's best men, not his daughter.

If they wanted the best, why am I here?

Paul knew the answer, but he didn't buy it. Maria was here because she believed in the romance of her existence, in the great cause. She was also here because according to Colonel Valdez she had the best small unit tactical mind of anyone in his army. Calling these ragtag people Paul had seen an army was stretching it. They were all so thin.

It was due to the Chinese occupation. Those like Maria and her six guerillas possessed fifth-class cards, if they owned a card at all. It meant they ate enough to keep breathing, but moving or working, that was another matter.

The world was starving to death due to glaciation. Because of it, the population was knocking on America's door, demanding food.

Lee reached the top of the hill and crouched beside Paul. He mopped sweat with his sleeve and his nostrils made whistling noises. Lee was too tough to open his mouth and pant, at least beside a Marine who had beaten him up the hill.

William Lee, aka "Wolverine" to his 75th Ranger Regiment buddies. He was shorter than Paul and built like a pit bull. Those muscles were all useful, even the ones bunched on the side of his jaw. In Hawaii, Lee had bitten off the nose of a

22

White Tiger commando, giving Lee time to draw his knife and gut the Chinese killer.

Probably because of his fanatical attitudes, Lee consistently produced results. In Hawaii, he had been the sole survivor of the "Night of the Generals." It had been a daring mission behind enemy lines, putting five Rangers of Chinese extraction into a conference room of high-ranking enemy commanders. All the generals had died, according to Lee, one bayoneted in the throat. Since only Lee had made it back, his version of the story had become official history.

Paul and Lee were here because of General Ochoa, who ran SOCOM. Ochoa believed in an old pro football adage: get big playmakers on your team, men who excel under pressure during playoff or Super Bowl performances and let them play a lot. Guided by his theorem, Ochoa had handpicked Paul and Lee for this off-the-cuff mission.

"You two have achieved the biggest successes to date. Paul, you helped slow the enemy on the North Slope of Alaska. And Lee, killing those Chinese generals in Hawaii—it makes me smile every time I think about you sticking one of those bastards in the throat. Your task this time is straightforward. We need to find out what 'Blue Swan' is and why the Chinese think it's so important. You're going into Mexico and getting our country a Blue Swan to study."

As they crouched on the dark hilltop in Mexico, Lee's whistling lessened. Paul hoisted his rucksack higher on his shoulders so the straps eased some of their pressure.

Lee leaned forward like an eager bloodhound. "I hear them," he said, meaning the Chinese.

"Be good to get an air-visual," Paul said, "and know how they're deployed."

"Next you'll be asking for a quad to drive down to the road."

"Better get going," Paul said.

Lee grunted as he forced himself upright. Gripping his rucksack's straps, he began stiff-legged down the hill.

Paul could hear the convoy easily now, the roar of approaching trucks. The Chinese were coming, the Chinese who ran Mexico with an iron fist, the Chinese who had invaded

Alaska seven years ago and swept every American satellite from space three years ago and who had launched a cyber-attack on his country. The U.S. had never been the same since.

Maria Valdez climbed beside him, crouching onto one knee. Sweat streaked her thin face. She never wore a helmet or a hat and she'd tied her long dark hair into a ponytail. She was pretty with those intense black eyes, but she never smiled and her voice was like a whiplash. She panted with an open mouth. In that regard, she wasn't proud like Lee. Her eyes narrowed and she turned to Paul.

"They're almost here," she said.

The mission had called for plenty of time to deploy. But there had been a patrol in the way. The nine of them had detoured, eating up too much precious time.

Thinking about it made Paul weary. If they couldn't even get this part of it right, he doubted the extraction would work.

Maria looked back the way she'd climbed. Cupping her hands around her mouth, she shouted, "Jose, Lupe, Jorge, hurry! Set up the machine gun."

She meant the .50 caliber Browning. She would man it, as she was the best shot among the guerillas.

"Luis, Benito and Freddy," she said, "get your RPGs ready. I want you in the ditch with the Marine."

The six guerillas toiled up the hill. Although thin and malnourished, they were hard-eyed partisans, Mexicans dedicated to throwing off the hated oppressor. Each of them had his own harrowing tale of abuse, of soul-crushing horror that usually involved a lost wife, daughter or sister, sometimes all three. The enemy avidly sought female companions, as their country had the worst man-to-woman imbalance in the world. More than one U.S. commentator said the Chinese lust for conquest was simply a primal urge belonging to the Stone Age—a hunt for wives. The Chinese had an ironclad law, permitting a family a single child only. Too many of them yearned for a male offspring, meaning they aborted the girls, the reason for the great imbalance.

Maria turned back to Paul, blowing her breath in his face. It smelled of sunflower seeds. She had littered the spent shells on the way here like an old time baseball player.

24

"We must kill every one of them," Maria said, with her eyes flashing as she spoke.

Paul cocked his head. He heard grinding gears. The big vehicles downshifted as they toiled uphill. General Ochoa's people had chosen this location with care.

Kill every one of them.

Lee was two-thirds of the way down the hill. The Ranger had a custom-built mine to deploy. He had two, but by the sounds, Lee would be lucky to get one emplaced.

"Over there," Paul said, pointing halfway down the hill. "That position will give you—"

"I know where to put my machine gun!" Maria snapped.

Sure, lady. "Wait until Lee explodes the first mine before you begin firing," Paul said.

Maria grabbed a fistful of his jacket and leaned close so their lips almost touched. "We've gone over the plan, amigo. Now you're wasting time because you insist on treating me like a child. Go! Get set up so we can kill Chinese."

This wasn't about killing Chinese, although Paul didn't tell Maria. "Good luck," he said.

Maria sneered. "I am not a pagan. I do not desire *luck.*" She pulled a gold chain from around her neck with a small crucifix on the end. She kissed it. "I pray that *Christos* bless us against the atheist invaders. Tonight, let us send them all to Hell!"

"Works for me," Paul said. He gripped his AT4, grunted as he stood and started down the hill.

Behind him, three guerillas followed, each of them carrying a Chinese RPG, long ago patterned off the successful Russian RPG-7. Maria and her team started for a position midway down the slope.

Lee had already dumped his rucksack in the ditch and knelt on the road. With a drill, he bored into the blacktop.

Can he get two mines in? We need two if we're to have a hope.

Long yellow grass rustled against Paul's jeans, while his boots scraped over half-buried rocks. He was dressed like a civilian, but it would fool no one. He'd declined regular body armor. It would give him away as an American but more

25

importantly, it would rob him of mobility, maybe the ability to have made the 16-mile march this quickly.

In the darkness, gears ground once more as trucks downshifted yet again. It was an ominous sound. The convoy, the armored trucks and IFVs, were almost up into sight from their steep climb. In their entire route, it was steepest over that lip, meaning the convoy would be down to a crawl once they reached this location.

Paul raised his AT4 and broke into something resembling a sprint. The rucksack bounced up and down, causing brutal agony to his shoulders.

The AT4 was an 84mm unguided, portable, single-shot recoilless smoothbore weapon, a successor to the old LAW rocket. It weighed nearly fifteen pounds and his fired a HEAT projectile that could penetrate up to 16.5 inches of steel. The tactical trick tonight was going to be a simple one. The mine would blow the first vehicle. Paul's AT4 would take out the last one, trapping the rest between them on the narrow road. The guerillas, Maria with the Browning, and U.S. Air Force drones would kill the rest. It was a KISS plan: Keep It Simple, Stupid. That was the best kind of plan in battle where the simple became difficult.

The air burned down Paul's throat as he ran down the slope and his legs wobbled. Damn, he was tired. He needed to get into position. He—

The first Chinese vehicle climbed over the lip, appearing on the road below. It was an armored hover and by the mass of antenna on top, Paul bet it was a drone. The hover would be worthless off-road, but it had come quietly and faster than any truck or IFV. What a balls-up. Chinese convoy operations called for a drone crusher to lead. Everyone knew that. The planners had expected a crusher, not a hover.

No! Lee was still on the road. The hover likely had motion sensors, as much a robotic vehicle as an operator-driven drone.

Paul dove and he splayed his legs, dragging his feet, hoping to keep from tumbling. He grunted as the slanted ground slammed against him and his rucksack drove him down harder. He bounced and his steel-toed boots dragged in the dirt, kicking up stones.

Lee sprinted for the ditch. The Ranger pumped his arms as his feet flew. The hover's heavy machine gun opened up with a stream of red tracers. Lee dove and jerked in the air as bullets ripped into him. The dive became a ragged tumble. He hit the ground and more tracers riddled his corpse, each one like a giant repeatedly slapping a doll, turning him over, and over.

Why had the Chinese brought a hover drone?

Paul didn't have time to shake his head. The answer was too obvious. The mine was now out of play, as Lee had the activation-switch. Maybe one of the operators in Arizona could trigger it. First, the stealth drones would have to be in position. Paul hadn't seen nor heard anything in the starry sky, nor had he communicated with the operators lately. Chinese detection gear was among the best and they therefore had decided to keep talk to a minimum.

Letting go of the AT4, Paul jerked quick-releases, shifted his shoulders and rolled the rucksack onto the ground. His fingers roved over pockets. He'd practiced this drill a thousand times. He ripped open a zipper and dragged out a laser-designator.

One of the guerillas crashed onto the ground beside him, readying a RPG. On the road, the drone raced for Lee's corpse.

Cursing silently, Paul shoved the designator against his shoulder. It was built like a small carbine. He dug out a satellite phone and jammed it against his right ear. He punched the auto-dial, hearing it buzz.

"Echo one?" an operator asked.

The hover slowed as a port opened. Was it going to collect Lee? Before Paul could learn the answer, Lee rolled over so he faced his killer.

No way. Paul watched. It was ghastly. Lee smiled with red teeth. *That's blood. His mouth is full of blood.*

Lee gripped something with both hands. His thumbs jammed down. The mine he'd planted in the road did its job as a coiled spring launched it airborne.

Paul thrust his face into the ground. An explosion rocked the world. Seconds later, debris rained with heavy pelting sounds.

27

After counting to three, Paul lifted his head and spotted the drone. It burned, flipped onto its side, a pile of junk now. Of Sergeant Lee of the 75th Ranger Regiment, there was no sign. In the end, Lee hadn't needed the false tooth and cyanide capsule. The Ranger, he'd never have to worry about torture.

Paul blinked several times, hating the suddenness of the loss. Then he realized he heard heavy trucks braking, doing it out of sight. Did they stop on the steep part of the road just out of visual? He heard a clang. It sounded an awful lot like an IFV's ramp crashing down. The shouts of Chinese infantry confirmed Paul's suspicion.

The IEDs and the RPGs, together with the AT4 and Hellfire III missiles—

The first Chinese soldier climbed into view onto the road. He moved in that crouched-over manner of cautious soldiery. Helmet, body armor and cradling a QBZ-95 assault rifle—it used a caseless cartridge, the propellant a part of the bullet. That meant more ammo per magazine.

A second soldier appeared. They scanned the road and began eyeing the stony, grassy slopes on either side. Surely, they could see how beautiful of an ambush site this was. A third soldier appeared over the lip.

How many were there? Six per Infantry Fighting Vehicle meant—

The game changed then. Maybe opening communication with the operators—the drone pilots—in Arizona did it. How long had the American stealth drones been waiting? The CIA officer had told them the ones for this mission were super-quiet. But Paul figured he should have at least heard something up in the darkness if the drones were here. The Marine Corps used drones and Paul always heard them long before he'd seen them. Tonight, it was different, very different, a good surprise.

Maybe America finally had a few secret weapons of its own.

The first that Paul, and likely those soldiers down there, knew about the drones was the flare of a launching Hellfire III missile as it appeared in the dark sky. It blossomed into existence like a shooting star. There was a streak as the missile sped earthward and then out of sight. Paul figured the Chinese

28

vehicles had stopped on the steepest part of the road, warned by the hover that enemy combatants waited for them here. A terrific explosion illuminated the night as if a giant had lit an arc welder. It was brightly white and hurt Paul's eyes. The Chinese that Paul could see—their bulky armor with the oversized chest plates starkly visible now—glanced back and then hit the ground. They crawled away from the strike.

Another Hellfire III erupted into existence. Did that mean there was a second circling stealth drone, or did the missile come from the same craft that had fired the first? One thing was certain, the Air Force had made it here without a hitch. It was good to know something worked right on their side.

Several new Chinese soldiers appeared on the road. They ran up over the lip at speed. Two of them dropped their assault rifles and leaned over as they gripped their knees, panting. A different soldier appeared, striding into view. He blew a whistle. The noise was sharp and commanding. The others straightened, the two picking up their dropped weapons.

On the other side of the lip, out of Paul's sight, Chinese anti-air rockets fire-balled upward into the darkness. Maybe to show them who had the biggest balls tonight, two more Hellfire missiles appeared, streaking down.

An explosion in the starry sky—brief but deadly illumination—showed a Chinese hit.

"Sergeant Lee?" the operator asked.

Paul realized he still held the satellite phone against his ear. "Gunnery Sergeant Kavanagh here," he said. It always surprised him how calm his voice sounded during these things.

"You blew the mine too soon," the operator said.

Did they have a higher drone up there watching the proceedings? Just how many drones had the Air Force been able to slip through the Chinese defenses? The enemy border bristled with radar, missiles, lasers, flak guns, AWACS planes and jet fighters and even with "distant" satellite recon. If the Air Force could get all these stealth drones through, why had they used only two commandos?

"Looks like you're right about the mine," Paul said.

"Is your screen up?"

"Just a minute," Paul said. This felt too surreal, it always did. He pulled a computer scroll out of the rucksack, flicking a switch that stiffened it. A second later he viewed the situation from one of the drones that used night vision. Trucks burned on the steep road. Chinese infantry fired assault rifles into the air. Each shot looked like a spark on the screen. Paul spotted a Marauder-sized light tank. No, not a tank. The vehicle swiveled a pair of anti-air cannons and began chugging radar-guided flak into the sky. Out of the corner of Paul's eye, he witnessed an explosion, which indicated a hit, another dead American UCAV: Unmanned Combat Air Vehicle. A different drone targeted the enemy. Paul watched his screen as crosshairs centered on the Chinese vehicle and as a Hellfire streaked down and obliterated the cannons.

"Do you have visual?" the operator asked.

"Sure do," Paul said.

"We're putting down another barrage," the operator said. "Then you have to go in, finish them and find the Blue Swan container. We have to take care of some enemy air headed your way."

Oh yeah, sure, no problem. "Have you counted the number of enemy infantry?" Paul asked.

"That's going to change right now," the operator said. "Keep your head down."

Several things happened at once. Maria Valdez on her midway position on the hill opened up with the .50 caliber Browning. She was four football-field lengths away from the nearest enemy. The Chinese officer with the whistle went down in a heap. The others hit the dirt a second time and swiveled on their bellies toward the machine gun. Several crawled like mad for shielding rocks. Others opened up, firing back at Maria.

That's a mistake. The Chinese were pinned on the road, easy targets for the Browning, which had greater accuracy at range than the assault rifles. In the next eight seconds, Maria killed two more enemy as her slugs ripped through body armor like pencils through paper.

Then the sun appeared—a monstrous light half-hidden by the steep slope. Paul clawed the earth, pressing his body against its protective soil. Concussion arrived with the sound. It

30

lifted Paul, flipped and threw him against the soil so he rolled. Thunder boomed and shook the bones in his body.

No one had told him about this. Was the Air Force using nukes? Or was this one of their nifty fuel-air bombs, the kind that sprayed a mist of explosive gassy liquid and ignited?

"They're all yours now," a gloating man said into his ringing ear.

Paul was only vaguely aware that he still held onto the satellite phone. *All mine? What do I want with them?* "Roger," he said. "How about keeping the spy plane up there so I can see what they're doing?"

"We still have to extract you," the operator said.

Paul scowled. That wasn't an answer. Then he realized it was. The spy plane—the drone—would stay to guide the extraction vehicles. They had to get "Blue Swan" back into America so the techs could pull it apart and figure out its great secret.

Maria's Browning kept chugging. Every fifth bullet was a tracer—a red light—helping guide the thin deadly line into desperate Chinese.

That was a problem, as desperate soldiers made dangerous ones. Several fired back from rocks near the lip. One of them, probably more, had radios. They would summon help, which might be helos, enemy drones or even jets to lay down old-fashioned napalm.

Paul checked the screen and choked on what he saw. While coughing, he saw movement among the burning Chinese vehicles on the steep part of the road. That was the problem with resorting only to bombs. The earth was a big place, with many folds and seams for anxious men to hide. It meant, as it always had, that infantry needed to go in to finish a task. Trouble was, his infantry was six skeletal guerillas and one bloodthirsty chick against—Paul counted at least ten more Chinese on the screen. Those in the rocks made another four. Fourteen alerted, body-armored enemies against their eight were poor odds.

It was only a matter of seconds before the Chinese in the rocks spotted him out here in the open. Some of them, at least, must have night vision equipment.

31

"Yeah," Paul said.

He dragged the fifteen-pound AT4 to him. It had a HEAT round, made to disable an armored vehicle. He removed the safety pin at the rear of the tube. That unblocked the firing rod. He lifted it over his shoulder, moving his legs to the side. Otherwise, the back-blast would burn them. He moved back the front and rear covers so the iron sights popped into firing position. With quick precision, he moved the firing rod, cocking the lever forward and over the top to the right side. He sighted the largest boulder behind which the four Chinese hid. Taking a breath and holding it, Paul used his thumb and pressed the forward red firing button.

With a whoosh and the heat of back-blast, the round blew out of the tube. Time seemed to stand still. The 84mm round struck the boulder, exploding it and killing several Chinese.

Maria swung the tripod-mounted Browning and worked over the dead. She caught one man crawling for new cover.

"Let's go!" Paul shouted. "We have to beat the others who are trying to climb up to the lip. If we do, we can pick them off."

He grabbed his assault rifle and ripped open a flap on his belt as he ran. Lee had loved bayonets fixed to the end of his assault rifle. The idea of sticking the enemy had always seemed to excite the Ranger. Paul had read studies. Less than one percent of combat deaths were due to bayonet. The gleaming blade on the end looked fierce, but that was about it.

Paul drew a long sound suppressor out of his pouch. On the run, he screwed it onto his assault rifle. The "silencer" tonight had little to do with quiet shots and everything toward hiding muzzle flash. If he used full auto-fire, the sound suppressor would quickly overheat and become useless. His idea was aimed fire while keeping hidden from the enemy, hopefully long enough to kill all of them before they figured out his position.

Paul heard his own labored breathing and the crunch of his boots. Behind him followed three guerillas. He glanced over his shoulder. Two carried their RPGs. The smart one had a submachine gun out. Could he count on them to help him? A further twist showed him Maria on the slope. Her team

32

dismantled the .50 caliber. That was a mistake. He could have used her to give fallback cover. She wanted to kill Chinese, however, and that meant moving the heavy machine gun forward. It was hard to fault her desire.

With his mouth open, as hot air burned down his throat, Paul sprinted for the lip, the edge that would show him the steep road and the burning vehicles. Ten Chinese soldiers were coming up, and he was sure that reinforcements were on their way from somewhere. He had to get this "Blue Swan" and be long gone, or he was going to end up in a torture chamber, worked over by experts.

He failed to win the footrace. A Chinese soldier stumbled over the lip and onto the visible road. If Maria still had her position, she could have killed the man.

Paul slid to a halt while still on the slope, tore off the night vision goggles and brought the assault rifle's butt to his shoulder. He panted, knelt and winced as a stone pressed painfully against his kneecap. He shifted his position and peered through the night vision scope. The man kept moving in his scope, in and out of sight because Pau's hard breathing moved his rifle too much. Paul took a deep breath, let it halfway out and held it, feeling as if he was underwater while trying to do it and while desperately needing air.

Concentrate. Squeeze the trigger.

The kick slammed against his shoulder. The soldier went down. Paul strained to see through the scope. The soldier crawled for cover. He'd just knocked the man down, likely hitting body armor.

Like a basketball player taking his second free throw—one who had missed the first shot—Paul aimed with greater deliberation and squeezed the trigger.

The Chinese soldier jerked and sagged, and half his face was missing as he lay on the ground.

War is Hell.

Paul glanced back at his help. The three guerillas lay on the ground. They must have stopped when he stopped, which was a natural reaction. That wasn't going to win them the needed position, nor garner them the "Blue Swan" whatever it proved to be.

"Go, go, go!" Paul shouted at the three.

Time was everything now. Forgetting to pick up his night vision goggles, Paul stood and ran for the road and for the lip. After four steps, he realized his mistake, but it was too late to go back. He had nine Chinese soldiers to kill if he was going to get home to Cheri and his son Mike.

Enemy gunfire erupted from the lip, each barrel blazing flame as several Chinese shot at once. They had to be on their bellies, wisely using cover.

Paul dove for the second time tonight. This time, he was hardly aware of striking the ground. Without the rucksack, it was like jumping onto a mattress. Behind him, a guerilla cried out in mortal agony. Paul didn't need to look back to know one of the guerillas was down.

Paul crawled and the dirt around him spit. A bullet whined past his head. Paul jumped up and ran crouched-over, yearning to reach a half-buried boulder. Something hot struck his left leg. He stumbled, but managed to keep his feet. Then he jumped, pulled the assault rifle close to his chest and shoulder, and rolled. More bullets hissed like wasps. Chips of rock struck his face.

He looked back and couldn't see the three guerillas. He lay stretched out behind his boulder, momentarily safe from Chinese fire. He checked himself, but couldn't find the satellite phone. He must have dropped it somewhere. Fortunately, he still had the scroll. Rolling it open, he studied the situation from the vantage of the patrolling drone. The nine Chinese were lying in a line on the lip, using it like a trench. Each wore body armor and each fired a QBZ-95. The only good thing was Maria. She'd set up the Browning again.

Paul glanced behind him just as the Browning opened up. The .50 caliber had much greater range, greater reach, than the enemy weapons.

"Okay," Paul whispered to himself, looking at the screen again. His three guerillas were down. By the angle and stillness of their bodies, they each looked dead.

How much ammo did Maria have? The answer would be the same every time: not enough.

"You have to use her Browning while you can," he told himself.

Paul pressed his forehead against the hard-packed ground. He had to *think*. He had to use what he had, which was what exactly? He had intel on the enemy, suppressing fire for a few more minutes and some night vision with his scope. The enemy must have night vision, too, but they couldn't see him here behind the rock. For the moment, they didn't have any UAVs. He had to use that against them. What made the most sense?

It came to him. It was obvious.

Paul took a deep breath, rolled the scroll and jammed it back into a pouch. Then he began to slither on his belly, using the rocks and boulders as a shield. His goal was simplicity. He had to get behind the Chinese and pick them off.

The next few minutes strained Paul's stamina. Sweat kept dripping into his eyes. The rough ground tore through the fabric of his shirt at the elbows. The stony ground did the same to his flesh. He bled, but that didn't matter now. Maybe in some future life it would matter. In the here and now, he kept using his elbows as he slithered for his destination.

Fortunately, Maria kept the enemy busy. Her team had carried extra ammo, which she now used prodigiously. Maybe she was smart after all. Maybe the colonel had known what he was doing sending his little girl.

Did Colonel Valdez love America? Paul had his doubts. Instead, the colonel's logic must have been cold and inflexible. On her own, Mexico could never free herself from the Chinese. The country was prostrate and shackled: a victim to the world's greatest power. To gain freedom, Mexico needed America as strong as possible. If the Chinese could breach the US's "Maginot Line" on the border and begin tearing chunks of agricultural land from the U.S., it would show the rest of the world it was possible. The South American Federation would join in the attack. The German Dominion would likely drop airmobile brigades to secure an eastern state for itself as it launched its hovers from Cuba. If "Blue Swan" really was a weapon that could allow the Chinese to breach the world's strongest defensive line, Colonel Valdez would want the Americans to find out about it so they could fix the problem.

35

That would be enough of a reason to send his little girl into the fray.

Victory can't come down to this little firefight, can it?

Paul gripped his assault rifle as he eased onto his feet. Blood dripped from his elbows. Below him to the left, he spied the burning vehicles on the steep hill road. They were all in a line, and they illuminated the nine Chinese prone on the road's lip and to the right and left of the road. Straight below Paul were rocks and shale. He was roughly three hundred yards away from the Chinese.

Gripping the assault rifle, Paul began to climb down the rough slope. He should have kept his night vision goggles. Instead, he had to move slowly, testing rocks with his feet, pulling back when one shifted. If one clattered too loudly, one of the Chinese might look over and see him.

How long did he have until enemy reinforcements showed up? The fact this was a "Blue Swan" convoy probably meant not long. He might already be out of time.

Paul blinked sweat out of his eyes. He wasn't going to get it done like this. He was going to have risk to win. First taking a deep breath, he propelled himself off his rock, jumping down. He strained to see in the darkness, using the distant firelight as best he could.

He landed on a boulder and almost pitched off it. He couldn't windmill his arms to keep his balance—they gripped his rifle—so he jumped again, sailing downward. He landed and a rock slipped out from under his left foot. His ankle twisted and he let himself go limp, crumpling onto the boulders, landing on his side. He crawled, panting, expecting bullets to rain against him. When they failed to materialize, he climbed to his feet. His left ankle throbbed. He set down the rifle and untied the boot's laces. His fingers felt thick and useless. His heart hammered.

You have to keep moving. You can't stand out here exposed like this.

With stiff fingers, he jerked the laces tighter, knotting them quickly. He grabbed the assault rifle, jumped down ten feet and landed hard on a flat boulder. He winced at the pain shooting up his left leg. He plopped onto his butt and slid over the

36

boulder's side, landing on dirt. Using the night vision scope, he examined the terrain. Okay. He began trotting. Each time he put pressure on the left foot, his ankle flared with agony. Sweat streaked his face and his left hip began to hurt.

Finally, Paul lay behind a boulder, below and to the side of the nine Chinese by about one hundred and fifty yards. His mouth was bone dry so that his tongue felt raspy against the roof of his mouth.

He climbed to a crouch behind a boulder, unhooked a canteen and guzzled. He waited, and he guzzled again. Sweat drenched his clothes. He was shaking. The idea of crawling away and getting the hell out of here kept appearing more appealing by the second. White Tiger commandos were surely on their way. Enemy jets could drop napalm on everything. The Chinese were ruthless that way.

"Bastards," he muttered, picking up the assault rifle.

He rested his bloody elbows on the boulder, bringing up the scope and taking several deep breaths. He needed calm. He needed steadiness. He put two extra magazines beside him. He didn't want to waste time later unhooking them from his belt. He peered through the scope, judging the situation. Maria must almost be out of ammo by now. Once he started firing...

"Get it done," he whispered.

Through his night vision scope, Paul Kavanagh sighted the leftmost Chinese lying on the ground. The soldier had pulled back from the lip, clutching his QBZ-95 between his knees.

Carefully, slowly, Paul squeezed the trigger. The assault rifle kicked, and the Chinese soldier lay back, his throat obliterated.

Paul was in the zone and continued firing with deliberate precision. When the third Chinese soldier shouted, standing up before Paul's second shot put him down forever, the others finally noticed. The fourth went down with shattered teeth and a gaping hole in the back of his neck. The rest began firing downslope, spraying bullets, seeking Paul. It was a good thing he'd screwed on the sound suppressor, hiding his muzzle flashes.

It took the entire second magazine to kill the fifth and sixth soldiers.

Maybe the remaining three Chinese had enough of the silent killer who hid behind them. One bolted up over the lip. Maria's Browning chattered a long burst and there came a terrible scream. She still had bullets.

The last two Chinese took off running away from Paul. He stood up and fired fast, sending bullet after bullet, chipping rock beside them and spitting dirt by their feet, but failing to nail either. They got away and both of them carried weapons.

Will they double back to fight?

Paul shook his head. He didn't know, but he felt soiled by the encounter. Sniper-fire killing always did that to him. The day he truly began to enjoy deliberate butchery, he felt, would be the day he was a destroyer and no longer a soldier simply doing his duty.

Blue Swan. It was time to search for the miracle weapon.

Slinging the rifle's strap over his shoulder, Paul limped toward the burning vehicles. It would be just his luck that this was the wrong convoy. There was only one way to find out.

By the time he reached the Chinese vehicles, his bad ankle made walking an act of pure will. He didn't need to check the IFVs or the big troop trucks. The smell of cooked flesh coming from them nauseated him. He'd never gotten used to that, or the look of the dead, some with melted faces or bone sticking up around blackened flesh.

Whatever bomb the Air Force had used was brutal. Likely, it was one of the new secret weapons people blogged about these days. America had lost the Arctic Circle oil rigs and Hawaii, but they weren't going to lose the mainland. Soon now, the world and the Chinese in particular were going to learn what old-fashioned Yankee ingenuity meant. That was one of the problems, however. The East—meaning the PAA and sometimes India—had greater manufacturing ability than the rest of the world. The East had also shown the niftiest battlefield hardware in both Alaska and Hawaii.

Paul limped toward a long-bed vehicle, what looked like a big missile carrier. This must be "Blue Swan," a new kind of missile. Pulling out a digital camera, Paul began taking pictures. The thing was huge.

A shout brought him around.

38

He spied Maria on the lip of the road. She waved, and Paul realized the last burning vehicles illuminated him. It showed, at least, that the two surviving Chinese hadn't doubled back. Only one of the original six guerillas stood with Maria. The two of them began down the road toward him.

Paul heard approaching helicopters then, a loud whomp-whomp sound. Those couldn't be the Air Force, at least not the American Air Force.

Biting his lower lip with indecision, Paul stood beside the damaged missile carrier for three seconds. Then he bolted toward the carrier bed. Despite his ankle, he climbed the flatbed and took close-up shots of the crumpled nosecone, the warhead. Fluids leaked from it. He poured water out of a canteen and collected some of the warhead fluid. He also aimed the camera at Chinese characters on the warhead, clicking like mad.

Maria's shout brought him around. She cupped her hands, yelling, "The White Tigers are coming!" Then she pointed up into the air.

Paul needed the satellite phone. Did America have any more air-fighting drones here? What was he supposed to do now?

Then Paul received the greatest shock of the night. He looked up sharply as he heard a faint sound. The strangest helicopter he'd ever seen hovered about sixty feet above him. It had four rotors at four equidistant points. Did it have a cloaking device? Or had it moved soundlessly? He heard it now, a whispering noise. This was incredible.

It dropped lower so he could see an undercarriage bay door open. A rope ladder slithered down toward him.

The CIA officer hadn't said anything about this. Was he supposed to climb up into the helicopter?

The rope ladder almost struck his shoulder the first time. The craft maneuvered into a better position and now the ladder touched his shoulder. Paul didn't need any more invitation. He grabbed rope, hoisted up and got a foot onto a rung. He climbed toward the bay door. It took him a second to realize that as he climbed the craft lifted higher.

"What about Maria?" he shouted.

No one poked a head out of the bay door to look down and answer. There was only the whistling wind and the dropping ground. It was too late to let go, so Paul kept climbing. He looked down and saw Maria staring at him. She turned to the guerilla. They talked, and they ran back up the road.

Paul saw the first enemy helicopter. It was small and black, with a machine gunner sitting with his weapon to the side. The vehicle belonged to the White Tigers. Paul knew because he'd seen these in Hawaii hunting American commandos.

A second helo appeared. The machine gunners didn't blaze at Maria. She kept sprinting for safety as the guerilla beside her stopped, knelt and aimed his assault rifle at a helo. The two gunners opened up then. One of them at least proved himself a marksman. The guerilla pitched violently to the ground, riddled with exploding bullets as his body turned into gory ruin.

Do they know it's Colonel Valdez's daughter?

Paul shuddered and he kept climbing. He stopped just before reaching the bay door, because he spied Chinese characters painted on the bottom of this machine.

They tricked me.

He went cold inside until he wondered if Americans had painted that on the drone in order to fool the enemy.

Paul stared at the ground. It was a long drop. The wind whistled past his face, making his eyes water. It wasn't hot anymore, but getting cold.

I guess there's only one way to find out. Paul climbed the last few rungs of the ladder and reached the door. He pulled himself within.

The rope ladder coiled in fast, a roller whizzing with automated speed. His last sight was a concussion grenade knocking Maria off her feet. Then the hatch shut with a clang and a light appeared. Paul spied three small seats and little else, no windows, no speakers, just walls. He secured himself in a seat, buckling in. Either this was a clever enemy trick or the newest American extraction drone. The idea of waiting to find out made Paul's gut seethe.

"How about telling me what's going on?" he said in the cramped area.

No one answered.

Scowling, Paul folded his arms and tried to make himself comfortable. It was impossible. He kept thinking about Maria Valdez in the hands of Chinese Intelligence.

-2-
The Darkness

MEXICO CITY, MEXICO

Captain Wei sat in his office, smoking an American cigarette as he stared into space. The smoke curled from the glowing tip, adding to the office's fumes. As he smoked, Wei blanked his mind, trying not to think about anything.

He was an interrogator for *Dong Dianshan*—East Lightning. Originally, they had been China's Party Security Service. With the creation of the Pan Asian Alliance, their powers had broadened. They were particularly apt at extracting information from reluctant individuals and getting to the root of a matter.

Wei was a small man with large ears and careworn lines on his face. He'd practiced his trade for uncounted years. He wore the customary brown uniform with red belts and an armband with a three-pronged lightning bolt.

A buzzer on the littered desk sounded. Captain Wei checked his cell phone and sighed. His ten minutes of solitude was over. He sucked on the cigarette a last time, inhaling deeply. The American cigarettes were good. He exhaled while mashing the cigarette into an overflowing ashtray.

He opened a drawer and reached to the back, unhooking a hidden container. He opened it, staring at five blue pills. It was going to be a long interrogation, and according to the information he had received, Maria Valdez was a tough-minded partisan. Captain Wei sighed, shaking his head. He was weary beyond endurance with his tasks. Yes, he was good at it, perhaps the best in Mexico. But it was so tedious and predictable. Worse, his tasks had begun to bother him. This mutilation of flesh and twisting a person's psyche, it hurt the soul—

Wei had been reaching for a pill. Now, his hand froze. Did humans possess souls? It was a preposterous notion. Humans were like any other animal, a mass of biological tissue with electrical nerve endings, a meat-sack of noxious fumes. People excreted, vomited, sweated and urinated, a wretched pile of filth that groveled under too much pain. Everyone broke. It used to be intriguing figuring out how to do it.

"No," Wei whispered. His dark eyes had been reflective. Now the reptilian look appeared, revealing him as the predator he was.

The tips of his thumb and forefinger pinched a blue pill. He deposited the pill onto the tip of his tongue, using his tongue to roll the pill back. He gulped, swallowing. A tiny smile played on the edges of mouth. Soon, the drug would numb the pestering qualms that had become stronger this last year. One patient had told him these qualms were his conscience. As he aged—the patient had said—he must realize the end of this existence was much nearer than, say, seven years ago.

"Seven?" Wei had snapped. He'd wanted to know why the patient had picked the number seven. Seven years ago, he'd interrogated Henry Wu, who had been an insignificant worm, a former American caught on video during a Chinese food riot. It had been then that the first glimmer of...unease, yes, unease had begun with his various interrogations. Seven years ago, Wei had increased the number of cigarettes he smoked and the number of whiskey shots he gulped. These days, whiskey was not enough. He needed the blue pills to ease him through each tedious day. Unfortunately, these cost cash and he had begun taking more of them lately.

The desk buzzer sounded a second time.

Captain Wei straightened his uniform and marched for the door. It was time to fix the little traitor and pry information out of her.

He strode down a long corridor, a flight of stairs and passed several open windows. Mexico City seethed with traffic, with small cars thirty years out of date, with thousands of bicyclists and tens of thousands of pedestrians. Smoke stacks chugged black fumes into the air from coal furnaces. Yet farther away in the center of the city gleamed new glass towers, thanks to the latest construction boom with the influx of Chinese troops. Mexico was a land of extremes, with the basest poverty and the most incredible wealth.

Captain Wei left the windows behind, opening a door and descending to the basement. The first tendrils of drugged numbing soothed his bad mood. By the time he reached the patient's door, the feeling had changed his mood altogether.

You are a meat-sack, Maria Valdez, one I will turn into a quivering hulk, a fountain of information.

Wei opened the door, expecting a number of quite predictable possibilities. The patient lay strapped to a table, naked, defenseless and primed for interrogation. An operative—a man—had shaved off every particle of the patient's hair. Wei found that most effective with females. The operative had also attached a host of leads to sensitive body-areas. Maria Valdez should have pleaded with him now or glared in defiance or stared into space, in shock, or sobbed uncontrollably. She did none of these things. Instead, with eyes closed, the patient whispered, speaking to an imaginary entity, it appeared.

Wei scowled, with his good feeling evaporating. Invisible entities did not exist. There was only power and the scramble to be the inflictor of pain instead of the receiver. It was the law of the jungle, of tooth and claw.

"Leave us," Wei told the operative.

The man bowed his head, hurrying for the door, never once lifting his gaze off the floor.

Wei listened for and heard the snick of the closing door. "Maria Valdez," he said sharply.

The patient ignored him as she kept on whispering.

44

That would not do, no, no. Wei strode to the controls and tapped a pain inducer.

The patient grunted and her eyes bulged open. She twisted on the table. She was shapely, if too thin and bony for Wei's tastes. She was also too tall, taller than he was—something he intensely disliked.

"Do I have your attention?" Wei asked in a considerate tone. It unbalanced and often unhinged patients to hear the solicitude in his voice and yet receive agony from his hands.

"I'm here," she said, whatever that was supposed to mean.

They both spoke English, as Wei had taken language courses and become proficient in the American usage.

Wei now forced himself to smile. "I'm sure you understand the situation."

"Yes! You're one of the *pigs* invading my country."

"My dear, please allow me to interject a factual point. You are the one who exudes a noxious odor. I refer to your sweat. We Chinese do not possess the same pig-like glands that you do."

"Go to Hell!"

Captain Wei smiled, stepping away from the controls. He put a gentle hand on her left thigh, causing the patient to stiffen.

"You are in Hell, my dear," he said.

"Wrong! In Hell, no one drinks beer."

Wei frowned. What an odd statement. Was she already unhinged? "I do not care for your attitude."

"That's because you're an invading hog," she said.

"Maria," he said, squeezing her thigh. It made her stiffen. He would teach her respect. Oh, she would learn to curb her tongue. First, he would begin her disorientation through soft speech. "You must not think of me as your enemy. I am here to help you."

"You're a worthless liar."

A flicker of annoyance entered his eyes. "I can make your existence gruesome or I can ease your suffering. It is my choice. Fortunately for you, my dear, I am easy to please. All I ask is for a few tidbits of information from you."

45

"I understand. I have what you want. But you have nothing I want except for your death, and I don't think you'll do me the favor of slitting your ugly throat."

Wei smiled faintly. "You are a veritable she-tiger, but you are also a liar."

"I curse you in the name of God."

Wei's smile slipped as he removed his hand from her thigh. Scowling, he went to the controls. He looked up at her. She grinned viciously, mocking him.

No, that would not do. He was in charge here. He would show her.

Captain Wei began to tap the controls hard with his fingertips. He winced once because he'd cut the nail down too much the other day on his left-hand middle finger. Then Maria Valdez screamed and thrashed on the table, causing him to forget about his own discomfort. Wei continued to inflict pain for some time, delighting in her various octaves. Finally, Maria slumped, unconscious.

Turning away, Wei stared up at the ceiling. What had overcome him? He'd never lost control of his emotions like this before. He was an interrogator, one of the best—no, *the* best in Mexico. He had a long list of questions his superiors wanted answered, yet now he'd needlessly tired out his patient. He should have already received a litany of her lies so he could compare her later answers and begin to pry out the truth. Never once during the torment had she cried out, offering to speak to end the pain. Obviously, the direct approach was the wrong method with this one. He must practice subtlety.

Wei cracked his knuckles and stepped beside a medical board. He selected a hypodermic needle and a vial of AE7. She was stubborn, possessing a core belief system that added to her rigid worldview. A double dose, yes, she would need a greater dosage to force her thoughts into a fantasy delusion. Then she would begin to tell him what he needed to learn.

Thirty seconds later, Wei slid the needle into her flesh, sinking the plunger as he pumped the drug into her bloodstream. It would take time before the AE7 brought her to the required state. Using his cell phone, he checked the time. Ah, he could go into the other room and smoke a cigarette.

46

Captain Wei slipped into the hall, entering an empty room. He found that his hands were shaking. How odd. Taking a pack of Lucky Strikes, he extracted a cigarette, stuck it between his lips and used his lighter. Soon, he stared blankly at the ceiling, occasionally watching the smoke curl. He refused to think about her words, her foolish curse or the way her body had contorted on the table. He had seen such things a thousand, a million times before. Instead, he smoked, emptying himself of thoughts, of emotions and emptying himself of the tedium of life. Mechanically, he shook out a second and later a third cigarette, enjoying them in the solitude of the basement.

The effects of the blue pill must have dulled his sense of time. Much later and with a start, Captain Wei took out his cell phone, checking it. Thirty-seven minutes had passed.

The small East Lightning officer rushed out of the smoky room and ran to the interrogation chamber. Sometimes, there were bad reactions to AE7. He had forgotten that and his dismissal of a watching operative.

Captain Wei threw open the door. "No," he whispered. He rushed to the table. Maria Valdez lay still, with a serene smile on her face. He checked her pulse and snatched his hand away, horrified. She was already cold. He hated everything about corpses, their stiffness, their chill, their—

"No," he said again. Wei blinked rapidly. What was he going to do? Higher command wished to know many things concerning her sabotage. Now—

Rushing to the computer, Wei sat down. He ran his fingers through his hair and logged in. Time. He had to register her time of death, her answers, her—

Wei licked his lips. What had he read about her earlier?

You need to think. You need to cover yourself. Is this her curse starting to work?

The thought sobered him. He needed a cigarette. No. He needed to use his years of expertise, giving High Command what it feared most. That way, they would worry more about the repercussions of her sabotage than how he had interrogated her.

Captain Wei of East Lightning began typing fabricated answers, turning dead guerillas into American commandos. It was clear by Wei's false answers that some Americans had escaped with knowledge of Blue Swan. The leak of the convoy's route and time of travel—it had occurred according to what Wei wrote because of a traitor on the Occupation Staff. Wei hated the Chinese Army, the way many soldiers looked at him with distain when they thought he wasn't looking. Yes. Wei grinned as he typed. The Americans had suborned this person because of his relatives living in North America. High Command would devour that, as they feared Chinese-Americans infiltrating their ranks.

Wei became thoughtful. How should he word this? Hmm. In his zeal to uncover more, there had been an accident. Yes, he had injected her with—

"No." He needed a doctor. There would be an autopsy. Wei considered ordering the body incinerated, but that would be a risk. He had already broken protocol ordering the operative away. Any more deviations would invite a full-scale investigation, just the thing he was trying to avoid.

Wei stared at his answers, checking them, looking for flaws or red flags. Returning to his office first and fortifying himself with another blue pill, he returned to the corpse and called for the resident doctor. He would say little, waiting for the doctor to tell him why the patient had died. Then he would concoct the end of the story and hope no one ever dug too deeply into what had really happened.

LAS VEGAS TESTING GROUNDS, NEVADA

A defeated Stan Higgins sat in his base house at his desk. It was in a small cubicle and blocked by a closed door. He could hear his wife in the other room watching *Hartford Wives*. She couldn't believe the news and had blanked it out. She escaped into the never-land of TV soap operas.

Stan stared at a computer screen, studying the judge's sentence: induction into a Detention Center until someone posted a ten thousand new-dollar bail. Stan massaged his forehead. Where was he supposed to get enough money to pay for his son's bail? Why had the young fool gone and protested?

Why couldn't Jake stick to his engineering studies? It had been hard enough gathering the tuition costs.

In his day, kids got student loans from the government. With the Sovereign Debt Depression that had gone the way of the dinosaur. Now, people had to scrape enough together to send their children to college. It meant fewer people went to college, making high school more important again for a person's future.

Stan closed his eyes. He felt the weight of his years. Three weeks ago, he'd turned fifty. He couldn't believe it—fifty! He still lifted weights, played basketball, ping-pong and ran occasionally. More than anything, the trouble was recuperation. He didn't heal like he used to and his left knee bothered him. He couldn't play basketball on cement courts anymore. Even blacktop hurt the knee. Wooden floors were the best. The truth, he should give up basketball. Otherwise, he was begging for a ripped tendon or a torn muscle.

Yet even ping-pong pained the bad knee when he lunged to slam the ball. If he slammed the ball too many times in a game, it made his shoulder hurt for the next two days.

Who would figure that ping-pong could hurt a man, even an aging athlete? It was ridiculous. Maybe he could learn to play like some of those experts he'd seen in Las Vegas last year. One old man with white hair had hardly moved. He had been an old geezer in every way except that he'd hit the ball just so and it did magical things, spinning off at bizarre angles, making the younger players leap around like fools. The trouble was Stan had never played that way. He liked speed, to drill the ball as hard as he could.

"Ten thousand new-dollars," Stan muttered, attempting to focus on the computer screen. His son had been accepted to Cal Poly in San Luis Obispo. That was one of the best places to earn an engineering degree. Now Jake had gone and openly protested the President's state of emergency. Even if Stan posted the bail, Jake would probably get kicked out of Cal Poly. Losing his Student Status, they would likely draft him into a Militia battalion.

"I don't have ten thousand new-dollars," Stan told himself.

49

Lines appeared in his forehead. Should he have remained in Anchorage? On his teaching salary and with the extra pay from the National Guard—

Stan blew out his cheeks in depression. So much had changed since the Alaskan War. What had that been, seven years ago now?

He had a theory about why time moved faster the older you got. When you were ten years old, a year represented one tenth of your life. When you were fifty, one year represented one fiftieth of your life. Therefore, one year was shorter the older you became. But none of that was going to help him post bail.

Laughter rang out from the TV, sounding like a drunken hyena. No doubt, it was over a joke that wasn't even funny. Shows still used laugh tracks just as when he'd been a kid. Stan wanted to yell at his wife to turn down the TV. She knew he was in here thinking about how to free Jake from the Detention Center. If someone spent too long there, officials stamped their driver's license with "Resister Status."

Stan massaged his forehead. He'd always wanted Jake to succeed. He wanted to give Jake every advantage he could. It wasn't like the old days. Good jobs were hard to come by now. An engineering degree from Cal Poly would have gone a long way toward making sure the boy avoided the Army, whether Regular or Militia.

Stan bared his teeth. The Army: fighting…killing…running from overwhelming odds, from enemy tanks. He'd never told anyone about his nightmares, not his wife, not Jose and for sure not the base psychologist who diagnosed each of them in the experimental unit, seeing if they were still mentally fit for duty. About once a month in his dreams, he relived the worst horrors of the Alaskan War. He dreaded the nightmares: the screech of Chinese shells, watching long-dead friends burn to death and fearing the terrible tri-turreted tanks rumbling toward him, knowing that every shell he fired would bounce off the incredible armor.

Lately his wife had begun asking if he was okay. He'd wake up in the morning hollow-eyed, or he'd start up from sleep sweating. He made up all kinds of excuses. Now, sitting here, Stan wondered if he was going the route of his dad. Old

Mack Higgins had gone around the bend—crazy in the head. These days, Stan had a greater appreciation as to why it might have happened.

"The apple doesn't fall far from the tree," Stan quoted to himself. He dreaded the idea of going crazy. For sure, he wasn't going to tell the base psychologist anything she might use against him.

Stan blew out his cheeks. He was a captain in an experimental unit. Seven years ago, he had been a captain in the Alaskan National Guard, in one of the few tank units there. He had received the Medal of Honor for helping stop the Chinese Invasion into Anchorage. Some people said his actions had been critical for victory. Afterward the Army Chief of Staff invited Stan to accept a commission in the Regular Army. Since Stan's expertise had been Armor, he'd entered that branch of the service and had soon found himself in the experimental department.

With that kind of start—even though he'd been old by Army reckoning—he should have risen in rank. Allen had just received a promotion from captain to major. Stan had been counting on getting the promotion. With better pay, could he go to a bank and finance ten thousand?

"Seven years of service," Stan muttered, as he rubbed his forehead. Now that he thought about it that was too long for a man of his age and expertise and with the Medal of Honor. He knew what was wrong. The colonel in charge of the experimental unit disliked him and his methods and Stan wasn't good at politicking, at butt kissing.

Stan slammed his fists onto the desk, jarring the computer screen.

Once, the TV volume would have lowered if he did that. His wife would have asked if everything was okay. Now, the volume increased. She didn't want to think about Jake being in the Detention Center.

"Ten thousand new-dollars," Stan whispered.

Maybe he could call Crane. The man was a former National Guard Colonel who belonged to the John Glen Corporation, a military-funded think tank in D.C. Crane had known him during the Alaskan War. Crane knew his nickname of

51

"Professor" and Crane had said many times that he appreciated Stan's military historical knowledge. "John Glen could use a man like you, Stan."

The last offer had come two years ago. Stan had been too absorbed then in the experimental unit, in the Mark I Behemoth battle tank. The Behemoth dwarfed all known tanks. It was a three hundred ton monstrosity, three times the size of a Chinese tri-turreted tank.

Stan flexed his hands. Two years ago, the possibilities of the Behemoth had excited him. Now he needed ten thousand new-dollars. Besides, the Army had passed him over yet again. He had learned that the Chief of Staff who had invited him into the Army—President Clark had twisted the officer's arm. The truth was the Army didn't want a man they considered a maverick at best and a hotheaded, insubordinate fool at worst. Which was funny really, because Stan knew himself to be a plodding man who always tried to do the right thing. There was nothing maverick about him, unless seeing historical parallels from time to time in a given situation was considered eccentric.

Stan stared at the judge's ruling as his mind raced from one thought to the next. He wanted to feel appreciated, as when he taught high school in Alaska. He was afraid that remaining in the military would only intensify his nightmares. Lastly, the bugs in the Mark I Behemoth—it was possible the three hundred ton tank would never see action and would never fulfill the destiny the U.S. needed against the threatening aggressors.

Stan tapped the screen, removing the judge's decision. With his mouth in a grim line of determination, Stan began writing an email to Crane, seeing if the John Glen Corporation still had a spot for a fifty-year-old captain. If there was such a spot, he would have to talk to the base colonel tomorrow about resigning his commission.

What would Jose say about that? What would his tankers tell him? How was he going to cope with the coming guilt as he bailed out this near to war?

You have to think about your son. Besides, you're an old man now. War—leave that to the young, to the strong. You need to understand that your days of action are over.

The idea made Stan miserable. No one liked to admit he was old. But it was time to face reality. He had to do whatever he could to bail Jake out of the Detention Center.

BEIJING, P.R.C.

Marshal Shin Nung's stomach seethed even though outwardly he seemed placid as he sat in a window seat of a large military helicopter.

Nung was sixty-six years old and a hero of the Alaskan and Siberian Wars. His hover/armored thrust across the Arctic ice to Prudhoe Bay had succeeded after a fashion, although it had been bloody and costly. His armored thrust in Siberia years earlier had captured Yakutsk and effectively ended the conflict.

He was the commander of the First Front, of the three Armies on the Californian-Mexican border: the most heavily defended real estate in the world.

Even at sixty-six, Nung still had blunt features and an aggressive stare, though he was more jowly than seven years ago. In his distant youth he had studied at the Russian Military Academy in Moscow. It had been a lonely existence and had earned him the reputation among the Chinese military that he was half-Russian, a terrible slur.

Nung allowed himself a bitter smile. Many in the Army hated him because he had continually achieved success through his adherence to headlong attack, as the Russians used to teach. Once, the old Chairman had backed him. Now the new Chairman known simply as the "Leader" felt obligated to him. During the Alaskan War, they had shared the task of securing Dead Horse, particularly the oil fields there.

Jian Hong was Greater China's "semi-divine" Leader, if one believed the propaganda messages. It was foolish to disagree openly. That was one lesson Nung had learned: to keep dangerous truths to himself.

Marshal Nung flew out of Mao Zedong Airport in Beijing, having arrived from Mexico, from near the American border actually. He was to attend an emergency session of the Ruling Committee. He knew why: the Americans had broken the

53

secret of Blue Swan. It was a terrible blow to Chinese plans, or it could be. Marshal Nung knew the answer to the present dilemma. He usually knew what to do in an emergency. It was his gift and curse to see farther than those around him could. Once, he would have openly declared to anyone who cared to listen what should be done. At sixty-six, he had learned a modicum of wisdom. These days, he kept such opinions to himself and practiced mediations in order to keep his once explosive temper in check.

Nung stared out of the helicopter's window. Below him, Beijing spread out in all its glory. It was rush hour, he supposed. Enormous Chinese cars crawled along the wide avenues and city streets. Many flew large flags with the single Chinese star, showing their patriotism. The vehicles moved past giant glass towers, monumental buildings and titanic statues, products of the Leader's mania for size and grandeur, and of the largest and longest construction boom in history. Beijing was the chief city in the world, the center of civilization, the Middle Kingdom. It was a riot of colors, boasting the most people, the most cars, the most billionaires and the highest concentration of political power.

The rich here maintained private zoos and botanical gardens of gargantuan size. The Leader's polar bears had been pictured in several documentaries, and he had often shown his favor by gifting a lucky official a prime polar bear cub. No longer did masses of pedestrians clog Beijing's sidewalks, nor did bicycles clutter the streets as in many foreign cities. Mexico City had seemed like an overturned ant colony with its tens of thousands of bicyclists. Everyone in Beijing went by car at least, if only in a taxi.

The helicopter's intercom crackled. "Sir," the pilot said. "In case you were wondering, those are two Air Force jets pacing us."

Nung stared out of the window. He spied a J-25 air superiority fighter. Sunlight winked off the craft's canopy.

The pilot banked the helicopter. They were headed for the Leader's summer palace outside the city. Nung closed his eyes, willing his seething stomach to settle down. The next few hours…they might well decide the fate of the world for many years to come.

***

Twenty minutes later, the helicopter banked once more and lurched, going down toward a landing pad in a vast garden of gingko trees. Nearby, there stood a huge palace dominating a luxurious villa. Grecian marble and Californian redwoods predominated as building material. There were gold inlaid fountains, a pagoda and even a large bronze Buddha with half-lidded eyes.

Armored cars ringed the landing pad. Each car bore a lion head on the hood and on the sides. Those belonged to the Leader's Lion Guard, his personal security apparatus.

Without looking at the Army security team in the helicopter with him, Nung said, "Maintain decorum throughout the proceedings and on no account will you take offense at anything said."

His chief of security, a large man with sloping shoulders, turned a stern face toward him, nodding once. The man never wasted words and Nung appreciated that.

A last lurch told him the helicopter had landed. Together, Nung and his security detail strode down the helicopter's carpeted walkway.

Now it begins. Now I enter the political world with its thousands of murky undercurrents.

First divesting his security personnel of weapons, Lion Guardsmen hustled them to waiting cars. The Leader's mania against assassins real and imagined was well known among those in power.

The chief Lion Guardsman, a hulking specimen, stepped up, blocking the sunlight. He bowed before Nung, although there was nothing conciliatory about it. "I must frisk you, sir," the giant said in a deep voice.

Nung froze for an instant. This was a grave indignity for a man of his rank. He resisted the impulse to turn to his security chief—the man wasn't there, but going away toward a confinement cell. For the first time in years, Nung had no security. It was a strange feeling, as if he'd left his fly open or forgotten to put on his tie.

"There is no need to touch me," Nung said gruffly, handing the man his service pistol.

"I'm afraid there is, sir." The Lion Guardsman had hard, pitiless eyes.

He's enjoying this.

"If you would lift your arms..."

Nung complied, enduring the shame of a pat down. The man groped everywhere, running his fingers down and under his buttocks. This was an insult, and it almost broke Nung's resolve. He clenched his teeth, telling himself the rumors must be true then that the latest assassination attempt against Jian Hong had come within centimeters of success.

Once finished with the frisk, the Lion Guardsman looked down at him, smiling faintly before motioning to an armored car. It was a short drive to the palace. Soon, Nung marched down corridors and climbed what seemed like endless flights of stairs.

The hulking Lion Guardsman snapped his fingers. The four flanking Nung turned, and soon they entered a new corridor with portraits of the Leader and the old Chairman in their earlier days. The corridor led to maple double doors with golden handles. The chief guardsman took out a whistle and blew a shrill blast. He yanked open both doors to reveal a cavernous chamber with giant chandeliers and an enormous conference table among other grand furniture.

The chief guardsman shouted in a loud voice, "Marshal Shin Nung of the First Front!" The guardsman stepped back and the four soldiers ground their rifle butts onto the corridor's marble floor.

Nung raised his eyebrows as he peered into the chamber. The Leader—Jian Hong—sat at the farthest end of the conference table. He was a medium-sized man with dark hair, darker eyes and wearing a black suit of the finest silk. The Leader motioned him within.

Once more, Nung complied and the doors shut behind him.

The five other members of the Ruling Committee already attended the Leader, sitting along the table's sides. There was Deng Fong the Foreign Minister, in his early eighties but with the smooth skin of a baby. He had received skin-tucks, but laser surgery could do nothing for his weak left eye, which had closed and marred his otherwise "youthful" features. The other four members held varying posts, although Nung knew each by the man's main occupation. There was the Police Minister, the Army Chief of Staff, the Navy Minister and the Agricultural Minister.

The Leader had attained the highest office, Nung knew, but he did not yet wield supreme power as the old Chairman once had. Deng resisted the Leader and was still too powerful to simply oust or assassinate without serious repercussions. The Navy and Agricultural Ministers often sided with Deng. Perhaps as important, many of China's subject states and allies trusted Deng's good judgment. The Japanese particularly liked him, which meant the Koreans hated the Foreign Minister. The Koreans had never forgotten how arrogantly the Japanese had ruled over them before and during World War II. The most powerful Southeast Asian allies took their cue from Deng and might well leave the Pan Asian Alliance if he simply dropped from sight. The same could be said for the German Dominion Chancellor.

"We have been waiting for you," the Leader said.

Nung nodded respectfully.

"You will sit there," the Leader said, pointing at a chair farthest from him.

Nung marched to the chair, noting his place had a computer scroll. As he sat, Nung greeted the Army Chief of Staff, an old foe named Marshal Kao: his tall shoulders were bowed with age. Kao hardly acknowledged him, turning away to tap the screen of his own computer scroll.

"We have been waiting for you, Marshal Nung," the Leader repeated. "We have a momentous decision to make, an ominous choice with worldwide repercussions." He scanned the others, a frown changing his features, making him seem sterner than Nung remembered.

Jian Hong had always been known as a clever man, a keen intriguer and quick-witted in speech. Over seven years ago, he had been Deng Fong's protégée, a "young" climber in the Socialist-Nationalist Party. Back then, Jian had accepted the post of Agricultural Minister and failed to meet harvest quotas due to increasing glaciation. Then he had backed the Alaskan attack and through it had gained fame, most of it by Nung's actions on the Arctic ice. Nung had never challenged the official story, as it gave him a powerful patron on the Ruling Committee. Despite the Army Chief of Staff's hatred, Nung had risen high these past seven years. If he succeeded in his coming tasks...there was no telling how high he could reach, perhaps even to the Ruling Committee itself. The past seven years had shown him that nothing was impossible.

After the Alaskan War, the old Chairman had deteriorated. He'd summoned his nephew, a Vice-Admiral who had botched most of his tasks during the war. Nevertheless, trusting blood over ability, the Chairman had raised his nephew, granting him the post of commander of the Lion Guard and becoming the Chairman's Representative on the Ruling Committee. The nephew, a lazy man with a strong streak of cruelty, had surprisingly risen to the task. The youngster—a man of forty-three—had begun intriguing immediately. He kept the Chairman secluded and soon began to shuffle his own people into higher and more important posts. The final straw had been when the nephew took the post of Minister of the Navy for himself. Out of fear, Jian and Deng had allied against him. During the height of the short Hawaiian Campaign, the Chairman's nephew fatally crashed into the side of a mountain, everyone in his transport plane burning to death. Afterward, news leaked out that the Chairman had been dead in his underground bunker several months already.

Nung used to wonder if that was true. If it was false, who would have dared to kill the Chairman? The answer to such a question could be found in who had benefited the most from the Chairman's passing. Jian Hong, the Leader, would be that person. Perhaps that's why Jian feared assassination so desperately. People often feared in others what they themselves would most likely attempt.

The Leader now stood and put his manicured fingertips on the table. Their reflective quality matched the shiny tabletop, as if each tried to outdo the other.

"I have summoned the Ruling Committee and Marshal Nung so we can decide today what to do with the Americans.

58

By now, each of you has read the secret report from East Lightning. The Americans managed to infiltrate elite commandos behind our lines in Mexico. In some fashion, they learned about Blue Swan. A convoy transporting a Blue Swan missile was destroyed en route. Worse, pieces of the warhead were ferried back to America. My analysts inform me that we must presume the Americans have uncovered the missile's purpose. If that is so, they can conceivably counter its action in the coming conflict."

The Leader glanced at the others, finally focusing on Deng. "Do you have a comment, Foreign Minister?"

"May I ask about the nature of Blue Swan?"

"Marshal Nung, would you explain the situation, the reason why we needed the missile?" the Leader asked.

Nung folded his hands on the table, clearing his throat and leaning forward so he could look at Deng.

"Sir, the Americans have heavily fortified the southern border, particularly the Californian-Mexican portion of it. There is no Rio Grande River Line there and California is a rich prize by any standard. In a starving world, its agricultural benefits—"

"I am aware of California's food value, General," Deng said.

Nung blinked, wanting to say, "It's Marshal, sir," but not daring to correct someone so powerful and vengeful. It was too soon to say that the Leader would outlast his most dangerous foe.

"Please, stick to the issue of the military need for Blue Swan," Deng said.

Nung bowed his head, keeping his features placid. It was the Chinese way.

Marshal Kao glanced at him, and the old man's right eyebrow twitched the tiniest fraction.

Nung recognized why. The others in the Army thought of him as the "Russian Bear," easily angered and unable to respond in a civilized manner. By civilized they of course meant Chinese.

"Many of the Americans have dubbed the California fortification as the 'Maginot Line'," Nung said. "The reference is to the pre-World War II French fortification. Everyone considered the Maginot Line impenetrable, even the Germans who eventually attacked around the defensive line and conquered France through blitzkrieg, which means 'lightning war'."

"Your Front is stationed across from this 'Maginot Line'?" Deng asked.

"Yes, Foreign Minister."

"Are the American fortifications *impenetrable*?" Deng asked.

"It is a matter of cost," Nung said, "the price paid in flesh and blood to smash through an obstacle. No, the fortification cannot stop our attack in an absolute sense, but it will make such an assault incredibly costly."

"Blue Swan will negate these defenses?" Deng asked the Leader.

"Marshal Kao?" the Leader asked.

Nung sat back as the old marshal told the others that the scientists agreed the missiles would indeed negate the majority of the defenses."

"But not all?" asked Deng.

"The missile will nullify the technological wonders emplaced by the Americans," Kao said. "The missiles will not harm the machine gun nests or disintegrate the concrete pill boxes or embankments there."

"How does our wonder weapon achieve this miracle?" Deng asked.

Kao glanced at the Leader.

"Please, tell us, Marshal," the Leader said.

"The missiles will emit a heavy electro-magnetic pulse," Kao said.

Deng sat up sharply like an angry panda bear. His weak eye attempted to open, failing in that but making the lashes quiver. "We're using tactical nuclear weapons?"

"No!" the Leader said. "Greater China shall never use nuclear weapons without heavy provocation. Firstly, it is unethical. Secondly, we want to conquer America for its agricultural usage. How does it profit us to irradiate the wheat fields and poultry farms that we so desperately need?"

"If I might digress for a moment…" Deng said.

The Leader stared at the older man, finally nodding.

"Why attack America at all?" Deng asked. "Meet with them. Exchange a lessening of our military forces in Mexico for reinstating their food tribute. It was a brilliant concept to put such a heavy concentration of troops into Mexico and prod the Americans to buying us off with grain. I happily concede that I was wrong in opposing the idea. I feared what is now occurring—that we would be fatally tempted into putting too many soldiers there and attacking America because our forces are so handily in position."

"It heartens me to hear you admit your error," the Leader said. "You are a man of stature, Foreign Minister. By our Mexico occupation, we have pushed the Americans and found them to be a hollow people indeed."

"Not quite hollow," Deng said. "Their ABM lasers destroyed many of our satellites. The Americans reacted more aggressively than we thought possible for them."

"A tiny victory that we allowed them," the Leader said with a wave of his hand. "We all can note that Alaska nearly fell to us seven years ago. If not for the former Chairman's nephew and his blunders, we would have added Prudhoe Bay and Anchorage to our conquests. Even with the man's blunders, we successively smashed American carriers, reaping the reward in the Hawaiian Campaign by demolishing America's surface fleet.

"The Americans are clever, however. It makes sense, as they must have been clever to fool the world all these years. I believe the Americans play for time while they build up their land forces."

"I agree with you," Deng said.

The Leader blinked in astonishment. "That meant they gave us foodstuffs to purchase time. Then President Sims cut off the food shipments, leading me to believe he thinks America strong enough to defend itself."

"Again, I would agree with you," Deng said. "My thought, however, is that instead of attempting a continental conquest we offer the Americans an alliance. Let us replace hostility with peace. The Europeans are investing heavily in several of

61

the Saharan countries, thinking to turn deserts into paradises. If successful, I suspect they will attempt to increase their economic zone, possibly replacing it with an empire to challenge us, especially after we've weakened ourselves with a North American War. Consider. We've placed much more of our military into North America than they have in Cuba. The South American Federation holds no true love for the PAA. They are simply greedy vultures, eager to reap the rewards that others, namely ourselves, have worked to produce. Let us offer the Americans an alliance and gain the use of their relative plenty, making an end run around our so-called allies. Now is the perfect moment to achieve this."

"No," the Leader said. "It is far too late for that. We attacked Alaska and took Hawaii from them. We destroyed their satellites, cyber-attacked their industries and helped terrorists set off a nuclear weapon on their soil. They hate us, Foreign Minister. The Americans thirst for vengeance. Their rearmament proves it."

"They fear us," Deng said. "They are simply trying to defend themselves from three giant coalitions. There are eleven million soldiers in Mexico, if one counts the Mexican Home Army. That is reason for the Americans to fear."

"With such forces in place," the Leader said, "now is the time to attack. We have kicked America when she was down. We must never let her get back up to gain vengeance against us."

"This is not the school yard," Deng said, "but international politics."

The Leader shook his head, glancing at the others. "You must not forget that our analysts agree on the coming forecast. The glaciation will continue, likely worsening for many years to come. The world starves, Foreign Minister. In the end, farmland equals power. China has stepped onto the path of conquest, gathering the world's best farmlands. One does not step off that path without serious repercussions. Now is the moment in time for us to build a peaceful world. We must break the Americans before they recover their power. We must add their lands to our Imperium."

"President Sims has given them hope again," Deng said. "He is a strong man busy uniting his countrymen. I think we have given them too much time to strengthen their defenses to now want a continental war."

"It is the reason why we have powerful allies," the Leader said. "The South American Federation adds millions of troops to our side. The Mexican Home Army adds another million. Once the German Dominion ferries greater numbers to Cuba, our combined might will dwarf the American defenses into insignificance."

"Am I the only one who thinks this continental war a grave risk?" Deng asked the others.

"With your permission, Leader?" the Navy Minister asked Jian.

"Speak," the Leader said coldly.

"Our merchant marine is finding it increasingly difficult to supply our Occupation Army in Mexico. A war would only increase the risk of stretching our naval supply line too thin. American submarines would likely operate against us, ensuring substantial losses."

"What about you, Agriculture Minister?" the Leader asked.

The minister did not look up as he stared at the table. "We could use American farmland, Leader. This accursed glaciation freezes our rice fields while leaving the North Americans untouched. It is a travesty of nature."

"Permit me to disagree," Deng said. He glanced sidelong at the Agriculture Minister, his usual ally in these debates. "Our masses are fed and relatively content. What we—"

"We live on a razor's edge of existence," the Leader said. "The European and Russian heartlands have begun to freeze, due to the change of the warm Gulf Stream that once helped heat them. They along with the Americans once produced the masses of foodstuffs to an already hungry world. India no longer exports any foodstuff. Thailand used to export great quantities of rice. Now it can barely feed its people. The Germans hope to turn deserts into paradises, but it is a pricey gamble. We all harvest the sea more than ever. The problem is that China uses too much of its wealth buying up the meager resources of other lands. What happens when the greedy in those lands no longer wish to sell to us? No. We must conquer the American breadbasket. In this dark age of growing cold, it is the only answer to our food dilemma."

Deng bowed his head. "You paint a glum picture, Leader, and I suspect you may be right."

"Then do not fight against me, Foreign Minister."

Deng shook his head. "I ask your permission to disagree. I do not fight you, Leader. My blood simply runs cold when I think about a continental war in North America. You spoke of them being a hollow people. Their war record says differently. We learned that in Korea in the last century during the early 1950s."

"Bah," the Leader said. "We used primitive weapons back then and nearly defeated the American alliance."

"Initially we drove them headlong in retreat from the Yalu River," Deng said. "I have studied the records. Afterward, they slaughtered us in great numbers. It was a bloodbath."

"All the more reason to attack now that we have better weapons and more numerous allies," the Leader said. "Let us remember Korea and gain our revenge on the bloody-handed Americans."

"But if we have lost the use of Blue Swan..." Deng said.

The Leader stiffened, and he slapped the palm of his hand against the table so his ring clicked against the wood. "We have not lost it. We have only lost the surprise of it."

Marshal Nung cleared his throat. He had been waiting for them to get around to this.

The Leader scowled, looking down the table, until he noticed who had made the noise. "You have a point to make, Marshal?"

"Leader, Ministers," Nung said. "We may have lost some of the surprise of Blue Swan, but not all of it."

Deng glanced at his computer scroll, reading something there before addressing Nung. "The East Lightning report clearly indicates the Americans escaped with most of the warhead. They will know what the missile does. Or do you disagree with me on that?"

"No, Foreign Minister," Nung said. "I agree with your assessment." He had read the report many times. It was too bad

64

Military Intelligence hadn't interrogated the woman. Why had East Lightning murdered her to extract such valuable information?

Deng appeared perplexed. "You just said the surprise won't be lost. Or do you deny that?"

"I was speaking in a strategical sense," Nung said. "If commandos managed to take some of the warhead, it will still take time for American scientists to uncover the missile's function."

"Or so you hope," Deng said.

"Even if the Americans know exactly what we're going to do with the missile," Nung said, "it won't help them if we attack immediately."

Silence filled the chamber. Nung smiled inwardly, although outwardly he remained placid. A truism of war was to boldly attack and gain surprise. Surprise left people in shock, unable to react. Under those conditions even bolder attacks won a commander everything. He was beginning to suspect that this truism worked in other fields as well.

"Attack immediately?" Deng asked softly.

"Again, Foreign Minister, I am speaking strategically," Nung said. "It would take another two weeks perhaps seventeen days to ready my Front's assault troops and position reinforcements for a continuous attack." He had been working out the parameters over the Pacific Ocean, realizing this was the opportunity of a lifetime. "During the final preparation week, even given the Americans knowing about Blue Swan, they will not be able to change their deployments significantly enough to change the outcome of a swift assault."

Marshal Kao had turned toward him. The old man opened his mouth, likely to blister the idea with a scathing rebuttal. Few in Chinese High Command cared for hasty perpetrations, preferring carefully calculated plans and setups. Kao particularly wanted every situation known to the smallest detail. It made for plodding, unimaginative strategies.

"A moment, Marshal Kao," the Leader said in a silky voice. "Let Marshal Nung continue."

"I have a hologram of the conceived assault," Nung said. His Front had trained for such an attack. They were ready,

65

well, almost ready. Something always needed greater priming. This was his moment, though. He could feel it.

"Yes, by all means," the Leader said, "show us your plan."

Nung took a computer stick from his pocket. His hand trembled, although probably only he noticed. He willed his hand still, inserting the stick into the scroll. He began tapping the screen. In thirty seconds, a holomap appeared above the center of the table.

"Notice please," Nung said, "the heavy enemy fortification along the border. There are massive concrete emplacements, minefields, artillery pits and SAM sites. Behind the initial fortification is a vast network of trenches, supply dumps and more troop concentrations. We will wash these fortifications with multiple electromagnetic pulses, nullifying the majority of their systems. Then we will send in waves of special infantry to fix them in place."

"A moment," Deng said. "*Fix them in place*, not destroy them?"

"Correct, Foreign Minister. Because of Blue Swan, we will break through their lines in hours rather than in days or weeks. This will occur in key areas. Afterward, we will sweep around them, trapping the bulk of their forces. Because we have fixed them in place, they will be unable to withdraw at the critical moment. That is important, for the Americans have made a fundamental error."

Nung studied the others. He saw it on their faces. They wanted to know what this error consisted of.

"The Americans have put too many troops in their forward lines," Nung said. "In California, that is well over six hundred thousand at our last estimate. Once those troops are trapped and nullified, the state will fall to us like a ripe fruit. Such a blow at such speed will critically weaken the rest of the country."

Deng recovered the quickest. He asked, "You will sweep aside the Americans as our troops swept the enemy from the Yalu River Line in 1950?"

Before Nung could answer, Marshal Kao spoke up. "I am not convinced attacking fortified lines is wise. The Army will be trading blood for blood. Yes, we have more troops, but

66

fortifications are a force multiplier. This sounds like a battle of attrition where you eventually hope the Americans to wilt in place so you may advance."

"I feel that I must agree," Deng said. "I had expected brilliant maneuvers from you, Nung. You're supposedly our best mobile fighter. This plan strikes me as two sumo wrestlers pushing and shoving against each other, trying to exhaust the other instead of using clever moves."

Nung had to glance down at his scroll, forcing away his scowl. *Win them over by keeping your voice level and showing them what this attack brings.* Nung looked up, his features nearly placid. "As Marshal Kao suggests, the Americans expect to slaughter our troops on their fortification. The Blue Swan pulses will change that. Even so, breaking through their line at speed may prove costly, but that will allow us to encircle them and turn it into a battle of annihilation. You must remember that they do not expect an attack there. The surprise of our assault might well unhinge their resolve."

"I doubt it," Deng said.

A wash of emotional heat welled up in Nung. "Foreign Minister, doing the unexpected often shakes an opponent's confidence. It is an ancient dictum of warfare and has done more to win more battles than any other factor." He clicked his scroll. "I would like to read to you what Sun Tzu had to say."

Sun Tzu had written *The Art of War* two and a half thousand years ago. His work was considered as the quintessential treatise on Chinese thoughts concerning war.

Nung quoted, "All warfare is based on deception. Hence, when able to attack, we must seem unable; when using our forces, we must seem inactive; when we are near, we must make the enemy believe we are far away; when far away, we must make him believe we are near."

Nung looked up. "The Americans believe themselves safe behind their defenses. Therefore, that is exactly where we shall begin the grand assault."

"And if your bloodbath means the Americans pour reinforcements there?" Deng said.

Nung allowed himself a faint smile.

"You would desire such a thing?" Deng asked, sounding surprised.

"Not a bloodbath, as you suggest, but their pouring reinforcements south," Nung said.

"Why?"

Nung began to manipulate his computer scroll. The six members of the Ruling Committee watched his plan unfold on the holomap. It involved an armor thrust swinging well east of the southern Californian urban areas and heading straight for LA and the all-important Grapevine pass to Central California.

"A clever plan," the Leader said later. "I am impressed."

"Yes, yes, very clever," Deng said. "Yet several matters outside the scope of the assault bother me. I do not wish to appear pessimistic…"

"I called this meeting so we could air our thoughts," the Leader said. "We six guide Greater China to glory and world dominance. I hold the reins of final authority, but I desire your input and need your cooperation and, hopefully, your enthusiasm. To that end, I would rather hear your disagreements here so I can have the opportunity to persuade you."

Deng nodded. "I have been to Berlin, Tehran and Brasilia. I have spoken with our allies and have received the privilege of listening to their generals. The Germans and their allies are still reluctant to attack America. Yes, they have sent airmobile and hover brigades to Cuba. They have moved a battle fleet into the mid-Atlantic, but they are still uncommitted to an assault. The South American Federation lusts after American farmlands. Of that, I have no doubt. Their military prowess, however, *is* in doubt. I am not a military expert, but I have been led to believe that our other fronts are not yet ready to assault the Rio Grande Line in Arizona, New Mexico and Texas."

"Marshal Kao?" the Leader asked.

Old Marshal Kao, with his aesthetic features, bowed solemnly. He had an unusually sharp nose for a Chinese citizen. There were rumors it had been bio-sculpted, and the thin shininess of the flesh at the base of his nose suggested the rumor was true.

"Leader," Kao said, "the Expeditionary Army in Mexico stands ready to achieve the greatest conquest in history. We have six million soldiers of the highest quality, each man keenly devoted and trained to—"

"How long until the Army can attack all along the line from California to Texas?" the Leader asked.

"Marshal Nung is a hasty soldier," Kao said. "It is his trademark and the reason perhaps why he seems to excel on a fluid battlefield. He has given us a...an incredible plan for taking California. The bulk of the Blue Swan missiles have been allocated to his front. More missiles will be en route from the factories for the New Mexico and Texas fronts in the coming months. The missiles are in limited supply, unfortunately. Thus, the attacks there will commence along conventional lines."

"Can the other fronts be ready to attack in two weeks?" the Leader demanded.

Marshal Kao fidgeted, highlighting his long fingers. He was an accomplished violinist. "The other Front commanders will need another month at least, Leader. I would prefer another six weeks."

The Leader turned to Nung. "What can the Americans do in another month? I mean those facing you in California and with their having learned about Blue Swan."

"In a month, they can change many things," Nung admitted.

"Too much?" asked the Leader.

"The possibility occurs. The greatest danger would be their pulling units out of the fortifications and placing them in strategic reserve."

"What else could they do?" the Leader asked.

"If they were wise," Nung said, "the Americans would harden what electronics they could. More importantly, they would bring massive quantities of simpler weapons to the fortified line and widen the depth of their defense. That would take time, but a month would be better for them than a mere two weeks."

"Why haven't they already done that?" Deng asked. "The Americans are not fools."

"I would suspect cost and time," Nung said. "They have a limited supply of both and must balance each decision for maximum effectiveness."

Deng turned to the Leader. "If the rest of the Army cannot attack, it will leave Marshal Nung's forces open to a concentration of American forces. Despite the brilliance of the plan, his three armies cannot face the full weight of American might."

"If the Leader would permit me to speak to the issue?" Nung asked.

"By all means," the Leader said.

"Foreign Minister Deng raises cogent points," Nung said. "But I do not believe they are insurmountable obstacles. One, the Americans will not know we are unready to attack into Texas, New Mexico and Arizona. We should use selected areas and have our troops there perform demonstrations of force. We must deceive the Americans into thinking we are about to unleash our mass into Texas. Greater troop movement and open supply rearrangements will focus their attention to the wrong sector."

The Leader nodded thoughtfully.

"Likely, the Americans do not realize the Germans want more time," Nung said. "With our demonstrations, the Americans will anticipate an assault on the wrong front, holding their various theater reserves in place. Therefore—"

"Will they do that if California is about to fall?" Deng asked. "Won't they instead risk depleting inactive fronts and rush those reinforcements to hurl your armies back into Mexico?"

"There are three reasons why I don't believe so," Nung said. "First, the speed of our assault will strategically surprise the Americans. We will not give them the time to shift those reserves. In other words, by the time they think about doing as you suggest, we will have conquered the Golden State and sealed it tight."

"And if your attack fails to keep the pace of your desired speed?" Deng asked. "It is my understanding that clever military plans seldom survive contact with the enemy."

Nung bristled. Who had reached Prudhoe Bay despite every impediment set before him? Who had won the Siberian War? The answer was *he* had through his swift attacks.

While clearing his throat, Nung squared his shoulders. "Foreign Minister, Leader, I stake my reputation on achieving a swift and California-conquering assault."

The others stared at him, and Nung realized his temper had gotten the better of him. He had spoken too bluntly and too boldly, too much like a Russian barbarian—at least how the others would view it.

"The second reason," Nung said, deciding to drive ahead with his analysis, "is the nature of California. Much of it sits behind the Sierra Nevada Mountains. If it looks as if it will fall, the Americans might decide to try to seal us in the Golden State. That, too, will weaken their resolve toward sending other theater reserves into California."

"How does their sealing us in California help us?" Deng asked. "This sounds like a reason to leave California alone and concentrate on a greater conquest by driving through Texas into the American heartland."

"As you've stated earlier," Nung said, "we are attempting a continental conquest. You do not shove an entire cake into your mouth to eat, but slice off pieces, eating a little at a time. First, their attempt to seal us in California would help us defend what we conquer. It would help us digest California. Californian foodstuffs are also important in their own right. Central California particularly produces great quantities of agricultural goods. However, if the Americans are so foolish as to strip their other fronts of reserves to save California—"

"And thereby smash one of our fronts," Deng said, "as they defeat your armies in detail. I had been led to believe that the coordination of *all* our assaults would be what would lead us to victory."

"That would be optimum, of course," Nung said. "But, as I was about to say, I also mean to send airmobile troops to the Sierra Nevada mountain passes, stopping or slowing any reinforcements into California."

"This is possible?" Deng asked. "Will you also stake your reputation on this?"

"I will!" Nung said.

Deng sat back, staring at him.

"You spoke of a third reason," the Leader said.

Nung bowed to the Navy Minister. "I do not presume upon naval matters. But I have been wondered about something."

"Tell us," the Leader said.

"Can I show you rather?" Nung asked.

The Leader gestured for him to do so.

For the next half hour, Nung outlined an amphibious assault he had worked out toward securing the Monterey Bay coastal region, the Bay Area and then a strong thrust into the Central Californian Valley.

"The question becomes," said Deng, "how long until the Navy could gather the needed forces to attempt such a thing?"

The Navy Minister licked his lips. "Leader, the Navy could attempt this amphibious assault in three weeks, perhaps sooner."

Deng's head swiveled around as he stared in shock at the Navy Minister. The man was supposed to be his staunchest political ally.

The Leader sat back in his chair, looking like a satisfied cat licking its paws.

Nung had spoken via satellite phone with the Leader during his Pacific crossing. It had been his suggestion about how to turn the Navy into the Leader's ally in this.

"Marshal Nung," the Leader said. "You have spoken boldly and honestly. I appreciate your candor, your enthusiasm and your military skill. What you are suggesting is breathtaking in scope. You have achieved near military miracles in the past. Yet it seems to me that your forces are too small to grasp this amazing prize. What additional units do you feel you would need to insure the conquest of California?"

"To make the continuous assault against the fortified areas a certainty, I would need the 19th and 33rd Reserve Armies," Nung said. "They are presently in the strategic reserve and simply need dedicated transports to reach my front. For my armored thrust, I would require the addition of the 233rd Tank Corps. It is presently in the Third Front and would need to be sent via rail. I would hope they would begin to entrain several days from now. Once the assault has commenced, I would also need the transfer of the 7th Army from Arizona. For the duration of the campaign, I require the dedication of the 10th, 13th and 18th Air Fleets."

Marshal Kao flexed his violinist's fingers. They were long and had large knuckles. It seemed impossible he could ever slip his gold wedding ring off its finger. He now tapped on his scroll. After reading what was there, Kao looked up, scowling. "Combined with the amphibious invasion, that amounts to over two million troops: a third of our Expeditionary Force."

"That is correct," Nung said.

Marshal Kao blinked repeatedly.

"We have moved six million soldiers into Mexico," the Leader said. "The South Americans have moved three million. The Germans, I believe, will become greedy and eager to slice off their portion of America once we show them the possibility of it."

"Storming and capturing California is a grave risk," Deng said.

"And yet, as Marshal Nung has pointed out," the Leader said, "it is a risk in a limited theater of war."

"Provided his airmobile brigades can block the strategic passes in the Sierra Nevada Mountains," Deng said.

"It is a risk," Nung admitted. "That is why we need the Blue Swan missiles. They are the key to the assault. We must smash through the border defenses at speed and trap the bulk of California's armies there. That will panic the Americans and make the amphibious assault that much more deadly to enemy morale."

With half-lidded eyes, Deng stared at Nung as if taking his measure. "I happen to recall the Arctic crossing seven years ago. You delayed then. Why won't you delay again at precisely the wrong moment?"

Marshal Nung opened his mouth in anger. Those delays had not been because of him. They had been because of—

The Leader cleared his throat.

Nung glanced at the Leader. A cold feeling crept through him. He'd almost told these men the truth. That would have ruined everything.

"I have learned from Jian Hong," Nung said. "I will not make the same mistake twice."

"Sir," Marshal Kao asked the Leader. "I wonder if we might add one precaution, especially as we recall that you had to prod Marshal Nung seven years ago."

"Yes?" the Leader asked.

"I would like to send Field Marshal Gang to the First Front," Kao said. "Gang would report to us—the Ruling Committee—particularly if he sees that Marshal Nung is spending our troops too liberally against the enemy fortifications. Also, if he feels that the Marshal is stalling, Gang could report that to us as well."

"I object," Nung said. "Divided commands are a serious impediment to—"

"Excuse me," Kao said. "I am not speaking about a divided command. Marshal Gang would be an observer only. Surely, you cannot object to the Ruling Committee having its own personal representative at your front?"

"The implications—" Nung said.

"I would feel better if Marshal Gang joined the First Front," Deng said. "It would alleviate my last qualms and help me to convince our allies. Naturally, we would have to empower the marshal to act in an emergency."

The Leader drummed his fingers on the table. Very well," he said. "Marshal Gang will return with you, Marshal Nung. He will observe, and he will be granted emergency powers, provided the need occurs." The Leader glanced at the others in turn before looking at Nung again. "In two weeks, you will unleash the greatest assault in history, smashing the Americans."

Nung nodded, delighted at the prospect but wondering how much Marshal Gang was going to try to interfere with him.

-3-
Deployments

OCEANSIDE, CALIFORNIA

Paul Kavanagh ran along the beach, trying to outdistance his guilt. His angular features were contorted with concentration. He repeatedly went over in his mind what had happened in Mexico.

Beside him, ocean waves rolled in, crashing against the sand, with swirls of cold saltwater and white foam reaching for his running shoes. In the water, tanned surfers rode the waves. They seemed like humanoid seals to Paul, moving with such ease and grace. He'd surfed a few times. The freedom of lying there on his board as the water rolled under him...it had been magical, among the most peaceful moments of his life.

The thud of his feet and the roar of the ocean couldn't absolve him of guilt, couldn't even hide it for long. He'd abandoned Maria Valdez to the Chinese. It hadn't been his choice. He hadn't known the helicopter drone was going to take off with only him in it. He'd thought it would pick up Maria and the last guerilla. There had been three seats in the drone.

Paul wore mirrored sunglasses, but he didn't bother glancing at the beauties lying on the sand on their towels. Most would have already untied the back of their bikinis to get rid of tan lines. Today—actually, ever since coming back from

Mexico—he wasn't interested in any of these women. Running, pumping weights, drinking beer interested him, anything to exhaust him or take his mind off lifting away as White Tigers fired shock grenades at Maria Valdez, knocking her unconscious.

By phone, he had complained to General Ochoa about the drone. The four-star general had told him he'd look into it. The drone was supposed to have picked up all survivors, not just him.

You don't leave your own on the battlefield. It was a Marine saying that had long ago been drilled into him.

Paul flung his head to the side so sweat flew off. He kept his thumbs "out." When you clutched your thumbs with your other fingers while running that meant you were about to flag, to quit. He now forced himself to swing his arms in rhythm and keep his knees up. He was too old to allow himself to get out of shape. If he wanted to succeed at his recon duties, he had to keep in top condition.

Years ago, many years ago, he had arrived in Camp Pendleton for basic training. It was only a few miles down the beach from here. That had been a grueling time for most of the recruits, but he'd excelled at it. While on leave, he'd met Cheri in Oceanside. She had been lying on the beach, one of the babes with her string bikini untied. He needed to call her later this evening. She wanted to know where they were posting him next. He still didn't know. General Ochoa—

Hey! What was this? An MP in his white helmet stood fifty yards down the beach, waving his arm at him. Several sunbathers had propped themselves up onto their elbows to stare at the man.

What do they want with me now?

Figuring this would be the end of his run today, Paul accelerated. He sprinted for the MP. The initial burst made him feel as if he was flying. He loved it. The sand whizzed by in a blur. He felt like a young god, as if he could run forever. Then it hit him: the long run and the demand he'd already placed on his aging body. His lungs wanted more air and his legs lost their feather-like lift. Paul snarled, forcing himself to run just as fast. It lacked the same effortless joy, though.

Keep it up to the MP. Sprint to there.

Paul did through raw stubbornness—it might have been his greatest attribute. He sprinted past the MP.

"Hey!" the man yelled at him.

Paul slowed and then stopped. He gasped for air as sweat appeared. The cool ocean breeze felt good on his skin. He turned around as sweat bathed his face.

"Paul Kavanagh?" the MP asked.

"That's me."

"You're to come with me, Gunnery Sergeant."

"Is there trouble or am I in it?" Paul asked.

The MP shrugged, which made the strap over his shoulder creak with a leathery sound. "I'm just carrying out orders. I'm to take you straight to Camp Pendleton, to the Commandant's office."

"You can't tell me anything?"

The MP shook his head.

"Sure. Let me get my stuff down the beach."

"We need to leave right away," the MP said. "I was told that was to be without exception."

Paul thought about it and shrugged. He had his key with him. What did a towel and water bottle matter? "Do you want me to follow on my motorcycle?"

"I want you come with me. We'll have someone else bring in your bike."

"Sounds serious," Paul said. "What's up?"

"Don't know, just that I'm supposed to get you."

The MP was young, maybe twenty-one.

"Let's go then," Paul said, marching across the hot sand, heading for the nearest set of stairs up to the road.

***

It was a short trip to Camp Pendleton. He'd been detached from his unit for some time. The last he heard, they were training near the Oregon border. He'd gone to D.C., meeting other special ops members for the secret missions so dear to General Ochoa.

Instead of heading for the Commandant's office, the MP took him to the base stockade.

"You didn't tell me I was under arrest," Paul said.

77

"You're not."

"Then why—"

"Security. We're to keep you safe."

"What are you talking about?"

"That's all I know. If anyone tries for you, I'm to shoot him, or her, if it comes to that."

"Who wants to shoot me?" Paul asked.

"You're probably going to find out soon enough." The MP braked in front of the stockade. "Go ahead. I have to park this."

Paul got out, checked in with the clerk inside, who stood and motioned to three armored MPs.

"This way," the senior MP said.

Several minutes later, Paul found himself in the basement, in a small interrogation room, staring at a computer screen. The door was locked and two of the MPs stood outside as guards.

"Now what did I do?" Paul muttered. He sat at the table, looking at the screen. It had several card games on it. He chose spider solitaire. In the middle of his seventh game, the cards dissolved and he found himself staring at General Ochoa.

"Sir?" Paul asked. "Is there some problem, what is going on?"

General Ochoa was a thickset man with straight dark hair and brown Aztec skin. He never smiled and had a particularly intense stare. Paul could easily imagine Ochoa as a gang leader, able to outface any opponent. Long ago, his ancestors had fought the Spanish conquistadors. Wielding nothing but obsidian-tipped swords and wearing feather armor, the Aztecs had furiously attacked Spanish knights in steel-plated armor, swinging Toledo-forged swords and backed by cannons roaring grapeshot. The Aztecs had lost in the end, but not because of a lack of courage or daring. The greatest feat of honor an Aztec flower warrior could achieve in battle was capturing an enemy for ritual slaughter later on the pyramids. Thus, during the hotly contested fights, the Aztec champions had often subdued a Spaniard and begun to drag him away. That gave the other Spaniards time to rescue their companion. Their only goal was to kill as many Indians as possible and take their wealth. Although General Ochoa had Aztec genes, in outlook he was

78

pure conquistador, wanting to kill as many of America's enemies as possible.

"Yes, there's a problem," General Ochoa said. "It concerns Maria Valdez."

Paul frowned as the guilt resurfaced. *You ran away, Marine. You left a comrade when you might have rescued her.* He had vowed seven years ago never to leave anyone again. Back then, he'd have to leave a friend on the Arctic ice in order to survive. The grim decision still ate at him. Whenever he drank too much, he had a habit of rethinking seven-year-old options. He would turn the problem over in his mind like a rat on a spinning wheel.

"I should have let go of the ladder and dropped down to help her," Paul said.

General Ochoa nodded, his face remaining emotionless like an ancient block of wood. "I thought you would believe something so romantically foolish."

"I didn't kiss her," Paul said.

"Not that kind of romantic. You're a soldier. You're special ops, the very best we have. You, more than anyone else, should understand the true nature of war. It's a dirty business. It's bloody and without remorse. I read your report. You shot Chinese from behind. That wasn't very sporting of you."

"If I hadn't done that they would have killed us, sir."

"Again, you miss the point. You did the right thing ambushing them, shooting them from behind. You also had no choice with the drone. If you had done anything else, we wouldn't have learned what we did."

"What did we learn?"

General Ochoa shook his head. "It's classified, but what you brought back will go a long way toward defending California. And that will go a long way to keeping this country ours."

"That's something, at least."

General Ochoa snorted. "Your mission will probably end up being the most important single event against the Chinese threat. You proved my theory right. For the big play, you need big play players. You may have fixed everything by what you found."

"So...why am I in this stockade?" Paul asked.

Ochoa nodded. "You're not in military trouble, if that's what you're thinking. It's the nature of the mission rebounding on you. Maria Valdez was captured."

"Are the Chinese trying to strong-arm Colonel Valdez with her?"

"No," Ochoa said. "They've already informed the Colonel of her death and have shipped him most of her body parts."

"What? That's sick."

"It's meant to break the Colonel's spirit," Ochoa said. "My sources tell me he's raging. His aides have hidden all his sidearms and they've told his guards to keep theirs at home for a few days. They fear he might turn suicidal or maybe shoot one of them. My sources also tell me he's angry with his aides for not stopping him from sending his daughter on the mission."

Paul thought what he'd feel like if the Chinese sent him his son's body parts. Imagine opening a package and finding a bloody ear, knowing you'd tweaked that ear more than once. Or taking a hand out of a box and recognizing an old burn mark on the back your son had gotten when he brushed the hand against a hot light bulb. Paul shuddered. He'd want to nuke China.

"The Chinese are remorseless," Ochoa said. "They mean to win no matter what they have to do. We have to fight just as hard, as ruthlessly."

Paul nodded. If he had to, he would take his wife and son to the hills, to the mountains, and resist the Chinese until his dying day.

"Unfortunately for you," Ochoa said, "Colonel Valdez has asked for your presence at his headquarters."

"Me?" Paul asked. "Oh. Does he want me to tell him how Maria fought until the very end?"

"If only that were it," Ochoa said. "He specifically wants your head detached from your shoulders. He wants your head on a pike so he can plant it on his daughter's grave."

"Is that a joke?"

Ochoa shook his head.

Paul leaned back and tore his eyes from the screen. He sat in a prison cell. Two MPs guarded his locked door. A sinking feeling twisted his gut.

"Colonel Valdez and his Free Mexico Army are important to American survival," Paul said.

"True."

"They're more important than a single Marine such as me," Paul added.

"Are you volunteering to visit Colonel Valdez?"

Paul frowned, thinking about Cheri, about his promise to her. He meant to protect his country. But giving up his head…

"Whether you're volunteering or not," Ochoa said, "doesn't matter. The U.S. military does not hand over its soldiers to other countries in order to have their heads removed."

At least not openly, we don't, Paul thought.

"I had you brought to Camp Pendleton as a security measure," Ochoa said. "My fear is that Colonel Valdez will have allocated hit men to take you out and bring him your head. Valdez killed President Felipe with assassins."

"I remember," Paul said.

"The Colonel has survived these years because he is a hard man. He has learned how to make people respect him. He also knows the border area and has many contacts in the Southwestern states."

"So where are you sending me?" Paul asked. "My unit is in Oregon."

"Actually, your unit is in Florida practicing in the Everglades."

"Are we worried about GD commandos?" Paul asked.

"More than that," Ochoa said. "But you're not headed for Florida."

"Okay."

"I'm placing you on Colonel Norman's staff. You're going to be his bodyguard."

"I don't get it."

"It's easy enough," Ochoa said. "Keep Colonel John Norman alive. He's supposed to be one of our defense wizards and the Joint Chiefs want him advising our generals down

81

there. It seems there's to be an emergency shuffle of military arrangements on the border."

"The colonel is in California then?"

"He's already inspecting the so-called 'Great Wall of America.' You have heard of it, I hope."

"Who hasn't?" Paul said.

"I'm sending you to him tonight. You'll be his shadow, Paul."

"Okay, but why am I really going?"

"I just told you."

"Who's going to try to kill a colonel that he needs a bodyguard?" Paul asked. "Isn't that what MPs are for?"

"You and I both know Chinese Intelligence has penetrated our country."

Paul nodded. President Sims and his communication teams often spoke about that, naming it as one of the key reasons for the state of emergency.

"It's also common Chinese military doctrine to try to paralyze an enemy by first assassinating his key commanders," Ochoa said. "I would expect them to know about Colonel Norman. Likely, the Chinese will use White Tigers to strike commanding generals and anyone else they think is important enough. It's an excellent idea, actually. We'll be doing the same thing soon."

"You're going to send me into Mexico to shoot Chinese commanders?" Paul asked, thinking about Lee in Hawaii.

"It's a distinct possibility."

"With the help of Colonel Valdez's guerillas to guide my team?" asked Paul.

Ochoa frowned. "We'll have to see if the Colonel has calmed down enough by then concerning you."

Right. The general was putting him on ice, keeping him nearby in case America needed to give Valdez a present to keep him interested in helping them. They would never just send him gift-wrapped. No. They would send him across the border on a mission and let him fall into Valdez's hands. If it was a matter of American survival…could he blame them?

Yeah, 'cause it's my head.

"You think the Chinese are going to attack sometime soon?" Paul asked.

Ochoa's frown departed, giving his features the ancient wood quality.

Is that his poker face?

"Would you ship six million soldiers across the Pacific to just sit on their thumbs?" Ochoa asked.

"It got them free wheat."

"Keep yourself out of trouble, Gunnery Sergeant, and keep Colonel Norman alive. I don't care what you have to do to see it done. Am I making myself clear?"

"Yes, sir," Paul said. *You're giving me a makeshift chore to keep me near Colonel Valdez, or you're hanging me out as a target for the Colonel's hit men.*

"Good luck, Marine. I think you're going to need it."

"Yeah," Paul said, believing exactly that.

NORTHERN MEXICO

Fighter Rank Zhu Peng of the White Tiger Commandos lay on the hard ground. His nose bled and his head rang from the rock-hard punch of First Rank Tian Jintao, the hit that had dropped him.

The others of their squad watched silently, waiting to see what he would do.

Zhu blinked while on the ground, trying to focus. He had always been too late and too little for just about everything. His parents had been in their fifties when they'd had him. Each had died before his twelfth birthday. He had gone therefore to the State home for orphans. Unfortunately, he had been a skinny child; some might have said malnourished. He had been an easy target to pick on and he might have retreated into himself except for an old soldier who had lost a leg in the Siberian War. The man was the orphan home's janitor. Many had considered the janitor a lack-wit. But the old soldier had let Zhu watch TV with him down in the basement. He had also taught Zhu a few Shaolin martial arts moves. With those, Zhu had fought back against his tormenters. It had meant corporal

83

punishment in the yard by the headmaster, a beating on the buttocks by cane. He had cried; more like sobbed. The others had laughed later and therefore he had been even more of an outcast than before. It had meant many lonely hours watching TV with the old soldier.

The man's combat stories had fired Zhu's imagination. It had led him to join the White Tigers, China's elite commandos.

The *Bai Hu Tezhongbing* were unique to Socialist-Nationalist China. They had been the first to implement the new enlisted rankings. The White Tigers had dispensed with the old order of private, corporal and sergeant. Instead, it went Fighter Rank, Soldier Rank and First Rank. Several years later, the Chinese Army, Navy and National Militia had incorporated the new enlisted rankings. In everything military, the *Bai Hu* led the way.

Too little and too late—Zhu Peng lay on the hard ground in Mexico. He had just arrived from China, from basic jetpack training in the Jing Mountains. Normal *Bai Hu* military procedure kept each White Tiger squad together. Like other militaries around the world, the Chinese had found that men fought hardest for their comrades, to save them and to keep his fellow soldiers' respect. Zhu was a replacement for a White Tiger killed by a Mexican saboteur. Zhu was the new man. Worse, he was the thinnest and weakest of the squad. This afternoon, the First Rank had decided to test his quality. In other words, to give Zhu a beating so he understood that he wasn't wanted.

Zhu clenched his teeth, even though it made his bleeding nose throb with pain. With the palms of his hands, he shoved up against the ground, feeling the grains of sand press against his flesh. Something at the corner of his eye blurred—it was the First Rank's booted foot coming for him. He could see the frayed laces.

The steel toe caught Zhu in the chest. It was like a hammer. It flipped him onto his back as he gasped for air.

Tian Jintao peered down at him from what seemed like a great height. Tian had bulging muscles and he knew how to use them with his dreadful coordination. Tian had a thick neck and a tiger-tail tattoo under his left eye. He was naked from the

84

waist up, wearing camouflage pants and combat boots. Tall cactuses ringed the hard-packed ground around them.

"You are too small, Zhu Peng," the First Rank told him. "You are also too slow. You will get the rest of us killed in combat."

The other squad-members muttered agreement.

"How did you ever pass White Tiger training?" Tian asked.

Zhu had been told before it was due to the war, to the mass mobilization of Chinese soldiers. The quality of the *Bai Hu* was not what it used to be. That he had made it this far showed that.

"I'm going to stomp on you," Tian said, raising his left knee.

Zhu swiveled while remaining on his back. He lashed out with a foot, almost catching Tian by surprise. At the last moment Tian hopped up. When he landed, he lashed out, kicking Zhu in the side with a terrific thud.

"Yes, a good beating," Tian said matter-of-factly. "That's exactly what you need."

"Get rid of the new boy!" one of the others shouted. "We don't want a skinny runt like him in our squad."

Tian swung his foot back to kick again.

From on the ground, Zhu threw two fistfuls of dirt up at the First Rank. He slithered away and hurried to his feet. His nose dripped blood, his chest throbbed and it felt as if one of his ribs was broken. The multiple pains stole his courage. He wanted to run away so the beating would end.

"That's a good trick, new boy." Tian took a combat stance, moving toward Zhu sideways, circling him.

The sight of Tian closing in, knowing there was going to be more pain—Zhu's eyelids flickered and his mouth opened slightly.

It made Tian pause.

Zhu took a combat stance. He was thin, a mere one-sixty in American pounds. Tian was two-ten and only an inch taller.

"I'm going to hurt you," Tian said, smiling.

Zhu shouted desperately, launching a flying kick. Tian evaded, punching Zhu in the side of the head, knocking him down so Zhu thudded onto the hard ground.

"Had enough, Fighter Rank?" Tian asked from above.

Zhu struggled to a sitting position, spitting dirt. He shouted, more a scream of frustration and shame. On his hands and knees, he charged Tian. He caught the First Rank by surprise, throwing his weight against the man as he clutched both legs. He toppled Tian so the man crashed onto his butt.

The others watched in silence.

As Tian kicked, Zhu released his tormenter's legs. He grabbed a rock as his fingers tightened like wires around it. He lifted the rock and lurched at his enemy. He was going to smash Tian Jintao's face.

Before that happened, Tian made it to his knees and his fist caught Zhu under the jaw. Zhu dropped the rock as he crumpled to the ground. He lay there, stunned, with ringing in his ears.

"He's too stupid to quit," someone observed.

"He's also much too skinny," someone else said.

"The Americans will kill him the first time we fight."

"I don't think he'll run away, at least."

"He won't get the chance because the Americans will kill him like that." Someone snapped his fingers.

"I think he meant to kill you, First Rank. It's clear he has no sense of proportion."

"Yes," Tian Jintao said. "The new boy knows how to hate. That's better than crying."

"I saw tears in his eyes. He feels pain too much."

"He's weak," Tian Jintao said. "Now that he's in Mexico, he can eat more. Let him put some muscle on his bones. Who knows what will happen." He paused before saying, "Anyway, he's ours, and we know now he's too stupid to quit. If he can actually control his jetpack, we can at least use him to ferry supplies."

"That's true. He can ferry supplies."

"Yes. If he can't fight, he can still be useful as an errand boy."

"Wake up, Fighter Rank," Tian said. "It's time we got back to base."

Water poured onto Zhu's head and despite the ringing in his ears, the world came back into focus. First Rank Tian held out his hand. Zhu took it, helped up to his feet.

Then the world spun and he staggered, trying to remain standing. The world spun worse and Zhu shuddered as his body spasmed. He vomited in front of the others, shamed. When he wiped his mouth, trying to focus his blurring vision, Tian nodded. Tian didn't smile, but he acknowledged him.

"You belong to Red Squad," Tian said. "You are too weak, too small and too slow to fight well. I think it is only that you are too stupid to quit that you made it into the White Tigers. From now on, you will carry our supplies."

Zhu bowed his head, and that made him vomit again. His cheeks burned as shame consumed him. When he straightened, the others slung their canteen straps over his head. Then, as a group, they began to run back to camp. Zhu struggled to keep up with them, weighted down by the canteens and slowed by the pounding in his head. Doggedly, he followed. He belonged to Red Squad *Bai Hu*, and he would die rather than shame himself by failing to bring the others their supplies.

LAS VEGAS TESTING GROUNDS, NEVADA

While wearing dark sunglasses, Captain Stan Higgins's shoulders slumped as he bounced about in his seat. He rode in an old Humvee back to base, with the big tires crunching over sand and gravel. A scowling, sunglasses-wearing Jose drove them through a bright desert.

Jose was short and fat and he had been with Stan in Alaska, the gunner of their M1A2 tank. After the war, Jose had followed him into the Army, remaining as his gunner, but now of an X1 Behemoth. Jose's youngest son ran his old mechanic shop in Anchorage. Because of his roly-poly physique, Jose was always wheedling another yearlong exemption for the Army's weight limit. That he was the unit's best gunner had something to do with his success gaining it. As did his mechanical skills. In the Alaskan National Guard, Jose had often worked late at night to keep their M1A2s running. Of

87

course, no one had expected an old, fat, ex-National Guardsman to be able to help on the latest technological marvel on the testing grounds. Yet Jose had done that three times already, his "fix" finding its way into the Behemoth's tech manual each time.

Stan had just told Jose about his decision to leave the Army and go to D.C. as a John Glen analyst.

The Humvee roared through the desert sands of the testing ground. They passed rocks and darting lizards, leaving a billowing sand cloud behind them.

"I can help you," Jose said.

"Huh?" asked Stan. He lifted his chin off his chest. He'd been thinking about how he was going to tell the colonel his decision as soon as they returned to base.

"I can give you a loan," Jose said. "How much did you say your son needed?"

"Ten thousand new dollars," Stan said.

Jose glanced at him. "I don't have that kind of money."

Stan shook his head. "I never expected you to give me money or a loan for that matter."

Jose tightened his grip of the steering wheel. His fat shoulders hunched up and his head leaned forward. "I could take out a mortgage on the shop."

"No," Stan said. "I could never—"

"You can't leave the Army! We need you."

"Believe me, it isn't something I want to do." Stan frowned, wondering if that was true. He loved tanks but he was sick of taking orders from a martinet like Colonel Wilson.

Over three hundred years ago, there had been a Jean *Martinet*, the Inspector General of the army of the Sun King, Louis XIV of France. The Inspector General had been a stickler for rules and etiquette beyond that of common sense. His brand of insanity had coined a word—martinet—and Colonel Wilson could have been a reincarnation of the Sun King's old Inspector General.

It would be good to leave the testing grounds, Stan decided as the top of his head struck the Humvee's ceiling.

"Sorry," Jose said. The front left tire had hit and climbed a large rock, shaking the Humvee.

Stan grunted his acceptance of the apology. Imagine—no more silly orders, no more snapping off precise salutes or penning time-wasting reports for the colonel. He wouldn't have to endure the colonel's scathing words either. The Army wasn't like the Alaskan National Guard. It had been informal in Alaska, working with the same men for years. Here, a man like Colonel Wilson could torpedo those under him, making life miserable enough so the joy leaked away. Sure, the colonel was smart, and he knew more about electromagnetic projectiles than just about any one. The colonel had a Ph.D. on the subject and years of experimental research. He lacked leadership skills and military acumen, however. Stan would hate to see the colonel try to maneuver the Behemoths in battle.

"There has to be something I can do," Jose said.

Stan blinked himself out of his reverie, glancing at his friend. Jose had a round head. He'd been losing hair and was almost bald now. Because of that, the man always wore a cap. This one was an old hunting cap with furry earflaps that were badly frayed on the ends.

Jose turned to him. "If I mortgage my shop—"

"No!" Stan said, louder than he'd meant to.

Jose winced as if Stan had hit him.

"Look," Stan said. "It…it is against regulations for me to accept a loan from one of my men, especially a large loan. I appreciate the offer, though. I really do."

"We need you," Jose said, watching the desert, swerving to miss a rock.

As he swayed in his seat, Stan shook his head. "There are still too many glitches in the Behemoths to take them into combat. That's all you'd really need me for, fighting Chinese. The colonel can take care of the experiments here. Besides, the Chinese aren't stupid enough to start a continental war with us."

"There are six million reasons why I disagree," Jose said.

"Yeah, I know," Stan said. He peered out his side window. There was a jackrabbit out there, running away, zigzagging. You never did that in combat. If you needed to get somewhere, you ran hard to reach safety. There wasn't any of that goofing around with zigzagging. Stupid rabbit.

89

Stan remembered reading an article about Bernard Montgomery, the English Field Marshal who had defeated Rommel at El Alamein during World War II. Montgomery had said:

"Rule 1, on page 1 of the book of war, is 'Do not march on Moscow.' Various people have tried it, Napoleon and Hitler, and it is no good. This is the first rule. I do not know whether your Lordships will know Rule 2 of war. It is 'Do not go fighting with your land armies in China.' It is a vast country, with no clearly defined objectives."

Stan would have liked to add Rule 3. Do not bring your land armies to America to fight because we will whip your ass.

Yes, the Chinese had six millions soldiers, with Mexican allies and with millions of South American Federation soldiers. But the U.S. was a big place with many tough fighters and American determination. Stan frowned. Would the Chinese dare attack? Yes, the Chinese had knocked out the satellites, cyber-assaulted and helped terrorists ignited a nuke. The scope of a land war, though, dwarfed the imagination. It would be World War III, and for what?

Stan's frown deepened. The Chinese talked about food, but that was just an excuse. It was about power, about being the biggest dog on the block. The truth was that some men loved to fight. History showed that some men or nations rose up to conquer. The Assyrians, the Persians, Macedonians, Romans…it was a long list. They conquered for a time and finally settled down again, becoming like everyone else once more. Was this China's era? Was it their turn to collect nations like trophies on their belt and kill millions?

"They won't attack us," Stan said. He had to believe that. He hated the idea of running out on his men if the Chinese were really going to attack. Why had his son protested Sims? Why couldn't his boy keep his head down and get on with his studies? The young were always so reckless.

"You keep saying the Chinese won't attack, Professor. So how come I don't believe you really mean it?"

"It's foolish to attack us," Stan muttered.

"Like you said many times, 'People are fools'."

90

"The expenditure in money, blood and treasure," Stan said, "it would beggar them."

"Maybe they mean to beggar us," Jose said.

"No. They want our farmland. The world does, too. In the end, it would be wiser and more productive for them to find new ways to grow food. Look at what the Germans are doing in Saharan Africa. That's the right way to fix this mess. But that takes too much thought for most people. Besides, men with nifty weapons like to use them. They figure, 'It's easy. We'll just conquer the Americans and steal their bread. They aren't what they used to be.' But invading a country, it seldom goes how you think it will. Ask the Iraqis about that after they invaded Iran in 1980."

"So you're staying?" Jose asked.

Stan closed his eyes. The truth, he could probably do more good at John Glen than he could do here. Congressmen would listen to him. Maybe he could even help shape policy. What was he going to do out here, driving these overweight tanks with their nitpicky problems and commanded by Colonel Martinet himself?

His wife wanted him to leave. His son desperately needed him to leave. From John Glen, if nothing else, he could pull strings. Crane had already said the corporation had a policy about helping relatives in trouble with the government. Besides, Stan thought, he could no longer endure the humiliation of serving here, not with being passed over yet again for major.

"I can't stay, Jose. I'm sorry."

***

Colonel Walter Wilson sat behind his mammoth desk staring at Stan.

Everything in the office was at right angles to everything else. The photographs on the wall showing Wilson with various dignitaries or superior officers were perfectly aligned. The desk and everything on the desk sat precisely at the right spot. There was no dust, no dirt and absolutely no sand on anything. The colonel's shirt and jacket were impeccably pressed. His shoes shone. His black hair looked as if he'd just left the barber's shop and his pinkish skin showed that he zealously kept the sun's rays from damaging his cells.

"You have three minutes," the colonel said.

It was three minutes to twelve and Stan and everyone on base knew that the colonel would be in the officer's mess sipping a glass of wine as he watched the waiter march out to take his order at 12:05. It took four minutes to walk from the office to the officer's mess, and it took one minute for the colonel to walk into the mess and reach his chair at his table. Thus, he could now afford Stan three minutes.

Stan wiped his brow. He was still sweating. The air conditioner in the Humvee had quit working several days ago. His jacket was stifling. Why couldn't Wilson lower the temperature in here?

Stan wondered if Wilson had read how Douglas MacArthur had changed his clothes several times a day. MacArthur had seldom appeared to sweat or show any sign that heat bothered him. He had simply changed shirts, and thus they had usually been free of stains.

A trickle of sweat worked down Stan's back, letting him know he was nothing like Douglas MacArthur or Colonel Wilson.

"Sir—" Stan said.

"You'd better hurry up," Wilson said. "You have two minutes and thirty-five seconds. I suggest you use the time judiciously."

Stan wiped his brow again as his heart thudded. This was just so damn hard to say. *Just do it then. Get it over with, already.*

"I'm resigning my commission, sir," Stan blurted.

Wilson couldn't sit any straighter, as he already sat ramrod stiff. He placed his hands on the desk, spreading his fingers until they were all equidistantly apart from each other.

"Is this more of your Alaskan humor?" Wilson asked.

"No, sir, I'm...I'm going to John Glen in D.C. It's a think tank, sir."

Wilson frowned. He had a long face. The frown put two vertical lines between his eyes. One of those lines was slanted off-center. Stan had never noticed that before.

92

Wilson is off-center. He tries, but he isn't straight like he wants to be. I wonder what the colonel is trying to hide.

"You're quitting the Army during its darkest hour, is that it?" Wilson asked.

"No, sir, that's not it."

Wilson snorted in derision. "If you resign your commission it means you're quitting the military, the Army. That is what you're saying, is it not?"

"No, sir, it means I'll be able to help my son. He's in a Detention Center."

Wilson's chin lifted as he made a scoffing noise. "Our country is the on the brink of war facing ten million enemy soldiers and that's the best excuse you can find to scamper away in fear. Let your son stew there and learn a valuable lesson about patriotism."

"There isn't going to be a war," Stan said. If he said it enough times, he might even come to believe it. *Why, Jake, why?*

"Ah, more or your gifted historical insight, is it?" Wilson asked.

"Yes, sir, that's right."

"Ah, we have grown bold now, Captain."

"No sir. What I think—"

Wilson held up a long-fingered hand. "I do not accept criticism from a quitter. Nor do I accept criticism after the fact. If you had wanted to criticize, you should have done so while under my command."

"I did criticize your actions," Stan said with heat. "It's why you failed yet again to help promote me to major."

"So, you're sulking over that, are you? This talk about your boy is merely your cover story."

Stan's eyes narrowed and he scooted forward on his chair until he felt the edge against his butt. If he moved forward any more he'd slip off. The heat in his chest now leaped onto his tongue, igniting it. "You're a coward, Wilson. You hide behind your rank and use rules to gloss over your mistakes. I've read about your kind. Now I've seen your kind in action. What you need is a life. Look at this office. Why is everything so perfectly set? Imagine the time it takes to worry and fuss with all that."

Wilson leaned back in his chair, tapping his chin with his two index fingers pressed together.

"I always knew you were a fake, Captain. The Medal of Honor, it was a prop a former President used to hide...I'm still not sure what he was hiding. But I know it was something." Wilson shrugged. "It doesn't matter that you wish to scamper away at this time, you still have obligations."

"I'll stay until my replacement is sent out," Stan said. Would Wilson try to keep him against his will? Had the President signed a new order about such things?

"I will expedite the matter, of that you can be sure," Wilson said. "The Army doesn't need your kind. Good riddance to you, I say."

Stan nodded, turning from Wilson. *I can't believe it. We're acting like boys, not men. The Chinese won't attack, I can't afford for them to attack.*

"Ah. I see that your time is up, Captain. Or should I say, Mr. Higgins?"

"No, it is still Captain for a few more days," Stan said.

"Hmm," Wilson said. "Good day then, Captain. Be sure to fill out the proper paperwork and to finish your report on the X1 Five. Dismissed!" he said, standing.

Stan stood too, feeling more defeated than ever.

FIRST FRONT HEADQUARTERS, MEXICO

Marshal Nung's right hand ached. He had signed hundreds of operational orders today. The bureaucratic procedures needed to move masses of munitions and troops stole precious time from reflective thought. Two millions soldiers and their support troops all carefully coordinated into one—

Nung shook his head. He sat at his desk surrounded by his staff, all of them busily at work. The rustle of cloth, the tapping of screens, typing, breathing, sipping drinks, munching on snacks added to the hive-like quality. Nung imagined himself as the chief ant in a vast colony, issuing orders that would send

94

thousands of scurrying couriers onto their motorcycles to various divisions and corps headquarters. Most of his orders were personally given by hand, making it impossible for the Americans to intercept or decode them. The little things like this often won a diligent commander immortality on the battlefield. In the end, it was worth taking such pains. Even old Marshal Gang had seen the wisdom of that.

Gang...Nung shook his head. He didn't want to think about Kao's intriguer. He had more important things to spend his time on.

We're busy ants. Nung grinned. He used to watch ants as a child outside Shanghai. He would catch a fly in their house, with his little and quite grubby fingers on the window. Once caught, he'd carefully pulled off the fly's wings. The fly's legs crawling inside his cupped hand used to make him laugh because it tickled his skin. He'd taken the wingless fly and dropped it onto a busy ant hole. How the ants had swarmed upon the struggling fly, biting its squirming legs and then its head. That's what he wanted to do to the Americans, immobilize them so he could pick them to pieces. The Blue Swan missiles would be like his little fingers pulling off the wings. That would leave the Americans defenseless against his massed ant assault.

It had been so much easier as a child catching the fly on the window glass as it buzzed to escape. Today, his eyes hurt from reading endless reports and his back was stiff from sitting in this chair too long.

He wished to lead from the front again, driving in a command vehicle as he raced with his troops to the objective. Exhorting exhausted and dispirited soldiers had once been his specialty. Drive, drive, drive toward the enemy, smashing anything that dared stand in the way. He'd done that in Siberia and on the North Slope of Alaska. Could he exhort his front to do the same thing in California?

There was so much to do, and his troops needed to do it secretly, or as secretly as possible.

Can we fool the Americans?

Clearly, six million Chinese on the border made it impossible to surprise the enemy in a true sense. Yet there had

95

been endless American alerts these past two years. East Lighting had discovered that much at least about the enemy. The alerts, the crying wolf, had sapped the American populace and perhaps the enemy generals. Now it was a matter of moving hundreds of thousands of troops in a chess game along a thousand mile border. A technological surprise could give him the needed edge. A hidden massing in the critical sector would ensure the surprise obliterated a million or more American soldiers and give him California. Perhaps it would give China the entire West Coast.

Would Blue Swan work as advertised? It had succeeded during the tests in the Gobi Desert. Had those been genuine tests or had some aspects of the tests been rigged so the person in charge would look good on a bureaucratic report? That was a problem. He had to trust others to do their job well.

He rubbed his throbbing hand, digging a thumb into the sore palm. It was a good plan, but it would demand competent execution by his troops. If he could lead each of the critical attacks from the front, ah, then he would win because he knew how to make soldiers *fight*. Now he had to trust others to act as he would, to act in an aggressive manner. He had worked hard these past two years weeding out the cautious commanders in his Front. He had prepositioned mountains of supplies and his troops had trained endlessly these past five months.

The Americans have their own problems. You must remember that.

In the old days, both sides would have watched the other through satellites. Those days were over for both of them. Chinese satellites watched much of the world, but not wherever the enemy ABM lasers could reach. The Americans didn't have satellites, at least not for more than several hours after launching. Chinese lasers or missiles took them down. The American drones, on the other hand, were still a problem.

Marshal Nung blew out his cheeks. He would have to decide later today how many Chinese drones to use to study the American defenses. Too many would alert them of an attack. Too few would leave his army open to defensive surprises.

I must think carefully. At all costs, I must gain tactical surprise and hopefully operational surprise as well.

96

If only he could read the enemy's mind. Nung grinned mirthlessly. War was the ultimate contest and in a week, in nine more days perhaps, he would initiate the greatest battle in human history with a full-scale invasion of California.

Cracking his knuckles, Nung picked up the next thing to sign. Hmm, penal battalions, he needed more East Lightning commissioners to ensure discipline. This could be a delicate topic.

Nung made a face as if sucking on a lemon. He had little love for East Lightning, particularly learning to hate them from the assault across the Arctic ice seven years ago. Still, the police had their uses, and he would need more penal battalions, especially during the initial attacks. He lacked enough special infantry. The Leader had promised him more, but they had not been forthcoming. Gang had sent back a negative dispatch to the Ruling Committee concerning the need. The Marshal had interfered against him, and it likely wouldn't be the last time, either. Only an observer—Nung understood that Kao meant Marshal Gang as a threat to take over the First Front if he failed. He could never give Marshal Gang that reason.

Hmm. Perhaps penal battalions would have to take the place of special infantry.

With a flourish, Nung signed his name. He needed more commissioners, which meant East Lightning. With this signature, he would get more because the Leader backed his plan. Let East Lightning worry about where to get extra men. They didn't even need to be excellent commissioners. At this point, he needed more warm bodies to feed the coming furnace.

MEXICO CITY, MEXICO

Captain Wei sat in his office, with the back of his head resting on the cushioned top of his chair. It stretched the muscles under his jaw, especially a tight knot parallel with his left ear. His eyes were closed and a cigarette dangled between his lips. He sucked on the cigarette, attempting to empty his mind of thoughts.

Today, that proved impossible. His report on Maria Valdez had climbed the rungs of power and importance. It had reached all the way to the Ruling Committee itself where, he'd heard, generals had swayed the Leader toward immediate war.

With his eyes closed, Wei frowned.

Usually while he smoked, the lines in his forehead eased away because he would drift into non-thought. He would relax as his qualms or worries disappeared, floating away with his smoke.

The Maria Valdez report had reached the Ruling Committee. His words, his pretense—according to what he'd learned—had actually affected state policy. He found that unsettling, believing nothing good could come from it.

Wei drew smoke into his lungs. He wanted peace, non-thoughts, not anxiety concerning his actions. Why did he let this information bother him? Could it be Maria's curse taking effect?

Exhaling smoke, Wei sneered. Silently, he mocked the concept of karma. Perhaps it was a useful tool to help keep fools in line. Let them think their bad actions rebounded on them later. Let fear keep them on a "pure" path of action. Ha! A simple scrutiny of life showed the folly of such thinking. The powerful trampled others in their quest for influence, fame and money. Thieves prospered, some of them running the largest banks in the world. Adulterers ruled nations. Mass killers received medals and politicians stoked voters lust for other people's money. The entire idea of the redistribution of wealth was nothing more than coveting what others possessed and then stealing it from them, all while praising yourself at how noble such theft was. Karma—it was a ridiculous idea.

It's as foolish as Maria Valdez's curse. She died. I'm safe and alive, and now my report will win me a promotion. I have nothing to worry about.

It he was lucky, he might actually leave this barbaric land and return home to civilization.

While resting his head on the back of the chair, Captain Wei heard a faint sound. His sneer shifted to a frown. Usually, it was quiet up here in *Dong Dianshan* headquarters. Who

98

dared to march about in the halls? Yes, those were shoes—boots, he realized.

Are their soldiers in the halls?

No, that was preposterous. The outer guards would have fought to the death before admitting the military into East Lightning Headquarters. The outer guards were chosen specimens, hypnotically motivated and thus fearless fighters even against outrageous odds. If the military had attempted to enter these halls, he would have heard gunfire.

The sound of marching grew louder. It was in cadence, too. Likely, that meant several jackbooted thugs trained to move in step. What were they doing here?

Wei inhaled so the tip of his cigarette wobbled as it glowed. Cadenced steps of booted thugs—

Wei sat up and opened his eyes. He blew smoke out of his nostrils and mashed the cigarette in his overflowing ashtray. He still had half the cigarette to smoke, too. It was the only one of its kind in the tray. All the other stubs had been smoked down to the end. Wei hated wasting cigarettes.

He'd heard such cadenced steps before from Easting Lighting personnel. The Guardian Inspector kept armored enforcers with her wherever she went. They often marched like that, with boots crashing down against the tiles. If she was in the halls—Wei blinked rapidly. The Guardian Inspector was second-in-command of East Lightning personnel in Mexico. Why would she be here in his halls?

Wei recalled the doctor's sly sidelong glances as the man had probed Maria Valdez's corpse. The doctor's silence during the examination had unnerved Wei enough to mention several of the doctor's indiscretions he'd committed this past year.

For many years now, Wei had found it useful keeping a dossier on his underlings, on anyone who could write a report about him. Would the doctor have been foolish enough to write or speak to others about his suspicions concerning Maria's death?

Wei released his crumpled cigarette as his office door swung open. There was no polite tapping on it first by his secretary. No one would barge in here like this unless he or she wielded power. Therefore, Wei raised his eyebrows in an

99

attentive manner, in the way an East Lightning operative should do before his superiors.

Three red-armored enforcers strode into the room. They were big men in body armor and enclosed helmets with darkened visors. Each cradled a close-combat carbine, an ugly-barreled weapon with a pitted end. They took up station in his cramped quarters and leveled the carbines at him.

Inadvertently, Wei touched his constricting chest. Those pitted barrels...

The Guardian Inspector entered the office, confirming Wei's worst fear. She was taller than he was, average-sized for a Chinese woman. Her hair was short, barely covering her ears. She wore a scarlet uniform with brown straps, reversing the normal East Lightning uniform. A short brown cape was draped over her shoulders and pigskin gloves clad her hands. She had a peasant girl's features. They were too wide in Chinese terms to be called beautiful. Even so, she had a pleasing face, with incredibly dark eyes of a compelling nature. They made her seem like a night creature, a seductress who would leave his bloodless corpse for jackals or rats to quarrel over.

She stopped before his desk and regarded him. "Captain Wei," she said.

He recovered from his shock enough so his chair scraped back. He stood, saluting smartly in the accepted manner.

"Sit," she said, while unpinning her cloak. She let it drape over a chair and then sat down.

Wei sat stiffly, putting his hands on the desk, waiting.

"You're surprised to see me," she said.

Wei nodded. How could it be otherwise?

"The carbines," she gestured at her enforcers. "Do they unnerve you?"

"Innocent men need not fear," Wei said, quoting an East Lightning maxim.

Her smile became cruel. "It surprises me then that you are not a quivering wreck on the floor."

Wei blinked several times. He wanted a cigarette. No, he needed a pill as his heart thudded. "Your words wound me," he managed to say.

While staring into his eyes, she shook her head. "It is my policy to never utter false words or to bandy in jest with those I'm about to destroy."

His throat tightened. What had gone wrong? The doctor—he would kill the man before this was over. He would escape and hunt the weasel to the earth, using a knife to castrate the informer and stuffing the man's—

"May I inquire as to what this is about?" Wei forced himself to ask. He needed to concentrate, not escape into revenge fantasies.

"Poor Wei," she said. "You wish to maintain dignity in your final hour. You have hidden like a snake among us all these years. I wonder now upon the number and magnitude of your transgressions."

"Guardian Inspector?" he asked. He would slice open the doctor's belly and pull out the man's—

"We know about your drug addiction," she said.

Wei stared at her and he almost let his shoulders slump in relief. He had to suppress a caw of laughter. Drug addiction, this was about drug addiction? No one could torture people long and escape some form of relaxant. East Lightning knew this. Oh, they all spoke about hard men determined to do the unwanted tasks because this was the hour of China's greatness. But the truth was no one was hard enough except for a psychopath.

"Ah," the Guardian Inspector said. She was watching him closely. "You interest me, Captain. You're relieved at the charge, not worried as you should be."

"I assure you—"

"No!" she said. "Do not assure me of anything. You are a snake, Captain Wei. You have abused your privileged post in order to practice a loathsome habit. How can we trust your judgment if you're addled with drugs? You are an addict. You ingest drugs to sustain yourself instead of hardening your resolve for the good of the State. You have stained yourself. You are no longer worthy of your rank or your station. I begin to wonder now about this report of yours concerning Maria Valdez."

Was she playing him like a mongoose with a cobra? That must be it. It couldn't really be about drug addiction. Besides, he wasn't an addict. He merely used the pills to ease his burden. He was hard inside. He did work for the good of the State. China was everything and he was nothing, an ant tirelessly working for the nation, for the people.

The Guardian Inspector shrugged. "By his actions, our Great Leader has stamped your Maria Valdez report with approval."

"Ah," Wei said. "That disproves your charge then. My hard work—"

She held up a gloved hand. The glove was thin leather with little holes running up and down the fingers. The gesture was menacing, as it seemed to Wei that if she should drop her hand too quickly, the three enforcers would open fire.

"Your report has reached too high for us to dig too deeply into it," she said. "But is there anything you wish to tell me about it, anything you wish to confess?"

He tried to appear contrite, but it was so foreign to him. He had dominated shackled patients too long, perhaps. He had always been in control.

"It is true I have sipped a drink to…to pass the time," he said.

"You were going to say something else. Tell me what it was. Confess to me, Captain, and you may find mercy."

Wei smiled softly. Did the Guardian Inspector not realize she spoke to the premier extractor of truths? He sifted truth and lies many times a week. He would never tell her that he took the blue pills to dull his conscience. No! That wasn't even true. He took the pills in order to pass the tedium of life. But he would never tell her that, either. It would simply be too dangerous. High-ranking, East Lighting operatives knew nothing about mercy except that it was a word for fools and weaklings.

"You are a snake," she said, as if pronouncing judgment on him. "Despite your glorious service to China, we must punish you, Captain. We are impartial, the dog and broom of the Socialist-Nationalist Revolution. We sniff out troublemakers and sweep them away."

102

Wei's throat felt gritty. He told himself it was the smoke of his cigarette. Yet if that was so, why hadn't his throat ever felt this way before?

"I have never performed less than excellently while, ah, ingesting a stimulant," he said.

"I'm sure that's a lie," she said. "Thus, it proves to me how low you've fallen from the height of dedicated service. Even in my presence, you dare to act like a snake, a liar and a drug addict."

"Not an addict," he protested.

"Spare both of us any breast-beating of innocence. You are charged, found guilty and will now hear your sentence, your punishment."

Wei hid his surprise. The charge of drug addiction in East Lightning usually brought swift death. He had been waiting for bullets to smash his body.

"You are surprised," she said, nodding, "as am I. Left up to me, my enforcers would kill you like a pig. Yet it is true that you have performed several notable services for China. Thus, you will have a chance at rehabilitation."

"Thank you," he said.

She shook her head. "I doubt you'll thank me a week from now. You are being reassigned, Captain."

"May I ask where?"

"To a penal battalion," she said.

He frowned. "I thought only the military possessed those."

She smiled like a hungry leopard. "You will join a shock battalion. It is a fancy title for those who clear minefields."

"I'm untrained in such—"

She held up her hand again.

The three guards grew tense. Wei noticed one smiling in anticipation under his visor. The man was just tall enough for him to spot it. Wei gulped, dreading to know what a bullet entering his body felt like.

"The mine clearing is a simple process," she said. "The battalion runs across it, exploding the mines with their feet. If you survive that, you will then become shock troops, charging enemy strongholds."

"But—"

She stared at him, wilting his speech.

"You will still be East Lightning. You will be one of the enforcers, guarding and goading the penal troops to courageous acts of bravery. I'm told these troops often turn their guns and grenades on their enforcers. So you will need to remain vigilant. If you become drug-addled while performing your duties, well, we both know what will happen: Your commanding officer will draw his gun and shoot you in the head."

Wei sat back. This was disastrous. What had he ever done to deserve this? It was viciously unfair.

"If you survive a year of combat," the Guardian Inspector said, "I shall review your case. If I find you have purged yourself of this filthy drug habit, I will reinstate you in your regular command."

"Thank you," Wei managed to say.

"But we both know that you will not survive," she said. "Good-bye, Captain Wei. Remember, if you can, to always act like an East Lightning hero, rooting out traitors to the State."

She slings jokes into my teeth in my hour of doom. I will remember this.

The Guardian Inspector stood. Wei sat in his chair, staring helplessly at her, wishing he could order her stripped and secured to an informant table. He would spend days on her, days of agony for this mocking bitch.

"Help him," the Guardian Inspector told her enforcers.

Each man slid his carbine into a large holster. Then, as one, they came around the desk, putting their iron-strong hands on him. With unnecessary brutality, they dragged Wei out of the chair, out of the office and propelled him down the corridor. He stumbled his way toward a penal battalion, one that would no doubt soon see military action.

LAREDO, TEXAS

Colonel Valdez sat in a dark room, smoking a cigar. When the glowing tip brightened as he inhaled, it showed hard, dark eyes and a pitted forehead. As a young man he had contracted

104

chicken pox, and it had ravaged his features. The rage in his heart over his daughter's death and dismemberment had changed to ice, and like a glacier, he remorselessly ground toward his goal in his mind.

He would have to leave Laredo soon. He seldom stayed in one locale for more than two days. The Chinese wanted him, but not nearly as badly as the new puppet President of Mexico did. The war of assassins between them continued despite the Americans and the Chinese. It was a ruthless contest between warring tribes, and Valdez had the weaker hand. Yet he had survived the SNP due to cunning, ruthlessness and the ability to instill fierce loyalty in his people.

"Maria," he whispered.

The Chinese had sent him her parts piece by piece. He would make them pay. He would discover who had done this thing and he would do terrible things to them. The Americans had come to him earlier, begging for his best man. Instead, he had given them his daughter, because she had known the countryside better than any of his men did. He had told the CIA man that he wanted his daughter back. Oh, the CIA man had assured him she would be safe because America was sending its best men with her. He had been a fool to believe that or believe they would take care of his daughter. He had learned the man's name. Yes. Paul Kavanagh the Marine had flown free, leaving his daughter behind to face the torturers.

Now Valdez waited for critical news concerning Kavanagh's whereabouts.

He took the cigar out of his mouth and rolled it between his fingers. Four years ago, he had renamed his ragtag guerillas the Free Mexico Army. He had fled to America for sanctuary, although he'd continued to send assassins and guerillas into his native land. Surprisingly, his army had grown from Mexican nationals in America and from those escaping the Chinese prison across the Rio Grande. American advisors had trained his men until he had over sixty thousand soldiers on U.S. soil. America desperately needed allies and needed trained fighters. His sixty thousand made him a force, and the Americans hoped that someday he could incite a Mexican uprising and return to his country as its new leader. Because of that, the Americans catered to him on many issues. He had contacts among them and could learn hidden things, such as where they had put Paul Kavanagh.

While inhaling, with the hot smoke tickling the back of his throat and the taste causing saliva to congeal, Valdez's eyes burned like icy motes of hate. The CIA man had told him Marines never left their own on the battlefield. That was a lie, and people lied to Cesar Valdez at their peril.

There was a knock on the door.

"Yes," Valdez said.

The door creaked open and one-eyed Torres stared at him. Torres, the Oakland Raiders fan, looked like the football team's logo, although minus the helmet. "The Marine is in California, Colonel," Torres told him.

"You are sure of this?" Valdez asked.

"One hundred percent sure."

Valdez considered this, finally saying, "California is a large state."

Torres nodded, and his smile was grim. "The Marine is guarding a man from Washington who tours the front."

Valdez inhaled so the cigar glowed fiery, and he nodded. "The Chinese have snipers, yes?"

"It is true," Torres said.

"Perhaps as this Washington man tours the front, Chinese snipers will kill him. It has happened before. Yes. I like it. The Marine guarding the Washington man—no one will care what happens to him if Chinese snipers kill the important one."

"And if the Americans learn we did this?" Torres asked.

The cigar glowed once more. "The Americans failed to protect Maria. You know what happens when people fail me?"

Torres nodded.

"Send Romo," the colonel said. "He is our best killer and he is near the bastard who failed my daughter. Forge a pass, allowing Romo to go where he pleases."

"The Americans are nervous, Colonel. Security has been tightening."

Valdez stared at Torres. The man looked down, nodding quickly. "It will be as you say, Colonel."

106

"I want Kavanagh's head. If Romo cannot bring it to me, I want pictures of Kavanagh suffering brutally before he dies. I want to see a dagger planted in his eye, planted to the hilt."

Torres nodded once more.

"Go. Do this. Then we leave Laredo tonight. I do not like the reports from Mexico. The Chinese in this sector are up to something."

"Yes, Colonel," Torres said. He softly closed the door behind him.

After several glows of the cigar, Valdez whispered in a voice few would have recognized. "Maria, my darling girl, I will avenge you and then I will free our country from the foreigner. This I vow to you, my child. This I vow by the Madonna."

-4-
The Abyss

LAREDO, TEXAS

Sino-American Border Skirmish

(NNI) In the early morning hours of May 17, a thunderous crashing boom awoke soldiers of the Free Mexico Army and General Kemp's Fifth Corps.

The Chinese claim American provocations have forced their hand. "It was an entry point for terrorists coming into allied land to commit murder and mayhem," the Chinese ambassador said later. "We will defend the SNP Revolution, with brutal force, if we must. China, the entire Pan Asian Alliance and the South American Federation stand shoulder to shoulder with allied Mexico. American provocations must end here and now. Otherwise, China will act and end them through force of arms."

American artillery responded to the bombardment. According to embedded sources, Chinese counter-artillery erupted soon thereafter, creating considerable confusion among the Americans. The indications appear obvious. The Chinese have planned this artillery barrage thoughtfully and carefully, perhaps with a greater intent in mind.

Considerable troop movement behind Chinese lines has heightened fear and worry in Laredo and in San Antonio, and, one would suspect, among higher American Command.

"Is this the Big One?" soldiers are asking, and likely, many in the country are wondering the same thing.

SAN YSIDRO, CALIFORNIA

"What's wrong, honey," Cheri asked on the computer screen. "You look troubled. Are you in Texas, by any chance?"

Paul shook his sweaty head. He wore regular body armor, with a combat helmet and assault rifle on the table beside the screen. He was Colonel Norman's "bodyguard," but had done precious little of that this past week. Mainly, he drove the colonel's truck everywhere. It was a gray Dodge with reinforced sides, ballistic glass windshields and bullet-resistant tires. The man said he liked the truck's comfort and this colonel seemed to get what he liked.

Colonel Norman spent most of his time in conference with generals. Paul had never been in those meetings nor even stood near the door. He drove from one headquarter to another. A few times the colonel went on a sightseeing tour, with five Humvees of staff officers following behind the bouncing Dodge.

"You look upset," Cheri said. "Is it about the news?"

Paul had heard about the Chinese artillery attack in Texas on the Fifth Corps there. The colonel had commented earlier that NNI's writer had gotten it wrong. It hadn't been a "barrage," but a "fire assault." Barrages assisted defensive or offensive troops by providing a wall of fire, or there was a standing barrage of smoke shells or poison gas to screen or prevent enemy movement or observation. Near Laredo, the Chinese shells had targeted strongholds, fortifications and American artillery parks. It had been concentrated on targets for the obvious purpose of destruction. It implied an impending attack on Kemp's Fifth Corps, which guarded the route from Laredo to San Antonio deeper in Texas.

That had worried Colonel Norman. If the Chinese attacked in Texas, what were their plans along the SoCal border? It wasn't adding up for the expert from Washington.

Paul had listened to talk before the artillery attack in Texas. Colonel Norman and the SoCal generals were worried about the Chinese in their sector. According to scuttlebutt, Paul had learned the Chinese had expended too many drones along the border for it to simply be routine reconnaissance. Night traffic near the border had increased, too.

Paul knew the veteran ground-pounders were telling each other it was another Chinese fake. The artillery fire-assault in Texas proved that, according to the vets. If anything big were going to happen, it would be in Texas. It made more strategic sense to happen there, anyway. If the Chinese broke through in Texas, they could possibly split the United States in two by driving deep into the flat American heartland. It was good attacking country because it was hard to defend, with no choke points. The vets here had agreed: the Chinese weren't going to hit the strongest American defense: the SoCal Fortifications. No way, the Chinese were obviously probing for the soft spot in America's underbelly.

"Paul?" his wife asked, via the computer screen.

While grinning at her, Paul noticed that Cheri had aged since the Alaskan War. They'd been separated during it, getting back together afterward. She had gained weight since that time, but Paul usually had trouble noticing. When he looked at her, he saw his wife as the small, beautiful woman with long dark hair and a gymnast's grace he'd first married. She was still all that, but with more curves and sometimes with tired eyes. They looked puffy today, probably because of worry after reading about the Chinese provocation.

It had been too long since he'd seen or talked with his wife. He knew she would be worried sick about him, so he'd taken the risk of calling her. This was BS, his driving a colonel around all week. If they wanted to jail him for this call with Cheri...let them. He'd had enough of playing chauffeur to a closed-mouthed DC staff officer.

"Are you okay?" he asked.

"I haven't heard from you for weeks. I was beginning to worry."

Yeah, he'd guessed right. News of Chinese military action had terrified her. It hardly mattered what front it had taken place on, either. That it had happened is what mattered to his wife.

Of course, he wasn't supposed to be talking to her now, but the comm-shack was empty. It was small, with three tables crowded together and piled with equipment, including a small refrigerator. He'd checked earlier and found rows of blue Pepsi cans and a single M&Ms package with a torn corner and half the candies missing. Paul had said he was coming here to get out of the heat. It was like the old days out there in the nineties. The colonel had ducked into a bunker to hold yet another conference, this time with the commanding general of the John J. Montgomery Freeway: Interstate 5. The freeway went all the way to the Mexican border three miles from here.

"I've been busy," Paul told his wife.

"You've been reassigned then?"

"You could say that."

"Are you in a safe place at least?" She frowned. "I've been watching the news about the Texas attack. The TV shows huge flashes on the horizon. It's the Chinese guns booming. I don't know why, but we're all on high alert here. Maybe they think the entire border will erupt."

Paul frowned.

"I know, I know," Cheri said, "you're going to tell me we've been through high alerts at least once a month for the last two years. But this one feels different. People are acting serious. I'm seeing that on TV. Oh. Maybe you haven't heard, but the Germans have massed hovers off the Cuban coast in a war game."

"You're paying too much attention to the news, honey. It's not like you."

"We're scared," Cheri said. "The neighbors are talking, wondering what we should do if the Chinese really do attack. What do you think, honey, should we be worried, or is the attack going to happen in Texas?"

111

Paul rubbed his chin. For several years now, the Chinese had lined up on the border, but no guns had opened up like had happened outside Laredo. If the Chinese attacked in Texas, would they also attack in California?

Cheri and his thirteen-year-old son Mike lived in Greater LA, in Newhall near Magic Mountain. Newhall was at the northern tip of LA, almost to the Grapevine, the mountain pass to Bakersfield on the other side. If Texas showed this was the Big One—the beginning of a Chinese invasion—LA would eventually become a prime target.

"Maybe you should visit your mother," Paul said.

Cheri's eyes widened. "In Colorado?" she asked. "You know we can't afford the gas. I checked, by the way. Since the news, it's already two dollars more per gallon."

"Well—"

"Tell me what's wrong, honey. Is the alert accurate this time? Has the war finally started but none of us realize it yet?"

"Maybe."

Her mouth firmed. "Paul, where are you?"

"I'm not supposed to tell you."

"You'd better tell me this instant. If you're near there, in Texas, I mean…"

His bitterness came bubbling up and he began to say more than he should. Besides, a few artillery shots in Texas wasn't World War III. Playing chauffer down here, it sucked and he hated it.

"They're screwing with me, Cheri. I don't know what's up, exactly. I'm near the border and—"

"In Texas?" she asked.

"No, I'm in California near Tijuana."

"Oh, so you're close. A couple hours driving and you could be home."

"I suppose."

"You don't want to come home?" she asked.

"I'd love to, baby. But they're not about to let me go sightseeing. They're screwing with me."

"What do you mean?"

"It's complicated. But I'm serious about you leaving. Cash out our savings and head to Colorado. I've been hearing

112

strange things down here. This colonel, he's a special ace from D.C."

"The Chinese are attacking in SoCal?" Cheri whispered.

"No, that's not what I'm saying. Maybe it's happening everywhere, in Texas, too. I don't know. But High Command must be worried about the Chinese, enough anyway so this ace is here to make sure everything is ready for them."

"Hey!" a tech corporal shouted. "Who are you talking to?"

Paul looked up. A scrawny kid of a soldier held the door open, letting out the shack's cool air. This was one of the few air-conditioned places in Ninth Division's Headquarters.

"Take a hike," Paul told him. "This is a private conversation."

The skinny corporal sputtered. "This is my shack. You can't tell me what to do. And if you're talking to civilians— that's a court martial offense."

Paul grinned at the corporal. It made the kid gulp nervously. Maybe the tech saw something in Paul he didn't like.

"I'm getting my lieutenant," the corporal said.

"Good," Paul said. "Run along."

The corporal glared at him, stepped back and slammed the door.

"What was that about?" Cheri asked.

"Can't talk long, honey," Paul said. He shouldn't be talking to her, but he'd wanted to calm her and he'd had enough BS. He was sick of it and he was worried. "I want you to listen carefully. Is Mike home?"

"No. He's at school."

Paul scowled.

It made Cheri pale as her small hand flew to her mouth. "Is it really happening? Are the neighbors right?"

All the little things he'd heard, the colonel's worry, the generals acting weird and now this softening up destruction in Texas—it jelled for Paul then. "I think it is," he said.

"Why aren't they telling us? All the talking heads are saying to remain calm. They're saying that artillery fire like what's going on in Texas without any Chinese saturation bombing means it must be a misunderstanding."

"It's about panic, I guess. They don't want a mass exodus from SoCal clogging up the freeways."

"Are the Chinese monitoring you?" Cheri asked.

President Sims had executive-ordered all kind of new laws on communications and dealings with the enemy. Sims had taken the growing chaos of these past twenty years and tried to instill greater discipline into the country. He'd raised militia armies to help beef the forces facing the more numerous enemy. The emergency powers he'd acquired—Cheri must realize he was taking a risk today by talking to her. But that couldn't be helped now.

"Empty the account—"

"You listen to me, soldier," Cheri said. "I want you to listen real good."

Paul's heart ached. He wanted to hug his wife. He wanted to kiss her, to feel her under him as they made love.

"I miss you," he whispered.

She nodded, but her features had become businesslike. "I want your attention, mister."

"Yeah?" he asked.

"Paul, please. You have to listen to me. You promised Mike and me that you would come home."

"Don't worry, sweets."

"I am worried. You're down there on the border. If this thing in Texas blows up, it might rage like an out-of-control forest fire. The entire border could erupt with war and you would be in the middle of it."

"I know how to take care of myself."

"This is different. The enemy has too many soldiers this time. This isn't like Alaska. This is like another World War."

"Honey—"

"Paul, you swore you'd come home to me. I want you to kiss me again. I want you to hold me. I want you to whisper in my ear that you love me."

"I do love you."

"Tell me in person. Do whatever you have to do to get to me."

"It's a long way to Colorado."

"I'm not going there until you come home," Cheri said. "Do you understand?"

"Don't be stubborn, sweets. I can't just get up and leave. I have to do my duty, my part to save our country."

"I'm not moving until you get here. I swear that, Paul."

He stared into her eyes, seeing her seriousness and tiny golden flecks in the irises. He'd told her before those flecks meant she was a love goddess. She'd always laughed with delight at that. But she wasn't laughing now. Cheri could be stubborn, maybe not stubborn like him, but stubborn enough.

"I'll come home to you, sweets. I promise you. First, I have earn my pay."

"You'll come home in one piece?" she asked.

"Yeah." Through the window, Paul saw a lieutenant marching toward the shack. The tech corporal spoke animatedly, waving his arms as he hurried beside the man. "Honey, I have to go. I love you. Kiss Mike for me. Tell him to take care of you until I get there."

"When is that going to be?"

"Maybe sooner than you think," he said. If the Chinese were coming through Texas, where would it end? He still hadn't told her about Colonel Valdez and possible hit men, but he didn't want to worry her more than he needed. He wanted to laugh then. What did hit men matter when World War III was threatening?

"Love," he said.

"Love," she said. And the way she said it slammed his heart. He put his fingertips on the screen. She put up hers.

"I need you, baby," he said.

"Ditto," she said.

The door began to open. "Bye, sweets. See you soon." Paul cut the connection.

"Who are you talking to?" a lanky lieutenant asked.

Paul stood up, grabbing his helmet and assault rifle off the table.

"I asked you a question, Gunnery Sergeant."

"Yeah you did," Paul said. "I was talking to my wife."

The lieutenant and corporal exchanged startled glances. The lieutenant told Paul, "That's a court martial offense."

115

"Better hurry then," Paul said. "Me and the colonel are taking off soon."

"Do you think I'm joking?"

"No. I think—" Paul cut himself off. "Sorry, sir. I'm a bit bitter, that's all. I haven't seen my wife for over six months due to hard training for what turned out to be a little exercise in Mexico. I'm not sure I'm going to make it home now. So I took the opportunity to call her."

"I'll have to report it," the lieutenant said.

"You do that."

"You'll have to wait here for the MPs."

"Nope," Paul said. "But you get them if you have to. I'm driving the colonel to his next stop-off."

"Do you mean Colonel Norman?" the lieutenant asked in something approaching awe.

"That's him," Paul said.

"You're his driver?"

"Bodyguard."

"What does Norman need a bodyguard for?" the lieutenant asked.

"Mexican hit men," Paul said.

The lieutenant and corporal traded another glance. The lieutenant lost more of his stiffness. "Are you pulling my chain?"

"That's right," Paul said.

The lieutenant nodded. "Okay. That makes more sense. Who were you really talking to?"

"Are we done here?" Paul asked.

"I saw a pretty woman on the screen," the corporal told the officer.

"There aren't any pretty women in the Army?" the lieutenant asked.

The corporal looked crestfallen.

Paul nodded to them as he squeezed past. He shoved the helmet onto his head and opened the door. As he stepped outside, the heat hit like a wall.

"Colonel Norman," the lieutenant said to the corporal, before Paul shut the door.

116

He strode across pavement. There were acres of it with the occasional concrete building and pillbox. Here and there, a Humvee or Stryker waited between white parking lines. Paul spied Interstate 5. It was still usable here, but nearer the border, bulldozers and other earth-moving equipment had turned the freeway into overturned chunks of concrete. Paul couldn't see that, however, as a big earthen berm blocked sight of the Mexican border three miles to the south. Beyond the berm were other trenches, fortifications and minefields. Miles to the rear were massed artillery tubes in hardened bunkers, together with laser emplacements, flak guns and giant reflectors.

Paul strode for the colonel's pickup. Were the Chinese really thinking about attacking? What did it mean the enemy had started something in Texas? Maybe it was just another game of chicken. He hoped so.

Texas—and they send a DC hotshot here. What's really going on?

LAREDO, TEXAS

Rising Tension

(NNI) Since the first barrage three days ago, PAA artillery fire has escalated into hours-long thundering against sections of the Texas fortifications. Crack SAF armor units have begun to mass, while long supply columns of Chinese trucks fill the roads.

President Sims has called for talks in Geneva. Chairman Hong has demanded two pre-conditions: the surrender of Colonel Valdez and the dismantling of the Free Mexico Army.

The Chinese Foreign Minister said, "Once Mexico needs no longer fear these terrorist assaults from the criminal Valdez, then Chinese soldiers can stand down, knowing the border is secure."

President Sims replied. "We're not the ones who started this, but we will end it if we have to. America doesn't respond to threats and we know how to defend ourselves. The war in Alaska proved that. I urge Chairman Hong to think long and

117

hard therefore and then meet with me in Geneva so we can solve this problem reasonably."

American troops are on high alert in Texas and Militia and Army Reserves are reporting for duty.

"The President is right," General Kemp was quoted as saying. "If the Chinese cross the border, we're going to teach them foreign boys how to be good patriots and die for their country."

LANGLEY, VIRGINIA

"You're to come with me," Johnson said.

Anna Chen looked up in surprise at her boss. She sat hunched over her e-reader, studying data in her CIA cubicle. Ever since the Laredo Incident, everyone had been working overtime.

"Sir?" she asked.

"Take your e-reader and come with me," Johnson said.

She grabbed the reader, stood and winced because her back was so stiff. "Just a minute," she whispered.

Johnson turned, frowning at her as she stretched and popped her back. "Are you through?" he asked.

She nodded, secretly pleased at annoying him. For the past two and a half weeks, he had avoided her, only greeting her once with a monosyllabic grunt. She took it to mean that her report on Blue Swan had achieved something. Realizing that had emboldened her while writing up other reports. She'd become fascinated with the spy in Mexico City. He was a veritable fund of knowledge concerning Chinese usage of Mexican roads and routes. According to him, the Chinese had practically stopped all civilian traffic in the Baja-Californian north during night. That implied mass movement of either supplies or troops, which in turn implied what…an imminent attack in SoCal timed with the Texas Situation? She had written her reports that way; she was more certain than ever that she was right.

Johnson led her past other cubicles to his office door. He opened it and said, "Go."

118

"Sir?" she asked.

"Go inside."

"After you, sir," she said.

He scowled and pointed within.

Confused, Anna stepped into his office without him. A man sat in her boss's chair. It took a second before Anna realized the Director of the CIA sat there.

Dr. Samuel Levin was a wizened figure of legend, with uncombed, thick white hair jutting in disorder. The hair with its many points was like an anarchist's crown or some strange wizard's hat. It made Levin seem as if he was an ancient in his second childhood, peering at people with quizzical eyes. His neck looked too skinny to hold up his large head and crown.

"Director?" Anna asked.

"Shut the door and sit down," Levin said.

"Should I call in Mr. Johnson?"

"You're a smart woman, Anna."

She hesitated and finally nodded, shutting the door with Johnson still outside and sitting down in a chair before the desk.

Levin scratched an ear as he peered at her. The quizzical eyes seemed to ask a hundred questions. He seemed like one of those youths with an insatiable number of queries, wanting to know everything. He didn't disappoint, either.

"Anna, how do you know the Chinese are going to attack in Southern California?"

His lack of small talk startled her. If that's how he wanted to proceed…it was fine with her. "I don't *know*," she said. "But it is my strong assessment."

He smiled like a fox from Aesop's Fables, one of those sly creatures able to talk crows into dropping their grapes.

"Your reports are like a blizzard of warnings," he said. "You're a veritable prophetess of doom concerning California when everyone else knows it's one of the few quiet fronts we have. The situation grows increasingly worse in Texas and drone reports show a massing of GD hovers off the Florida Keys. When he should be concentrating on Texas and possibly Florida, the President keeps asking about California."

"Because of my reports?" asked Anna.

119

"I believe that's what I just implied."

"Why hasn't anyone told me?"

Director Levin used his pinky finger to scratch the inside of his ear. "You're on a short list of undesirables. It isn't my list, but your ethnicity has more than a few people worried. Fortunately for you, the President recalls that you were on Clark's staff during the war."

"The Alaskan War?" Anna asked.

"It's the only war that counts with the President."

"Yes, sir, I think I understand."

"I believe you do. Not that it matters. The point of our little meeting tonight is for you to tell me why you think the Chinese are about to invade California. Why not invade Texas—where the sheer volume of shells used has shattered large sections of the Laredo Fortifications? The Pan Asian Alliance and the South American Federation have openly moved large forces into position to exploit any breakthroughs there."

"I realize that, sir. Still, it's unlike Chinese generals to advertise their moves so openly. They like to use surprises, to use decoys."

Levin shrugged. "Perhaps they know we know that. Therefore, acting like a decoy, pretending to be a decoy, these troops in Texas are actually the real thing: an invasion force meant to drive a wedge into our underbelly."

"I suppose it's possible," Anna said.

"But you deem it unlikely?"

"Yes, sir," she said.

"And this is because…?"

"Marshal Kao helps formulate much of China's strategy."

"Tell me about him," Levin said.

"He's the Minister of Defense on the Ruling Committee," Anna said. "He works closely with Chairman Hong. Frankly, what you're seeing in Texas, it isn't like Marshal Kao."

"Maybe it's someone else's plan."

"Maybe," she said.

Levin pursed his lips. "Give me another reason."

"I'm troubled by the amount of dedicated road usage in the Baja-California region of Mexico. The usage implies massive shipments of troops, supplies, or most likely both. I'm not talking about corps-level movements as appears to be happening in Texas, but something much larger."

"You've been following the situation in Texas?" Levin asked.

"A little," Anna said.

"You like to keep your finger on the pulse?"

"If you want to put it like that," she said.

"Hmm," he said, scratching his ear again. "If this is all so simple to see, why doesn't anyone else see it?"

"The data is always there, sir."

"Meaning what?" Levin asked.

Anna took a deep breath. "That most intelligence agencies have the facts of this or that on the enemy but simply don't trust the data. It's only clear to everyone once a thing happens. They say hindsight is twenty-twenty. Then people say, 'Look. The evidence was right there in front of them all along. It must have been a conspiracy that kept it hidden.' But there usually isn't a conspiracy. It's just that no one believed the reports or the obvious was so obvious that it had everyone's attention. In this instance I mean Texas."

"I believe I'd already figured out what you meant," Levin said.

Anna nodded. "In this instance, I happen to trust our spy in Mexico City, the one in traffic control. He has shown a continuous and massive shutdown of northern roads in the Baja-California area. That implies a mass—"

"I know what it implies," Levin said. "The trouble is that no one else agrees with him."

"Exactly," Anna said. "The massing GD hovers, the artillery attacks near Laredo and the movement toward the Texas Front of SAF armor—some of the same units that so brilliantly conquered Argentina—have diverted everyone's attention on everywhere but California. And that is why I think an attack is imminent against the SoCal Fortifications."

"You're not telling me everything," Levin said.

Anna looked away. "No, sir, I'm not."

"Well…tell me the rest."

Licking her lips, Anna said, "I'm not a military historian, sir."

"No?"

"But the Battle of the Bulge is a good example of my final reason. There, the Germans practiced strict communication discipline. The critical factor was the movement of troops and supplies into attack positions. The Germans did that secretly, too, usually only moving at night."

"I'm with you so far."

"The Chinese are practicing strict communication control. I also believe they're aware of every satellite shot into space and drone flight sent into their territory. That means to me they're trying to be very secret about what they're doing near the SoCal border. The artillery in Texas and the GD hovers, that's to throw us off."

"I see. And you're the only one in America smart enough to see through these Chinese and German deceptions?"

"No, sir," Anna said. "You see it and I expect that so does the President. That's why he's sent you to talk to me."

"Ah. You're a smart girl, Anna."

"And you're a smart man, sir."

Levin grinned. "You're coming with me."

"Okay. Can I ask where I'm going?"

"To every meeting I have with the War Council. You're going to be my aide. You're also going to help me understand what the Chinese are thinking, just like you helped President Clark seven years ago."

"Then you do believe the Chinese are going to attack in SoCal?"

"I pray I'm wrong. The President hopes I'm wrong, but probably not for the reasons why you would think. If Blue Swan does what we expect..."

Anna perked up. "You sent someone to look at the Blue Swan convoy then?"

"As a matter of fact—yes, we did. It's why I'm talking to you."

"The military operation happened because of my report?"

The CIA Director nodded.

Anna grinned, feeling appreciated and as if she had done something useful. "So what does Blue Swan do?"

"Our technicians were fortunate, as our commando didn't bring back much in way of evidence. Luckily, one of the techs—let's just leave at this: we're ninety percent certain the missiles melt electronics through EMP. And they do this without needing a nuclear explosion."

Anna's eyes became large. Oh, that was clever.

"It means a national disaster could be in the making," Levin said. "We're hoping the Chinese drag their heels using their advantage. They should have already moved. We keep expecting EMP missiles in Texas, but that hasn't happened. The Chinese appear to be waiting for something. We'd like to figure out what and then see if we can thwart them."

"I can tell you what they're waiting for," Anna said. "They want to line up all their ducks in a row."

"Explain that, please."

"In this, the Chinese are more like Russians than World War II Germans. The Germans liked to take bold gambles. The Russians bet on sure things. The Chinese will want to make sure they have enough to win big, instead of going too soon and ruining their chances of conquest."

"This is your opinion why?"

"Years and years of study and research on the Chinese and their character," she said.

Levin scratched his ear again, with the pinky fingertip disappearing from view and shaking vigorously so it reminded Anna of a dog. But this man was one smart dog.

"Let us suppose you're right. The hovers and the Texas artillery attacks are decoys meant to fix our attention. What does that say about California, especially knowing that Marshal Nung is in charge of the First Front?"

"Nung means you're likely not going to get as much time to get ready as if it were someone else," Anna said.

Levin looked away as his grin vanished. He seemed old then. "Right," he whispered. Looking up, he said, "Get your purse, Ms. Chen, and then let's go."

"Any place in particular?" Anna asked.

Levin nodded. "White House Bunker Number Five."

"Sir?"

"The President wants you at the War Council meeting as they decide what to do about Texas and Florida."

NORTHERN MEXICO

In the darkness of night, Zhu Peng lurched upward in flight. His Qui 1000 jets expelled air with tremendous force. The jetpack shook his frail body and lifted him with terrifying ease. He rested his right elbow on a flight pad, his right hand using the control-throttle. It was delicate work and needed extreme precision. This is why he had passed the White Tiger tests. Among his pod of recruits, he had proved the best in flight.

Zhu wore an Eagle helmet, top-of-the-line in quality and with the latest technology. It had a HUD display with night vision built into the visor. He had a shoulder-mount grenade launcher. He turned his head, with crosshairs in his helmet showing him where the grenade would go. By pressing a button in his left hand, the launcher electromagnetically propelled the grenade and reloaded his weapon. Assault rifles had their uses, but were harder to wield well during flight. The idea of the grenade launcher was to clear a landing zone for an Eagle soldier.

Eagle Team doctrine had changed since the Alaskan War, although Zhu knew little about that. The trainers had taught him present doctrine, not past. In the air, jetpack troops were vulnerable to enemy fire, just as paratroopers in the past had hung like ripe fruit floating down to earth. The jetpack was for maneuver while away from the enemy. While fighting, every Eagle soldier tried to land as quickly as possible and use cover like a regular combatant.

Pop up. Then get down fast.

"Fighter Rank." The words crackled in Zhu's headphones. It was Tian Jintao.

Using his chin, Zhu flicked on communications. "Here, First Rank."

"'Here,' he says," Tian told the others. "Give me your exact coordinates, recruit."

Zhu did.

"Come down at mark 3, dash 42," Tian said.

Zhu read the coordinates on the HUD. Ah, this was a tricky maneuver. He twisted his wrist and throttled down, dipping, his body spinning to the left. He thrust harder, lifting now, and twisted again so he plunged toward the given coordinates.

"Impressive," he heard over the headphones.

"Anyone can fly," Tian said. "It's fighting that counts."

"He's supply and doesn't have to fight," someone else said.

"He's one of ours," Tian told the others. "So he must do everything right."

The dark ground rushed up to greet Zhu. Landing was hardest. Landing while weighted down made it even more difficult. Zhu grinned as his boots touched down light as a feather. He was gifted at this, a—

Something hard smashed against his side, hurling him down so his visor hit a rock.

Zhu groaned.

"Up, up!" Tian shouted. "The enemy is upon us. We're heading to mark 3, dash 41."

Zhu crawled to his feet. On the ground lay a dud grenade. The First Rank must have fired it at him. Despite the dinylon armor, his side throbbed.

"You must be ready for anything, Fighter Rank," Tian said over the headphones.

Zhu grunted a response. Just when—he twisted the throttle, rising above another projectile shot at him.

"He learns quickly, First Rank."

"But can he fight?" Tian asked.

"We'll find out soon enough."

Zhu nodded. They were training hard. Word had filtered down to them that a combat assault was about to take place in several days. No one knew the hour, but everyone knew the Big One was almost here. Invasion: California, it was really going to happen and Zhu would be in the initial assault, killing American High Command personnel.

"Fighter Rank!" Tian shouted.

"Here, First Rank," Zhu said.

"Quit dreaming. You're off course by several meters. I expect perfection from my men."

Zhu squeezed his eyes shut and then opened them wide. He was going to excel. He was a White Tiger, an elite jetpack killer. The trainers had taught him that he would live or die with his squad mates. He would show the others. He would, even if he was too skinny to fight as well as they did. He would train until he could fire his grenades as well as any of them, or he would die trying.

WASHINGTON, D.C.

Anna sat down beside Director Levin at the circular conference table. She couldn't believe it. Little had changed since the last time she had come down to White House Bunker Number Five. Oh, there were a few more fancy computers and a holoimage in the center of the table, but nothing fundamentally different.

She recognized General Alan: the Chairman of the Joint Chiefs of Staff, the highest-ranking military man in the chamber. He was thin and wore glasses, and frowned upon sight of her. General Alan had been here during Clark's term as President. From a few tidbits that she'd heard before, Anna believed Alan was Sino-phobic.

There were others here: the Secretary of State, of Defense, the President's advisors and the top general of the Air Force, the Army and Strategic Command.

President Sims was a plump man with wispy blond hair attempting to cover his balding spot in front. He had splotchy features, only looking a little like the man who appeared on the TV and billboards. The eyes told a different story. They were pale blue, alert like a hawk and spoke about a man willing to make tough decisions. He had done just that in Alaska seven years ago. The thin mouth was downturned, showing worry. Again, that was nothing like his TV appearances. On TV, on political ads and on the internet he always appeared confident. He spoke in a forthright manner then, looking like someone the American people could trust with their children's lives.

He has good image-makers, Anna realized. *I wonder what he's like in person.*

126

No one introduced her, although several members frowned in her direction. Levin glanced at her once, as if to say, "Don't worry about a thing, smart girl. You're here under the President's wing."

Anna wondered what would happen to her if she gave advice that proved disastrous. The President's wing might not stretch so far then. She might be on her own among an increasingly xenophobic group. If the Japanese had actually landed on the U.S. mainland during World War II, what would have happened to all the interned Japanese-Americans?

Under the table, Anna rubbed her shoes together so they rustled. What an unpleasant prospect. Should she hedge her bets? Should she tell the others what they wanted to hear? It would be the safest course. She studied the computer scroll before looking up.

A major was speaking. The woman was one of General Alan's aides. Using a holopad, the major changed the holoimage in the center of the table. She was running strength figures along the Mexican-American border, the entirety of it, not just in Texas. The enemy had a 1.75 to 1 advantage in numbers. That counted the U.S. Militia brigades. Some were better than others. According to the major, they expected some militia units to crumple upon contact with the enemy.

Can you count soldiers like you would cordwood? Anna didn't think so.

One of the problems was tanks. The PAA and the SAF in Mexico had a three to one advantage in tanks, and the major said a substantial advantage in quality, too. That could spell true calamity if the enemy armor broke free in Texas or New Mexico. They might drive for hundreds of miles, creating a gap America could never hope to close, forever dividing the country in two.

"A moment," the President said. "What about our new Behemoth tanks?"

The major glanced at General Alan.

Alan cleared his throat. "Sir, the Behemoths are experimental, with too many teething problems. It will be six months, maybe nine months to a year before they're ready for combat."

"Seeing as what we're dealing with in Texas, we're probably not going to have that long." Sims glanced around the chamber, appearing thoughtful. "I remember the tri-turreted tanks in Alaska, the T-66. They were pure murder. I hate the idea of superior Chinese technology chewing up our boys again. I want those Behemoths in combat."

"I understand, sir," Alan said. "I'll set up a video conference so you can speak to the colonel of the experimental team."

The President nodded. "Keep talking," he told the major.

In artillery and mortar tubes, the enemy coalition had a four to one advantage. They were seeing what that meant in and around Laredo. The enemy had already destroyed too many American guns. Towed artillery was nearly useless in these duels, dying soon after firing. It was "shoot and scoot" on the Texas plains.

Once the Germans added their hovers and airmobile brigades, the numbers would skew even more sharply against America. GD aircraft were just as good as the Chinese, their pilots probably better.

We're like one giant Alamo, Anna realized.

"We need time," Sims said. "The Chairman didn't bite on my Geneva offer. I thought for sure he would demand a reinstatement of the food tribute. I could have talked for weeks, gaining us time. I want other ideas from you people."

Some spoke about a preemptive strike against Mexican railheads, stalling the Chinese buildup against Laredo. Others suggested taking artillery from quiet fronts and massing them and surprising the coming Chinese thrust with a wall of raining steel.

"You can't take anything from Florida," the Army Chief of Staff said, a big man with flushed features. He looked like a beer drinker. "For that matter, it would be a damn stupid idea to strip soldiers from Louisiana or Georgia. The Germans are coming. They want revenge for what we did to them in World Wars I and II."

There came a pause in the conversation. CIA Director Levin cleared his throat. "We have some minority analysis that indicates a possibility that we should consider one disturbing possibility. The Laredo artillery attack and the GD demonstration may be meant as decoys to the real assault."

General Alan shook his head. "I think you're being too subtle. Remember, the World War II Germans thought the D-Day Invasion into Normandy was a feint. They held back their reserves, waiting for the real attack to occur. In the end, they waited too long to strike at the beachheads. It seems clear to me what happened in Texas. A Chinese general started shooting too soon. How do you keep control of six million soldiers? Believe me; it's difficult. Since he started firing, the Chinese are massing sooner than they intended, deciding to push through with the assault."

"I don't know about 'massing'," the Air Force Chief of Staff said. He was a tall man with a nose like a hawk and a thin mustache, looking like the old French General Charles De Gaulle. "The Chinese are 'moving' troops into the sector. I don't believe they're moving as many bodies as we're supposed to think they are."

"Bah!" General Alan said. "And you believe your drones have spotted everything?"

"Enough to get a picture of what's happening," the Air Force General snapped. His name was O'Connor.

"Gentlemen," the President said, "please. I don't want pointless bickering. Instead, I would like to address the possibly of a Chinese offensive in California."

"Sir?" General Alan asked. "The evidence is plain. An offensive has already begun in Texas."

"I wouldn't call it an offensive just yet," the President said. "After years of waiting that's the best the Chinese can do?"

"It's very methodical," Alan said. "It's chewing up our fortifications and whittling down our artillery at little cost to them, other than a massive expenditure of shells."

"It's also giving us time to harden our defenses behind the attacked area," Sims said. "No, as devastating as it is, the artillery bombardment isn't a real attack. The Chinese have yet to send in their infantry to take ground. It feels far too much as if they're orchestrating an attack to fix our attention in Texas."

"I wonder if the German General Staff had similar arguments about the D-Day Invasion," Alan said.

Sims scowled at his hands. He sat like that for a time. Finally, looking up, he said, "Ms. Chen, explain to us your reason for your continuously grim reports concerning California."

Anna's head snapped up. Everyone looked at her, some with hostility. Steeling herself, she began to speak, telling them what she'd told Director Levin. The spy in Mexico City reported a shutdown of civilian road usage at night in northern Baja to California. It occurred, the spy believed, so the Chinese could move troops and supplies to the border.

General Alan shrugged. "The biggest war in history has started and we're worried because the Chinese military has closed the roads nearest our border? I expect attacks in California. Yes, we must prepare there. But I'm much more worried about Texas where men are dying. Our reports indicate the Chinese weren't one hundred percent ready to attack there. Yet they have massed—"

"Moved, not massed," Air Force General O'Connor said.

General Alan slapped a hand on the table.

"Gentlemen," the President said. "I would like to point out that Ms. Chen was correct about Chinese actions seven years ago. Back then, she tried to warn Clark or one of his top people about the impending attack. None of them listened to her. I don't plan making the same mistake. She is an expert on Chinese behavior. It is, I believe, her report that allowed us to find out about Blue Swan."

"That is correct," Director Levin said.

"Blue Swan," Sims said. "I haven't heard anything about evidence of Blue Swan missiles in Texas. Yet we know some are near the SoCal border. The EMP missiles seem to me like a potentially war-winning weapon. It would be logical to believe that wherever the Chinese put the Blue Swan missiles, that is where they plan to break through our defenses."

No one said a word for a time after the President's statement.

Finally, General Alan glanced at his aide—the major— before addressing the President. "Sir, suppose this is the truth. Suppose the growing Texas firestorm is a Chinese ploy to divert our attention. Suppose the German Dominion is helping them trick us by sending their hovers out to sea. What does that mean for Southern California?"

O'Connor spoke up. "It means the Chinese have improved EMP devices to throw against us."

"Highly improved," Levin added.

General Alan glanced from the Air Force General to the CIA Director. "Suppose Blue Swan knocks out much of our electronics on the SoCal front. What does that mean to us?"

"You're supposed to tell us what it means," Sims said.

General Alan glanced at the major.

"With your permission, sir," she said.

The President nodded.

"Sir," the major said, "We're laying old-fashioned fiber optic lines between various headquarters and their artillery parks in the SoCal Fortifications."

"That isn't exactly correct," Director Levin said.

The major blushed and she glanced at General Alan. Alan glanced at her with raised eyebrows. She leaned toward him, whispering in his ear so her red lips almost touched his skin. She did it as if she was his lover imparting precious secrets.

"Let me correct the statement," General Alan said a moment later. "We've *begun* placing fiber optics. It is unfortunately taking us longer than we thought it would. We've also scoured warehouses for old land mines, simple pressure mines. Our stockpiles are low, I'm afraid. Usually, we send factory-made mines straight to the front, where the troops emplace them. My point, sir, is that up until now little has changed in the Southern California Fortifications. Because of the sheer size of the fortifications and the hundreds of thousands of troops there, these things take time."

"We don't have time," Sims said. "Texas shows us that."

"That's the real problem, sir. We're not ready to face the Blue Swan missiles—if the missiles do what our scientists believe they might. But what if this is all an elaborate bluff by Chinese Intelligence."

"Speak plainly, General."

General Alan glanced at Anna. "No offense intended, sir, but can we trust everyone in the chamber?"

131

Sims's pale blue eyes focused sharply on the Chairman of the Joint Chiefs of Staff. "Do you believe Ms. Chen is a traitor? Is that what you're saying?"

"I have no way of knowing that, sir," General Alan said. "She has not gone through the military's vetting program as most of us here have."

"Other than her Chinese heritage," Sims said, "what suggests to you that Ms. Chen might be a traitor?"

General Alan frowned and he drummed his fingers on the table. The frown vanished and his features tightened. He leaned his head forward in an aggressive manner.

"Blue Swan suggests it, sir. This entire scenario is too incredible to believe. It would seem, given this technological marvel, that we should pull back our troops from our carefully built defenses. That would be better than exposing an Army Group worth of soldiers to heightened EMP missiles. Yet if that's true, then we know why Ms. Chen found out about the convoy when no one else could. The Chinese *want* us to leave our defenses without their having to fire a shot."

"No," Sims said. "I don't see it that way."

"If we stay," Alan said, "and Blue Swan does indeed melt our electronics, it could be a military disaster."

"Sir," Director Levin asked, "If I may?"

Sims nodded to the wizened CIA Director.

Levin directed his words to General Alan, "Trying to withdraw our troops from the fortifications as the missiles hit would be an even greater disaster."

The Chairman of the Joint Chiefs pursed his thin lips, nodding a moment later. "I grant you that."

"Therefore," Levin said, "no matter what, we must hold the line."

"Hold without communications?" General Alan asked. "Hold with many critical components burned out? Oh, I grant you we may be able to harden with field-expedients some electronics if they give us enough time. Depending on the strength of the EMP, many weapons systems would simply shut down. You don't hold under those conditions. You die. But as I said, it strikes me as too incredible that China has such missiles. I think we are being bluffed by Chinese Intelligence."

"What you're suggesting is ridiculous," Levin said. "Ms. Chen has often been proven right in her assessments. The Chinese have advanced technology. We know that. The Blue Swan missile exists. Your recon man Kavanagh discovered the one as the Chinese quietly brought it to the SoCal Front. These are all facts."

Anna watched the debate, appalled at the exchange concerning her reliability. It was hard to accept that anyone could think of her as a traitor.

"I believe Blue Swan exists," the President said. "I do not accept that it is a bluff. Therefore, what are your suggestions for defeating it?"

General Alan blinked at the President. Finally, he said, "If these missiles truly exist, sir, if the Chinese possess them in number, our entire front could melt away in a matter of days. We could lose California before the war is even a week old."

"If we attempted to pull back to redeploy farther from the border and the Chinese attacked, the front would be just as damaged," Sims said.

The Chairman of the Joint Chiefs grew still. He showed surprise, shock and then wonderment. "Sir, you believe the missiles are real. Yet you seem to be suggesting we let our troops absorb the electronic attack. Are you saying then we let our troops die where they stand, given this thing works? That's an entire Army Group you're talking about. We can't spare that many soldiers and hope to hold everywhere else."

Anna watched in fascination. President Sims's eyes hardened with determination. The splotchy features began to transform into an approximation of what she'd seen on TV before. With a little makeup, yes, he would look like the war-hero President the country had learned to trust.

"We don't have any good choices," the President said. "I didn't have good choices in Alaska, either, but we beat the Chinese before Anchorage. We can beat them again if we all pull together. Yes, the world has gathered into growing packs of jackals and those packs are sniffing at our door."

He's making a speech. We need strategy now, not speeches, Anna thought.

"George Washington beat the British," Sims declared. "Lincoln defeated the South. Wilson brought down the Kaiser's Germany and Roosevelt defeated the Third Reich and the Japanese. Well, I didn't become President to let the world dismember my country. I'm here to tell you that we're going to outthink and outfight the Chinese. They have a jump on us. A possible jump," he said, glancing first at the major, Anna and then the rest of the people in the chamber. "This jump is a technological missile of unusual proportions. We can't afford to leave our border fortifications in SoCal and we can't afford to let the enemy saturate us and roll over hundreds of thousands of our best soldiers. Therefore, this is what we're going to do. As quietly and quickly as possible, we're going to withdraw our mobile forces out of the missile's radius of damage."

"What *is* the radius?" General Alan asked.

No one answered.

President Sims licked his lips. "Right," he said. "We begin pulling out our best mobile formations from their positions near the fortifications. We pull out those in the second and third line, too. I want them well out of the EMP radius. Those mobile formations will redeploy well behind the front, maybe even near southern LA. If the Chinese attack and shatter our defenses, we hope our soldiers there fight tenaciously to buy the rest of the county time. If we must, we plug the holes with the mobile forces."

"If this all happens as we fear," General Alan said, "we'll need greater reserves in California than we presently have. But if we're wrong, and the attack in Texas is the real thing, we'll have outmaneuvered ourselves by thinning that front or by not placing our extra reserves there."

The President stared at the Chairman of the Joint Chiefs. Slowly, reluctantly it seemed like to Anna, Sims nodded. "We're going to have to take a risk somewhere and speed up the hardening of our electronics among the troops on the border. Send a few reserve divisions to California; put the rest near the Texas Front."

General Alan wrote on his computer pad.

President Sims glanced around the conference table. "We have to change the defenses on the Californian border. More pressure mines that are not vulnerable to EPM instead of our quake and sleeper variety. More fiber optics lines embedded in the ground so there are some backup communications if the EMP hits. Look into what they did in World War I. I seem to recall reading about dispatch runners."

"It will take time to retrain our troops into using something so antiquated," Alan said.

"We don't have time," Sims said. "We need to scrape up troops wherever we can." He scowled. "I know, I know. We don't dare take them from Texas or Florida. Yes," he said, as if to himself. "I want the experimental Behemoth tanks in California."

"Sir?" Alan asked.

"This could be what we've been dreading for several years now," Sims said. "We have to pull out all the stops to face what I think is the coming storm. I don't care if these Behemoths have teething problems. I want them in California with the reserve troops. That's what I did in Alaska. I used everything I had to buy us time until reinforcements arrived. We'll have to scrape together our own reinforcements. Mainly, we're going to have to fight hard with what we have and exploit every Chinese mistake."

"And if they don't make mistakes?" General Alan asked.

"Everyone makes mistakes," Sims said. "We're all human, and I've never met a perfect one of us yet. Nor do I think I'm going to any time soon."

"Yes, sir," General Alan said. "And if this Blue Swan situation is an entire bluff?"

"Then we'll fall down on our knees and thank God," Sims said. "Then we'll concentrate against the Chinese in Texas and the Germans in Florida, if the Huns are arrogant enough to attack us. Are there any questions?"

"I have one," Air Force General O'Connor said.

The President tapped a computer stylus twice on the table before pointing the tip at the general.

"We keep talking about absorbing the EMP missiles," O'Connor said. "I think there's another answer. We need to

135

move or mass our anti-missile lasers and rockets there. The Blue Swan missiles can't hurt us if we knock them down before they broadcast their electromagnetic pulses."

"General Alan?" the President asked.

"In theory it's the right move."

"But in practice?" the President asked.

"Massing anti-missile units in SoCal means we open them to the same EMP that will melt all the other electronics. The same holds true for our air cover."

"We can't just let them hit us!" O'Connor shouted. "That means we're abandoning our boys on the line. My planes and fighter drones can save the situation."

"We're not going to abandon anyone," the President said.

"We're saying that, sir, but—"

The President slammed a fist onto the table. The chamber became deathly silent.

"Are you accusing me of double-talk?" the President asked the Air Force General.

"No, sir," O'Connor said crisply.

"Good, because I'm not going to abandon anyone," Sims said. "We'll bring more lasers and anti-missile systems to the SoCal Fortifications. We'll bring more fighters, too. But we're not going to denude ourselves of cover elsewhere."

"How much extra cover are we talking about?" General Alan asked. "It isn't as if we have enough tactical lasers or flak guns. Which front do we take them from?"

"I have an idea," Anna heard herself saying.

Director Levin stared at her and he shook his head minutely.

"Concerning military strategy?" General Alan asked in a scornful manner.

"Mr. President?" Anna asked.

"Go ahead," Sims said.

Anna's stomach tightened. It was a risk to talk, as others could pin her idea's failure on her. It was a chancy thing she was about to suggest.

"Well," the President asked, "what's your idea?"

"Sir, General O'Connor has spoken my thought: why wait for the Chinese to strike with Blue Swan? He advocates knocking down the missiles, and that's better than letting them strike. But my question is why let them launch at all."

General Alan laughed. "Are you advocating that we *attack* the Chinese?"

"In a manner of speaking, yes," Anna said.

"Ah," General Alan said. "And just how will you conjure up this army? I'm very curious. If our analysis is correct, the Chinese have thirty-five thousand artillery and mortar tubes massed on the SoCal border, while we have a paltry eleven thousand. They have a clear three to one advantage over us in artillery, tanks and I imagine planes and probably a two to one advantage in numbers."

"I'm not a military expert," Anna said.

"No, no, tell us your plan," General Alan said. "Anna Chen, the Chinese expert, can predict the future and instruct us in the military arts. By all means, enlighten us, please."

President Sims frowned at the Chairman of the Joint Chiefs.

Anna looked down and she could feel her face heating up. She should have kept her mouth shut. What had she been thinking?

"You have to tell us now," Levin whispered. "You can't let the general bully you."

Anna swallowed, looking up. "Sir," she told the President. "It seems to me that America cannot allow the launching of Blue Swan. We don't have the numbers to launch a conventional attack—"

"Nuclear weapons?" the Army General asked. He scowled, but he nodded. "I concur, sir. We *have* to go nuclear."

"No!" Anna said, horrified. "I'm not talking about nuclear weapons."

"What then?" the President asked.

"Commando teams," she said.

General Alan frowned severely, shaking his head. "How do we know where these missiles are? And how do you propose getting our special forces teams down on the ground with the missiles?"

"The spy in Mexico City might be able to help us pinpoint the missiles' locations," Anna said. "As for getting our commandos in, I don't have the answer to that. I just know that we have to do whatever we can to stop the Blue Swan missiles from hitting the SoCal Fortifications."

President Sims sat as if shocked. His nostrils widened and he began to nod. "I hate to order anyone so deep into the midst of the enemy. Those missiles are sure to be heavily guarded. Yet, I don't see any other way."

"It would be suicide to send commandos at those missiles now," General Alan said.

"We can only ask for volunteers," Sims said.

"Sir…" General Alan said.

Sims stared at the Chairman of the Joint Chiefs. His eyes had become red-rimmed. "I don't know what else you would have me do. It's a gamble, a terrible risk, but with several hundred men only, maybe two or three thousand commandos all together."

"How do you sneak them in, sir?" Alan asked.

"A mass aerial assault," O'Connor said grimly. "We saturate the Chinese with drones, all we have. Behind them, we use helos to insert the commandos. Once on the ground, they should know what to do."

"It's mass suicide," Alan said.

"It's better than letting an entire Army Group die on the fortifications," Sims said.

"Our drone losses would be staggering," Alan said. "That would likely give the Chinese control of the air for the duration. We've known the air situation will be critical. To then knowingly burn up our air assets on the first day of battle…it is madness, sir."

"Our backs are to the wall," Sims said. "Yes, it's suicide to send those men, but if this works we'll actually have a chance at holding California. Ms. Chen, it's a brilliant plan."

"Maybe," General Alan said. He stared at Anna as if remembering her face for a future showdown.

"'Maybe' is better than certain defeat," the President said. "How much time do we have until the Chinese launch?" he asked Levin.

"I don't know," the CIA Director said.

"Give me a ball park estimate."

138

"A day," Levin said, cautiously, "several days, less than a week, I'm certain."

Sims ran his fingers through his thinning hair. "In two days we must strike. It's madness, but so is Blue Swan." He took a deep breath. "We have a plan now, a slim hope to save the situation. Let's get to work."

LAS VEGAS TESTING GROUNDS, NEVADA

Early the next morning, Stan Higgins walked solemnly around his X1 Behemoth #5 for what would likely be for the last time. The monster tank was in the desert where Jose, the driver and he had left it yesterday. Las Vegas's mountains rose in the distance as the sun worked to show itself, the first rays lighting the edges of the mountaintops.

Stan sipped coffee from a Styrofoam cup. It tasted good and was an antidote against the desert chill. He wore a coat and waited for Jose to gather his tools in the Humvee.

Yesterday, the Behemoth had engine trouble again. It had been having problems of this sort for several weeks. After hours of exhausting work, they had headed to base for the night. He hadn't told the colonel about the trouble. He didn't want to speak to the man again until he was a civilian, out from under Wilson's control.

Stan took another sip of coffee. He'd told his wife what he'd told Wilson the other day about leaving for John Glen. She'd hardly heard him. All she could think about was Jake in the Detention Center, together with the other "non-patriots."

Scowling at the tank's extra-wide treads, Stan wondered if maybe it was good for Jake to stew in the Detention Center for a while. Maybe he'd been too easy on the boy. Let Jake know that there were consequences to his actions like protesting the President. He didn't want to leave Jake there, but what harm would there be for a few months?

The loss of his education, for one thing.

Stan pried off the coffee's plastic cover and enjoyed the aroma as it steamed into the cold desert air. He sipped more, as it had cooled just enough for him to enjoy.

If Jake didn't care about his education, why should he fret so much about it? The boy was old enough to vote, to drink beer and go away to school. Maybe this was the best thing for him. People didn't treasure what came too easily. Jake had worked a half-time summer job, but otherwise, Stan had paid for the tuition.

Stan drained the cup. Who was he trying to kid? Himself, it seemed like. The boy was in trouble. Jake might never get another shot at a college education. The laws were harsh regarding non-patriotic protesting. The longer he stayed in a Detention Center, the heavier the mark on his record. In the eyes of most, it meant that he lacked friends and family. That equated to a loner who likely didn't love his country. The police watched such "miscreants" and bosses didn't have to worry about discrimination suits if they failed to hire anyone with a three-stamp mark.

"I have to get him out of there," Stan muttered. He went to drink more coffee and discovered the cup was empty. Stan crumbled the Styrofoam in irritation. He almost threw the pieces into the desert. But that would be littering. Instead, he put them in his jacket pocket. He would throw away the cup later on base.

Frowning, Stan eyed the beast, the Behemoth tank. It was a marvel all right, and this might be the last time he had to deal with it. His chest—

Stan rubbed his chest, feeling a sore spot. He didn't want to leave. The entire operational idea behind the Behemoth—

Stan's lips peeled back. He remembered Alaska and their M1A2 tanks. They had been good tanks, if too old. The Chinese tri-turreted tanks had played havoc with them. Better armor, better guns, better shells—the enemy had outclassed them in every category.

The Behemoth was supposed to be the great surprise. It was supposed to be the equalizer, the antidote to enemy numbers. China had far more and better quality tanks. What did that leave America? Not much chance of winning, had been Stan's answer.

The tri-turreted tank—the T-66—weighed one hundred tons. The Behemoth was three hundred tons. Stan rubbed his hands. The specs on these things: they told their own story.

It was fifteen by six by four and mounted 260cm of armor. It had nine auto-cannons, seven auto-machine guns and an onboard radar and AI to track enemy missiles and shells. Given enough flight time, the Behemoth could knock down incoming missiles and most shells. Whatever came close had to survive the forty beehive launchers. Those fired tungsten flechettes, a spray of shotgun-like metal that often knocked down or deflected an enemy projectile enough to skew its impact against the heavy armor. It was the super-thick armor and the sheer mass of beehives that was supposed to make the Behemoth more than a big, expensive target.

The special power plant in the Behemoth was also huge. It had to be to move all that mass. The three-hundred ton machine had magnetically balanced hydraulic suspension and a weapon unlike anything else in the world. Instead of shells, the Behemoth fired a force cannon. Some people called it a rail gun. It was high-tech and it was amazing—if everything worked like it was supposed to. The force cannon needed the Behemoth's mighty engine to juice it, and the new batteries that stored power for extended shooting.

The Chinese had many fancy weapons, but Stan bet the Chinese didn't have anything like the Behemoth. Stan crunched over gravel and he slapped the treads. It would have been interesting fighting in the Behemoth.

Too bad you'll never get to use it against them.

It would be good to get some real payback against the Chinese tankers. There were too many nightmares that included Stan's friends murdered once again by the T-66 tri-turreted tank.

"You're too old for this," Stan muttered to himself. "Jake did you a favor getting you out of this before the Big One."

Then why did he feel so terrible, as if he was running out on his friends and his country during everyone's darkest hour?

"Professor!" Jose shouted from the Humvee.

"What's wrong?" Stan shouted back.

Jose stuck his head out of a window. "The colonel just radioed. He wants you back at base and he wants you there now."

"Do you know what it's about?"

"Not a clue, Professor. What do you want to do?"

Stan rubbed the giant tread. What did Wilson want now? He sighed, wanting to make the stickler wait, but not wanting to cause problems for Jose and Ted, their young driver.

"Sure!" Stan shouted. "Radio Wilson that we're on our way in."

**

Forty-five minutes later, Stan sat in Colonel Wilson's tidy office. From behind his desk, the colonel watched him, with his index fingers tapping his chin.

"We were fixing our tank," Stan said. Wilson hadn't asked where he'd been or why he had been late. The colonel had simply pointed at the chair as Stan entered.

Stan decided to wait it out. He was through with Wilson anyway. Not that he planned to tell him any more of his faults. Once was enough.

Wilson breathed deeply through his nostrils. As if annoyed, he turned his computer screen so it faced Stan.

Stan raised an eyebrow. Wilson breathed deeply again, saying nothing. Bending closer, Stan began to read the print on the screen. In a moment, it felt as if his blood froze. It was hard to focus on the words.

"Do you understand the message's significance?" Wilson asked in a brittle tone.

"The Army can't refuse my resignation," Stan said.

Wilson snorted. "You're with us for the duration, Captain. You will remain under my command until either you or I die."

"But—"

"Dismissed," Wilson said.

Stan stared at him.

"You are dismissed," the colonel said. "You do remember military discipline, I hope."

Nodding, Stan stood. He could fight this, he supposed. Yet how would that help Jake? The President had signed an order. The experimental unit had been activated and cancelled all

142

leaves of absence, resignations—the unit was headed for California, for active duty.

Why would they send us there? The big tanks were hard to move. There were only a few railcars big enough to carry the Behemoths and almost no bridges. If the railroad over the mountains were destroyed, why, that would strand the Behemoths in California. They had snorkel gear so the giant tank could ford or cruise underwater through the largest rivers.

"John Glen will have to wait to enjoy the pleasure of your company," Wilson said.

Stan swallowed a retort. It was like swallowing a big pill that refused to go down. He had to work at it, his throat muscles going up and down. The colonel sounded vindictive. He shook his head.

"You're refusing orders?" Wilson asked.

"No, sir," Stan said, giving an over-crisp, sarcastic salute. He was sure Wilson didn't get it. He'd have to think this over. The unit had been activated. What did the President think was going to happen that he wanted these so-very-prone-to-breakdown-tanks in California?

"I'd better get back to my tank, sir. I need to get the engine running if they're moving us."

"Hmm," Wilson said. "Yes, see to it, Captain."

Stan spun on his heel and marched for the door. Did this mean he was going to war, that the country was? He couldn't believe it.

-5-
Into the Abyss

SAN YSIDRO, CALIFORNIA

"Gunnery Sergeant," General Ochoa said, nodding a greeting.

"Hello, sir," Paul said warily. He was in one of the Ninth Division's comm-shacks, the same one he'd used to speak to Cheri. After a tiring day at the border with Colonel Norman, Paul had headed for the showers. The lanky lieutenant he'd bluffed before told him he had a special message.

Now Paul stared at the grim-faced Ochoa. "Do you have bad news, sir?"

"I'm afraid I do," Ochoa said. "I've been giving the news to others all day long."

"Is it my wife?" Paul asked.

"What?" Ochoa asked. "No," he said a moment later. "It's about the survival of the United States as we know it."

"Oh." Paul's shoulders loosened. He had been worried sick it was about Cheri or Mike. "Go ahead, sir. Let's hear it."

General Ochoa frowned before explaining the nature of Blue Swan.

"Okay," Paul said. "I get it. EMP leaves us sitting ducks for the Chinese. What does that have to do with me?"

Ochoa nodded crisply, although he spoke hesitantly. "We need commandos to, ah…"

Paul laughed mirthlessly as the problem and plan crystalized in his mind. "You want American kamikazes to take out the enemy missiles, is that it?"

Ochoa stared at him, finally nodding.

"But those missiles are likely in the middle of enemy formations across the border in Mexico."

"We've begun pinpointing them," Ochoa said.

"And how have you done that, sir?"

"The CIA—"

Paul had worked with the CIA for some time now, ever since Hawaii, in fact. "Oh," he said. "You mean you're guessing."

Ochoa stopped speaking, which left his mouth open. He closed his mouth and hunched toward the screen. "I won't lie to you, Kavanagh. Ah...these are educated guesses by the smartest people we have."

"Great," Paul said.

"Can I count on you for this?"

Paul turned away. *They want me back in Mexico. If this Chinese thingamajig works...then we're all dead anyway.* He faced Ochoa. "When would we go in, sir?" This was going to take a lot of precision training.

"Twenty-four hours from now," Ochoa said.

Paul felt himself go cold. *We're trying to stay alive by our fingernails.* "This is getting better by the minute," he said. "You're throwing men together—strangers—to go in and die for a wild hope."

"It's a gamble and it's a raw deal for you. But we need you, Gunnery Sergeant. Your country needs you."

"Just like the U.S. needed me in Hawaii?"

Scowling, Ochoa said, "The truth is you're probably a dead man if you agree to this. The trouble is that if you don't agree, our country could be dead before we start the fight. This is one of those times..." Ochoa cleared his throat. "Sergeant, we've been flat-out beaten before the fighting starts by a war-changing enemy weapon. The intelligence community believes the Chinese only have a limited number of these missiles. We've yet to spot any facing Texas. Now if—"

"I'll do it," Paul said. "I'm in, sir. I want to get it done."

Ochoa blinked several times. "You know what this means?"

"Yeah, that I get to do the job I was trained for. This driving around as a chauffeur—it's a waste of my time."

Ochoa looked away. He shook his head. When he looked back, his eyes had hardened. "You're a good man, Kavanagh. I'm emailing you the plan on your secure account. Study it, refine it if you can think of anything better for your team, and then tomorrow night you're going in."

"Yeah," Paul said, "that's just wonderful. I can hardly wait."

FIRST FRONT HEADQUARTERS, MEXICO

Marshal Nung clasped his hands behind his back as a green light bathed his features. He stood over a computerized situation map of the Mexican-Californian border. Around the glowing table stood his staff officers and old Marshal Gang, the Ruling Committee's observer.

Marshal Gang was big for a Chinese officer, with wrinkled skin and rows of gaudy medals on his chest.

"We still need several more days, sir," General Pi told Nung, his logistical wizard. Pi looked haggard, with red-rimmed eyes and a drooping mouth. He was the eternal pessimist and therefore an oddity among Nung's officers.

Nung breathed deeply, expanding his chest and making his medals clink against each other. He looked up at Pi and shook his head.

Pi's frown deepened. "The Third Corps needs more—"

"Listen to me," Nung said. His voice was raw from lack of sleep. Since his return from China he had been everywhere, inspecting, threatening, cajoling and watching. Through force of will he attempted to move two million men and their supplies into attack position. It was a daunting task. Even with a brilliant, hard-working staff, there was simply too much to do and too little time to do it in.

Fortunately, they had prepositioned masses of supplies months ago. The Americans had noticed then and the enemy had gone into alert status. Over time, the Americans became accustomed to his maneuvers. The enemy was on alert again, but Nung suspected that many Americans must think of it as routine, especially as the action had already started in Texas.

Nung breathed once more, staring at the green screen. Two million soldiers and their support groups. Masses of artillery shells, masses of bullets, body armor, boots, jackets, rifles and millions of tons of rations—there was no end to his soldiers' needs. Tanks, armored cars, IFVs, hovers, fighter jets, bombers, missiles and the tens of thousands of drones, it boggled the imagination how much fuel he needed.

The diversionary attack in Texas had absorbed an amazing amount of materiel, but it would be as nothing compared to his needs.

The Americans had mass, too, but not as much, never close to equal to what he possessed. Besides, the enemy had vast frontages to guard, never certain where his enemy might land an amphibious invasion.

"The Chinese hammer falls here, comrades," Nung told his officers. "We will crack the Californian defenses. First, we must smash the American air cover and destroy radar stations, anti-missile launchers, laser and flak sites. Then we will unleash Blue Swan and send in the Eagle Teams. Only then will the wave assaults wash over the shattered and shaken Americans. One swift blow given with tremendous force will shatter the American defenses into a million pieces. Ah, then comrades, then our tanks will lunge into the Californian hinterland and win the war before the Americans have time to recover."

"It is a bold plan," Marshal Gang said.

Nung nodded, accepting the compliment.

"Yet I wonder if the Americans will wilt as you hope," Gang said.

Nung squinted at the frowning marshal. "Without communications, without their vaulted command and control, with Chinese soldiers en masse, flowing over, around and behind them—yes, the Americans will wilt as I expect," Nung said. "They will run from us in terror. Their entire defensive line will shatter like a brittle vase. I have promised our Great

Leader this and I intend to see it achieved. Ceaseless assaults, comrades," he said, turning to his officers. "Mass and more mass will swamp the American soldiers. Therefore, even though we haven't achieved perfection in all our divisions, we will launch the assault two days from now. Two days, comrades, and the greatest battle in history will begin.

SAN YSIDRO, CALIFORNIA

Marshal Nung was wrong. The start of the war would not begin in two days, but one night earlier under cover of darkness.

Paul Kavanagh stood with his new team in the glare of bright lamplights. Moths flew up there by the lights, motes of anarchy showing the senselessness of fate. This was an ad hoc group of soldiers. He had four former Marine Recon drill instructors from Camp Pendleton. They had been plucked from their training duties. He had six Rangers and five Free Mexico assassins. According to their records, they were the best Colonel Valdez possessed. Their leader was a man named Romo.

He was a dark-skinned native with sharp features. He was shorter than Paul, with his hair shaved to his scalp and with the eyes of a stone cold killer. Romo had an earring, with a small feather dangling and he walked with the silky grace of a jaguar.

Paul had shaken hands with each of his men. All had squeezed back. One or two had looked away; three of the Free Mexico soldiers had shifted uneasily. Romo had shaken hands normally.

"You are Paul Kavanagh?" Romo asked.

"Do I know you?"

Romo shook his head.

"Do you know me?"

"Si," Romo said, hardly moving his lips as he spoke, but always staring into his eyes.

Paul knew it then. "Colonel Valdez sent you?"

"Si."

"He wants my head or something like that?"

148

"Si."

"And you're the one who's going to bring it in?"

With the tip of the fingers of his left hand, Romo touched his feather. "Si," he said.

"Okay," Paul said, "fine. But answer me this."

Romo barely shifted his shoulders in a shrug.

"First, what's with the feather?"

Romo became utterly still.

"I don't see too many Mexican soldiers wearing those," Paul said.

"I am Apache from my mother's side.

Paul raised his eyebrows, and he nodded. "Good enough. Will you obey my orders until we destroy our Blue Swan missile?"

Romo glanced at his four men, each of them carefully listening to the conversation. "You and me," he told Paul, "we kill the Chinese first, si."

Paul stared into Romo's eyes, and he felt a chill along his spine as if someone had put a cold blade against his back. The man was grim death, a stone killer. As Paul stared into those pitiless eyes, he considered drawing a knife and gutting the man on the spot. But since none of them were coming back alive, he figured why bother.

The conversation with Romo had taken place many hours ago. Now Paul adjusted his body armor. He looked around at the lamp-washed concrete at the waiting helicopters. They were sleek and fast, representing the latest in American insertion technology.

This was the land of the free, eh. Yeah, it was his land. His wife and boy were in LA. If the Blue Swan missiles worked and demolished the SoCal Fortifications…then his family was meat. This way, they had a chance.

"Love you, babe," he whispered. Paul picked up his combination assault rifle/grenade launcher and with his rucksack secured, he jogged for his waiting jet-assisted helo. Romo and several of his killers followed. So did the Recon Marines. The rest of the Free Mexico soldiers and Rangers headed for the second helicopter. They were sixteen commandos bent on destroying a Blue Swan launcher—if it

149

existed and if the planners had really pinpointed the thing's location.

SAN DIEGO, CALIFORNIA

Flight Lieutenant Harris cracked his knuckles. He sat in a padded chair, staring at his screen and while wearing virtual reality goggles. In the same room were ten other men and women like him. Each was a drone operator.

Their drone was the Viper 10 air-superiority Unmanned Combat Vehicle. Lieutenant Harris rolled his shoulders, trying to make himself more comfortable. He didn't like flying if he was stiff.

The V-10 was half the size of an F-35, the Air Force's main single-engine fighter. Because the UCAV lacked a pilot, it needed less space and a smaller engine to do the same task. It could also take more Gs and be ordered to do suicidal things without losing a valuable pilot.

Lieutenant Harris squeezed his eyes shut and then he concentrated. Tonight, they were headed into enemy air space. Tonight, the drones were going to hunt for trouble.

What are we doing, huh? Doesn't the brass upstairs know we're going to take severe loses doing this?

Lieutenant Harris shrugged and then settled back, finding his comfort zone. He would do his best. He knew how much the V-10s cost. And if they failed, it was likely he wouldn't make it out of San Diego alive before the Chinese came.

"Here we go," the lieutenant whispered, taxiing his drone down a runway.

All across Southern California, other UCAVs, fighters, bombers and wild weasels launched into the darkness. From Vandenberg Air Force Base, a Titan VII rocket lifted a three-package satellite into space. No one expected those to last long, just long enough to give them vital intelligence.

AWACS planes remained well behind the border. They were critical in detecting enemy low and fast flyers—strike, recon and interceptor aircraft, even ground-to-air weapons and cruise missiles. The Airborne-Warning-And-Control System

150

aircraft used look-down phased-array radar and computers to find low-flying enemy against all the ground clutter. The computers had gotten better since the Alaskan War, making it easier for AWACS and radar stations to spot enemy aircraft.

Because both sides lacked reliable satellites near the combat zone, they also fell back on using their AWACS and high-flying drones to control their planes and provide an integrated operating picture through secure datalinks. In other words, the AWACS were flying air battle control centers.

A terrible truism affected modern warfare, particularly in air combat. If one could see the enemy, one could kill the enemy nine times out of ten. It was why both sides used stealth craft. Special alloys and polymers, anti-radar paint and ingenious construction meant that most Chinese and American aircraft gave back very small radar signatures. Ever-improving radar and computers helped each side spot the faint returns, often pinpointing positions with lethal precision. It was a constant cat and mouse game.

As he sat in his seat in San Diego, Lieutenant Harris watched through his VR goggles as his V-10 waited twenty miles from the border. There were hundreds of Chinese aircraft up on the other side. The majority of those were fighter drones guarding Chinese air space.

Harris licked his lips. He'd never flown in combat before, although he had logged plenty of hours in simulated battle. There were four critical factors to air fights and to interception missions in particular. The side with superior eyes and ears, the detection devices and electronic counter measures—ECM— usually maneuvered into superior attack positions. The second factor was that the side with better tactics, including tactical or strategic surprise, gained an edge. Third, the side with more skilled pilots had an advantage. Lastly, numbers, sheer mass of planes over the enemy gave a striking advantage.

Lieutenant Harris wiped a wrist across his mouth. America had none of these advantages here. The Chinese particularly were rich as a people and a nation. They had bought the best planes and drones and logged hundreds of hours, perfecting their pilots. Perhaps, America would have tactical surprise tonight—

"Look at that," a drone operator said.

Harris stopped breathing as he watched his split screen. One side showed him what the V-10's cameras "saw." The other was an aerial map of SoCal. The red dots—the Chinese—began to fill the "southern" edge of his screen. More kept appearing, making it a blizzard over there.

"Look at them."

"I'm looking," Harris said.

As he did, American wild weasels surged to the forefront. They jammed enemy radar and applied other electronic counter-measures. They attempted to blind the Chinese by throwing a blanket over their early warning stations. Behind the wild weasels followed heavier "Buffalo" drones. These launched flocks of anti-radar missiles, with the missiles zeroing in on Chinese radar and other air-detection stations. These rode the enemy radar beams straight down to their targets. Even if the enemy turned the beams off as a countermeasure, the missiles remembered where their targets were and struck them anyway.

The command came then and Lieutenant Harris and his fellow operators launched their V-10s for the Mexican-Californian border.

Harris took his drone low. He didn't want to lose his UCAV to enemy flak, tac-lasers or SAMs. Flying low and fast was the way to avoid most of those. The trouble was that this was one of the thickest SAM belts in the world.

Like a swarm of angry bees, the American V-10s raced over the border and lifted their noses to engage the enemy drones, firing anti-air missiles and cannons.

Lieutenant Harris had other orders. As his fellow V-10s engaged the enemy, he raced deeper into Mexico at treetop level. Through his VR goggles, he saw endless splashes and flares of brilliant light. Those were enemy and friendly kills. Twice his threat-receiver blinked, warning him of enemy radar lock-on. Harris released chaff and an echo decoy. It gave off a V-10 signature. Seconds later, a nearby explosion rocked his drone.

In his padded chair in San Diego, Harris's head wobbled. The action was more noticeable to him because of the weight of his headgear. It felt as if he was in a gym doing a neck exercise. The motion was a reaction to the feedback vibration of the VR system. *They almost got me.*

Fortunately his threat receiver was quiet now. He'd shaken the radar fix. Grimly, Harris took his drone even lower. He passed a brick building, flashing over it by a mere fifty meters. Since it was a drone, he could take greater chances than a regular pilot could.

His target was an enemy AWACS plane, which stayed well behind the border by several hundred miles. The Chinese had ten up now and could put up more. But that would take time. Whoever had greater air control and better eyes gained a critical advantage for as long as it lasted. And AWACS were high-value targets, expensive, full of specialists, and hard to replace.

The minutes ticked by. The threat receiver blinked. Harris released another packet of chaff. He was deep behind the giant air battle going on over the border. Enemy lasers flashed there, cutting down American aircraft. A thousand Chinese SAMs made it a pilot's nightmare.

"Come on, baby," Harris whispered. He wiped a sweaty palm on his pants.

Minutes passed. He was far behind the giant air battle now. He needed to reach the AWACS. There were others like him, he knew, hunting their own AWACS craft. Would any of them make it? If not…it was over for their side.

More time passed. Then it got sticky. A buzzing in his ear told Harris Chinese radar had fixed on him tight. Back here, that would likely mean SAMs.

Harris released his last packet of chaff and two echo decoys. He didn't have any more now. If the nearby AWACS was smart, it would be turning retrograde, trying to escape.

Harris checked his fuel level. If he used afterburners to catch the enemy, he'd never make it back. "Let's kiss this bastard," he said. It was all or nothing tonight.

He kicked in the afterburners and the V-10 became the bat out of hell. Twelve miles from target, ten, eight—Harris lifted his drone sharply. The target acquisition indicator growled in his ear. In his VR goggles, a crosshairs fixed on the enemy

AWACS five miles away. Yeah, it was fleeing, racing for the ground, hoping to get lost in the clutter.

"This is with love, baby," Harris said. He toggled and fired two Sun-stinger missiles. They launched from the V-10 and flashed at the enemy, rapidly building speed at a terrible velocity. A ray burned in the darkness—visible on the V-10's infrared scanner—and one Sun-stinger disintegrated.

They have a dedicated tac-laser, no doubt. I don't like that.

The enemy AWACS was diving hard and it was expelling chaff like a snowfall. Would American electronics in the Sun-stinger defeat that?

Harris watched avidly through his VR goggles. He licked his lips. "Come on," he whispered.

The speeding Sun-stinger exploded against the enemy's tail. It was pure ecstasy. *I love it.* The large plane simply dropped for the ground. There wouldn't be any saving it now.

"Hit," Harris said.

Seconds later, a Chinese SAM scored its own hit, killing his V-10 and taking Lieutenant Harris's drone out of the opening air battle of the war.

FIRST FRONT HEADQUARTERS, MEXICO

Marshal Nung shrugged on his jacket as he entered the underground command bunker. His hair was still messed up from sleep. He had taken several tranks earlier in order to get a good night's sleep before the beginning of tomorrow's invasion. Now he threw two amphetamines into his mouth, slugged back some tea and swallowed the lumps. Afterward, he accepted his military cap from an aide and jammed into onto his head.

"Report!" he barked, noticing that for once Marshal Gang wasn't here "observing."

"The Americans," General Pi said, looking up from the green command screen. "They're throwing their air at us. It is most bewildering."

Nung scowled. "A night before our big assault and they attack? That doesn't make sense. Did they know what we are going to do?"

General Pi shook his narrow face. "No, Marshal. Our lasers and flak are decimating them, and our drones are killing the rest. They're throwing away what air force they have. It doesn't make sense."

"What about enemy missiles?" Nung asked.

"They've taken out a few radar stations. Well, a large number of them, but not enough to affect the overall efficiency of our tac-lasers."

"Sir, they've launched satellites," an operator said. The man watched on one of the many screens in the room.

"Call Space Command," Nung said.

"We have, sir," Pi said. "Space Command is targeting the satellites with strategic lasers. The American won't be watching us from space for long."

"Are they attempting to create lanes in our airspace for nuclear-tipped missiles?" Nung asked. That was the only thing that made sense to him.

"That is also my impression, sir," General Pi said. "Otherwise, this is a meaningless attack."

"No," Nung said, scowling at the computer table. "It isn't meaningless. The Americans aren't fools." He stared at the situational map as Pi kept changing screen shots. "I find it hard to accept they would go nuclear," Nung said. "We would shoot down many of those missiles. Afterward, China might well launch a retaliatory strike. But if they're not going nuclear…" Nung became thoughtful. "Give me a strategic look of the Mexican-Californian border."

Pi touched the screen, bringing up the strategic map of Southern California.

Nung scowled at it. "Show me the destroyed radar installations."

Pi tapped the screen several times. Tiny pink lines like threads appeared on the screen.

"Where do those lines lead?" Nung asked.

Pi shook his head.

For the next fifteen minutes, they monitored the air battle.

"Why aren't the American fighters retreating?" Nung asked. "This is amazing. They're handing us their air force." He felt the amphetamines beginning to kick in. The fuzziness around his mind slipped away, focusing his thoughts. "Compute the ratios of destroyed aircraft between our two sides."

General Pi tapped a computer screen. Several moments later, he said, "We've destroyed half their attacking craft, sir, drones and planes. For every one of ours they've destroyed, we've shot down four. As you say, it's a slaughter. The only real negative is the number of our AWACS they destroyed."

"Sir!" a comm-officer said, swiveling in his chair.

Marshal Nung nodded at the officer.

"The Americans have landed commando teams on our side of the border."

"Landed where?" Nung asked. His face felt tingly. He adjusted his hat, beginning to feel jittery. "Well, landed where?" he asked.

The officer pressed a hand over his earpiece. He looked up. "Sir, one team landed at a cruise missile installation, another at a Black Thunder park and yet another at a Blue Swan launching site."

"Blue Swan," Nung said. "That's it!" He adjusted his hat again and moved his mouth. His face felt as if ants crawled over it. Why did his skin feel so tight?

"What is it, sir?" Pi asked. The general looked concerned.

Marshal Nung blinked in surprise. What was wrong with him? He felt odd, off. It must be the combination of the tranks and amphetamines.

"Sir?" asked Pi. "Do you feel well?"

"The Americans have discovered Blue Swan," Nung said. "They're trying to destroy the missiles before we launch them."

"Destroy the launching sites with commandos?" asked General Pi. "It would be suicide for them, and we know the Americans are not suicidal."

Nung's heart began hammering. Sweat appeared on his face, particularly at the inner corners of his eyes. Yes, he could feel the tranks fighting the amphetamines. He blinked groggily as sweat stung his eyes, and he tried to understand what this

156

meant. Beside him, General Pi was babbling about something. Nung focused on the man's words.

"Launch now, sir?" Pi asked.

"What are you talking about?" Nung asked. The hammering of his heart increased. He clutched the edge of the computer table. Was he having a heart attack? He couldn't have one now. This was the greatest battle of his life. Though force of will, he listened to Pi, staring at the man.

"Sir," Pi said, sounding worried.

"Concentrate on the battle," Nung snapped.

Pi nodded nervously. "If the Americans are destroying the Blue Swan missiles, sir, shouldn't we launch them while we can?"

Nung glanced at the green situational map. His heart was tripping fast and he felt cold, yet sweat continued to ooze onto his skin. That wasn't important now. He had decisions to make. The Americans...they were attacking—"Yes!" he shouted. "Order the personnel to launch all Blue Swam missiles now! This is an emergency. They are to immediately launch the missiles."

After shouting, Marshal Nung lost his grip on the table. His strength simply vanished. In slow motion, the bulldog soldier toppled backward onto the tiled floor.

FORWARD EDGE OF THE BATTLE AREA, MEXICO

Paul swayed in his seat as the Cherokee helicopter banked hard. Below, the dark ground swept past. The sound of firing in the distance—missiles, artillery and rockets—penetrated the whomp-whomp of the helicopter's blades. Red light flared, artillery no doubt, and smaller, brighter flares that indicated explosions.

They flew at treetop level, trying to come in under the enemy radar. It made them vulnerable to ground fire. But they flew so fast that enemy soldiers only had a moment's glance and then they were past.

The Cherokee was the latest in American innovations. No nation used helicopters like the U.S. This one was faster and sleeker than anything seen so far and it maneuvered with afterburner tri-jets.

The Cherokee shook now from counter-fire, its automated flechette launchers firing. Paul glanced outside. A contrail closed toward them, showing a speeding missile. Then, where the missile had been, a brilliant flash stole his night vision. Seconds later, the helicopter shuddered from the concussion.

The flechette launchers had done their job, knocking down an enemy missile that would have blown them out of the battle.

Paul watched the ground pass. They must be in Mexico by now or close enough so it didn't matter. A hundred thoughts tumbled through his mind. Would he ever see his wife again? When should he shoot Romo and his killers? Did Valdez want to torture him? How did the CIA know where the Chinese had hidden their secret weapons? He doubted their team would get anywhere close to one of these Blue Swans. What were the odds, ten percent, fifteen? Just how many doomsday missiles did they have to destroy—all the commandos together—to have to make this crazy operation worthwhile?

He didn't know the answers to any of his questions. So he let his gut churn with pre-battle jitters. It was always like this. He figured if he ever stopped feeling nervous before a mission then he would have stopped being alive.

I'll be a corpse. Yeah, then I'll know peace.

The helo shuddered again with another brilliant flash. Seconds later the craft slewed hard as if a giant had batted it. The noise from the blades changed. It wasn't whomp-whomp-whomp now, but sounded wounded.

"We're going to crash!" a Marine shouted in Paul's ear.

Paul clutched his restraining straps. His stomach did flips. Would they topple, tumble and burst into flame? Would he feel anything? Damn, he hated this. He should have deserted and headed for LA. He would have loved to hold his wife one more time. He had things he wanted to tell his son. He should have taken the time when he had the chance. This was so screwed up.

The helo slewed one way and then another, and then, incredibly, they straightened, more or less. The back end kept fishtailing. One of the Free Mexico soldiers vomited. Another was as pale as a corpse. The Cherokee kept heading in the same direction as before. It was crazy.

"It ain't our time just yet!" Paul shouted into the compartment.

Romo stared at him. The man had dead eyes. It was creepy. Didn't it bother him they had almost eaten it?

Paul leaned across the small aisle and shoved his face close to Romo. "What's wrong? You don't care if you die?"

Nothing changed in those dead eyes. Slowly, Romo shook his head.

Paul grinned. "I'll be doing you a favor later."

One eyebrow lifted the tiniest fraction.

Paul sat back. He'd said enough. Now he leaned toward the edge of the open compartment. The glows and flashes were brighter out there.

"Shit!" he said.

The Cherokee flashed over enemy soldiers crouched low. They looked up, and Paul got a momentary glance of Chinese faces.

We're in enemy territory all right.

"Almost there," the pilot said over the intercom.

Paul blew out his cheeks and he saw Romo staring at him. With his thumb, Romo slowly sliced it across his throat.

"That's right!" Paul shouted. "We're about to kill us some Chinese. We're still on with our deal?"

Romo just stared at him.

"What deal?" Frank asked, one of the Marine Recon drill sergeants.

For just a second, Paul wanted to tell the Marine why Romo was here. Then he realized it would probably start a gun-battle in the helo. That wouldn't be any good. They had a job to do. America needed these Blue Swans destroyed. How many commandos needed to die in order to give the SoCal soldiers a chance of stopping the Chinese?

You have no idea; do you, Marine?

"Ten seconds!" the pilot shouted.

At that moment, a terrific explosion occurred just ahead of them. The concussion hit a second later as the Cherokee

159

swerved hard. Paul stared outside. The lead helicopter was gone, debris raining onto the ground a bare forty feet below.

His body went cold inside. He would mourn them later, if he could. Now, he just felt cold, like his emotions had died.

"Eight men left!" Paul shouted into the compartment. He pumped his fist, glancing from man to man. If his emotions had died, it still meant he could fake it. He needed these boys ready for battle. "Semper Fi!" he roared.

Frank, the Marine Recon sergeant, roared it back at him.

The Cherokee started down, coming in among twenty trucks and armed Chinese soldiers firing their weapons.

The Cherokee's beehives launched together and in a continuous chug, chug, flooding the air with thousands of tungsten flechettes the size and shape of fishhooks. The Cherokee shuddered from the launchings and Paul was certain the helo would simply disintegrate. Instead, as trucks bloomed into fireballs below and as Chinese soldiers toppled into gory ruins, the helicopter slammed against the ground, bounced up and hit again, skidding.

This time Paul had clenched his teeth, the muscles in his jaws beginning to throb from the intensity. Even so, he jerked this way and that, his body slamming against the restraining straps or pressed into the cushioned seat.

"We're down!" the pilot shouted.

Paul's head rang and it felt as if someone had played basketball on his muscles. He was sore and tired before anything had begun. That didn't matter now. He jerked his release so the restraints dropped away. "Go, go, go!" he shouted. He flipped a visor over his eyes and thrust himself out of his seat and for open ground. A dreadful lurch was his only reward and warning—he tumbled out of the helo and hit the ground with his chest. He lay stunned for several seconds, with his lungs locked from the impact. Hands pulled him up from the straps on his back. One strap pressed near his throat, making him cough and unlocking his lungs. Behind him, crouched on one knee, the Marine Recon sergeants fired at the enemy, at Chinese hiding among the burning vehicles. Romo did the same thing.

"We need cover!" Paul shouted. He tried his HUD visor, but there was nothing overhead looking down. No American drones, satellites or AWACS to give him any intel on the enemy. He was going to have to do this the old-fashioned way.

Forcing himself to concentrate, Paul scanned the wreckages around him. Not every truck or IFV burned. There! Enemy soldiers crawled for what looked like a perfectly useable IFV. With his undercarriage grenade launcher, he shot a grenade at the moving clump of Chinese—lousy bastards. He grunted as he climbed to his feet—he'd been kneeling—and ran at them. As he did, he pumped another grenade into the chamber and fired. An explosion and screams told him about his success.

"There, there, to your left," a sergeant shouted in his ear via his helmet's radio.

Paul saw it, a Blue Swan launcher. It was big: the launch vehicle and the straight-up missile with twenty cables snaking from it. He wasn't an expert, but the thing looked ready to fly. Several Chinese technicians—they wore blue overalls—argued as they stood by a command board. Chinese soldiers surrounded the techs. The enemy fired, spewing sparks from the muzzle of their assault rifles.

Dirt spit around Paul. He grunted and flew backward as a round stuck him in the chest. Another *whanged* off his helmet and it was hard to think. Paul crawled behind a fuzzy burning object, thankful for his body armor.

The pilot put us right on top of them. This is the craziest op I've ever been on.

At that moment, their Cherokee blew up in a spectacular blast, creating several secondary explosions. The blast hit Paul in the back of the head and slammed him onto the ground. There was a roaring sound in his ears. It might have been him shouting, he didn't know. Nothing made sense, just blurry motion and heat up and down his body. Why did his chest throb like that?

The next thing Paul realized was him crawling, firing, crawling and firing again. He looked back. A Chinese soldier rushed Romo from the side. The Mexican Apache was toast. Before he thought things through, Paul swung his gun and fired, cutting down the enemy. Romo saw it, and there was something in his eyes. Maybe he realized Paul had just saved his life.

The Chinese were doing a damn good job of defending the arguing techs. What was it with them anyway? Why didn't they just fire their toy? It was always something.

By crawling and eating dirt—Paul spit several times—he reached what had seemed at first like a perfectly good Chinese IFV. It wasn't. There were neat little holes in it from gun rounds—those must have come from the Cherokee's pilot. Enemy infantry lay in gory ruin around it. Some of them must have not worn body armor. That was stupid but fortunate. Paul thrust himself to his feet and raced into the cramped vehicle. He banged against a rail and bumped his head twice. Good thing he still wore his helmet. By releasing his rucksack, he climbed up into the cupola.

With a savage grin, he drew back the bolt of its 12.7mm machine gun. He swiveled it around, sighted and pressed his thumbs on the butterfly triggers. The hammering sounds and the shivering of the gun was pure delight. He mowed down the soldiers guarding the technicians. Next, he shot the Chinese in blue overalls as they tried to run like mice. All was fair in war, right? Lastly, he poured bullet after bullet into the Blue Swam missile. Some of them were incendiary bullets. The freak had wanted to fly, huh. And it had wanted to broadcast its electromagnetic pulse on his fellow citizens.

"No tonight, Johnny Boy," Paul said under his breath.

An explosion ended it as the missile's fuel ignited. Paul slid down into the IFV and rolled himself into a fetal position. A second later, the thirty-ton IFV rocked violently, sending Paul tumbling around like a bowling ball. He didn't see the very end. The missile fell like an axed tree on speed, hurling itself onto the soil and crumpling. The last Chinese died in a hail of Marine and Mexican assassin bullets.

Soon thereafter, bullet silence allowed the survivors to hear the sound of roaring flames.

Paul crawled out of the IFV. His head throbbed and he staggered as he walked. The enemy was dead and the missile destroyed. According to Paul's count, including him, there were two Marines and two Free Mexico soldiers left alive behind enemy lines. One of the Mexicans—of course—was Romo. It was probably stupid to have saved the man's life earlier.

Was this act two between Romo and him? Or did the man still want to work together in order to get back to the good old U.S. of A?

It was time to find out.

FIRST FRONT HEADQUARTERS, MEXICO

Marshal Nung groaned as he sat up. His eyesight was blotchy and breathing had become a chore. There was a painful knot on his head where he'd banged it on the floor.

Medics hovered over him. One of them finished attaching an IV-drip to his arm.

"General," Nung said in a hoarse voice.

A nervous General Pi glanced down at him. The man looked harried, out of his depth. At logistics, he was excellent. Making battlefield decisions—no, he would give command to Marshal Gang.

"Help me stand," Nung said in a hoarse voice.

"Begging your pardon, Marshal," the chief medic said, "but I suggest—"

"I've given you an order," Nung growled. Anger washed though him. A sharp pain in his head made him wince. His lung muscles locked up and he gasped.

"Please, sir," the medic said, kneeling beside him, rubbing his chest.

With weak fingers, Nung grasped the medic's arm. "Stand," he managed to gasp. "Help me. I order you."

The medic stared at him, judging the odds perhaps at what would happen to him if he disobeyed. Finally, the medic nodded and motioned to his helpers. Together, the three medics helped Nung to his feet.

"Report," Nung whispered, as the pain in his head throbbed. Why was the chamber tilting and spinning?

General Pi looked at him in horror. "Marshal, I recommend that you—"

Even though it hurt, Nung shook his head. He knew now that he must leash his anger. He must maintain his composure or his body would betray him a second time. A catastrophe threatened. If Marshal Gang reported this...the Ruling Committee might summon him home. He knew what to do to win, and he must do it and show all of them that he was the greatest commander China possessed.

First taking several calming breaths, Nung glanced at the computer map. Unfortunately, he couldn't make any sense of it. It kept blurring, hurting his eyes.

"Blue Swan," Nung managed to say.

General Pi licked his mouth, bobbing his head. "The missiles are about to launch, sir, although on an ad hoc basis. We lack full coordination, I'm afraid. I have ordered our fighter drones into California in order to clear the space and swamp American anti-air defenses. For the same reason, I am also in the process of launching cruise missiles."

Nung tried to gather his thoughts. It was like an old fisherman trying to draw a net too heavy with tuna. He lacked the strength. His willpower kept slipping. "Procedure," he said.

"I know, sir," Pi said. "I'm trying to follow your plan. But it is chaos tonight. Some of the Blue Swan launchers have been destroyed."

"How...how many?" whispered Nung. This was terrible.

"We're still in the process of discovering that, sir."

Nung blinked several times. When did breathing become so difficult? He swayed, and the medics eyed each other.

"Sit," Nung told them. "There." He tried to indicate with his chin. He was simply too weak to lift his arms to point.

The medics moved him toward an open chair before a screen. Nung shuffled his feet. He felt so old, so desperately weak.

"Rest," Nung whispered.

"Yes, sir," the chief medic said. "You must rest here and gather your strength."

FORWARD EDGE OF THE BATTLE AREA, CALIFORNIA

164

As the night progressed, the air battle went heavily against the Americans. The surviving V-10s retreated from Mexican air space, racing for home. The Chinese fighter drones followed, although most had already launched their air-to-air missiles and expended their cannon shells.

Two American drones watched the battle from a great distance away near the stratosphere. Each had long, thin wings and many, black bubble canopies along the length of its fuselage. Hidden in each bubble was a sensor.

The three satellites were drifting junk in the stratosphere, clusters of twisted metal.

Then a Chinese strategic laser outside Monterrey, Mexico reached up and burned one of the high-flying drones, searing off a thin wing. There was hardly any noise this high up. The drone had drifted too near Mexican air space, but now it began a long tumble to the Earth below. That left one drone and three American AWACS hundreds of miles behind the border.

With the data from these sources, the JFC of California realized the Chinese were up to something. They had gone from defense to offense. Therefore, he gave the order. Waiting F-35s entered the fray.

Major Max Grumman gritted his teeth as he signaled his acceptance of the order. He had been watching the air battle for the past half hour. Drones. He hated them. They took the glory out of air combat. The great aces of World War I and II, the Vietnam jet-jocks and the heroes of the Alaskan War, he'd read about them avidly. Like his fellow pilots, he knew that UCAVs could never replace the man on the spot in his fighter plane.

The night was rich with stars and the ground was far below. Grumman banked and took the F-35 down.

His screen lit up with targets. Look at them, drones by the dozen, small and lethal. They could turn tighter and take any Gs their operators gave them. Yeah, drones had advantages, but desk boys weren't jet-jocks.

"Little pricks," Grumman said under his breath.

He activated a Sun-stinger. It was a lovely new missile, the latest thing in the American arsenal.

165

"You watching me through your cameras, desk-boy?" asked Grumman.

He began the targeting sequence. One of them jittery, fast-flying little pricks, ah, right in his crosshairs.

The F-35 shuddered as a Sun-stinger dropped loose from a wing. The heavy missile dropped and its engine ignited. The burn was a hard glow, and the missile zoomed into the night after its target.

Grumman watched on his targeting HUD. The little prick, it moved quickly, the jittery bastard. Then, a winking light on his screen indicated a hit and a kill.

Grumman's gritted teeth turned into a faint smile as the Chinese drone ceased to exist. There were a million of them, though. This was like an old Star Wars movie. He shook his head, the edge of the oxygen mask pressing against his cheek. It was time to work, time to play the ultimate game. How could a desk-boy in Mexico City know anything about that?

In quick succession, Grumman launched two more missiles, getting two more kills in less than a minute. That's how you did it. That's how you owned the sky.

"It's a turkey shoot!" he shouted over the radio.

Even as he said it, he studied the operational screen. Look at that. Three kills and the Chinese pricks just kept on coming. Tonight, he was going to become an ace—five kills. He just needed two more now. A turkey shoot was the right place to be in order to enter the hall of air-ace heroes.

Major Grumman might not have thought that if he'd known the Chinese plan. Like him, most of the F-35s fired their Sun-stingers, taking a dreadful toll of nearly dry—of offensive armament—enemy fighter drones.

The drones bored in, firing their remaining air-to-air missiles and if they made it close enough, using up their last cannon shells.

Grumman swore then.

"J-25s," the ground-control operator said in his headphones. "They're coming up fast behind the drones."

The J-25 was the Chinese air-superiority fighter. Like sharks using a shoal of herring, they'd hidden behind the drones. The J-25s were armed, fresh and loaded for American pilots.

Major Grumman's stomach tightened as he heard the growl of his threat indicator. Enemy radar had locked onto him. He launched chaff, a decoy and looked up into the starry night. Something flashed toward him. It came as fast as an enemy missile. Then he realized the truth, saw it for just a moment.

"Drone!" he snarled. Where had it come from? With his thumb, he readied his cannon.

The drone's cannon fired first, quick blooms of light at shutter-speed, sending death and destruction. The operator in Mexicali had been waiting for this. The drone's shells punctured Grumman's F-35, a fragment of metal slicing into his back and severing several arteries.

The air battle turned savage after that. American tac-lasers, flak and SAMs devoured hordes of Chinese drones. U.S. officers and men alike shouted in glee at their stations. Many of them pumped their fists, although a few wondered how much more ordnance the Chinese would keep pouring at them. This was just too bloody much and it was a sign of enemy wealth.

Then enemy ARMs exploded a dozen American radar stations. In a matter of minutes, a half dozen more disappeared. The J-25s engaged the F-35s. There were too many Chinese, with more fuel and missiles. After twenty minutes, the F-35s were either dead or running away.

Waiting Chinese bombers screamed in, released smart bombs and then flashed away along the ground. American C-RAM systems chugged steadily. Several times an explosion created a greater fireball as an enemy bomber plowed into the earth and ignited, sending a column of fire up into the night.

Larger Chinese aircraft now fired air-to-ground missiles, flocks of them. The heavy missiles bored through flak, defensive explosions and screens of flechette clouds: tungsten particles that disintegrated many of the lethal cargoes. Half the missiles never made it to target. The others chewed up tac-laser sites, SAM launchers and radar installations. It was a bloody start to a savage attack, as the Chinese refused to quit and just kept on coming.

Because of this, more Chinese cruise missiles made it through the defensive belt than might have otherwise, even as they died. The enemy mass swamped the American defenses, overwhelmed it and poured through in sickening numbers, raining death and destruction, and bringing shock and awe.

It was then the first Blue Swan missile arrived. Like a cruise missile, it flew nap-of-the-earth, over hills, through valleys and scraping treetops. Its onboard sensors and AI allowed it to avoid nearby enemy defenses, aided by defensive chaff and decoys and through plain speed when it could.

In a few places, the air battle still raged hot above the destruction, although the Americans had seriously dwindled in number. In its flight, the Blue Swan missile passed burning anti-air installations and a damaged radar site.

Then one of the American AWACS two hundred miles away bounced a radar beam off it. The missile was of especially stealthy construction, however, and the faint return signal wasn't enough for the AWACS' computers. Six and a half miles later, a powerful ground-based American radar station in Escondido located the advancing missile.

Two SAMs left their launchers, accelerating to Mach 7. If they had launched sooner, they might have reached the Blue Swan missile. Maybe. The fact was they failed to reach it in time. Three miles into the border, over Fourth Corps of the American Sixth Army, the Blue Swan warhead exploded.

Everything worked perfectly inside the warhead core—the missile had been manufactured and tested in Tokyo, Japan. A massive electromagnetic pulse blew outward from it, radiating like an exploding sun. The pulse washed over American minefields, over artillery, mortar tubes, troops, thousands of computers, hundreds of tanks, Strykers, IFVs, a veritable host of electronic equipment. The EMP also struck nearby drones, fighters and bombers. It even reached a following Blue Swan, incapacitating the missile so it plunged into a hill and disintegrated. The latest technological marvel wrecked masses of American equipment and weapons systems, and it took a bite out of Chinese air assets.

The single Blue Swan missile created confusion everywhere, on both sides, on and behind the battlefield. But it wasn't over. There were more Blue Swan missiles on the way.

The Americans couldn't know it yet—they might never learn, in fact—but five commando teams had succeeded in destroying their targeted missiles. The rest of the teams died, some attacking the wrong site, usually dying in the process, or they never made it through the Chinese air defenses. Their helos became junk, the commandos gory chunks of meat. It was a bloodbath of lost commando teams and lost equipment.

But the five destroyed Blue Swan missiles were only part of the damage. The *fact* of the attack did more than the five teams achieved individually. In the haste and confusion of the night launch, three Chinese technician teams blew up their own missiles. Improper launch timing meant that Chinese EMP rendered two other missiles incapable, while American ground-to-air defenses shot down four more. That was not counting the five missiles that simply failed to work as advertised. For one reason or another—a faulty component, incorrect computations or a malfunctioning AI—five missiles never detonated or never even made it near their targets.

That left a paltry six Blue Swans. Those six created unprecedented damage, chaos and confusion. In the radius of the EMP, air and a great deal of ground equipment and mines simply ceased functioning, with their electronics fused or burned out.

Both Chinese and American air took appalling losses as drones, fighters and bombers plummeted, crashing, crumbling and igniting as they struck ground. Several explosions started forest fires.

Amid the burning radar stations and the dying tac-laser casements and SAM locations, the SoCal border defenses had electronic gaps. They were black holes where nothing electrical worked: cell phones, dead; radar, dead; vehicle starters, dead; tank systems, dead; artillery sighting equipment, dead, all dead and useless junk now.

These "black-hole" gaps were uneven in nature. Two Blue Swan missiles had exploded near each other, making it the largest dead zone. One other missile EMP yield was low, while another had caused three times as much radiation as expected.

In the majority of the SoCal Fortifications, the electronics were shielded well enough to work normally. In others, panic and confusion had already begun. Soldiers there wondered if the end had come. What was going on? Why couldn't they talk to anyone and why had their equipment simply died?

Those six Blue Swan missiles initiated the first phase of the great Chinese assault into California. It was less than Marshal Nung would have wanted but much more than President Sims could accept. Whether it was a success or a failure was still to be determined by the second phase about to begin in several hours.

-6-
The SoCal Fortifications

FIRST FRONT HEADQUARTERS, MEXICO

Despite his infirmities and weakness, Marshal Nung struggled to awareness. He found himself lying in bed, with medical equipment surrounding him and with tubes attached to his arms.

He lay still for several seconds, attempting to collect his thoughts. The attack began tonight. He must return to his post and oversee the greatest assault in history. He couldn't let General Pi make the key operational decisions. He couldn't let Marshal Gang report this and take over command.

This is my hour in the sun. You must be at your post.

Nung opened his eyes to signal the nurse fiddling with one of the machines. This was odd. He couldn't lift his arm. Nor did she seem to be aware of his efforts.

Concentrate, Nung. Will your body into obedience.

He cleared his throat and he concentrated, but it brought zero results. *This is ridiculous.* In desperation, he thought back to his younger years. The others in school had always looked upon him as the country oaf. They had mocked him. But he had shown all of them by studiously applying himself and excelling at everything he did. It had only made things worse, as he had been too outspoken about his successes. Upon entering the military, his troubles in that regard had worsened. The petty intriguers, the legion of yes-men, he had found himself hating all of them and striving night and day. They had sent him to Moscow, and oh, how he had applied himself. The others of his military class had hated him the more for it. Only the Chairman of yesteryear had really appreciated him.

The old man had loved a winner is why. But you aren't winning in the sick bed, Nung. If you fail now...Gang and his kind will use that against you. The mockers will have beaten you.

Anger surged through Marshal Nung, the old anger that had helped him overcome a thousand obstacles. He squeezed his fingers together so the nails bit into his palm. Although his arm shook, he raised it and wriggled his fingers.

The nurse noticed, and she came to him, her eyes filled with concern.

"Help me into a wheelchair," Nung said in a soft whisper.

"But, sir, you're unwell. You must rest and regain your strength."

"No," he whispered. "I have been resting. Now I want you to help me into a wheelchair."

"I must summon the doctor, sir. He might not agree to this."

"Go then. Hurry. But if he fails to show up soon, I will remember that you disobeyed me. And you must know what that means."

Her eyes widened in fear. She bowed hastily, turned and ran out of the room.

Letting his head fall back against the pillow, Nung stared up at the ceiling. This was simply another battle he had to win. His body wanted to betray him. It was old, and a combination of drugs had weakened him, maybe damaged some of the organs within. So be it. He didn't want longevity. He wanted to win this war. He yearned to capture California and open the way for Chinese glory. This was his hour and he would savor it and achieve even in his final moments of life. He would *not* wither away in a bed while his soldiers showed the world how you won a continent.

The door opened and the doctor walked in, a short man in a white uniform, with a stethoscope in lieu of a tie.

172

"Marshal Nung—" the doctor said in an authoritative tone.

Nung held up a hand. He did it easier this time. "You will listen to me, doctor," he said in a hoarse whisper. "You will remove this ridiculous gown and clothe me in my uniform. Then summon orderlies and they will lift me into a wheelchair."

The doctor blinked in confusion and hesitation. Slowly, he said, "I must object, sir."

"No. Do not object, because it simply tires me out. Instead, give me a mild stimulant so I can regain my energy."

"I cannot do that, as I do not wish to kill you, sir."

"Nor do I wish to die. Even so, you will obey me."

"Sir, your body is much too weak for stimulants of any kind."

"I have already deduced that and have decided to override your concerns. If I die in the line of duty, so be it. I accept that. Then let me die. Until such a time occurs, I command the First Front. I will do so in the command center, not here."

"Sir—"

Nung looked up at the ceiling. Nausea threatened. That shook his resolve and he almost decided to rest. It seemed then in his mind's eye that he saw hundreds of his past foes laughing at him. In the forefront, old Marshal Kao stood prominently. No. The others would not beat him. Nung willed down the nausea.

He whispered, "If you do not obey me, doctor, I will order my security officers to take you outside and shoot you."

The doctor stiffened, in shock and dismay, no doubt. He asked, "A mild stimulant, sir?"

"We're wasting time. Do as I have ordered."

"At once, Marshal."

It took fifteen minutes until Nung sat fully clothed in a mobile wheelchair. He decided it would take too much energy directing it with its confounded joystick control. Therefore, he drafted the beefiest orderly to push him.

"Take me to the Command Center," he said.

The orderly pushed him outside. The stars twinkled as the orderly took him from the medical center to the First Front's underground bunker. A long corridor led down, with harsh

173

florescent tubes lighting the way. In the main chamber, the staff officers turned in shock at his entrance. Big Marshal Gang stared at him from the head of the computer table.

Gang is already trying to usurp my command.

"Good to see you back, sir," General Pi said.

Nung grunted, deciding to save his strength.

"You should be resting," Gang said.

Nung ignored the man as he signaled the orderly. The beefy youth wheeled him to the green-glowing computer table. To Nung's dismay, it was too high for him to see while he sat in the wheelchair. This would not do.

"I'll order a ramp installed, sir," Pi said.

"No," Gang said. "You must return to the hospital and get better."

The staff officers glanced from Gang to Nung in his wheelchair.

This is the first test, eh.

"I command the First Front," Nung whispered.

"Maybe not after I make my report," Gang said.

"Then go," Nung said, "report. Until such time, you are merely to observe. Do not presume again."

Gang's eyes narrowed. He glanced at the staff officers. Slowly, he nodded. "I must make my report. If you will excuse me…?"

Nung managed the barest nod.

Gang left. So did officers to get the materials to make a ramp.

Ten minutes later, the orderly pushed the wheelchair up the installed ramp and locked clamps onto the wheels. Nung looked down from the same height as if he'd been standing. Seeing the screen at its strategic setting invigorated him.

Four armies waited for the great assault: sixty full divisions, with twenty thousand artillery tubes and ten thousand Marauder light tanks. The Fifth Army with the Pacific Ocean to its west would head for LA, masking San Diego and other coastal cities. The Eleventh Army lined up beside it and then the Nineteenth and Thirty-third Reserve Armies. Once the offensive began, the Seventh Army from the Third Front would become his operational reserve.

Ah, this was exhilarating indeed. The Twenty-third Tank Army waited to the east of the grand assault. The bulk of the T-66s were there, the famed Chinese tri-turreted tank. He had surprises for the Americans. He would give them a land-air-sea and human-robotic assault that would shatter their resolve and devour their soldiers. The 233rd Tank Corps would terrorize them when the time came. He could almost pity the Americans…until he recalled the bitter fighting on the Arctic ice seven years ago. That burned out any thoughts of mercy.

Time passed and Nung grew sleepy. After the fifth time his chin touched down against his chest, he sent the orderly to find the doctor. He couldn't let Gang see him like this. Soon, outside in the hall, the doctor administered a heavier stimulant.

Finally, zero hour arrived, and Marshal Nung gave the most important order of his life, initiating Operation Yellow Dragon.

Early on the morning on 21 April 2039 and all across the Mexican-Californian border, the Chinese unleashed the assault with a five-hour hurricane artillery bombardment. They only employed gas for the first two hours, striking American headquarters units and enemy artillery sites.

In the darkness, the thousands of artillery pieces created giant flashes of brilliance as they sent their shells screaming across the border. The thunder was awesome, a testament to Chinese power. This was the greatest concentration of artillery since the Battle of Kursk in World War II.

Resolve stiffened Marshal Nung's neck. He glanced around at his staff officers. He could only imagine what it must feel like for the shivering Americans in their fortifications. The bigger the enemy casement or bunker, the larger the shell or missile sent against it.

Once the artillery stopped, once the bombers unloaded their cargos, ah, then the special infantry divisions and the penal battalions would swamp the Americans who had dared believe they could halt Chinese excellence.

BEHIND ENEMY LINES, MEXICO

Paul woke up with an assault rifle pointed at his face. The open orifice showed the initial rifling, the grooves in the barrel that spun the bullets. His gaze climbed the barrel, stock and up to Romo's emotionless features and obsidian-chip eyes.

Behind fluttering leaves, the last stars were still out in the western portion of the twilight sky, although dawn had broken in the east. Paul ached everywhere and his head felt stuffed with cotton, making thinking a chore. He couldn't smell any oil or gasoline, gunpowder or the stink of cooked flesh. Oh yeah, he remembered stumbling away with the others, away from the wrecked Blue Swan launch-site. They'd headed for some trees and had found a stream. What had happened to Frank, the other Marine Recon sergeant? Why wasn't he here?

"Colonel Valdez wants you to suffer," Romo said in a low voice. "He wants you to pay for leaving his daughter behind."

Paul didn't see anything in those dark eyes other than a hungry wolf ready to kill. Romo must have learned to enjoy killing, and that would have been a long time ago. Paul had known a few Marines like that. They were the truly scary people. The enjoyment of killing had eaten away at their humanity. Shedding human blood, it changed you. There was no getting past that. It made you different. It was a beast, and if you failed to control the beast, it ate the good part of you while you were still alive. Yeah, that's what he saw looking into Romo's eyes: a stone cold killer about to do what he loved best.

Even so, Paul couldn't help but trying. "I didn't have any choice in leaving her. Before I knew it, my drone was taking off and Maria was still on the ground."

Romo's shoulders made the barest shift—his shrug of indifference.

"Doesn't matter, huh?" Paul asked.

"You're liked greased death in a fight," Romo said. "Back there at the launch-site…you were a Tasmanian devil. The Chinese had us pinned and you turned it around. It was impressive. You even helped me personally. I would like to use your prowess to help me reach America. But after watching what you did, I realize it would be foolish of me to give you a chance. The Colonel, he will free Mexico from the invader. He needs to shed his remorse for Maria. Your death will return his focus where it belongs."

"Sure it will. You bet. The Colonel, he's going to boot six million Chinese out of Mexico. What were the rest of us thinking?"

That brought a flicker of annoyance to Romo's hatchet features. He pushed the barrel against Paul's left cheek.

"You fled the battlefield, Gunnery Sergeant. You left Maria Valdez for the Chinese torturers. They abused her and cut her into pieces, mailing those to the Colonel."

"They're sick bastards," Paul said. He was about to say more, but he closed his mouth instead. What good would it do to tell Romo how it had eaten at him, leaving Maria? It had reminded him too much of the Arctic, out there on the pack ice. The Chinese had butchered Maria like an animal, huh. It figured.

"Put your hands behind your back," Romo said.

Paul laughed. "That's right, I'm going to let you hogtie me so you can play your games. Screw you, Romo. Shoot if you think you have to. Earn your pay."

Romo moved fast, taking the tip of the barrel away from Paul's cheek and swinging it down toward his leg. Paul figured he had nothing left to lose. He didn't see Frank or the other Mexican. It must mean it was just the two of them. Paul jerked his leg aside as Romo pulled the trigger. The bullet creased his pant leg and his flesh, leaving a furrow, but it failed to incapacitate. The assault-rifle's kick against Romo's shoulder gave Paul a fraction of a second to act, and he used it. He thrust himself at Romo and kicked up as hard as he could. It was an old-fashioned groin kick, catching the assassin even though Romo instinctively tried to block by twisting his hips and closing his legs.

The toe of Paul's boot did its job. Romo crumpled as only getting smashed in the balls could do. The assassin released the assault rifle and flopped onto the ground. He clutched his groin, groaning, rolling on the dirt.

Paul grabbed the rifle, put the barrel against Romo's head and started applying pressure to the trigger.

"Hey, what's going on?" That sounded like Frank.

Paul took two steps away from Romo and looked up. Frank the Recon Marine carried a canteen in each hand. Behind him was the other assassin. He had a heavy pistol in his hand, held against his leg.

"Our Mexicans were ordered to kill me because Valdez's daughter got captured on a mission I happened to survive," Paul said. "The Chinese chopped her up and mailed the parts to her father."

Frank swore under his breath.

Before Paul could tell him the same thing he'd told Romo, shots rang out from behind the other two. They came from the bushes fifty yards away. The Mexican gunman groaned and sagged down. Frank dove onto his belly.

Paul hit the dirt as bullets zinged past him. Bushes shook over there. Yeah, Paul spotted barrels poking out. He fired at a bush, slithering backward, firing and slithering some more.

Frank tried to do the same thing. Chinese fire hit him. With his assault rifle and as he shouted, Frank sprayed the bushes. The Chinese sprayed back. A round caught Frank in the face and the former drill sergeant deflated as death claimed him.

A second burst caused the gunman to scream in agony. It was a terrible sound. Maybe it rattled the Chinese soldiers. They stopped firing for a moment.

It gave Paul time to slither into hiding behind a grassy knoll. He popped up as Romo crawled after him. For the first time there was something new on the assassin's face. It was grim determination to survive. Paul fired at Chinese soldiers, giving the assassin cover. He wasn't sure why he helped Romo. Maybe the man's determination showed him that a portion of Romo's humanity yet remained.

A second later, the assassin panted beside Paul while peering up over the knoll.

The Chinese soldiers fired again, killing the gunman and ending the dreadful screaming.

"We got a problem," Paul said.

Romo eyed him strangely, with seemingly mixed emotions.

"You want to see me suffer and the Chinese want to kill me," Paul said.

"No…the problem is that you have a rifle and I don't."

178

"There's one out there," Paul said, indicating Frank's assault rifle.

Romo's nostrils widened. His head whipped forward as the Chinese started firing at them. Well, they fired at the grassy knoll, as both men ducked down. Bullets chewed the soil. How soon would it be until the Chinese fired some grenades?

"Do you know how many are out there?" Paul asked.

Romo shook his head.

Paul kept low. He needed to think, to use his wits and figure out what made the most sense. They were behind enemy lines—far behind them—and the Big One might have already started. Romo was a bastard, and Frank and the gunman were dead. Hmm. Those two might have died anyway. Yeah, the place must be crawling with Chinese for those soldiers to have stumbled on them like this.

Cheri. Mike. What was going to happen to his family? He had to make it back to LA and make sure they were okay.

Romo popped up his head, maybe to see what the enemy was doing. The action brought immediate fire. The assassin ducked behind the knoll as bullets plowed dirt and hissed overhead uncomfortably near.

Paul crawled up, shooting back as he pulled the trigger twice. It made his rifle kick, letting him know it was alive and well. If he didn't fire back, the Chinese might start getting brave. As he slid back behind the knoll, he noticed Romo with a knife in his hands, and turned his rifle toward him.

"No!" Romo said, holding up the knife, turning it sideways. "This isn't to kill you."

"You're going to fight them with it?" Paul asked with a sneer.

"We have to flee."

"I'm heading out alone," Paul said.

"Two are stronger than one," Romo said.

"Usually that's true. But I can't trust you. So no, one is better this time."

Romo nodded. "You should think this… Why did you help me just now?"

"Reflex, I guess. Don't let it bother you."

"That is the second time you helped, maybe saved my life."

"Yeah?" Paul asked.

Romo frowned intently. "I owe you a great debt. But I am the Colonel's man."

"Keep thinking about it. I'm leaving."

"No. Wait. You and I…we must become blood brothers."

Paul stared at the man. "Are you nuts? Blood brothers, like Indian mumbo-jumbo? You just tried to kill me."

"Not *Indian*," Romo said, "but White Mountain Apache."

"Apache like the little feather in your ear? Since you're Mexican, you must be Aztec."

The dead eyes came alive as if shutters opened into Romo's soul. It showed a blaze of emotion.

"Do not tell me what I am, white man. In the old days, Apaches often raided into Mexico. They took women, one of them my great grandmother."

Paul noticed a lull in the enemy gunfire. He lifted up and fired a burst, causing three Chinese soldiers to dive back into cover. He slid down and began crawling away. Romo crawled beside him, with the knife still in his hands.

"You feel you cannot trust me," Romo said as he crawled. "I understand. But you saved my life twice now. I owe you a debt, and I pay my debts, always. Besides, we need each other if we're going to make it back alive."

"I don't need you," Paul said. "I'll make it by myself."

"You are greased death, this I know. But you will need to sleep sometimes. Then you will need a lookout. I will need the same thing."

Figuring they were far enough away, Paul climbed to his feet and began to run past trees. He wore combat fatigues, his helmet and a few supplies on his belt. The rucksack was back at the temporary encampment with Frank and the gunman's corpses.

Romo ran tirelessly beside him.

Soon, Paul slowed to a walk. He heard shouting Chinese behind them. Last night had taken its toll. He had been battered, smashed and might have gotten a concussion. Yeah, he could probably use some help. Did it really matter to Romo he'd saved his life twice? The eyes before, they had shown the man's troubled thoughts.

Kill him. Get it over with, Marine.

As if reading his mind, Romo said, "I am sworn to the Colonel. But... He never saved my life. You have. Therefore, I will make you my blood brother. It means I will tell you before I kill you. I will give you a fair chance to defeat me."

"After what you did, you think I buy your Indian crap?"

"Apache," Romo said.

"Indian, Apache, Aztec, it doesn't matter to me. What you are is a vicious murderer without a conscience."

"I am a warrior defending my native land," Romo said. "Unlike my ancestors, I will never surrender."

Paul veered to the west. They had been headed north and the tress thinned out north. Right now, they needed to stay in this small forest.

After fifty more steps, Paul stopped. Romo stopped beside him, the knife still in the man's hand.

"So what's the deal anyway?" Paul asked.

"We each cut our hand."

"Maiming ourselves?" Paul asked. That sounded bright.

Romo shook his head. "A small cut, enough to bring blood. Then we clasp hands and speak the oath, the vow as my Apache ancestors used to do. We will become blood brothers. As such, we cannot kill each other except in a formal duel, either fist-to-fist or knife-to-knife."

"And you believe in this stuff?"

Romo stared at him.

For a moment, Paul seemed to see into the man's soul. This man was tribal, a barbarian really. He obviously believed in what he was saying.

"Ah, what the hell," Paul said. "We're dead men anyway." He shouldered the assault rifle and held up his hand.

Romo stared hard at him.

For a second, Paul thought, *he suckered you, you fool.*

Romo lifted his hand and made the cut. Then he pressed the razor-sharp knife against Paul's left palm and made a tiny incision. Blood oozed out. Romo clasped his bleeding hand against Paul's. Then he made his oath, his vow, calling Paul his blood bother.

181

Paul repeated the vow even though he felt like an idiot doing it. Afterward…

The two men stared at each other. It was a crazy feeling for Paul.

This killer is my blood brother. I've never had a brother before. This is weird. He knew a moment of sadness. It was too bad he was going to have to kill Romo after this was done.

"Come on," Paul said, with a burr in his voice. "Let's get the heck out of here before the Chinese find us."

SAN YSIDRO, CALIFORNIA

The thunder had stopped—an ending to the Chinese hurricane bombardment.

Now Chinese wild weasels lead the way into American air space. Advanced electronic counter measures and hard jamming attempted to confuse the enemy. Behind the wild weasels came bombers and fighter-bombers. Many sent ARMs into whatever operational radar stations the Americans still had and dared to use. Others released napalm or five-hundred pound bombs. The rest carried bunker-busters, seeking out those fortifications the artillery had failed to smash.

In selected areas—San Ysidro being one of those—sleek Chinese helicopters zoomed for enemy HQs. The poison gas had been to suppress the enemy commanders. These pinpoint missions were to kill the hopefully dazed Americans.

There were three types of helicopters. The first were the standoff hunter/killers, the Graceful Swans with their Annihilator missiles. They swooped across the battlefield, seeking American vehicles to destroy. The others were Gunhawks, transformed Chinese cargo helicopters. They each carried two 12.7mm machine guns and a 20mm auto-cannon in its nose. Each machine gun and cannon had a dedicated TV-fed operator. The Gunhawks' MO called for them to hover above American infantry at ten thousand feet, well out of enemy machine gun range. Aiming their weapons straight down, the Gunhawks would pour concentrated fire on any enemy trying to hide. It was similar in concept to the old "Puff the Magic Dragon" airplane of Vietnam, the Douglas AC-47 Spooky.

The last type of helicopter carried deadly cargos of White Tiger Eagle Teams. Their task: kill enemy commanders and radio networks. Lop off the head so the body—the American formations—could no longer act in a harmonized fashion. In other words, turn disciplined bodies of men into uncoordinated and isolated units so the Chinese could kill and capture them more easily.

Fighter Rank Zhu rode outside his specially fashioned helicopter. It was nicknamed the "Battle-Taxi." It lacked a regular cargo bay. Instead, it had a bubble for the pilot and four staggered poles swept back like a fighter-jet's wings. Each pole contained three seats and a motorcycle-style windshield. On each seat sat an Eagle Team member in full commando gear, ready for action.

Zhu crouched behind his windshield as the helo roared over the American landscape by a bare fifty meters. He had an eagle's view of the masses of vehicles crawling over the earth. IFVs, jeeps, missile launchers, light Marauder tanks, hovers, drones, trucks and masses of marching soldiers moved on the Americans. Soon, enemy ground objects flashed past: splintered trees, a trench-line and blasted casements.

Zhu's stomach churned. He was going to fight today. He would have to prove himself to the First Rank and the others. First, he would have to launch like an eagle.

Gripping his rest-bars, Zhu watched the terrain. He spied a running dog with something bloody in its fangs. Behind it followed three bigger dogs. They might have been barking. He laughed. It was exhilarating perched out here in the elements. These Z4 helicopters—the battle-taxis—were the latest in White Tiger commando operations. The old-style helos only allowed a few Eagle commandos to lift at a time. This allowed them all to leave at once and drop on the enemy.

"The longer you are in the air, the longer the enemy has to pick you off," the trainers had told Zhu. "You need to get down and fight."

Zhu nodded. He knew what to do now. The only trouble was...

I must not shame myself. I must fight bravely. I will show the others I deserve to be here.

Zhu wore an Eagle jetpack and dinylon body armor. He had his Eagle grenade launcher attached to his shoulder. On the jetpack was strapped his QZB-95 assault rifle. The First Rank carried a hand-held anti-air missile. Others had RPGs.

"Target in six kilometers," the pilot said over the helmet's earphones.

Zhu nodded, even though no one could see the gesture. He glanced at a fellow commando who sat on the same pole. The crouched White Tiger seemed like a rock.

Kill everyone was the order. In these engagements, they had no use for prisoners, no place to safely put them. It was kill or be killed.

"Five kilometers to target," the pilot said.

Zhu needed a drink of water and all of a sudden, he needed to take a piss. Just five more kilometers to the enemy? Dead Americans lay scattered on the ground. They looked like they were asleep. They must have lacked masks and been hit by poison gas.

I must not shame myself. I must show the First Rank that I am worthy to be an Eagle commando.

Something fast flashed underneath Zhu. It was long and it headed in the same direction they went.

"Cruise missile," someone said over the helmet radio.

"Two kilometers to target," the pilot said.

Zhu blinked three more times. Then a terrific explosion occurred ahead. *It must be the cruise missile.*

Overhead, Gunhawks raced for their hover positions. Graceful Swans—looking like giant mechanical wasps—now hung back. Zhu saw an Annihilator missile streak toward an American tracked vehicle.

"Get ready," First Rank Tian said.

Zhu's gut clenched and vomit acid burned the back of his throat. This was real. This wasn't practice. He began to shake, and shame as he'd never known it began to bubble inside him.

The battle-taxi sank toward the earth as they raced at a berm. There were puffs of smoke from the top of the fortification. Then American RPGs zoomed toward them.

Why so many? Zhu wanted to know. A major had told them that none of those enemy weapons would be operable today because of a new Chinese secret weapon.

The major lied to us. Zhu wondered why.

Almost simultaneously, two enemy shaped-charge grenades struck the battle-taxi nearest Zhu. Some Eagle fighters flew off the stricken helicopter. Other jetpack-soldiers plummeted earthward, to plow like javelins against the built-up berm.

Then Zhu's helicopter flashed over the berm. He twisted back. American soldiers stood in gun-pits, firing at the other helicopters.

"Fly!" First Rank Tian shouted in the headphones.

Zhu's muscles froze. He couldn't let go of the rest-bars. Beside him on the pole, an Eagle-commando launched upward and to the side with a whoosh of jetpack power.

I am shamed. I am forever shamed. Why couldn't he tear his fingers free? Was he that much of a coward?

Enemy fifty-caliber machine gun fire slammed into the battle-taxi, shaking it as holes appeared in the bubble canopy.

With a yelp of terror, Zhu released his rest-bars and jumped.

"Use your jetpack," Tian shouted in his headphones.

At the last moment and as he dropped with sickening speed, Zhu realized that Tian spoke to him. Despite his terror, with practiced smoothness, Zhu brought up his arm to the flight-pad. His hand gripped the throttle and he roared his jetpack to life. With a lifting pull on his shoulders and waist, Zhu braked his descent and then rose upward.

There were many Eagle commandos hanging in the air, moving on the enemy like a giant flock of deadly birds. The stricken battle-taxi turned, the pilot inside the shattered bubble bleeding profusely. The helicopter went down, its blades slicing the air a foot from where Zhu hovered.

I forgot to jet to the side.

"Down, down," Tian said, "land near the bunker."

To Zhu, it felt as if he was in a fog. Everything moved so slowly. His thoughts were jelly and his limbs hardly obeyed his mental commands.

Yes, the others of his squad sank toward a concrete bunker. It looked like a toy from up here. Vehicles were parked around it and there were shacks in various places. Americans ran outside, some of them kneeling, aiming weapons skyward and firing. Part of the bunker was hidden under desert soil.

Zhu twisted the throttle and sank toward the Americans. It felt surreal. Bullets whistled past him and grenades landed like bombs among them, tumbling some. Then everything became confusion. Eagle team commandos plummeted to the hard ground. One screaming commando struck another flyer under him and they both hit the ground hard enough to bounce. An American ran toward them, firing from the hip, shattering jetpack parts and helmets.

Zhu activated his grenade launcher. In a daze, he targeted enemy soldiers, lobbing grenades at them.

The ground rushed up. As if he were in a dream, he twisted the throttle again, lightly touching down. Then he was running, following Tian. The others shed their jetpacks. The packs hit the ground, sending up dirt. Some commandos sprawled onto the ground, firing assault rifles at the enemy. Others crouched over as they sprinted for burning vehicles or other hiding positions.

Zhu gasped as he ran. The jetpack was heavy and the straps dug into his shoulders. More Eagle Team commandos landed. This was an enemy HQ, the command center for the American Ninth Division.

Zhu saw a tall American with red hair and the eagles of a colonel. The man held an M-16 as he sprinted for a civilian-style pickup truck. Zhu fired a grenade into the colonel's chest, blowing the man off his feet. Nearby, Humvees revved into life.

First Rank Tian fired an RPG at one, exploding its hood.

The other Humvees carried .50 caliber machine guns. One American shook as he fired the big machine gun, killing two commandos of Zhu's squad. They toppled to the soil like rag dolls, with red holes on their chest. The American kept shooting them, desecrating their bodies. That was wrong. Without thinking about what he was doing, Zhu throttled up his jetpack. With a whoosh, he lifted into the air three meters and arrowed at the Humvee.

"What are you doing, Fighter Rank?" Tian asked. "Stay on the ground."

The man's voice penetrated Zhu's sub-conscious. What *was* he doing? He was flying during a firefight, exactly the wrong thing. Zhu watched in stupefaction as the American behind the .50 caliber swiveled the big machine gun up at him. The man grimaced like a manic. Zhu realized that he was a dead man.

Then an RPG hit the Humvee. It threw the American backward, his fingers sliding off the machine gun's butterfly triggers. Three seconds later Zhu landed behind the burning vehicle, turned and fired a grenade into another Humvee, one whose engine revved. Americans bailed from it a microsecond before the grenade exploded. Chinese assault rifle fire cut the Americans down.

"Shed your jetpack, Fighter Rank," Tian radioed Zhu. "We don't want any more heroics from you. Too many of us are dying."

"He's a real White Tiger," a Soldier Rank radioed.

"Did you see Zhu? That was amazing. We have a real fighter on our hands, First Rank."

In a daze, Zhu shed his jetpack. It fell back and hit the ground nozzles-first, spraying heat and air and making dirt puff up. He'd forgotten to shut if off completely. A sensor in the pack now initiated an emergency shutdown and Zhu began wondering who the others were talking about. It couldn't be him. His heart raced as he gulped air. Slowly, he lay down on the ground amid the burning American vehicles. From his position he began firing bursts from his assault rifle at the nearest enemy. When the magazine was empty, he wiped his sweaty brow and put in another one.

Soon, First Rank Tian ordered the squad up. Another squad launched multiple RPGs at the bunker's door, blasting it down.

"It's time to kill colonels and generals," Tian said.

In as big a daze as ever, Zhu climbed to his feet. He shouted with his squad members and charged the door, entering the bunker-clearing phase of the attack.

Fifteen minutes later, with blood and steaming gore splattered against the walls, it was over. With grenade and rifle fire, they had slaughtered the Ninth Division's general and HQ's staff, effectively destroying the coordination for twelve thousand American soldiers.

Only four Eagle Team members of Zhu's squad remained: him, First Rank Tian and two others. The cost in White Tigers had been heavier than expected, but the operation had been a success. It would no doubt help pave the way for next move in the grand Chinese assault.

BEHIND ENEMY LINES, MEXICO

With one knee on dirt, Paul leaned against an almond tree within an orchard. Romo knelt beside him as they eyed a two-story ranch house. A heavy military truck and a Chinese version of a Humvee sat on the U-shaped driveway to the side.

"We need food," Romo said.

The growl in Paul's stomach had led him to the same conclusion. They had trekked over seven miles by his calculation, having detoured three times to avoid enemy logistic support. Seven miles…that meant the border was still a good twenty miles away.

Normally, that wouldn't have worried Paul. He had often ranged far behind enemy lines, but this time he had no radio and no way of knowing if the Big One had begun. He was beginning to believe it had. The amount of traffic had surprised him.

Unfortunately, he had no supplies this time, no destination other than the American line. The longer they remained behind Chinese lines, the worse it was going to become. The odds weren't with them.

"You know what I think?" Paul said.

"We go in and kill them."

Paul glanced at Romo. The man looked tired, with hollowness around his eyes. "First, we only have one weapon and I only have three magazines for it. Second, there could be

Mexicans in the house, and I have no intention of killing them."

Romo shook his head. "Chinese vehicles are there, meaning Chinese soldiers lived in the house. The Mexicans were driven out long ago. And we have two weapons, as I have a knife."

"Okay, three weapons then. I have a knife, too. Are you sure no Mexicans are in the house?"

"I am positive," Romo said. "Come, we will surprise the Chinese."

"Unless there's a dog in the house," Paul said. "I'm surprised there aren't any dogs out here."

"They say Koreans and some Chinese eat dogs."

Paul had heard the same thing. Who would eat a dog? That was barbaric. Yeah, he could believe it, though. Food was scarce behind enemy lines; at least that's what he'd heard. That might cause some soldiers to butcher animals for the pot. Would they have butchered all the Mexican dogs?

Paul studied the barn, the back yard and the ranch house. The grass in the yard looked trampled. The dirt around the barn had a hundred tires tracks and now that he looked closely, he saw the barn had several scrapes as if brushed by heavy vehicles.

"They must have kept troops here," Paul said. And those troops had eaten the dogs, which was a good thing for the two of them. A dog would have sniffed them out or heard them by now and started barking.

"Why are those two vehicles still here?" Romo asked.

"A thousand reasons," Paul said. "Maybe one of the trucks had engine trouble and they stopped here. Maybe someone got sick. Maybe they were supposed to pick something up here. Maybe there are whores in the house and they wanted a quick one before heading out to battle."

Romo stared at the two vehicles. "I doubt the truck is a troop transport. It looks like something is in the truck."

A back door in the ranch house opened and three Chinese soldiers exited. One of them was talking and gesturing. Finally, the other two began laughing. A fourth man came out of the house. Instead of a helmet, he wore a hat with a single red star on it. He shut the door and inserted a key.

"He's locking up," Paul said.

Romo gripped Paul's shoulder. "Kill them."

"They're too far for me to hit all of them."

"I watched you in battle. You're a good shot. Kill them and we'll take the vehicles."

"And then?" asked Paul.

"No more talking. You must kill them. Look, the one is beginning another joke. The officer appears interested. You must take them out, as we don't have time to get closer. Besides, they'll see us if we try that."

Paul didn't like it. It was too far to take out four Chinese soldiers. Yeah, he could take out one maybe…if he had a sniper rifle and time to settle down for a good shot.

"Now," Romo urged him.

Resting the barrel of the assault rifle on a branch, Paul sighted the enemy. It was ninety yards, almost the full length of a football field. He had three magazines and that was it. Then he would be down to a knife just like Romo. If he took out the officer first—

Paul withdrew the assault rifle from the tree branch. It would be safer to let the Chinese leave. Afterward, they could break in and get some food."

"What are you doing?" Romo asked. "We must kill them and take their vehicles. We cannot hope to remain hidden more than a day or two. We may not get another chance like this."

Paul thought about that: take the vehicles. Yeah, that was a good idea. He watched the four Chinese soldiers. The joke-teller had gotten into his story. The other three watched him. The two enlisted men stood close. The officer—the man with the hat—stood farther away.

Taking his assault rifle, Paul began walking through the orchard. He didn't head toward the enemy, but moved parallel to them. He wanted the barn between them and him.

"This is risky," Romo said. He didn't run, but walked beside Paul.

Paul was through talking. The tingling in his arms had begun. Five more steps put the barn between them.

"Better hope there's no dog around," Paul said. *Or more enemy soldiers we're not seeing*. He sprinted for the back of the barn. Behind him, Romo followed. He heard the man's footsteps.

I hope it's a long joke.

As he reached the back of the barn and ran for a corner, he heard muffled laughter. Paul skidded slower and pressed his back against the barn. He peered around the corner. The back ranch yard wasn't visible, at least the part the four Chinese soldiers stood on wasn't. He probably didn't have much time left.

There was a scrape of leather against wood. He glanced the other way and saw Romo sliding along the barn with him.

"You should have stayed in the orchard," Paul said in a low voice. "That way, if I fail, you could get the heck out of here."

"And leave my blood brother?"

Paul glanced into Romo's eyes. That wasn't a joke. The man was dead serious. Dead—

Taking a deep breath, trying to steady his nerves, Paul pushed off the barn and walked for the ranch house. He passed the last corner of the barn. The four Chinese soldiers were splitting up, two walking toward the military truck and the officer and other enlisted man heading toward the Chinese Humvee.

Paul lifted the assault rifle, aimed at the officer and pulled the trigger. The butt slammed against his shoulder. The officer went down and the others turned in surprise. Paul fired again and hit the joke-teller, making the man stagger. Paul shot a third time, putting the jokester down. The two Chinese who had been heading for the truck stared at him. One clawed for his pistol. The other whirled around and sprinted for the truck. Paul shot him in the back, putting three bullets into him. The soldier lifted off his feet and smacked his forehead against the cab of the truck. He sagged, his chin striking the truck before he rolled onto the ground. An enemy bullet ricocheted off gravel, puffing dirt twenty feet in front of Paul. Pistols were terrible at range. They were even worse when caught by surprise.

"Drop your gun!" Paul shouted.

The Chinese soldier brought up his other hand, clutching his pistol two handed, aiming at Paul.

"Drop it!" Paul shouted.

The soldier fired. This time there was no ricochet. Instead, wood splintered in the barn. A quick-glance showed a bullet-hole ten feet up. The man had aimed far too high.

Paul fired, putting several slugs into the soldier's chest.

Romo clapped Paul on the shoulder. "Excellent."

Paul almost turned on him with a snarl. Instead, he nodded, feeling hollow inside. Those four, they never had a chance. They weren't all dead yet, but they were all down.

Romo strode for the four. Paul watched him. After Romo reached halfway, Paul realized what the man was going to do.

"Wait!" Paul shouted.

Romo never even turned around.

Paul wondered if he should do anything to stop Romo. This was war, right? The Chinese were invading America. They were heading for LA. They had to be. He hadn't started this. Then again, neither had those four started the war. He doubted they had any or much say in where they had ended up. Now it was over for them and over for their jokes.

Almost, Paul turned away. He stood there, holding his assault rifle as Romo checked each Chinese soldier. With two of them, Romo cut their throats, using his weapon, his knife.

The Chinese had stolen Romo's country. There was no pity in the man. Paul wondered what he would feel like if the Chinese, if the Pan Asian Alliance, the South American Federation and the German Dominion, conquered America. Maybe he would cut every enemy throat he could by that time. What had happened to Romo? Had he lost his wife, his children, his parents to the Chinese? Paul didn't know. What had made Romo so remorseless? There was a reason. Things didn't happen in a vacuum. The man was his blood brother. Maybe that meant it was his duty to find out.

Maybe. His first duty, though, was reaching his family. Yeah, maybe his first duty was to make sure the Chinese didn't reach his family. This was a battle for his home and his loved ones.

You'd better toughen up, Kavanagh, because if you lose this fight, if America loses it, then you're going to be ruled by a conquering power. Then you're never going to have a say in how your country is run.

How much of a say did he have now?

Paul shouldered his rifle and trudged across the dirt. He didn't want to become a butcher. But this was a dirty fight with no holds barred. He was going to do what he had to in order to win. The Chinese would kill his family in the snap of his fingers. It was like a man invading his home at night. You don't ask questions then—you picked up your gun and kept firing until they were dead.

Nodding, Paul could understand why Romo showed no mercy. He was fighting the invaders of Mexico. Colonel Valdez was fighting the invaders. They were shooting until the enemy was down.

Paul blew out his breath. It was his duty to fight as hard as he could. His family depended on him. Thousands, maybe millions of other American families depended on him, on all the soldiers to do their duty and defend the homeland.

"They're dead," Romo said.

"Grab their weapons," Paul said. "Pick one for yourself." He lifted the tarp at the back of the military truck. It was filled with giant crates, with missiles of some type. Paul couldn't read Chinese script. Modern warfare devoured ammo. To keep the attack going, the Chinese would have to pour supplies to their soldiers.

"Okay," Paul said, "which do you want to drive?"

Romo gave him a funny look.

"We're grabbing food," Paul said. "Then we're heading for the front. We're going to supply the Chinese."

"You're white and I'm Mexican."

"You think there aren't others like us transporting supplies for the Chinese?"

"Are you crazy?"

Paul grinned, although there was nothing humorous in it. "It's balls to the fire wall. If this is the first day of the assault, believe me, there will be plenty of confusion. Now is the time to get as close as we can to our side. Once we're close enough, we'll hoof it the rest of the way."

Romo shook his head.

That brought a true grin to Paul's face. "I'll take the truck. They won't look as closely at its driver. You take the Humvee. Are you ready?"

Romo stared at him a moment longer before nodding.

"Then let's get busy," Paul said. "We got a lot of miles ahead of us."

-7-
The Right Hook

WASHINGTON, D.C.

In horror, Anna Chen watched a holo-video as she sat in White House Bunker Number Five. It was the fourth day of battle in California and desperation like a sickness ran through the SoCal Command. Disaster threatened.

On the first day of battle, after the Blue Swan missiles struck, the enemy broke through the SoCal Fortifications at San Ysidro. Chinese Marauder tanks, IFVs and remote-control drones pushed through Chula Vista, chewing apart everything in their path. Nothing could stop them as they raced for San Diego. The Joint Forces Commander of California had shifted border formations, even though everything was chaos. Too many places lacked any communications. Others faced heavy assaults. Even so, a brigade of Abrams and Bradleys finally maneuvered in front of the advancing Chinese, and old Apache gunships expended salvos of Hellfire III missiles. It looked like the thrust for San Diego would fail.

Then, early that afternoon, a vast hover-armada had left Mexico. They swung out to sea and roared north. JFC California saw what was happening and sent strike fighters to pick them off. Unfortunately, the hovers had linked fire-control systems. From a distance, the fighters launched air-to-surface missiles, keeping well out of SAM range. The hovers'

195

integrated air defense system shot down most of the missiles, only losing a modest number of hovers. Then the Chinese swung toward land and hit San Diego. Too many of them were infantry carriers, unloading assault troops. A portion of the hover fleet had continued to La Jolla, landing infantry there and digging in on Interstate 5.

The Chinese continued to fight at night, pushing through Chula Vista, destroying the blocking brigade and linking up with the infantry on the outskirts of San Diego.

On the second day, as fierce conflicts continued along the border fortifications, U.S. armored and mechanized infantry reserves rushed south from LA. Many of these were the mobile units saved by the decision earlier to move them back from the main defensive line. They moved down Interstate 5 and clashed with Chinese advance units in Carlsbad on the coast. For the moment, the U.S. contained the relentless Chinese advance.

The SoCal Fortifications were in serious trouble, however. Like Atlas, they were supposed to be able to carry the world on their shoulders—the military had guaranteed the people that the Chinese would never be able to crack through there. The Blue Swan missiles had changed the equation. There were too many gaps in the line and the Chinese freely expended soldiers to force through dry beachheads. Like a mass of hungry jelly leaking through—particularly in the western portion of the fortifications—the Chinese were encircling the border formations and threatening to devour them.

It had called for a total effort and reorganization from JFC California. Battles raged and American and Chinese alike consumed vast amounts of materiel: artillery and tank shells, missiles and bullets. The destruction awed the participants. Burning vehicles, smashed fortifications with littered bodies made it a surreal landscape. Modern equipment had turned war into a merciless event. Laser sighting, heavier payloads and computer-assisted fire control produced unprecedented death and destruction. The carnage bewildered the combatants, quickly tiring all but the most hardened.

By the evening of the third day, the Americans had linked up the majority of their locally encircled formations in the SoCal Fortifications and secured their internal lines. It came at the cost of operational encirclement. The JFC of California had formed a large defensive area. But his few counterattacks had failed to dislodge the Chinese soldiers guarding the thrust from Tijuana to San Diego, La Jolla, Encinitas and Carlsbad. It meant that over six hundred thousand American troops were in the process of being cut off from the freeways and rail lines leading to LA. That would make it nearly impossible to send them reinforcements and supplies.

"It's turning into a giant Stalingrad," General Alan explained.

Early on the fourth day of battle, the U.S. Air Force reappeared in strength. Desperate American assaults from the air and on the ground failed to reopen I-5. Fifty-three wrecked M1A3s on the freeway showed the futility of the attacks. Instead, the Chinese continued to advance, using bulldozers to shove aside the useless American hulks. The Chinese advance was slower than before. Even so, fresh units and a continuous expenditure of material wore down the defenders.

"I've never seen anything like it," General Alan told those in the White House bunker. "The will to fight, to drive through—someone has inflamed the Chinese with a greater determination than we've ever seen before."

If that wasn't enough, news from the eastern SoCal Fortification had suddenly become ten times worse than the western drive on LA.

In the central to eastern SoCal Fortifications, no Blue Swan missiles had exploded. But now mass Chinese armor had broken through at Calexico. The city was near the eastern edge of the Californian border with Arizona. Instead of encircling the embattled Army Group and possibly annihilating it, the enemy armor had swept north past El Centro and raced for Brawley and the Salton Sea. According to General Alan, it looked as if the Chinese were using the desert to swing well east of the southern Californian urban areas. Instead, they were heading for the pass in Palm Springs on Interstate 10. If the massed armor could break though there, they would find LA nearly defenseless, as those forces had headed south to stave off the Chinese on Interstates 5 and 15. If LA fell now, that would irrevocably trap Army Group SoCal and possibly net the enemy nearly eight hundred thousand American troops.

General Alan explained why the fortifications at Calexico had fallen, showing them with the holo-vid. Like everyone else at the conference table, Anna knew the U.S. could not afford such losses this early in the war. It could mean having to retreat from California altogether.

Anna, President Sims and the others watched a Chinese wave assault. The Chinese attacked the fortifications like a horde of ants,. A steel curtain of enemy shells advanced ahead of the Chinese hordes. Missiles came down on the battered fortification in what must have been thunderous salvoes. Then Chinese died as American machine-gun strongpoints began firing. Mines blew up in a portion of the defenses. Still the Chinese came, hunched like turtles with their rucksacks and in their body armor.

"Look," the President said, pointing. "What's happening over there?"

General Alan—Chairman of the Joint Chiefs—nodded at his aide. She adjusted the holo-video. Where the President pointed, it now zoomed larger.

Anna watched in sick fascination. Heavily-armored Chinese—in some kind of exoskeleton-enhanced body armor—fired integral machine guns. The gun was part of the battle-suit. They shot down their own soldiers who had turned and fled from the exploding minefield. A few of those unlucky Chinese fired at their tormenters. One exoskeleton-enhanced soldier staggered backward from the slam of bullets. Once he righted himself, he continued to gun down the "cowardly" offenders.

"Those are Chinese officers killing their own men," the President said. "Is that correct?"

No one spoke until Anna felt compelled to say, "Yes, Mr. President. If you'll notice the insignia of the heavily-armored Chinese—the lightning bolt—those are East Lightning officers."

"Yes?" the President asked. "Is that significant?"

"The soldiers marching over the minefield must belong to a penal battalion," Anna said. "They are controlled by East

Lightning political commissars. Some of the soldiers...it looks as if they're trying to run away and that is not allowed."

"Incredible," the President said. "Why not capture and discipline them, using the soldiers again?"

Anna could have told him that the Chinese had more political offenders than they knew what to do with. In fact, they had too many males in general. Shooting them down like this was much easier and served as a bitter lesson to the others."

After another few moments, the President nodded to the major.

She adjusted the controls and the holo-vid resumed as before. Despite staggering enemy losses, the wave assault reached the Americans, swamping the defenders. Enemy armor now began to reinforce the attack.

General Alan spoke up. "Word of these wave assaults has spread among our troops. I have seen more than one report of badly shaken morale."

The President's features hardened. "This is an opportunity for us to bloody the Chinese. Surely our soldiers can see that."

"Maybe," General Alan said. "Mostly, they're terrified of finding themselves surrounded by the Chinese. There are already reports of enemy atrocities. The Chinese are letting some of their soldiers butcher prisoners."

President Sims rubbed his chin angrily. "We need to spread those reports far and wide to ensure our soldiers fight to the death and don't surrender."

Alan nodded.

"Continue with the battle report," the President said.

The largest enemy breakthrough had occurred at San Ysidro, one of the cornerstones of the SoCal Defenses. Chinese mechanized infantry had thrust through, battling remorselessly, using wave assaults when they had to. They were in Carlsbad now. Another branch was headed up Interstate 15 along the Escondido, Temecula route to LA.

"As we feared, sir," General Alan said, interrupting the major's report. "The Chinese launched another hover assault last night. They swung through the ocean and hit Camp Pendleton from the west early this morning. They have landed

199

infantry hovers, unloaded troops and have already gained footholds there."

The President ran his fingers through his hair as the general continued to talk.

The casualties had been brutal these past four days. With the amount of actual fighting—due to endless round-the-clock assaults—and the vast expenditure of munitions, these four days would have been like eight or even twelve days of the hottest World War II battles. Because of that, the entire southern front was buckling under the fierce Chinese assault.

Anna listened to General Alan wax eloquent about the battle. In his opinion, the Chinese kept attacking the trapped formations so they couldn't regroup and push north to LA. It was costly in Chinese lives, but it was ruthlessly brilliant if victory were the sole objective.

"If you'll notice this, sir," General Alan said, as he motioned to the major.

She brought up fresh images on the holo-vid.

"Tri-turreted tanks," the President said.

Anna grew concerned. This was the real reason for the meeting. On the holo-vid were masses of the triple-turreted tanks. They were big, one-hundred ton vehicles. They churned dust, creating billowing clouds. Behind them followed smaller, conventional tanks and missile-carriers and then fleets of trucks and fuel carriers.

"The Chinese have broken through in the east, sir," General Alan said. "They appear to be heading for the Salton Sea, which lies in the Coachella Valley. I would guess their objective is Palm Springs."

"We have to stop them before that," Sims said.

"Agreed, Mr. President," General Alan said. "We wish to unleash the last of the strategic reserve in Central California and rush it to Palm Springs. We have to stop those tanks or risk losing LA. Without LA, it will be over for Army Group SoCal."

"How big is this tank attack?" the President asked.

General Alan looked down at his hands before he said, "It looks to be several corps' worth, sir, making it a Tank Army.

There are literally thousands of enemy tanks rushing Palm Springs."

The President shook his head. "They'll annihilate our reserve armor."

"We have to slow them down before they get through to Palm Springs. We have to give the trapped Army Group time to break out to the north and head to LA. If the Chinese take LA and trap the forces south of the city, it means we simply won't have enough soldiers to hold the rest of the state."

"We shouldn't have massed so many troops on the border," Sims said.

"I agree with you, Mr. President. But if you'll recall, for political reasons, you had no other choice."

Sims nodded slowly. "Are there further suggestions on how to stop this Tank Army?"

Like many of the others, Anna looked down as the President glanced at her. She noticed beads of condensation on the nearest water-pitcher. One of those beads slid down onto the table, entering the pool of moisture there.

Like a drowning man, Sims picked up his glass of water, although he didn't drink. With a thud that startled Anna, the President slammed the glass back onto the table, causing water to splash up over the rim and drench his hand. "Yes!" he said. "Release the last of the strategic reserves in Central California."

Does all this spilled water signify something? Anna wondered.

In response to the President, General Alan tapped his computer screen.

"Sir," Anna asked, "what about the experimental tanks? Couldn't you send those to Palm Springs?"

The President brightened and asked General Alan, "Where are they?"

"They're also in the Central Valley, Mr. President."

"Why there?"

"Well, first, they're hard to move," General Alan said. "Most bridges can't support them. Secondly, we wanted to keep them secret until we'd perfected the tanks. Maybe California isn't the right place for them."

The President's scowl worsened.

"And finally, sir," General Alan said, speaking faster as the President opened his mouth. "We believe the Chinese are planning an amphibious assault. There are reports of an invasion armada somewhere in the Pacific. The San Francisco area makes the most sense. It's what I would do given Chinese numbers and capabilities."

President Sims shook his head. "If I were them, I would land in LA, make certain of taking it."

"LA is a possibility," General Alan conceded. "San Francisco seems more likely, given that the Chinese would like to stretch our forces to the breaking point."

"No," the President said. "If we lose LA now, it's over. We have to use everything in Central California. Send the Behemoths to Palm Springs."

"They might not make it in time," General Alan said.

"Send them," the President said gruffly.

General Alan nodded.

President Sims stared at a wall. He soon asked, "What's happening in Texas?"

The meeting now moved to the additional fronts.

As others talked, Anna tapped her computer scroll and studied the SoCal situation. Despite the commando gamble, the great Chinese surprise had worked. What would have happened if they hadn't learned about the Blue Swan missiles or not done anything to blunt the blow? Likely, the enemy attack would have been even more successful and she would be sitting in on a complete catastrophe. Would the central reserve armor slow the Chinese Tank Army? Could the SoCal formations break out of the trap? Maybe if the Americans fought in a superhuman fashion… Unfortunately, it was starting to appear as if someone on the other side knew exactly what to do to gain a supreme victory.

FRESNO, CALIFORNIA

Stan Higgins was nervous and sweaty. Grunts were loading the Behemoths onto tank carriers and the carriers would be ready to roll in another hour or so. He didn't have much time left.

Stan was in the Detention Reception Center in Fresno. The city was in the middle of the Central Valley, a dusty place with myriad irrigation canals feeding peach and almond orchards and mile after mile of wheat fields.

He had spoken to a government coordinator and now waited in a special cubicle with a computer screen. He could hear others in nearby cubicles speaking to relatives in the Central Detention Center in Colorado. These cubicles were the only way to communicate with someone in a Detention Center. The government, he knew, kept careful records of who spoke to detainees and how often they did it. Too much, and it went against your political profile.

The screen came to life and an officious, thick-lipped woman with a mole on her nose regarded him. She wore a tan uniform of a Detention warrant officer and a tan, military-style hat with a red band.

She glanced at something off screen by her hands, his profile, no doubt. "You're Captain Stan Higgins?" she asked.

"Yes, ma'am," Stan said.

"Hmm. You're in the Army?"

"That is correct."

"What is the nature of your call, Captain Higgins?"

He'd already told a Detention official here in Fresno why he was calling. He'd had to fill out several request forms to get this far. The warrant officer he was talking to must know that. Instead of saying any of that, Stan pasted the best smile he could on his face.

"I'd like to speak with my son, Jake Higgins."

"Hmm," she said, studying something. "I'm afraid that isn't possible. Your son is presently in solitary confinement. He has three more hours to serve on a five-day offense."

"What?" Stan asked.

The warrant officer frowned. "I'm not sure I like your tone, Captain Higgins. According to this," she said, tapping a computer scroll, "you're in the active military. Ah, I see you won the Medal of Honor in 2032, ah, in Alaska. You'll understand then what it means to follow orders."

203

"No," Stan said. "I received my medal for disobeying orders and doing what needed doing to beat the Chinese."

The warrant officer's frown hardened, and there was a gleam now in her dark eyes.

Stan knew he'd made a mistake. "Look. I'd just like to say a few words to my son before I go off to face the Chinese."

"You're in California?"

"Yes, that's right."

"Near the front?" she asked.

"Not yet, but I'll be there in a day at the latest."

"You realize that I cannot let your son out of solitary."

"Can I ask you what he did?"

"He assaulted a guard," the woman said.

"Jake did?" Stan asked, horrified to hear this. That was just like Jake's grandfather. "Did my son have a reason for the assault?"

"There is no good reason, Captain."

"No, I'm sure there isn't," Stan said. He needed another angle with the woman. "You know," he said, "The Chinese are attacking viciously. According to what I'm hearing, they mean to take the state in what looks like one fell swoop. I might die in the coming fight. I would really appreciate it if you would somehow see it in you to let me speak to my son before that happens."

"I'm sorry, no. He's in solitary confinement as I told you and I'm not authorized to break the rules. Despite your earlier statement about disregarding rules, we here in the Detention Center know how to achieve our tasks while coordinating with our superiors."

"I'm not condoning my son's actions. I would just dearly like to speak to him one more time. Maybe...maybe I could help straighten him out."

"I think you already had your chance, Captain, when your son lived with you for over twenty years."

Stan turned away, biting his lip. Couldn't they let him talk to his son? Jake only had three more hours to serve in solitary. What was wrong with these people? "Look," he said, facing the screen. "Do you have any children?"

"I have a daughter, as a matter of fact. But I don't see what that has to do with this."

"What if she was in a Detention Center and you had to go fight the Chinese."

"My daughter would never be sent to a Detention Center," the warrant officer said in brittle tone.

"I'm sure that's true," Stan said. "How about if the government had made a mistake in putting her there?"

The warrant officer's features tightened. She leaned closer into the screen. She had terrible skin and visible pours near her nose. "Are you suggesting the government made a mistake with your son?"

"No, of course not," Stan said. And then, his words just stopped. For a second, he wanted to lift the screen and smash it against the floor. He wanted to slug the woman—the warrant officer—in the face. He could hardly blame Jake for striking a guard if this is what they were like. Maybe he should be proud of his son for standing up for freedom. What was wrong with protesting anyway?

"You know, lady, I'm laying my life on the line for my country and for my family. In a way, I'm putting my body in harm's way for you and your daughter. And you can't even let me speak to my son for what might be the last time. That's un-American to me, just flat-out wrong."

"Would you like me to record your statement?" the woman asked.

"Yeah," Stan said, "go ahead and record it. Put it down. I said it and I meant it."

They stared at each other with growing hostility.

"Good-day, Captain Higgins," she said.

"I want to speak to your superior."

"No. I don't think you do."

"What's wrong? Are you afraid now?"

She stared at him. Then she glanced to the side. "My superior happens to be right here. Are you sure you'd like to speak to him, Captain?"

"Absolutely," Stan said.

The woman rose and stepped out of sight. There was muffled talk and a few moments later, a thin man sat down. He didn't need to frown, as his long face seemed to have frozen into a scowl.

"I'm afraid I cannot help you," the man said.

"I think you can," Stan said. "I'm in California."

"Sir, the only reason I'm talking with you is so that you understand we back our people to the hilt. We stand as one. Your son has seen fit to protest the President's actions. That is disloyalty to our country at a time of national emergency. Now he has struck a guard and he has found himself time for serious thinking in solitary confinement. We do not break the rules here in the Detention Center."

"Don't you have any heart?" Stan asked. "I might die in combat defending our beloved country and all I want to do is say a few words to my son. I fought in Alaska and won the Medal of Honor. Surely, that should count for something. If you've been following the news, you must realize the Chinese have turned this into a bloodbath. Let me tell him goodbye. As you have any mercy in your heart, I'm begging you to do this for a fellow American soldier."

The man stared at Stan. Finally, he nodded. "My father is in the Militia. He's a colonel. I would want him to say goodbye to me. Very well, Captain. I'll give you two minutes."

"Thank you," Stan said, surprised at this turnaround.

"Give us a few minutes here to coordinate the call," the man said. Then the screen went blank before Stan could say anything more.

For the next few minutes, time seemed to crawl along for Stan. Had they forgotten about him? Would they monitor the call? Yes, of course they would.

Oh, Jake, what have you gone and done?

Two minutes later, the screen resumed and his son stared at him. Jake was a younger version of Stan, with a thinner face and now with hollowed-out eyes. There was a strange gleam in Jake's eyes. It reminded Stan of his father.

He's been in solitary confinement for some time. Remember that.

"Dad?" Jake asked in a rough voice.

"Hello son. It's good to see you."

"Dad...I'm sorry about this."

206

Stan nodded because his throat tightened and he was afraid to say anything just then.

"I guess I went and protested the illegal—"

"Jake! Listen to me. Will you listen a bit?"

"Sure. Is everything okay?"

"No," Stan said, "I've been called up and chances are I'm going to face the Chinese soon."

"You said that wouldn't happen this time around."

Stan smiled sadly. "I didn't think it would. But they need our...they need us, I'm thinking. It must be pretty bad. Son...I love you. I want you to use your head from now on."

"You think I was wrong protesting the emergency decrees?"

"This is probably the wrong place to talk about that," Stan said.

"I know we're being monitored, Dad. That's why I'm protesting."

Stan nodded. His boy looked terrible. He looked used up, but he was standing for his rights. That took moral courage, something usually much more lacking in people than physical courage. Thinking about that made Stan's heart swell with pride.

"You're an American, son. I'm proud of you. Real Americans stand up for freedom and fight for what they believe in. We may not have the perfect system, Jake, but it is worth fighting for because the other side is ten times worse."

"I'm not arguing that."

"I know you're not. You watch yourself, son. Don't attack guards unless it's a matter of self-defense. I...I might not get to talk to you for a time."

"Dad...I'm proud of what you're doing, sir."

Stan nodded, afraid to speak again lest his voice betray what he was feeling.

"When they let me out of here, I'm going to join up."

Stan shook his head. "I'm not sure you can with a Detention mark on your record."

"They'll let me join a Militia. I'm going to fight then, and when I'm done, I'm going to study how to fix our system."

"Ten seconds left," a disembodied voice said.

"Good-bye, Jake. You take care of yourself."

"You too, Dad. Kick their asses, huh?"

Stan forced a grin. "I plan to."

"Show these invaders what it means to mess with real Americans."

Stan nodded. As he did, the screen faded and the thin official reappeared.

"Thanks," Stan told the man. "Watch over him for me—if you know what I mean?"

The man stared at him, and there was an odd look in his eyes. "Yes sir, Captain Higgins. Good luck to you."

"Thanks. I'm going to need it," Stan said, wondering if the tank carriers were ready yet.

SALTON SEA, CALIFORNIA

In a vast armada of armored power, the one-hundred ton T-66 tri-turreted tanks clanked through the desert sands beside the Salton Sea. Many of the commanders were half out of the main hatches, using binoculars to scan forward.

Before them, light Marauder tanks raced ahead, scouting for a sign of the enemy. To the rear of the 83rd Brigade clanked several UAV-launching vehicles. When the time came, they would give them tactical eyes and provide the armored thrust with airborne Annihilator platforms.

First Lieutenant Sheng commanded A platoon of Seventh Company: three T-66s at the head of the battalion.

Sheng wore a black tanker's uniform with a skull patch. He also wore black gloves and had a pair of powered goggles over his eyes. He'd waited a year for this chance to show the Americans what he could do to their paltry armor. They had nothing to compare to the T-66. He had studied the Alaskan Campaign of seven years ago. The frozen terrain up there had worked against the T-66. These desert sands would give Chinese armor its full scope.

First Lieutenant Sheng beamed with pride just thinking about it. His T-66 had two hundred centimeters of Tai composite armor in front. It also possessed three turrets. Each could traverse 180 degrees and each had a huge, 175mm smoothbore gun. They fired hypervelocity rocket-assisted shells against enemy tanks, and HEAT shells for lesser targets. Six 30mm auto-cannons and twenty beehive flechette defenders made the tank sudden death for any infantryman out in the open. Linked with the defense radar net, the massed T-66s could knock down or deflect most enemy shells. The main gun tubes could also fire Red Arrow anti-air rounds, making it a deadly proposition for attack-craft trying to take it on. The tank had a magnetically balanced hydraulic suspension, so Sheng's gunners could fire with astounding accuracy while moving at top speed.

Sheng dearly hoped the Americans were foolish enough to engage his tanks. It would mean kills on the battlefield. That might win him a medal, and the medal would definitely help him gain a marriage permit before he reached thirty. Sheng had worked hard to gain this position of honor. The colonel considered him the best first lieutenant in the battalion, the reason why he led the assault.

Sheng lifted his goggles and glanced back. The brigade's tanks churned a mighty cloud of dust. It rose and billowed, some of it drifting onto the sea to the brigade's right. There, the falling, raining particles speckled the water, creating ripples.

Incredibly, the Salton Sea was a manmade lake. In his spare hours, Sheng had studied the databases on it. In 1900, the Americans had built irrigation canals, diverting water from the Colorado River and into the Salton Sink, an ancient dry lakebed. American farmers had benefited from this until 1902, when floodwaters from the Colorado River overran a set of headgates for the Alamo Canal. The flood breached the Imperial Valley dike, among other damage. In the course of two years, two newly created rivers carried the entire volume of the Colorado into the Salton Sink. Only the completion of the Hoover Dam in 1935 had ended the periodic flooding of this area.

The Salton Sea was 69 meters below sea level and averaged 24 km by 56 km. It was California's largest lake and saltier than the ocean, although not as salty as the Great Salt Lake in Utah.

Taking out a rag, First Lieutenant Sheng wiped his mouth. The T-66s were headed for Palm Springs and then LA beyond. Afterward, Sheng hoped to be the first to race onto the Grapevine and over the pass to Bakersfield. They were going to overrun California. That's what the colonel had told them. They were going to meet up with Navy personnel in Sacramento, crushing any Americans foolish enough to engage the greatest tanks and the greatest army in the world.

Sheng grinned thinking about it, and then he checked a computer. The gauge showed they were in the red, meaning they were almost empty of diesel. He would need more fuel soon. They had been traveling fast for many hours. If the T-66 had a problem, it was a hog-like thirst for fuel. How long until the fuel carriers pulled up?

Dropping down into the interior, Sheng moved to the radio, deciding it was time to find out.

COACHELLA VALLEY, CALIFORNIA

In the late afternoon, Sergeant McGee shut down his Abrams M1A3 Main Battle Tank. He had half a tank of fuel left and wanted to conserve what he had.

In training, the instructors had hammered home the need to conserve fuel. After 2032, with the loss of the Arctic Ocean oil fields and the diminishment of Prudhoe Bay, finding enough oil and gas had become a problem. Extracting oil from shale had provided some of the answer. It proved harder to do on a commercial scale than expected. Synthetic oil from coal produced the rest. Despite this, the American Army seldom had enough fuel and thus everyone conserved wherever he could.

McGee was seven miles outside of Palm Springs, an advance unit of American armor. He was in a swing battalion of the U.S. Tenth Division, the second-to-last reserve formation in LA. The plan was simple enough, as McGee knew about it. Bradley Fighting Vehicles with advanced TOW missiles would engage the Chinese at range, four thousand meters or more. Self-propelled artillery would then hammer the enemy with direct fire of guided projectiles. Old Apache helicopters with advanced Hellfire III missiles would then pop up and try to destroy advancing T-66s, before falling back.

At that point, in the hoped-for confusion, Sergeant McGee and others would turn on their Abrams and attack the enemy flanks. The goal was to get in amongst enemy supply and headquarters vehicles and blow them to Hell. The key vehicles command wanted destroyed were the enemy fuel carriers. They had to stop the Chinese advance to Palm Springs, giving LA time for Central Californian reinforcements.

As he stood in the hatch, Sergeant McGee swallowed uneasily. The rumors coming down were all bad. The Chinese had encircled the fortifications on the border, trapping the bulk of Army Group SoCal. On the coast and a little inland, the enemy was driving up the interstates to LA. But the big right hook that would take out Southern California was coming through the desert past the Salton Sea.

"Sergeant!" his driver yelled up from within the tank.

McGee was resting in the hatch, with a pair of binoculars on his chest. He dipped down inside the tank. "What are you hollering for?"

The driver looked up. "The Chinese, Sarge, they've been spotted."

"Yeah?" McGee asked, trying to sound cool. He was twenty-three years old and was finding that hard to do right now.

"It looks like their advance elements will be in range of the Bradleys soon, maybe in twenty minutes, maybe sooner."

"T-66s?" McGee asked.

The driver shook his head. "Marauder tanks, Sarge."

McGee had to turn away from the driver, as the driver looked too scared, and that could be infectious. "We'll show them."

"Do you think so?" the driver asked.

"Yeah," McGee said, looking at the man again.

"They say a whole tank army is coming behind these vehicles. How are we going to face an army of enemy tanks? We're just a division, Sarge."

"Yeah, but we're *Tenth* Division. They've beefed us up to twenty thousand soldiers. We're going show the Chinese what it means to take on the Tenth."

The driver blinked so his entire face scrunched up. "I hope you're right. I don't want to die out here."

"No," McGee said, "neither do I."

SAN DIEGO, CALIFORNIA

Flight Lieutenant Harris shook his head. He wore VR goggles and sat in his chair in an Air Force bunker. Onscreen, he looked out of his new V-10 UCAV. He flew over the Coachella Valley, hunting for enemy fuel carriers.

What he should be doing was hunting for Chinese amphibious vehicles heading for San Diego. He and the other drone pilots were presently trapped behind enemy lines. It made him nervous. The idea of being shipped overseas to a Chinese POW camp terrified him. The Japanese of World War II, the North Koreans in the 1950s and the Vietnamese during the 60s all had terrible records as prison wardens. Harris didn't see why the Chinese would be any different.

He shook his head again, trying to drive the idea away. He needed to concentrate on the task. The Chinese were heading for Palm Springs, trying to slip into LA through the side door.

A ping in his ear alerted Harris.

Flipping on a different camera on his V-10, Harris looked down on the white sands below. It showed a billowing dust cloud. He used a thermal scanner. The image told him he could possibly have a fleet of fuel carriers. Unfortunately, air-defense vehicles roared alongside them.

Harris didn't want to lose another V-10. It would look bad on his record. But he knew this was important, critically so, he'd been told.

He chinned on his radio to the colonel in charge here in the San Diego bunker.

"You see them, sir," Harris said. "Do I wait for others or—"

212

"Kill them now, Lieutenant. Don't waste time. We have to stop the Chinese from refueling their heavies, if they haven't already done that."

"Yes, sir," Harris said.

If he'd been flying an F-35 or a ground-attack plane, the order might have been different. The Air Force didn't like suicidal pilots. UCAVs changed the rules.

"Here we go," Harris said to himself, using his joystick thumb-control. He piloted the V-10 down, down, down toward the fuel carriers. As he did, he primed the V-10's Hellfire III missiles.

From below and hidden in the dust cloud, enemy chain-guns opened up. They were like mini-volcanos and soon he spied eruptions of flames. They were hypnotic if he looked at them too long. He heard a growl in his ear from the threat indicator. The Chinese had radar lock on him. This time it didn't change a thing. Harris increased speed as he launched Hellfire after Hellfire. Their contrails burned brightly on his screen.

"Come on," Harris said, trying to get within cannon range.

On his thermal scanner, he saw the first hit. It was a massive explosion. He'd gotten a fuel carrier. Then came another explosion and another. He'd hit pay dirt, this time.

Harris whooped with delight. This would go on his record, too. He was making kills, critical kills.

At the last moment and on his screen, he saw a Chinese SAM barreling up at his craft. He hit a button, expelling chaff. This time it was too late. The SAM destroyed the V-10 and Harris lost his link to the Coachella Valley. He was back to being a pilot without a drone, but at least he was alive and he had helped the Army out there on the white sands facing the enemy sneak attack.

BAKERSFIELD, CALIFORNIA

On the flat Highway 99 north of Bakersfield, twenty massive tank carriers hauled twenty Behemoth tanks. It was the whole complement of the experimental vehicles. They were

213

spaced far apart on the highway and moved at a mere fifteen mph. If they tried moving any faster, they would risk blowing tires and tipping over.

Captain Stan Higgins sat in the back of the cab of the fifth hauler. He listened to reports from Tenth Armor Division outside of Palm Springs. They were supposed to delay the Chinese tank advance, giving the reinforcements from Central California time to reach Palm Springs.

Studying the desert terrain of the Coachella Valley, Stan realized it would be the perfect place for the Behemoths—if the tanks worked how they were supposed to, and if they had enough air cover.

Could Tenth Division halt the Chinese? Could the lone American formation give the rest of them enough time to get there and set up?

Time for what, though? What could twenty experimental tanks do against thousands of Chinese T-66s, the Chinese MBTs and the light Marauder tanks?

We need a miracle, Stan realized. *We need our own Blue Swan missiles.*

COACHELLA VALLEY, CALIFORNIA

With his head and shoulders outside the main hatch, Sergeant McGee heard the distant thunder of divisional artillery. There were flashes in the night. Seconds later came the booms.

Dark twilight had come over the desert. Several hours earlier, Bradley Fighting Vehicles had launched a salvo of TOW missiles at advancing Marauder tanks, killing some and driving the others back. It had brought about visible air duels above, more waiting and finally an enemy battalion of what command now knew had been drone light tanks. They had driven at the Bradleys at over forty mph. That had been a mistake: the head-on attack. The TOWs had demolished the drones, although it had seriously depleted the number of missiles the Bradleys had. Maybe that had been the idea.

214

McGee took comfort in the fact the Chinese could make mistakes. A tank drive against unknown forces…he could only imagine how difficult it was to coordinate everything.

Now word had come down. A large force of T-66 tanks was massed before the Bradleys and the enemy was massed against the flanking forces, too. In other words, there weren't going to be any American surprises. Instead, it looked as if a slugfest was in the making.

"Are they going to try to overrun us?" the driver asked McGee.

McGee had dropped down into the M1A3 tank.

Two low-powered blue lights lit the Abrams' interior. The blue light didn't steal their night vision. Of course, other lights glowed on the panels: red, green and yellow.

"The Chinese waited too long," McGee told the crew. He had to tell them something to cheer them up. "I don't know why they waited. They should have rushed us earlier when they had the chance. Now we have more artillery. Our side must be laying down sleeper mines. That will give the T-66s something to think about."

"You sure, Sarge?" the driver asked. "You don't think the Chinese have them a good plan?"

"No," McGee said. "They made a mistake waiting this long. Now we're going to bloody their noses and then fall back to our next prepared position. They played into our hands and now we're going to delay them as ordered."

LOS ANGELES, CALIFORNIA

Stan Higgins watched twilight turn into true night from the cab of his Behemoth-carrier. They had made it over the Grapevine at fifteen mph. Now they were in LA, the vast urban area.

What amazed him was they had only been stopped once, letting a faster formation race past.

He still listened to Tenth Division net. The Chinese had made desultory attacks, but nothing in force. What were they waiting for? It didn't make sense. Were the Chinese going to let the reinforcements set up outside Palm Springs? It seemed like a missed opportunity for them.

They had raced up the Coachella Valley, heading for the San Gorgonio Pass. It cut between the San Bernardino Mountains on the north and the San Jacinto Mountains to the south. San Gorgonio Pass was one of the deepest in America, the mountains on either side towering 9000 feet above the road. Palm Springs guarded the pass, while Greater San Bernardino was on the other side. Now was the moment for the Chinese to smash through.

"Keep waiting," Stan whispered.

Jose lifted his head. He'd been snoozing most of the trip. "You say something, Professor?"

"Go back to sleep," Stan said. "At this speed, we're still a long way out from Palm Springs."

"Sure, Professor, anything you say." Jose's head slumped back.

Stan stared out of the cab, watching LA go past outside the tank carrier's window.

COACHELLA VALLEY, CALIFORNIA

First Lieutenant Sheng had been chaffing at the bit most of the afternoon. It was dark now and still his platoon waited for the attack to commence, still waited for a fuel-carrier to fill up his T-66 tanks.

Motion caused one of the vehicle's outer lights to snap on. In the distance, Sheng spied a jackrabbit in the circle of light. Its long ears twitched, and with a bound, it dashed for cover.

Earlier, Sheng had listened to the major explaining the situation to them. "We will destroy them at a blow, shattering them utterly. We have watched the Americans trickle reinforcements to the Tenth Division. Yes, they have laid their artillery-spread minefields and they have strengthened themselves. We want to destroy them here in the desert so there will be fewer of them in the built-up areas later."

One swift and massive blow, yes, Sheng could understand that. But the major had been telling lies. The attack hadn't

216

occurred out of any brilliance. It hadn't occurred, Sheng suspected, because the Americans had destroyed too many fuel carriers. He'd heard about the air attacks, hundreds of little pinpricks that had hit a fuel-carrier one at a time. Command had ordered the other fuel carriers back until enough air support appeared. Finally, the fuel carriers were here, or so the major had told them.

The T-66 was like an alcoholic with an immense thirst. They needed fuel before they dared attack the Americans.

It took another hour before Sheng actually saw a fuel-carrier. Men attached a hose and gave him half-a-tank full.

"I need more," Sheng said, as a First Rank began disconnecting the hose.

"Sorry, sir," the First Rank said. "It's orders. Everyone only gets half-a-tank."

That seemed foolish to Sheng. It would be wiser to fill half the tanks all the way, so they could drive to LA without having to worry about another fuel gulp.

Because he was merely a first lieutenant, Sheng kept his thoughts to himself.

After the fuel carriers left, brigade waited another forty-five minutes. Finally, at 9:23 PM, the order came. They were finally going to destroy the American Tenth Division and open the way to Palm Springs and LA beyond.

FIRST FRONT HEADQUARTERS, MEXICO

From his wheelchair in the command center, Marshal Nung rubbed his eyes. He was impatient for the Tank Army to attack. The Americans had cleverly burned up more of their air, hunting through the desert for the most forward fuel carriers.

He should have remembered the tactic from what the enemy had done in Alaska. It was foolish to forget something so obvious. From now on, he would defend the fuel carriers with triple the anti-air units and with continuous air cover.

He mustn't allow the Americans to practice the same tactic on him again.

217

General Pi looked up from the glowing computer table. "Sleeper mines are taking a heavy toll of our Marauder drones, sir."

"Yes," Nung said. "I accept heavy losses in those cheap units now in order to achieve brilliance later. A hard and furious assault, General, that is what wins true glory."

"Yes, Marshal," Pi said.

From his wheelchair, Nung observed Marshal Gang frowning in the corner. He knew the man would record that statement and tell Ruling Committee member Kao about it.

As long as I'm advancing, no one will say anything. It is if I start to lose, that these words will haunt me. But I will not lose. That is the key.

"Unleash the T66s," Nung said. "It is time to shatter the Americans and let them truly know what it is to fear."

COACHELLA VALLEY, CALIFORNIA

Sergeant McGee had buttoned the M1A3, meaning he'd shut the outer hatch and was completely inside the tank. He now sat above and behind the gunner. His right hand rested on the pistol-grip handle. With it, he had override control of the turret—where it turned—and where the main gun pointed. He leaned into the brow-padded thermal sights, hunting for a target.

Tenth Division Command had just radioed. The Chinese heavies were finally advancing. The realization had twisted McGee's gut with fear. Was he going to die tonight? Was this it?

Get a grip, McGee. You're fighting for your country. Stand your ground and kill the Chinese.

Like the other M1A3s, McGee had carefully chosen his first spot. The tank used a small, grassy dune, putting the Abrams behind it in the "hull-down" position. It meant most of the tank used the sand as a shield. The turret was higher than the top of the dune and the gun-barrel depressed so it could fire straight at the enemy. It would make him a smaller sight on enemy thermals and the sand or dune would act as a shield against enemy shells. Well, the dune would stop a HEAT round, but he wasn't sure about the latest Chinese sabot round.

In the Abrams's thermal sights, he saw the first enemy tank—a T-66 by its size. It was nearly five thousands meters away. Behind it, others appeared, following the first monster. A squeeze of purified terror tightened McGee's chest. He'd heard stories about the tri-turreted tanks. The battalion didn't have a chance against them. But so what, huh? It was time to fight.

With the pistol grip, McGee adjusted the turret and put crosshairs on the target. The enemy tank was moving fast and would soon be in range.

"Gunner, sabot, tank," McGee said. It made him glad his voice still sounded level. Maybe he could fool the others, not letting them know he was worried sick.

The first order—"gunner"—alerted the crew. The second told them what kind of shell he wanted. The last was the target they aimed at.

McGee glanced at the gunner. The man had his own thermal sights, leaning his brow on the pad. The gunner shouted, "Identified," and took over control of the gun. With his left hand, the gunner flipped the switch on the fire control to "sabot." At the same time, he ensured the crosshairs were on target. He used the laser range finder. It shot a beam at the target and returned, giving them the precise distance. The M1A3's ballistic computer analyzed the type of ammo, the wind speed and direction, humanity and the angle of the tank relative to the horizontal plane. In microseconds, the computer showed the needed gun-tube elevation, which the gunner used to adjusted the mighty 120mm cannon.

While the gunner readied the gun, the loader—to McGee's left and below him—turned to the rear bustle. With his right knee, the loader hit a switch. A one-inch-thick blast door slid open, showing rows of main gun rounds. He pulled out a fifty-pound sabot round. With a grunt, he turned and his knee lifted off the switch. The blast door slid shut, sealing off the deadly rounds. The loader shoved the round into the breech and slid it home with his fist. The breech-lock knocked his fist out the way as it sealed the breech. Some loaders had lost fingers that way. The loader finally flipped the safety switch on the turret wall and shouted, "Up!" over the intercom.

Now McGee waited, letting the enemy come to poppa. Before the T-66 reached the gun's range, American artillery shells began falling on the enemy. This was perfect. McGee knew all about the enemy defensive systems. The T-66 had more than great armor, but included radar-directed flechettes and auto-cannons. The artillery shells might give the radar-guided defenses too many targets to monitor. Even better, the arty shells would possibly hit against the T-66s' tops. Just like the Abrams, the enemy's weakest armor was there. Unfortunately, enemy defensive systems began chugging at the steel hail.

After a wait that squeezed McGee's stomach tighter than a fist, the lead and targeted T-66 came into range.

"Fire!" McGee said.

The gunner shouted, "On the way!" and fired the round.

The M1A3 shook as the 120mm smoothbore gun fired the shell. The entire front of the tank seemed to lift.

The sabot round contained a cardboard casing around the gunpowder, which was burned up by the explosion. It meant that no hot brass shell landed inside the tank.

The kinetic energy sabot round exited the tube. The word *sabot* meant "wooden shoe" in French. The plastic "shoe" around the depleted uranium (DU) rod dropped away upon exiting the tube. Flight-stabilizing fins popped up, making the round look like a technological arrow. The arrow was a dense metal rod nearly two feet long.

Despite the artillery rain, Chinese flechettes flew as the round neared, but they missed, as did the auto-cannons tracking it by radar. Too many targets—this was great!

The DU round struck the T-66 with the mass and pressure equivalent to an NASCAR racer hitting a brick wall at 175 mph, all concentrated in an area the size of a golf ball.

The DU round punched through a turret. As it did, particles sheared off as the round penetrated. It was like a snake shedding its skin. The enormous pressure turned the projectiles white-hot. The peeled-off skins became fiery granules and were twice as dense as the steel that followed them. Those granules zinged around the compartment like a thousand white-hot BBs. They ignited everything they touched, killing the Chinese personnel and cooking off a round. In this instance, the pyrophoric effect resulted in a terrific explosion that ripped the turret from the T-66 and flipped the one-hundred ton tank onto its side, taking it out of the battle.

Back at the M1A3, McGee shouted, "Hit! We took out a T-66."

The crew shouted with glee, the driver pumping his fist in the air, showing off his high school ring. Then McGee targeted the next enemy tank and the procedure began all over again.

All along the line from their hull-down positions, American Abrams opened up, reaching out over four thousand meters. Some rounds hit, a few making kills like McGee. Others hit and only burned in partway. A few hit and bounced—the angle and new, super-dense skirts working as designed on the Chinese tanks. The T-66s knocked down some rounds with defensive fire or deflected the sabots just enough. A few of the sabots just plain missed.

As all this happened, McGee realized the enemy probably had as good a night vision as they had, maybe even better.

"Back her up!" McGee shouted to the driver. "And give me smoke."

The driver revved the gas turbine engine. The mighty seventy-ton tank lurched as it backed away from its dune and backed away from the advancing horde of Chinese monsters.

The Abrams lobbed smoke shells, creating dense clouds of it between them and the enemy.

The Abrams had two ways to make smoke. The first was how they were doing it, with the turret-mounted grenade dischargers. The second way was to inject a little fuel into the exhaust. That generated a heavy cloud of smoke.

Sergeant McGee pressed his forehead against the thermal sights. Night or day, they used them. They could "look" through most smoke and other interference. These smoke shells had tiny particles, however, making thermal imaging harder to achieve.

The opening battle raged against forty-two M1A3s and fifty-nine T-66s. The Chinese tanks now opened fire. On McGee's thermal sights, the firings were bright blooms.

Unfortunately, for McGee and his fellow tankers it wasn't sixty gun-tubes firing at the battalion, but one hundred and eighty. The Abrams had a 120mm tube. Each Chinese tank had three 175mm tubes and more advanced munitions.

Terrific explosions occurred outside McGee's Abrams. Titanic hammers beat at metal and it rained shattered and exploded M1A3s.

"Get us out of here!" McGee shouted, with his voice cracking.

"I'm trying, Sarge! I'm trying!"

McGee leaned his forehead against the thermal sights. When the T-66s fired in unison, it looked like Hell had erupted.

How are we supposed to stop this?

***

First Lieutenant Sheng sat in the commander's seat of the highest turret. He had several computer screens around him and wore safety straps as the T-66 roared at the retreating enemy.

The damned Americans had knocked out one of the platoon's T-66s. It was because of the artillery shells. There had simply been too many targets for the defensive radar to track at once. An Abrams had hit, blown a turret off one of his T-66s, which had caused the tank to fall onto its side, thereby taking it out of the battle.

Sheng wanted revenge, which overrode the small sense of concern humming in his head for his own safety.

These were China's premier tank. These models were better than the ones that had gone into Alaska seven years ago. The Americans—once they had built the greatest weapons. That had been before the Sovereign Debt Depression. After the Alaskan War, America had faced growing debt, secession troubles, sanction damage and the Chinese cyber-attack. Even better, a terrorist nuclear weapon had taken out Silicon Valley, once home to the world's highest technology. The American research and development had yet to advance as far as the great T-66. Yes, once the Americans had ruled the world's battlefields with their superior weapons. Now China ruled the battlefields, and tonight Sheng was going to show the has-beens what that meant.

The Americans fled from their hull-down positions, trying to use the dunes as cover for their escape. Sheng shook his head. He wasn't going to let that happen.

At his orders, the two tanks of his platoon revved to the right. They had brigade UAVs in the sky, spotting for them. He used the computer screens, waiting, watching—

"There!" Sheng shouted. He spied the enemy Abrams, the bastard who had killed one of his tanks. He'd "painted" the Abrams, using a computer-code marker.

"I want all three guns targeted on the painted Abrams," Sheng said.

The T-66 had three turrets and three guns, which meant a gunner and a loader for each. The main turret was slightly larger than the other two. It held the gunner, loader, Sheng and his radio operator. Each T-66, therefore, had eight crewmembers.

Now the three 175mm tubes aligned on the retreating Abrams.

The enemy tank's cannon boomed. Sheng witnessed the fact on one of his screens. The sabot round screamed across the distance between them and likely would have hit. The radar on the T-66 tracked it and two 30mm auto-cannons fired, knocking the American round out of the air.

"You cannot defeat us," Sheng said. "Yes, you are wise to flee, weak American tank."

Sheng heard the three gunners shout. They were ready.

For a second, he enjoyed the sensation of knowing he was going to kill the American. It was a delicious thing. Then Sheng said, "Fire."

The front of the one-hundred ton monster seemed to rise in air from the three cannons firing in unison. Three Chinese sabot rounds sped at hyper-velocity, rocket-assigned for greater speed and reach.

First Lieutenant Sheng watched on a thermal-imaging screen.

Sabot rounds hit the Abrams. Giant lava streams spewed out of blown enemy hatches. Those were solid columns of flame climbing into the night air. It meant one of the shells at least must have burned down the blast door to the enemy shell compartment. The American rounds began to cook off and the turret tore free from the main body, its 120mm tube spinning like a top. The Abrams engine shot out of the back like a squeezed bar of soap. Oh, this was impressive. This was pure joy to Sheng, better than porn.

"We are the conquerors," he told the main turret crew. "We are supreme, the lords of the battlefield."

The T-66 crew cheered.

Sheng allowed them the moment. Ten seconds later, he snapped an order. Tonight, they would smash Tenth Armor Division and open the way to LA.

***

Sergeant McGee's corpse was gone, devoured in the inferno that had destroyed his beloved M1A3. The battalion was dying and the hated enemy bloodied but advancing victoriously on Palm Springs.

PALM SPRINGS, CALIFORNIA

Captain Stan Higgins was wide-awake and on the move, directing his Behemoth down from the tank carrier.

It was 3:19 AM, cool and dark outside. Tenth Division was gone as an organized force, the vast majority of it was dead and littered on the white sands beyond Palm Springs. That meant wrecked Abrams, destroyed Bradleys and demolished Humvees, 155mm self-propelled artillery, Strykers and supply vehicles by the hundreds. Many of the hulks burned miles outside of Palm Springs. Close to eighteen thousand American soldiers were dead. Maybe seven hundred or so fled from the approaching T-66s. Less than a hundred still fought, firing a TOW here or a Javelin missile there. It meant the Chinese crept forward instead of racing into Palm Springs.

It helped that artillery fired from within the city. Several infantry battalions were also setting up in Palm Springs. There was a woeful lack of armor and very few Bradleys with their TOWs.

The last of the Apache gunships were dying, although they had managed to kill T-66s, about a dozen of them.

The Tank Army of the great Chinese right hook followed the conquering T-66s of the first wave.

Stan knew these things, and yet he calmly motioned the driver easy does it down the carrier's ramp.

Colonel Wilson marched up to him then. The man wore a red scarf around his neck, with the end whipping about at each step. In the wash of sodium streetlamps, he eyed Stan critically. "Your tank is down. Good. I want you to head out immediately. Captain Reece will go with you."

"Two tanks, sir?" Stan asked.

"We want to slow the Chinese down before they hit the city."

"This is our great moment, sir. I think—"

"Are you refusing orders, Captain?"

"No sir," Stan said. "I'm just thinking—"

"You leave the thinking to me," Wilson said. "I want you to obey orders for once."

"Yes sir," Stan said.

"Get out there and stop the forward advance. But don't go farther than our artillery shells can reach."

"Yes sir," Stan said. He hadn't intended to do that anyway.

Wilson eyed him critically, waiting. He finally asked, "Haven't you forgotten something, Captain?"

"No sir," Stan said, knowing what Wilson expected. "It isn't good practice to salute near the forward lines. The enemy likes to take out the officers. If I salute you, sir, I'm marking you for death."

Wilson blushed and nodded sharply. Without another word, he turned and strode away.

"The man's an ass," Jose muttered from behind Stan.

Stan shrugged. "He's our commanding officer, so we'll give him the respect he's due."

"Which is nothing, right?" Jose asked.

"Wrong," Stan said. "His commission and rank deserve respect. Now let's get going."

"Alone to face the enemy?" Jose asked.

225

"Didn't you hear? Captain Reece's Behemoth will be joining us. Now let's quit jawing. We have a job to do."

FIRST FRONT HEADQUARTERS, MEXICO

"I have reports, Marshal," General Pi said.

Nung blinked his eyes and lifted his chin off his chest. "What was that?" he asked groggily. Had he been sleeping?

"The American Tenth Division has been destroyed, sir. Our lead tankers have spotted Palm Springs. There are reports of new American formations setting up within city limits."

Nung nodded and smacked his lips before speaking. "I expected that. The Americans will have poured whatever they could find to block us. Now is the moment to shatter them just as we have destroyed the armored division. Afterward, we will drive onward to LA and greater glory."

"The attack is for China's greatness," Marshal Gang said in his deep voice.

Nung nodded, not for the first time hating the man's presence. "Here," Nung said, stabbing a finger on the computer map. "Here is the beginning of the march to American dismemberment. Once we are in LA, then we will turn our attack onto annihilating the trapped Army Group."

"Let the trapped troops wither on the vine," Gang suggested. "That is the wise move. As Sun Tzu has said, 'If the army does not have baggage and heavy equipment it will be lost; if it does not have provisions it will be lost; if it does not have stories it will be lost.' Therefore, the trapped Americans are now lost to their cause."

Nung scowled. Instead of answering with a sharp rebuttal or a Sun Tzu quote of his own, he let the statement go. The marshals who quoted the ancient sage on war didn't impress him. The Americans had said it better long ago: shock and awe. He had shocked the enemy, would continue to do so, and that awed them and made men's knees weak. That was the time to strike.

"Here," Nung said for the third time. "Here at Palm Springs is where the Americans will truly realize that we are invincible in battle and their cause doomed to ultimate failure."

PALM SPRINGS, CALIFORNIA

Stan sat in the commander's seat. For a three-hundred ton monster, there was surprisingly little space within the Behemoth.

So far, the engine worked and the treads stayed on the suspension system. They had been working hard these past days in Fresno, making sure all the little problems stayed away.

The Behemoth was something completely new. It was big because its engine was *massive*. The power plant had to be that way to feed the rail gun.

The Behemoth didn't use conventional gunpowder shells, although it had several .50 caliber machine guns and used the auto-cannons and beehive flechette launchers. It was a walking—rolling—supergun. There was nothing like it on Earth.

The rail gun was simple in a way. It had two magnetized rods lining the Behemoth's cannon. The projectile or "shell" completed the current between the two rods. The direction of the current expelled the round, firing the shell and breaking the current. The great difference was the incredible speed at which the electromagnetic cannon could eject the solid metal round.

Like the Abrams's sabot round it used kinetic energy, the same kind of energy that sent a bullet smashing through a man's body.

An M16 rifle fired a bullet at the muzzle velocity of 930 meters per second. The Behemoth's cannon fired its round at 3,500 m/s, over three times as fast. That was approximately Mach 10 at sea level.

The Behemoth's penetrator size and weight was much lower than an ordinary sabot round. It could therefore carry much more ammo onboard than otherwise. Nor did the crew need to worry about explosives in the tank. The greatest benefit was that at this velocity the rail-gun had much greater range, less bullet drop, faster time on target and less wind drift. In other words, it bypassed the physical limitations of conventional firearms. In fact, the rounds flew so fast, they ionized the air around them.

The Behemoth rail-gun theoretically fired farther, faster and with greater penetrating power than any comparable conventional gun. Its range was also much greater than the targeting precision, meaning it was easily possible to fire a Behemoth round over one hundred miles.

Stan blew out his cheeks and cracked his knuckles. The Behemoth clanked onto the desert sands, the treads rolling over a cactus so moisture squelched onto a nearby rock, wetting it. Captain Reece's tank followed behind them by fifty yards.

"How far are we going?" Jose asked.

"Eh, what's that?" Stan asked.

"How far are we going?"

"Several miles," Stan said.

No one talked after that. They listened to the steel monster rattle and clank. The Behemoth could theoretically perform marvels. Unfortunately, on the testing grounds the giant vehicles had broken down all the time.

Stan now pulled up a map and began studying the terrain. If he could find a level—

"Hello," Stan said.

Jose arched an eyebrow.

Stan got on the radio with Reece and they talked things over. Ten minutes later, the two giant tanks parked fifty yards apart.

There was a thin, last ditch screen of Americans ahead of them. Coming hard against these shreds of Tenth Division were the lead elements of two T-66 divisions.

"What else is there out here?" Reece asked over the radio.

"It's just us now," Stan said, "with artillery support once we call for it."

"I hope you know what you're doing, Higgins," Captain Reece said.

"I hope the Colonel knows what he's doing," Stan replied.

Captain Reece said nothing to that.

Stan studied the data on his screen. They had a high-flying drone in position. Ah, look at them, Chinese T-66 tanks plowing head-on. Using the computer to study the enemy, Stan counted one hundred and eleven tri-turreted tanks, seven miles out, a bit more than eleven thousand meters. They were just beginning to appear on the same horizontal plane as the two Behemoths and almost in effective range.

"I'd say we give them another eight hundred meters," Stan said, trying to sound more confident than he felt.

He knew it was important to get the maximum advantage out of a technological surprise as one could. The Germans had failed to do that during World War II with their newest Panther and Tiger tanks in 1943. Hitler had ordered the new tanks into combat before all their teething problems had been overcome. The Panthers and Tigers were supposed to be new wonder weapons, helping the Germans defeat the much more numerous Russian tanks. The new tanks had been thrown in too soon into the giant cauldron of the Battle of Kursk, the greatest tank battle of the war.

Are we throwing our Behemoths into the fray too soon?

If America lost California, but had time to perfect the Behemoth and enter battle for the first time with a hundred of them instead of twenty, or the two out here—

Stan shrugged. It didn't matter now. He was out here. On his screen, he watched the last Americans of the Tenth Division standing their ground in the desert and dying.

"Are you boys ready?" Stan asked his crew.

Jose, the gunner and the air/radio operator nodded or muttered a yes.

"Captain Reece," Stan said, "I suggest we open fire on the enemy."

"We should order some artillery down on them first," Reece said.

"Agreed," Stan said. He was feeling surreal. He was about to enter combat again. He hadn't fired in anger since Anchorage.

Can I do as well this time? Stan shook his head. He doubted he could, but he might halt the Chinese advance. He could buy the U.S. Army time to regroup and defend LA. It

229

might even save an entire Army Group, allowing them time to fight their way out of the trap.

Thirty seconds later, American artillery began to pound the enemy, who used onboard defensive armaments to shoot down the vast majority of artillery shells.

Stan checked the Behemoth's batteries. They were at full power. "Okay, rev up the engine."

The driver did just that.

"Target the nearest tank, Jose."

"Roger," Jose said, with his brow pressed against the high-powered thermal scanner.

The Behemoth had an auto-loader, which just dropped a round into position.

Stan's hands were clammy. They weren't in danger yet from the enemy. The T-66s had conventional ranges.

"Fire," Stan said.

The giant electromagnetic gun hummed with power. Then the current pumped the twin rods in the cannon. The round fired, and it exited with a hard surge that rocked the Behemoth. It was one of the reasons the tank needed its incredible weight. For every action, there was an equal reaction in the opposite direction.

Stan watched on the thermal screen. The round's flight time—it was incredibly short. Within two seconds, a T-66 lit up on the screen and exploded.

"Fire at will," Stan said. He felt as if his spirit stood outside of his body, watching him at work.

Stocky Jose proceeded to do just what he did best: target, laser-wash the enemy, wait for the chambered round and the crack of the shell going supersonic before it even exited the gun. The Behemoth rocked with violent force, expelling another of its incredibly hyper-fast rounds, reaching out around over ten thousand meters or six and a half miles.

Stan grinned at first, hit! A T-66 blew up. Seven seconds later, hit! On the thermal sights, a second T-66 lay on its side like a dead beast. Every seven seconds another hard surge sent a shell screaming across the desert, slamming into a Chinese tank.

It's working. The Behemoth is behaving, but for how long?

The smile slipped three minutes later. Stan kept a clicker, counting hits, counting kills. So far, Jose had destroyed twenty-three tri-turreted tanks, almost eight a minute. Reece probably had a similar count. Stan's smile slipped because a loud noise from the engine area made his gut clench.

"What's wrong?" Stan shouted.

"A generator," the driver said.

"Battery power is dropping," the radio operator said, who helped Jose right now.

Stan peered through the thermal scope. The Chinese were still coming. *Don't fail us now. God, help us.*

For the moment, he needn't have worried. Yet another hard surge rocked the Behemoth as a shell roared away. How long could they keep this up? Theoretically, a long time, but the desert tests had shown them not to expect that.

Even as Stan worried, shell after shell continued to drop into the chamber. The turret swiveled, the gun adjusted and the penetrator round reached supersonic speed as it raced at the oncoming Chinese.

COACHELLA VALLEY, CALIFORNIA

Soon after the giant enemy tanks opened fire, the order came down the Chinese line of command: Charge the enemy and destroy the technological marvels at close range.

First Lieutenant Sheng rode in his platoon's last T-66. The other two tanks were smoking hulks. Behind him thundered hundreds of tri-turreted tanks.

It was then Sheng learned the truth. The major told them over the company net. "It seems to be only two American tanks we're facing."

"Two?" Sheng said. That couldn't be right. Not two tanks. The way they fired, so fast, so accurately, each hit drilling though a T-66—these things were science fiction dreams.

"We will be in firing range soon," the major said. It was the last time Sheng heard from him, as the major's T-66 blew apart.

231

"Two American tanks are doing this?" Sheng asked aloud in wonder.

Sheng sat between his computer screens. Sweat soaked his back. How was this possible? Could the enemy have better weapons than China? No, that was impossible.

Three seconds later, his internal debated ended. An electromagnetically ejected penetrator round smashed into Sheng's tank. The velocity—white-hot BB-like sparks were the last things Sheng saw. One passed through his chest and First Lieutenant Sheng died. Immediately the T-66 generated an internal inferno and turrets popped off, spinning away onto the white sands.

**

Stan's Behemoth continued to malfunction, but in a more serious manner now. Sensors in the engine diagnosed trouble. It could begin a forced shutdown any second, stranding them out here.

"Not now," Stan said with a groan. "My engine is about to begin an involuntary shutdown," he said over the radio.

"Back up," Colonel Wilson said. "Get out of there. We're on our way with the rest of the regiment."

"Roger," Stan said. "Captain Reece should probably come with me."

"Negative," Wilson said.

"Sir—"

"I give the orders," Wilson said over the radio. "Now scoot."

Stan licked his lips. He had won his famed medal by—

"What are we doing, sir?" the driver asked.

Stan only gave it a moment's thought. An order was an order. "Okay," he said. "Let's move out." He immediately got on the radio with Captain Reece and told him the score. "I'm moving out," Stan told him. "Orders."

"Don't worry about us, Higgins."

Stan did worry. Why didn't the Colonel order Reece to come with him? Slowly, the Behemoth began to clank, retreating from the still sizable mob of enemy T-66s. It was the last time he spoke to Captain Reece and their crew.

232

Twenty T-66s made it within range, and they fired salvos of sabot rounds at Reece's Behemoth. The shells flew like angry wasps roaring with destruction. The defending beehive flechettes and auto-cannons took out most of the rounds. Most, but not all of them—with a terrific *clang* two penetrated the Behemoth from the side and blew the giant engine.

Stan's tank stopped by that time, the forced shutdown stranding them for the moment. The remaining T-66s started for him. They never reached that far, as the rest of the Behemoths had finally left Palm Springs and now closed with and destroyed the final enemy lunge at the city.

It ended the first battle for Palm Springs, leaving one dead Behemoth tank, two out due to technical difficulties other than engine trouble and three with engine trouble. In return, they had destroyed three hundred and fifty-nine T-66s and for the moment, at least, halted the right hook to Palm Springs and LA beyond.

-8-
The Cauldron

LA MESA, CALIFORNIA

Paul Kavanagh sat on a stuffed chair inside the lobby of a large hotel. For almost a week now, he'd been craving a Snickers bar. Ever since he and Romo had started back to the American lines, he'd been dreaming of the chewy insides.

Lying back on the chair, with his assault rifle propped beside him, Paul watched Romo stride nearer, Snickers bar in hand.

The Mexican assassin had gotten thinner and he looked out of place in the striped green uniform of an American Militia corporal. Paul also felt out of place wearing a similar uniform, although he had a sergeant's markings. But it made the Lieutenant happy, so what the heck, huh?

The Lieutenant had saved their lives…yeah, that was three days ago now—an eternity of fighting. Three days ago, Paul and Romo had been crawling nearer and nearer the battered American lines, slithering past rubble, endless drifting paper and strewn garbage. It sure hadn't been a line in the sand. The place had been many miles from the destroyed casements and smashed bunkers of the SoCal Border Fortifications they had crept past. It had been beyond the second and third trench lines. Dead and bloating bodies, with spilled intestines and thousands, no, *millions* of flies crawling over them—the dead had laid unburied in the maze of trench systems, American and Asian corpses alike. The flies had been clouds of greedy, buzzing testaments to the savage fighting.

Paul and Romo had been crawling through rubble, easing past watching Chinese gunners. They had slipped past a Chinese patrol in the streets of La Presa. Then one of the patrol members had spotted Romo. A buzz and a quick look upward had shown Paul a small UAV with Chinese markings. That had been just great, spotted by an enemy drone.

PAA bullets made the decision for them. Tired from days alone and from having walked endless miles after ditching the two stolen vehicles, they'd sprinted down the street for the American positions.

Machine gun fire coming from ahead of them struck the paving, chips of cement hitting Paul in the chest. Then, as suddenly as the firing had begun—the friendly machine guns aiming at their faces—it stopped.

Several seconds later, Paul discovered why. The Lieutenant had ordered his teenage machine gunners to stop firing. The man had recognized Paul and Romo as Americans.

The two kids behind the .50 caliber, they had watched Paul with wide, scared eyes. Paul had merely nodded to them. Then he'd jumped down right there beside them behind the sandbags. Paul had added his assault rifle fire against the Chinese patrol that led the probe against the shrinking American lines.

Paul and Romo had reached their destination, the one they had dreamed about for days, wondering if they would ever reach it. Since everything had been chaos three days ago, they'd donned the uniform of the Anaheim Militia Company that had saved them and joined the Lieutenant's woefully understrength platoon.

That had been three days and two cities ago of endless fighting.

"Catch," Romo said. He pitched the Snickers bar.

Paul caught it one-handed. The kids looked up from their card game around a low lobby table. They'd scooted big, overstuffed chairs up to it. From the corner of his eye, Paul noticed them watching.

There were four of them, what was left of the original Militia squad. They were painfully young, although two claimed to be juniors in college. The other two had worked in construction, meaning fortification workers, probably the grunts hauling material for the men who knew what they were doing. They were aged nineteen to twenty-one, kids really with old men's eyes now.

These four had looked into the face of death and it had aged them horribly. They tired fast during combat and recuperated even faster afterward. Paul had laid shoulder-to-shoulder with them on many occasions already. Whenever the Chinese artillery or missile poundings stopped, the wave attacks commenced.

Their Militia battalion had a third of its personnel left, maybe less. Not all of the missing were dead. At least half of the missing had taken off, either to surrender or go AWOL with the hordes of streaming refugees heading north. Paul and these four kids had seen what happened to those who tried to surrender to the enemy.

Americans with their hands on their heads had tried to approach enemy lines. Massed Chinese firepower had chopped them into bloody chunks of rat-meat.

"Hungry?" Paul asked, holding up the Snickers bar.

The four Militiamen turned away without answering, resuming their card game.

There was a gulf between Paul and them. It was mainly age—at least Paul liked to tell himself that. They were so young, pure even, with innocence leaking from them. They had illusions, so many illusions it had surprised Paul more than once. During one firefight, the machine gunner just quit firing.

"It's butchery," the kid had whispered.

Paul had let go of his assault rifle, shouldered the kid aside and taken over. He'd killed pinned down enemy soldiers. Even as the Chinese had broken and scrambled away, Paul kept firing. When he'd stopped, the kid had just stared at him with a terrified look.

Later, Romo told him what the stare had meant. "You are a killer, my brother."

"What?" Paul said.

"They are scared of you."

"That's crazy. We're on the same side."

"No, it is very sane," Romo said. The two of them had been outside the strongpoint, collecting Chinese weapons and ammo from the dead. Supplies had been drying up lately.

"We're all fighting the enemy," Paul said.

Romo smiled. It hadn't been a friendly thing, although the assassin had not aimed it at Paul in anger or disrespect.

"Do you know that ten percent of the fighter pilots make ninety percent of the kills?" Romo asked.

"Afraid I don't."

"Many soldiers do not fire their weapons during battle. Among the others who do fire, many of them aim anywhere than at the enemy. Most men do not like to kill other men. It is one of the reasons it takes many thousands of bullets to kill one enemy. It is also one of the reasons why artillery is the great killer in battle."

"Is that a fact?"

"Why are you angry?" Romo asked.

"No reason. Being called a killer, yeah, that's a real honor."

Romo's smile had become sad. "We are the wolves, amigo. We are the ten percent. The young ones, they realize this in you. It frightens them. They are brave. I do not mean to disrespect them. But they are not the natural warriors that you and I are."

"Maybe."

"Accept who you are, my brother. I have. It is you and me, and men like us, who will drive the invader back into the sea."

As Paul sat in the wrecked hotel, sitting in the stuffed chair, he used his teeth to tear open the bar's wrapper. He'd been craving this for days. Battle, being close to death, did that to you. Cravings would overcome him and he would just have to have whatever the thing was.

Paul bit into the bar and savored the gooey, caramel chocolate taste. Oh, this was wonderful, but it would go even better with an ice-cold glass of milk. But where was he going to find that in this sinkhole?

He wasn't a natural killer. That was a load of crap. He was just a soldier who wanted to see his wife and kid again. If a bunch of Chinese or other Asians was going to get in the way of that, well, he was going to kill them. They had killed enough of his countrymen that he figured he was entitled. Besides, they had invaded his home, his country. If someone entered his house with the intent to steal or rape, bam, he would drill them in the head. End of story.

Paul drew a deep breath through his nostrils and he realized that all he held was the wrapper. Shoot, he'd already finished the Snickers bar. He glanced sidelong at the kids. One of them *clicked* coins one on top of the other. If they hadn't been there, he would have licked the wrapper. But he couldn't do that if he was the big mojo killer.

From outside came a loud boom.

Paul grabbed his assault rifle and bolted upright. The kids dove for their weapons and Romo already ran for the holes in the hotel wall. Chinese IFVs had made similar noises this morning.

Romo crouched by a hole. Then he shouted back. "They brought tanks with them this time, two of them."

"Right," Paul said. He picked up a Chinese RPG. They had collected them this morning from the fallen enemy.

In seconds, Paul crouched by his own hole. An enemy IFV had made it close with its 30mm auto-cannons. The tracked carrier had held six infantrymen inside its "womb." The IFVs were nimble vehicles and heavily armed with four of those auto-cannons and two missile tubes. The Chinese liked to roar at their lines under heavy missile or artillery cover, pouring everything they had at the American positions. Then the back of the IFV would clang down and out would charge six armored Chinese infantry.

This time it was different. Two tanks clanked down the street. A host of antennae sprouted from each light tank. It told Paul these two were drones, remote-controlled vehicles. Each Marauder was smaller than an SUV and possessed a non-turreted 153mm gun.

"Hold your fire," Paul told the others. "Romo, grab an RPG and come with me."

"How long to you want us to wait?" asked the twenty-one year old Militia sergeant. He had pimples on his forehead and stood near the two with the .50 caliber.

"Give us a minute," Paul said. "Then fire at the tanks so the sensors know the vehicles are taking fire. Then scram, but be sure to take the machine gun with you. We're going to need it."

"Go where?"

"Deeper in the hotel," Paul said. "When you hear the explosions outside, you'd better come running fast. Set up the machine gun in a new position and get ready."

The pimple-faced sergeant nodded and rapped out orders to the other three.

Paul hefted two RPGs, one under each arm. Romo did the same thing. They trotted to the stairs and climbed, going to the third floor. Paul was panting by the time he approached a shattered window.

"They will have spotted these," Romo said.

"Yeah," Paul said. He set down one RPG and primed the other. Taking big gulps of air, he tried to steady himself. They would have to do this quickly: spot and fire.

Downstairs, the .50 caliber started up. Metallic hammering sounds told Paul the gunner was hitting one of the light tanks at least.

"Not too long," Paul said under his breath. As he finished speaking, the machine gun fire quit. These were good kids, the survivors of days of brutal, endless fighting. They had learned.

Paul glanced at Romo. The lean assassin stood poised beside his window. He was ready. He wanted to kill the enemy, even if it was only drone tanks.

The 153s boomed below, and the crash told Paul the shells had smashed into the hotel. Enemy machine gun fire started. He hoped the kids had retreated far enough.

Paul didn't say anything to Romo. The man knew what to do. Inside Paul's chest, the fear built, but so did the excitement. *One, two, three*, he told himself. At three, Paul stepped up to his window. The light tanks were below, perfect targets, showing him their lightly armored tops. Paul brought the RPG into line, using the iron sights, and he fired.

The backblast whooshed fire into the hotel room, starting a blaze on the rear wall. Romo fired his rocket launcher. Paul watched for a split second. His shaped-charge grenade slammed against the top of the Marauder, exploding. Paul felt the concussion, and he saw auto-cannons swiveling up at him. Romo's RPG round hammered the same vehicle and the auto-cannons froze.

"One down," Paul said. "Let's go." He picked up the remaining RPG from the rug and raced past flickering flames on the wall. This fire had bit into the wall and it looked like it might last. That was okay. Soon, the heat would hide them from enemy thermal sights. A blazing hotel, the Chinese would figure the Americans had evacuated it.

Paul grinned savagely thinking about it. Then he was on the stairs again. He climbed, his thighs burning as he raced for the roof. Outside, Chinese machine gun fire riddled something here, likely the windows they'd just used. The Chinese were so predictable you could have set your cell phone by them. Well, if he'd had a working cell phone.

With a heaving chest, Paul crashed against a door and strode onto the roof, heading for the edge. Romo was right behind him.

"Ready?" Paul wheezed.

"Go," Romo said.

They both stepped up to the edge of the roof. Six stories down, the light tank used its main cannon for what had to be the fourth time. Flame belched, the light tank shuddered and smoke billowed upward from the cannon. Machine gun fire from Chinese infantry nests hammered the hotel's windows. Soon, the IFVs would appear.

Paul aimed almost straight down and fired. The rocket-propelled grenade flew atop the tank, exploding. Once again, Romo did likewise. Both soldiers twisted and dove backward. Even as they did, armor-piercing bullets slammed against the roof, shattering brick and eating into the tar-covered top.

From on their chests, Paul and Romo grinned at each other.

"That will slow them down some," Paul said.

"Si."

"We'd better get back and help the kids."

240

"They are near their breaking point," Romo said. "Soon, we must leave them."

"Those four?" Paul asked, as he climbed to his feet.

"They are brave for such young men, but they are terrified and we are running out of ammo."

Paul cocked his head. Yeah, that was a problem. They needed more ammo. The Chinese, they just keep on coming, dying as they expended munitions at a prodigious rate and pushing the Americans into a smaller and smaller area.

"I'm not leaving the Lieutenant in the lurch," Paul said.

"Si, I understand. But he will break soon, too. It is inevitable."

"I don't agree."

Romo stared at him, and soon he shrugged. "Let us help the young ones."

"Yeah," Paul said, heading for the exit.

WASHINGTON, D.C.

In the subdued light, Anna Chen concentrated on her split-pea soup in order to avoid seeing the people staring at her. She was in Upscale, one of the most expensive restaurants in D.C. Across the red and white checkered cloth of the small table from her was Dr. Levin, Director of the CIA.

The old man forked more of his salad, popping an oily olive and some lettuce into his mouth. He smiled at her, nodding.

"Do you like the soup?" he asked.

"Oh yes, it's delicious, sir."

"Please, my dear, don't do that here. We're on a half-hour vacation, remember?"

She hunched her shoulders a little more, letting the spoon click against the bowl.

"I didn't mean that as a reprimand," he said.

"I know," she said, softly.

"What is it, my dear?"

She hesitated before leaning toward him. "The people, do you notice them staring at me."

241

Dr. Levin blinked in wonderment and glanced around. Several people looked down. One big Navy officer glared at him. The officer had a bloated face with red cheeks.

"Why do you suppose he's angry with me?" Levin asked her.

"Because you're with me," Anna said.

"Ah," he said, "because you're of Chinese descent?"

"Half of me is, yes."

Levin sighed, seemed as if he was going to say something profound and then he forked another bite of salad.

Anna thought she understood. Dr. Levin didn't share their feelings, although he understood. But what could he do about it here? The answer was clear. Nothing. Therefore, it was best to let the topic drop. A stubborn core in her didn't quite feel like letting it drop.

"Man is tribal," Anna pronounced.

"An unfortunate truth," Dr. Levin said.

Anna shrugged. "Perhaps it isn't as bad as we think."

"Would you elaborate, please?"

She smiled. She liked the Director. "Could you imagine if the entire planet lived under one political system?"

"Indeed. Most people yearn for just that."

"No sir, I'm afraid you're wrong."

He nodded as the waiter indicated the empty salad plate. The waiter took the plate.

"I'm done, too," Anna said.

The waiter took her bowl, balancing it on his arm and then pouring more coffee into the Director's cup.

After the waiter left, the Director said, "What I meant to say is that most political theorists wish for a one-world government."

"True, but I think it would be a catastrophe."

"Because of racism?" the Director asked.

"No sir, because it most certainly would eliminate the few precious freedoms certain people in various countries enjoy."

He added cream, stirred with a small silver spoon, laid the spoon aside and sipped his coffee. "Ah, this is perfect. It's why I come to Upscale. Now about this theory of yours…"

"It's simple, really. With many competing governments, there is always somewhere to flee if one system becomes too repressive. Power corrupts. A one-world government would place that much greater power into the hands of the person or the clique ruling it. There would be no competing system to oppose him or the clique."

"What about world peace? Isn't that something worth striving for?"

Anna shook her head. "It is an illusion, sir. Most militaries are used to kill their own people, to preserve those in power, and to repress those who are out of power. If there was a one-world government, I have no doubt those in power would use the military or the police to repress those they disliked. As I said earlier, man is tribal. If it isn't racism, it's competing ideas. For example, the abortionists and the pro-life people have divided into competing camps and cannot abide each other. Why do sports teams create such fierce loyalty? The reason is easy—men like to divide themselves by tribes. The Kansas City Chiefs fan hates the Oakland Raiders fan, who turns it around and hates the Chiefs fan right back."

"Hmm," Levin said. "I wish the Chinese used their military to kill their own people. That would be better them their coming to America to kill us."

"Believe me, they have killed their own in the past, and still do. But consider what China has done. The political theorists always seem to think that bigger governments or organizations are better. I disagree completely, by the way. Smaller countries are often better for the average citizen. China is now Greater China. That in turn has become the Pan Asian Alliance. But what if China was still divided into many small competing states? They would not have the unity to attack us as they're doing. Big countries field big armies. And eventually, those in power like to use their big armies to go conquering. Therefore, my belief is this: with greater unity there is a greater ability to harm."

"And to do good," Levin said. "America is big. If we weren't, the Chinese could sweep us aside."

"That's the problem. When one group gets big, the other side feels forced to do the same thing. In the end, it's seldom good for the regular people and their freedom."

Levin sipped his coffee. "I think I understand. You feel the racial hostility, the tribalism, as you like to put it. I suppose I would find such a situation embittering, too."

Anna shook her head. Couldn't he see what she was trying to say? "I'm a student of the human condition, sir. I try to study what is there, instead of what we would like to think is there. No one benefits from too much authority over others. Eventually, power works its insidious spell over the heart of the one who wields it."

"I hope you're not referring to the President," Levin said frostily.

Anna noticed his tone. Before she could correct him concerning her point, the waiter brought their meals. Dr. Levin had lobster. Anna had an eight-ounce piece of prime rib. The waiter set a small cup of horseradish beside her. Prime rib wasn't the same without it.

Levin bowed his head, praying silently before picking up his knife.

"I was speaking theoretically," Anna told him. "I support the President, but he is only human. I would not want him to possess unlimited power, no."

Levin nodded, popping a piece of lobster into his mouth. He closed his eyes as he chewed. After he swallowed, he said, "Please don't say such things to anyone else. I've come to appreciate your insights during the meetings. If you become too outspoken about the President having too much power, you'll find yourself in a Detention Center. And yes, I've begun noticing the stares directed toward you. If these people here are like this, I can only imagine what they'll be like in a Detention Center."

Thinking about that almost stole Anna's appetite. She so seldom ate out anymore that she refused to let this dampen her enjoyment. The Director's bodyguards waited in the lobby. At the snap of the old man's fingers, they would come running with guns drawn. With such protection, Anna had accepted his invitation to dine at Upscale. She never went out to eat alone these days, and she didn't trust the latest, commercial bodyguard services—not since what had happened the last time they had sent someone.

"Anna, the reason I've asked you to eat with me is that I have something I would like to share with you."

She looked up, startled and worried.

Levin glanced both ways before he said quietly, "I'm afraid the military has run out of ideas on how to save the situation in California."

His words surprised her.

"There's an invasion armada out there in the Pacific, waiting for something," Levin said. "The Chinese are annihilating Army Group SoCal and there doesn't seem to be anything General Alan can do about it."

"We are entraining reinforcements from other fronts," Anna said. "We've also shipped trainloads of munitions to LA to make sure they don't run out."

"It will all be too little, too late. General Alan knows that."

"Then why is he doing it?"

"If you're fighting a stronger person who is trying to kill you, does that mean you simply give up and let them do that?"

"I wouldn't think so," Anna said.

"There's your answer. That's what we're doing. We're fighting."

"The Behemoths have changed the equation," she said.

"Yes, for the moment that's true. But you've seen the data. Some of the enemy tanks that would have poured through to Palm Springs have now turned back on the eastern part of the embattled Army Group. I think whoever is making the decisions over there has decided to accelerate the destruction of our trapped soldiers. It's an inferno."

"I agreed with that," Anna said.

"Once the Army Group is gone, the Chinese will swamp the rest of the defenders in LA. There won't be enough reinforcements to save the state. We'll have lost, and that rather quickly, too."

"I suppose I do read the situation the same way, sir."

"Well that's just won't do!" Levin said, striking the table with a fist.

The dining area grew quiet. Anna could feel the stares even more than before.

Levin waited and took several more bites of lobster. He must not have prepared it well enough because Anna heard his teeth chewing and crushing shell. After people had stopped staring, Levin told her, "There's a way out of this impasse."

"Oh?"

Levin's eyes seemed to shine. "I'm going to suggest to the President that he use nuclear weapons to rebalance the situation."

A hollow feeling worked through Anna's chest.

"You don't agree with that?" Levin asked.

Anna didn't know what to say and barely managed to shake her head no.

"I see," Levin said. "Then you won't support me when the time comes?"

"Sir... Are you certain there's no other option? I mean, nuclear weapons will be a disaster. They may have helped us a little in Alaska, but we paid a terrible price using them."

"Give me another solution and I'll listen. The problem is that I don't see any other way to save the situation."

Anna bowed her head in thought. This was a challenge, wasn't it? Was there another way to save the situation? There had to be. Nuclear weapons might bring the end of the civilized world. It was a terrible risk. There had to be something she could do, some fact or other that would give them a chance. Who knew the Chinese better than she did? No one. Therefore, it was her responsibility to find the answer that might save the country.

She looked up at Levin. "Do you mean that, sir?"

"Eh?" he asked. He was cutting his lobster.

"Will you back me if I find you another way?"

Levin set down his fork and knife, leaning back, studying her. "I said I will listen. What do you hope to find?"

"I don't know."

"The prospect of nuclear war terrifies you, I can see."

"Sir, I think it should terrify everyone."

"Hmm," he said. Picking up his fork and knife, he went back to cutting his meal. As he forked a succulent piece of lobster, he eyed Anna again. "A nuclear explosive is just a bigger weapon."

"That's one way of looking at it, sir. Another might be as a civilization ending event."

"You think that one nuclear weapon will lead to another?"

"Yes I do. I also believe that radiation poisoning is a terrible way for the world to die."

Levin gave her a chilling smile. Who was this little old man?

"Then find another way, my dear, because I don't plan on letting anyone defeat my country. I'd rather destroy it than let Jian Hong's hordes have his way with it. I'd rather annihilate his armies with nuclear fire than surrender. We cannot let the Pan Asian Alliance smash through California with such ease. It will be the beginning of the end if that happens and I will not stand by and watch that occur. I'm certain I can convince the President of that."

Anna's appetite left for good. She would have to ask for a doggy bag, even though she had no dogs, but a Persian cat. *What can I possibly do that the Chairman of the Joint Chiefs of Staff cannot or the President of the United States?* She didn't know, but she did realize that she was going to work her thoughts overtime to finding an answer.

EL CAJON, CALIFORNIA

Captain Wei of East Lightning had a fixed smile on his face as he slid an enclosed helmet over his head. Today, they were going to try something new, something special for these infuriating American holdouts.

The attack had been going on for days. This was the twelfth or thirteenth wave assault. That meant…eight or nine days ago since command had launched the Blue Swan missiles. Eight, yes, it had been eight days ago and they were digging out these American holdouts.

Eight days, or a lifetime if one considered how many cowardly offenders he had gunned down. At first, he had found it difficult. And the fear in him standing at the rear of the battle-line so American soldiers could actually sight him with their sniper rifles—he had kept himself drugged ever since.

His battle-suit was the latest in combat technology. Certain White Tiger squads had them and East Lighting commissioners in the penal battalions.

He wore powered armor from head to toe. It was not science fiction armor. He had seen several Japanese movies about those. There, a soldier could jump fifty meters or run like a bullet train. He could do nothing so amazing, although what he did was spectacular enough.

The suit was mostly body armor, but of such weight that electric motors helped the wearer move. It was mostly heavy dinylon mesh with a carbide-ceramic corselet. With the helmet's CBR filter, it protected him from chemical or biological attacks. The visor in the helmet had a HUD and targeting crosshairs. He had several computers integrated into the suit, connecting him to the HQ net and various video feeds. He had two weapons. The first was an integral 5.56mm machine gun. All he had to do was turn his head and paint the crosshairs on a target and the ballistic computer did the rest, firing from his shoulder. Sound-suppressor plugs in his ears saved his hearing. He also had an electromagnetic grenade launcher. It, too, had a ballistic computer, adjusting for range, height and wind speed. He could lob the grenade over a hiding spot, raining death on whatever coward had thought to sit out the battle.

The powered armor was amazing, prohibitively expensive, and ran off the latest batteries. That was the suit's greatest drawback. The batteries supplied power for six hours. Then they needed recharging. With charged batteries and full magazines, however, he was a walking tank. Unfortunately, he lacked normal mobility and if his sensors failed, he became deaf to the world. It was the perfect thing for a political commissioner watching his penal soldiers from the back, ready to destroy those who lacked the zeal to continue attacking.

How the White Tiger specialists used their powered armor, Wei didn't know or care. In his company, three East Lighting commissioners had died, either slain by Americans or enraged political offenders who had turned their weapons on their betters. That had sobered the rest of them. At first, the East Light commissioners had feared their charges. Later, after shrugging off bullets and grenade fragments, Wei and several others had felt invincible. Watching a RPG penetrate the armor of a fellow commissioner had cured them of that battlefield malady. Still, they had learned how to motivate the penal soldiers to courageous acts of madness.

Now command had sent them a fresh batch of penal personnel. Some of these offenders already had combat experience. Wei had spoken with his lieutenants and first ranks. Some of the new men might be more dangerous than those they had *processed* so far.

Last night in an abandoned 7-11, Wei had received his inspiration.

"Why are we so eager to destroy Chinese citizens?" he asked the others.

They had remained silent, watching him carefully. The words he spoke, they were nearly heretical and therefore dangerous.

Wei had reached into a pocket and removed a blue pill. He had blue pills, red ones and yellow triangles that gave him fantastic hallucinations. Those he saved for his "let-down" times after battle, after killing too many of his offenders. Incredibly, shooting them outright had been much different than killing them on the torture table. Watching men crumple from his 5.56mm bullets, he had felt like a god inflicting such divine justice. It was an awesome sensation, but later gave him the shakes and a hollow feeling in his chest. At those times, to drive the emptiness away, that is when he'd popped the yellow triangles.

"Let us do as the Mongols once did," Wei had told the others last night.

"Do you mean Genghis Khan?" a thin lieutenant asked.

"Yes, yes," Wei said. "Genghis Khan was the greatest soldier in history. He was invincible in battle. Remember your studies, gentlemen."

The lieutenants, and the first ranks milling behind them, continued to look at him in wary silence.

"We are consuming soldiers at too fast a rate," Wei said. "That is what HQ has told us. Yet they also order us to clear minefields at once, or to storm a strongpoint and take it despite what casualties we might suffer. Excuses don't matter. Am I right?"

Two of the lieutenants nodded. The taller of them squeezed a cigarette between his fingers, the tip glowing red as smoke curled.

"Yes," Wei said. "I am right. Therefore, we have a contradiction. Win through at all costs but save personnel while you do so. The wave attacks have been succeeding, but at a terrible cost. Now I ask you, are we not the Chinese?"

"Yes," a lieutenant said.

"Yes," Wei said. "We learned at the hands of the greatest conqueror in history. Genghis Khan had his handful of Mongol warriors against China's millions. He could not afford to spend his men like water against Chinese cities. What did he do? None of you knows, eh?"

Wei had eyed them, these hardened butchers, and he had seen their curiosity. This was amazing, as several of them had been as drugged as he was.

"The plan was simple," Wei said. "The great Khan ordered his soldiers to gather Chinese peasants and captured city dwellers. These his soldiers drove with whips before them toward the besieged city walls. Enemy archers had a terrible choice, expended needed arrows to kill their fellow citizens or let the enemy get to the walls unscathed."

Wei had smiled at them, a smile that had shown all his teeth. He had been genuinely happy with his thought.

"Tomorrow," Wei told them, "we will gather a horde of Americans hiding in the ruins. Women and children, it doesn't matter to me. Warm bodies are all that counts. Then we will drive them at the American strongpoints, letting our penal soldiers mingle among them. If the American soldiers fire, they will kill their own and possibly save some of ours."

"What if the people try to run away?"

"We kill them," Wei said. "We mow them down."

The others looked at him. Then they looked at each other. Finally, those highest on drugs had grinned back at Wei.

Now morning was here and HQ had given him the order. They were supposed to wave-assault the American strongpoint that was holding the outskirts of El Cajon. The enemy had been adjusting, apparently trying to reshuffle their formations to gain strength to attack the northern-most Chinese. In other words, Army Group SoCal was trying to make a breakout in order to link-up with LA.

Inside his special body armor, Captain Wei grinned. His skin tingled and he felt good. He was pumped up. The men of his penal company had gathered nearly two hundred American civilians. With bayonets, they prodded the protesting mass up the street and toward the enemy strongpoint.

Last night, American artillery had laid quick-mines. Oh yes, the Americans were ready for a wave assault. But he doubted that they were ready for this.

"I am the son of Genghis Khan," Wei told himself. "I am the conqueror."

With his armor purring with battery power, Wei lurched out of the 7-11. He loved the clank of his footsteps. This was so different from the torture table. This was glorious.

Within the enclosed helmet, Wei frowned. The old way in Mexico City seemed like a world ago now. Yes, it had been much more peaceful, and safe. Now he was out on the battlefield. He shuddered. He remembered Maria Valdez and her hated curse. But there was no God and therefore no curse. Wei could do as he wanted on this Earth and no one would ever judge him for it. It was good to know that. Yes, very good, otherwise he might not have been able to devise such a clever tactic as the one he was about to spring on the defenders.

FIRST FRONT HEADQUARTERS, MEXICO

"Sir, can you hear me?"

Groggily, Marshal Nung opened burning, bloodshot eyes. For a moment, he didn't know where he was. Then he recognized his aide bending over him. Yes, he was in bed. The days of endless decisions and worry had wearied him. His body wasn't what it used to be. The doctor had finally convinced him that instead of stimulants and constant attention, what he needed was plenty of sleep. Then he could make wise decisions. The aide looking over him, Nung finally realized the man was worried.

"Is there trouble?" Nung whispered.

"Uh...Chairman Hong wishes to speak to you, sir."

"Help me up," Nung said.

The aide was a large man and easily pulled him to a sitting position. The wheelchair was at the foot of the bed. Nung had begun to hate the thing.

"Help me to my feet," Nung said.

The aide licked his lips.

"Do as I command," Nung said, for the first time speaking in his normal tone.

The aide gripped an elbow and helped Nung stand. A moment of disorientation followed. Then Nung felt better than he had since the "incident" with the tranks and amphetamines. With faltering steps, he stepped into the lavatory, turned on the facet and washed his hands and then his face. Oh, that felt good. Drying his hands, he returned into the bedroom. Maybe the doctor had known what he was talking about.

"Help me into my uniform," Nung said.

Ten minutes later, the aide wheeled Nung into the communication room. With a boiled egg in his stomach and a bowl of rice, Nung felt ready to tackle the Leader. As he ate, he listened to a situational report. The main forces continued to squeeze the SoCal Army Group as the Fifth Army coordinated with the Hover Command for another thrust up Interstate 5.

Nung rose up out of the wheelchair and had the aide put it out of visual range of the computer screen. Then he sat in a chair and activated the link. He spoke to the Leader's secretary and waited. Hopefully, this wouldn't take too long.

Three minutes later, Jian Hong appeared on the screen. The Leader's hair was jet black from the best hair dye. His face was wider than it used to be, evidence that the man had gained weight.

"I will make this brief," the Leader said.

Nung bowed his head. The Leader's tone troubled him.

"Marshal Kao has informed me of the situation," the Leader said. "The sudden and now complete blockage of the Palm Springs-Los Angeles route is a disturbing occurrence."

Kao! Nung thought. It seemed the old soldier on the Ruling Committee was always trying to torpedo him.

"It is accurate to say that the Americans surprised us," Nung said. "They have developed an amazing tank and potentially one that could do us great harm. Fortunately, they are few in number. We know this is true because otherwise they would have gone over to the attack. Notice, the Americans are content to hold the Palm Springs pass. Therefore, in truth, the few superlative tanks do not change the balance of military power or the precarious American position."

"Marshal Kao predicted you would say such things. He says you cannot see anything but for headlong assaults. Marshal Gang has concurred with this analysis."

Within his chest, Nung burned at these insults and he felt his blood pressure rising. Why did such small-minded men always try to interfere with his greatness? They feared, perhaps, to risk everything for glory and ultimate, spellbinding victory.

"With all due respect, Leader, the two marshals are old men who have the lost the spirit of the warrior. It pains me to say this, but they quail like the enfeebled worriers they are at the idea of taking a risk to win large."

"There is a risk?" the Leader asked.

"In war, one must always accept risks."

"Do you seek to teach me, Marshal Nung?"

"I do not, Leader. I am the servant of the State, the State you lead with consummate skill."

"Hmm. I find the latest reports disturbing. We have taken heavy causalities and expended massive amounts of munitions. Already, the Navy has rushed more supplies to Mexico. This rate of expenditure cannot continue indefinitely."

The battle has just begun, and already the Leader's nerves are shaky. I must proceed with caution.

"Sir," said Nung, "we have smashed the heaviest fortification on Earth and driven the Americans back in reeling disarray. We have surrounded the main Californian Army

253

Group and cut them off from their supply base, in this instance, Los Angeles. It is true we have accepted heavy causalities to achieve this. Yet we have far more troops than they do. Our factories churn out far more munitions."

"Marshal Kao suggests we use maneuver to defeat the Americans instead of attrition."

"Yes, these things are easy to say, Leader. Yet Marshal Kao does not know how to do such a thing. I do know, sir. I am outmaneuvering the Americans."

The Leader frowned, looking confused. "You admit to great losses and yet claim to be using clever maneuvers. Yet our boldest maneuver ended in a bloody defeat."

"I'm sure that is how Marshal Kao put it," Nung said. "The situation is actually quite different, sir."

"Your confidence is intriguing. I wish you to enlighten me, Marshal."

"The situation is this, Leader. We have stretched the Americans in California, doing so in a little more than a week. We are about to devour their main Army Group. The reason we are doing this is our relentless assault. It is costly now in men and munitions. Soon, we will reap our reward, obliterating the Army Group and then snatching California. Marshal Kao should be congratulating me for bringing the fight to the brink of annihilating victory, and this victory despite the unveiling of a truly impressive enemy weapon system."

"It amazes me how two marshals of China can see this in such a different light."

"I suspect that Marshal Kao sees that I am in the process of shattering two of my armies. I have hurled them at the enemy and in urban areas. Many would consider that rash. What they cannot see is that I will annihilate the Americans and still have armies to rush into the rest of the state, snatching Oregon and Washington and setting up our defenses in the Sierra Nevada Mountains. That will allow us to proceed with the next step in conquering a continent."

"What if the American Army Group breaks out of your trap?" the Leader asked.

"They will not break out. I am constantly attacking, lunging, grinding, refusing to give them time to regroup and escape."

The Leader tapped a computer stylus on the table. Then he lifted it and bumped the end against one of his teeth. "There are reports of new reinforcements from the rest of the U.S."

"Paltry sums, I believe. In any case, our amphibious assault in two days will change the equation even more in my favor."

"China's favor," the Leader said.

"That is what I meant, sir. My victory is China's victory."

"Hmm. Yes, I'm beginning to appreciate your overall theory. It is much different from what Marshal Kao tells me. You will continue with your relentless assaults. Shock and awe the Americans, Marshal. Grind their bones to dust so we may ready our other fronts for the truly great Battle for America."

"As you command, Leader," Nung said, his voice ringing. "We will grind their bones to dust."

EL CAJON, CALIFORNIA

"I don't know, Lieutenant. We ought to retreat from this spot."

Paul Kavanagh glanced at the frightened man behind the .50 caliber machine gun. The forty-something man was a new levy, fresh from a training camp that had given him two days instructions.

There were fifty militiamen and soldiers hiding behind what had once been a Wells Fargo bank, a retail outlet and a Baskin Robbins ice cream shop. The buildings were piles of rubble, dust, shattered boards and rotting flesh. Rats had begun to appear everywhere, wild-eyed feral cats and flies, always the flies.

The Anaheim Militia Company was now composed of people from all over Southern California. Two of them were from El Cajon, their latest stop in the endless retreat from the border.

"Division told us to hold," the Lieutenant told the man, the new Militia private. "So we're holding the line until they tell us otherwise."

The division had become an ad hoc grouping with a Militia battalion, a regular Infantry battalion, a company of mortars and a missile platoon, meaning three missile-carriers. It wasn't much to hold the line. But it had finally begun, the careful withdrawal of select units in order to build a reserve in the shrinking area of Army Group SoCal.

Paul figured the reserve was meant to hurl against the Chinese in order to drive to LA. They had to break out soon or the Army Group was going to succumb to a lack of ammo and supplies.

"We're exposed here, Lieutenant," the forty-something Militia private whined.

The Lieutenant stared at the man. The young Lieutenant had aged since La Mesa. He'd lost the four young kids of the platoon Paul and Romo had joined. They had died fighting, holding their post.

The forty-something squirmed uncomfortably. Yet he still managed to say, "We have to preserve ourselves so we have soldiers to keep the Chinese at bay."

"The Lieutenant still doesn't understand," Romo whispered. "But I will show him." The Mexican assassin rose from where he couched beside Paul. They had their own .50 caliber to serve and several RPGs, the last ones.

Romo sauntered beside the Lieutenant. "Can I speak to him, sir?"

The Lieutenant eyed Romo, finally nodding.

Romo crouched beside the wary, forty-something private. He began whispering, going so far as to pull out a knife and show it to the private. The older man paled, and he would no longer look in Romo's eyes.

"Si?" Romo asked him.

The forty-something private nodded quickly.

Romo rose, touched his helmet in respect to the Lieutenant and then sauntered back beside Paul.

"What did you tell him?" Paul asked.

"If he runs during combat I will feed him his balls."

"You showed him the knife you're going to do it with?"

"It always helps to show them the knife."

"I'm sure it does," Paul said. "Oh-oh, you hear that."

"Incoming!" Romo shouted.

"Everyone down!" the Lieutenant shouted. "And don't get up until you hear my whistle."

Paul crawled into a narrow slit trench. Seconds later, shells went screaming in and blew up rubble, dust, men and weapons. Concussions washed over Paul. Debris flew everywhere. The enemy pounded their position and likely all along the line and the mortar and artillery sites. No doubt drones buzzed up there, helping the enemy sight them.

Screwing his eyes shut, Paul endured. He hated artillery. It was so impersonal. It was just stupid fate and luck. Someday, his luck would run out, just as it had for Maria Valdez. Colonel Valdez should never have sent his daughter along.

Then an arty shell landed too close. The blast hurled Paul against the side of his trench. Hot shrapnel flew over him. He began shivering uncontrollably. *Cheri, Cheri, Cheri, I love you, babe. Can you ever forgive me, my love?*

"God!" he screamed, although he couldn't hear a word. "Let me live! Let me be with my wife again! God! Are you listening?"

Another shell came down. The explosion hurled Paul against the other side of his slit trench. He wore armor, a mesh vest. He wore a helmet, tough pants and heavy-duty boots. It would be like wet toilet paper if a piece of shrapnel caught him.

Suddenly, the artillery barrage ended.

Paul knew what it meant. The Chinese did these things like machines. Their attack procedure never varied. The trouble with him was that he just wanted to lie there. The peace of no shells coming in…he couldn't take any more of this. He didn't want to face yet another Chinese wave assault. He wanted—

Gritting his teeth, Paul rose to his knees. He was the first up. With ringing ears and moisture in his eyes, he crawled to the .50 caliber and set it back up. It had survived, although there were dings in it. He put it on the tripod mount and manhandled it to a position behind a smoking piece of rubble.

"Lieutenant!" Paul shouted. "The artillery prep is over. They're going to be coming soon."

Romo appeared beside him. The lean face looked more hollowed-out than ever and dirt smeared the assassin's face. The eyes lacked their normal wolfishness. The artillery shelling had shaken Romo. Who wouldn't be shaken by that?

A whistle blew. A turn of his head showed Paul the Lieutenant was up. The officer began kicking prone and shaking soldiers. The Lieutenant bent down, yanked a kid up and screamed in his face.

"Mother Mary," Romo whispered.

Something about the way Romo spoke made the hairs on the back of Paul's neck rise up. He didn't want to look, but he did. What he saw...

"No," Paul whispered. "They can't do that."

Except these Chinese were doing it. Soldiers herded civilians, American women and children straight at them. The enemy poked bayonets at the civilians. One of the soldiers drove his bayonet into a young woman, between her shoulder blades so the point jutted out of her chest. Her scream was paralyzing. Paul had never seen something like this, such gruesome barbarity.

"They're going to stumble over the minefield," the Lieutenant said.

Paul could feel the officer's hand on his right shoulder as the Lieutenant crouched behind him.

"This is murder," Paul heard himself say.

Romo cursed in Spanish. He turned to Paul, and there was fire in his eyes. "We cannot let them approach."

Paul felt the heart go out of him. "What are you suggesting?"

"Start firing, amigo. We must stop the Chinese."

"We can't fire on women and children," the Lieutenant said.

Paul found himself agreeing internally.

"Let's get out of here," the forty-something private said.

Romo cursed again. Using his elbows for propulsion, he slithered across shale, one of the dislodged stones tumbling into a shell-hole. Romo reached a forward observer. He

258

grabbed the man's speaker and shouted into it. After he was done, Romo slithered back to them behind the low wall of rubble.

"What did you report?" the dazed Lieutenant asked.

Seconds later, the answer came in a hail of mortar rounds.

"No," Paul said, staring at Romo.

The Mexican assassin stared hard at the wall of rubble. He seemed to be in another world right then.

The mortar rounds howled down, and soon the sounds of the wounded, dying and screaming civilians drove Paul to madness.

He went to the .50 caliber, to the butterfly button triggers. He aimed at the dinylon-armored Chinese and he fired at the enemy. He also hit American civilians, putting many out of their misery. All along the line, other Americans opened up. The Chinese climbed to their feet and they kept coming. Far behind them watched robots or at least they looked like robots.

"Battle suits," Paul said. He aimed his machine gun at them, but after a single burst, they moved out of his line of sight.

The other Chinese refused to break, firing assault rifles and grenade launchers in a suicidal frenzy. One by one, the defending Americans hiding in the rubble died, killed by bomb, lobbed grenade and bullet. In return, the few survivors reaped a dreadful harvest of Chinese penal soldiers.

Then all at once, even though they had worked far forward, the remaining wave assaulters threw themselves flat.

"Incoming!" Paul screamed in a raw throat. He fell flat, too, and a missile barrage thundered upon them. He felt himself lift and slam back against the ground. It left him limp, and then he lay still as one dead.

Soon, he heard the march of enemy feet. He heard Chinese curses and then he heard them crunching over rubble and climbing into their positions. Some Americans farther away took potshots at the enemy.

Harsh Chinese commands boomed nearby. It must have come from the battle-suited soldiers, the officers, likely.

Paul lay still like one dead. A Chinese soldier kicked him in the helmet, but Paul never flinched. He waited. He couldn't do anything more now. He waited as the soldiers moved past. Like a beast, a deadly wolf playing a last trick, he bided his time.

Then some instinct rose in Paul. He grabbed his assault rifle and lifted up to one knee. Enemy soldiers had their backs to him. Without hesitation, Paul opened up, cutting down the wave assaulters. Beside him, Romo did the same thing, together with the Lieutenant and a handful of others. Paul lobbed grenades and shot the enemy.

"We're doing it. We're—" Those were the Lieutenant's last words. He crumpled, torn apart by machine gun fire.

Time seemed to slow down for Paul Kavanagh. He whirled around. One of the battle-suited soldiers was less than fifty feet away. The man's armament was crazy. The machine gun was perched on the armored shoulder. The muzzle blast made the Chinese killer take a step back, and that produced a whine of motorized power.

It's powered armor. Paul didn't have any more time to think. He acted. He picked up his last RPG and didn't even bother with the iron sights. He did this the natural way by feel, and he pulled the trigger. The backblast felt good. The shaped-charge grenade did its trick. It blasted the powered-armored soldier and tore him apart.

***

Captain Wei of East Lightning flew backward, blasted off his feet by the crazy American with the RPG. His chest was wet and the world spun out of control.

Is this you, Maria Valdez? Is this your curse?

Then Captain Wei died, his soul headed to the next world, there to learn one of the most terrible truths of existence.

***

In El Cajon, among the littered dead, Paul Kavanagh and Romo crawled through gory rubble. Enemy machine gun fire from the surviving battle-suits sought to end their lives. Like hardened rats, like junkyard dogs, the two soldiers fled from superior armaments and firepower. The Chinese had broken through here, killing everyone in the Anaheim Militia Company except for these two interlopers, two killers who were turning out to be harder to butcher than an old governmental tax.

-9-
Amphibious Assault

Old Admiral Niu Ling commanded the invasion fleet from the supercarrier *Sung*.

The ship was massive, displacing one hundred and eight thousand tons. It was seven years older since the last time it had been in battle during the Alaskan War. The supercarrier had missed the Battle of Oahu in the Hawaiian Islands where the Chinese had annihilated the last American flattops. Instead, the super-ship had been near the coast of Australia with the waiting Chinese invasion fleet.

During the Alaskan War, *Sung* held ninety modern fighters, bombers, tankers and electronic warfare planes. This time, it held one hundred and sixty smaller UCAVs, giving it nearly double the punch it had seven years ago. There were five other supercarriers in the invasion fleet, giving China six altogether and a heavy influx of air power. Each floating airfield had its escort of cruisers, destroyers, supply-ships, submarines, helicopter-tenders and other necessary vessels.

Admiral Ling was old and he was still missing his left arm, as he'd rejected a prosthetic replacement. He'd lost the arm many years ago in a flight accident while he had attempted to land his plane on a carrier. The left side of his face was frozen flesh, although he had a new eye that gleamed with hideous life. Ling had found that the eye intimidated people more than his rank or age did.

He presently stood in the ship's command center, watching via screens as his UCAVs swept the San Francisco coastal regions, particularly the shores along Monterey Bay. The last time he'd led an invasion fleet against American territory, the enemy had launched Anti-Ship Ballistic Missiles (ASBMs) against his vessels. It had been a terrifying experience. This time, his fleet was better protected against such an attack. He wondered if the Americans realized this. Perhaps it was the reason why they had not yet launched a mass missile-assault against him.

The greater protection was due to new, laser-armed cruisers. Destroyers still used the SM-4 missiles and the fleet possessed COIL drones with chemical lasers that could shoot down incoming ballistic missiles. The cruisers were the latest in ASBM protection, their lasers heavier than the tactical variety used by the Army. These were midway in size and power between the strategic lasers for continental defense and the mobile lasers beaming targets on the battlefields of Southern California.

Even so, Ling's stomach churned with worry. He was far too old for this, but the Leader had insisted he command the assault. Now Ling had to risk his reputation one more time. Maybe if he had been younger, he would have liked the idea of a rematch against the Americans. All he could think about now was what a failure would mean for his son and grandson.

Yet how could he fail? The American Fleet of old was a dinosaur of the history books, its brittle bones littering the bottom of the oceans. From its glory days of invincible power, the vaunted American Fleet had become little more than a handful of fast attack boats like the Iranians used to use, and the still potent but far too few submarines. Yes, the Americans had air power, and they could surely gather it here in overwhelming strength and drive him away. But those airplanes and drones fought in Southern California in a life-or-death match or they waited in Texas and Florida for the great hammer to fall.

Ling smiled bleakly as he watched the screens. Chinese UCAVs blasted runways and destroyed radar installations. He watched a missile enter a large shack through the window and explode. The radar disk rotated wildly in the air before landing and shattering into pieces. The UCAVs shot down the few enemy drones that came up to challenge Chinese air superiority. Even better, they hunted for mobile military hardware to destroy and concentrated on American SAM and laser sites.

"The enemy appears to be defenseless before us, sir."

Ling didn't bother glancing at the Commodore who stood beside him. It was a younger, newer man, not his old friend who had been with him in Alaska. This man was far more political and lacked wisdom.

Still, Commodore Wu spoke truth. They had caught the Americans with their pants down around their ankles. Hmm, perhaps it was even worse than that for the enemy.

"Do you think this is a trap, sir?"

"No," Ling said.

"But why are they conceding—"

Short Commodore Wu failed to finish his thought as Ling turned his gaze upon the man. It was the left eye, of course. It gleamed with a metallic color. Worse, it moved like a twitching eyeball. It was a video recorder. In his quarters at night, Ling often downloaded the video and watched what had occurred around him during the day. It meant, in effect, that he had a photographic memory. It also seemed to terrorize his underlings as if he was a superior being, or as if perhaps he was a demon.

The knowledge gave Ling cold comfort. At least it stopped the otherwise endless chatter from these younger officers. Far too many of them had gained rank through political connections and knew how to scurry for favor. Too few of them had a warrior's instincts. Too few cared to risk an independent comment. Instead, they sought to figure out how he felt about a situation and then parrot it back to him.

"Where are their lasers?" Ling asked.

"Shipped south to the cauldron," Wu suggested.

"Or waiting until our amphibious boats, hovers and helicopters race for shore," Ling said.

"A grim possibility," Wu agreed.

Admiral Ling watched the UCAVs. His carriers were far too close to shore, but they had to be in order to give full air support to the landing. This was the most dangerous operation of war: landing on an enemy shore. So much could go wrong, and if it went wrong, it could go badly wrong. If that happened, there could be staggering losses to report to Chairman Jian Hong.

"It is time," Admiral Ling said.

"Sir?"

"Send the signal. It is time to unleash our amphibious assault against the Americans."

WASHINGTON, D.C.

Anna Chen entered the hushed command chamber together with Director Levin. They sat down at their places. Anna noticed that people avoiding looking at each other today. This was the great crisis, greater even than the encirclement of the SoCal Fortifications. The soldiers in SoCal fought an unequal battle, but they fought with courageous zeal and inflicted heavy damage on the enemy. On the Northern Californian coast it was different, turning into a full-scale rout and disaster.

The door opened and a powerful Marine entered the chamber. He said in a deep voice, "The President of the United States."

Chairs scraped back and everyone stood. President Sims strode in, with General Alan following. Sims had red eyes and he slumped his shoulders, as if the burden had become physically too much. He stared straight ahead, moving to his chair.

The Marine advanced and pulled the chair out for the President.

Sims sagged into his seat and slowly lifted his head. During most of the meetings, he had tight facial features. Today, his face looked doughy.

265

This is grinding him down, Anna realized. *The responsibility is devouring his strength.*

General Alan moved to his seat, conferring in a whisper with his aide, the major. Soon, the general looked up and said, "Sir?"

"Report," Sims said in a quiet voice.

The voice calmed Anna. It held power and it told her the President was far from giving up.

General Alan motioned to his aide. She turned on the holo-vid and began to speak in her professional style:

"The Chinese have made a massive amphibious assault into Monterey Bay. It's still unknown the exact number of naval infantry they landed. We mined those waters heavily, but the Chinese cleared paths through them at unprecedented rates. They did lose ships. If you will notice…"

She pointed at the holo-vid in the center of the conference table.

Anna watched absorbed. A squat-looking vessel moved through the water. Suddenly, a geyser of water blew thirty feet high beside it.

"One of our mines struck and destroyed a mine-sweeping ship," the major said. "The trouble is that the Chinese seem to have decided on an aggressive new policy."

"Meaning what?" Director Levin asked.

"Meaning that what we've seen in Southern California is holding true here, too. The Chinese seem to be accepting heavier casualties in the interest of speed. In Monterey Bay, they rushed minesweepers into the selected areas. That's interesting for several reasons. First, until quite recently, the Chinese possessed few minesweeping vessels. Now they have deployed them in great number and engaged them aggressively. We have reports, too, of many enemy underwater demolition teams. They saturated our shores with them to blow beach defenses and to climb onto land to patrol. Our people, particularly the local Militia companies, have inflicted losses on those demolition teams. That brought immediate air attack against the Militiamen."

Anna watched as two Chinese UCAVs flashed onto the holo-vid. Silvery containers tumbled from their underbellies.

266

The containers exploded onto American troops. The militiamen burned up in a holocaust of napalm. It was awful.

The President scowled and that tightened his skin.

"I'm afraid it gets worse," the major said. "From our studies, it appears the Chinese have learned effective amphibious assault doctrine. Their naval infantry hit the shores and their helicopters raced farther inland to block the major arteries against us. That is, blocking us from sending quick reinforcements against their beachheads.

"Now it's true that we've kept our remaining Northern California troops concentrated in the Bay Area. Unfortunately, terrain, Chinese air superiority and aggressive, inland assaults have blocked our soldiers from retaliating. That has allowed the enemy to grab the urban sites from Monterey to Santa Cruz, everywhere along the edge of Monterey Bay."

"I understand all this," the President said impatiently. "They're building up behind the local mountains and will likely launch an assault against the Bay Area soon. It will give the Chinese priceless ports."

"I'm afraid they've already taken port Santa Cruz. We were unable to demolish enough of the port's infrastructure as we had hoped."

The President stared at the major. She looked down. Slowly, the President turned his gaze onto General Alan. "Explain this to me."

The Chairman of the Joint Chiefs cleared his throat. "Sir, it was a simple matter of miscommunication. The speed of combat caught the local commander flat-footed."

"The Chinese have taken Santa Cruz intact?" the President asked.

"Unfortunately, sir, the speed of the Chinese amphibious assault caught the commander in Santa Cruz flat-footed."

"Don't repeat yourself," Sims said. "I want facts and I want them straight."

General Alan blushed and anger flashed across his thin face. "Yes, sir. This occurred because of a lethal combination of helicopter assaults and jetpack Eagle Teams in unprecedented numbers. Also, Chinese expenditure of cruise missiles and yet more commandos made it impossible to rush

267

troops from the Bay Area to the affected coast. Frankly, I believe we're seeing the entirety of the Chinese naval infantry. We've managed to slip a few drones out to sea and have spotted an enormous convoy of troopships approaching Santa Cruz. At least, we believe that's their destination."

"Continue," Sims said. "Tell me the worst of it."

"Sir, if those troopships unload their cargos of naval infantry and armor at Santa Cruz, they will swamp us if they can break out into the Bay Area. We entrained the bulk of the northern forces down south to stave off defeat in Palm Springs and LA."

"We must use our submarines," Sims said. "They have to sink the troopships. And our soldiers in the Bay Area need to contain the Chinese. The mountainous terrain between Santa Cruz and the Bay Area must become a death trap for the enemy."

"In theory that's an excellent idea, sir," General Alan said. "But the truth is that we need more troops. Without a fresh influx of soldiers, it will simply be a matter of time until the Chinese grind through into San Francisco and San Jose. The great danger then is that they will head inland into Central California."

"Yes, agreed," the President said.

"How many reinforcements are we talking about?" the Army Chief asked. He took off his hat and ran thick fingers through his hair, scratching the back of his head. "I have to tell you, the Germans are building up fast in Cuba. By my estimates, they're ready to go now. We don't want to strip ourselves bare from Georgia to Louisiana just so the Germans can do to us there what the Chinese are doing here. And I don't have to tell you about the South American Federation. They appear ready to mount a massive armor assault into Texas. They daily add to their tank formations along the border."

"Clearly," General Alan said, "the aggressors are trying to stretch us thin everywhere."

"They're not only *trying*," Sims said, "they're succeeding."

Silence descended on the chamber as the weight of the President's words settled.

Anna looked down as she rubbed her shoes together. They'd known the Chinese had an armada waiting out there. This went back to the Blue Swan missiles. Enough of them had hit and worked to turn the SoCal Fortifications porous. The engineers who had designed and built the defenses had boasted how they would hold back the world. That had been the great hope, and it had proven futile. For several years now, Sims had used the draft and he had created the Militia battalions. America had millions of soldiers under arms, but it still wasn't enough.

Anna noticed Levin then. The CIA Director sat right beside her. He drew squiggles on a piece of paper. With a lifting of his chin, Dr. Levin set down the pencil and cleared his throat.

"I have a suggestion," he said into the quiet chamber.

Sims stared at Levin. "Not yet," the President whispered. "I don't want to hear it yet."

"Better sooner than later, Mr. President," Levin said. "Let's nip this invasion in the bud and get on with the business of defeating the Chinese in Southern California."

With a touch of horror like a cold hand on her neck, Anna realized Levin meant the U.S. use of nuclear weapons.

"Not yet," the President repeated, his voice firming. "I want you to work out a troop transfer," he told General Alan. "We must send NorCal Command reinforcements. Then communicate to the Bay Area Commander that he is to bottle the Chinese in Santa Cruz."

"There are masses of refugees clogging all routes," Alan said. "They're making military movements difficult."

Sims shook his head. "I don't want the details on this now. I want the Chinese contained on the Monterey Bay coast."

"Sir," Levin said. "I respectfully would like to point out the need to stamp this invasion flat instead of merely *containing* it. Otherwise, it has the potential of becoming another front that we simply cannot afford to face. Don't we need every soldier we can spare in Southern California? You must free the trapped Army Group and you must free it now."

"He has a point, Mr. President," the Army Chief said. "If there was ever a time to use the nuclear option, this is it. An amphibious assault takes time for its commander to shake out

269

the troops and get them into place. The Chinese are using speed to throw us back to give them that time, and they have succeeded. If they're using Santa Cruz as the funnel point to land the bulk of their force, that is a perfect opportunity for us to smash tens of thousands of enemy soldiers and ships at one blow and free ourselves from a front we cannot afford."

Sims rubbed his face. "I don't understand this. We've put hundreds of thousands—millions—of new people in uniform. How can the Chinese swamp us so easily in these opening moves of the war?"

"It's plain to see how it happened, sir," Alan said. "The Chinese—or the PAA to be more exact—have hit us in a single and rather small locale. At least, this is true in continental terms. California needed more troops to hold against what appears to be one third of the PAA's power. We believed the extensive border fortifications would allow us to use fewer troops there than we otherwise would have deployed. Frankly sir, the reinforcements you wish to send to NorCal, we need them along the Texas, New Mexico and Arizona borders. Otherwise, we risk having more SoCal situations."

"And we need those troops in Georgia, Florida and Louisiana," the Army Chief added.

Sims sat up as he put his hands on the table. "We have to use the Behemoth tanks south of LA."

General Alan and the Army Chief exchanged glances.

He's diverting, Anna told herself. *The President doesn't want to make the great decision yet. Therefore, he's turning to matters he can truly control. I wish there was some way I could help shoulder his burden.*

"The, ah, Behemoths are a handful of tanks, sir," Alan said.

"Yes," Sims said, "they're the handful that stopped the Chinese outside of Palm Springs. Now I need them to perform another miracle."

"They achieved the miracle because of the range of their amazing cannons and the enemy was canalized," Alan said. "In the desert, they could use that advantage to its full scope. South of LA and the other urban areas, I'm afraid, will nullify their extreme range. They'll have to fight toe to toe, as it were. And we've already seen what that means. Once the T-66s got in range and were able to make side shots, they destroyed several Behemoths. The desert and prairies are the experimental tanks' natural habitat. Anywhere else and we risk their destruction. We only have about fifteen of them left in working or operational capacity."

"I understand your objections," Sims said. "But we don't have anything else that can smash through Chinese formations like they can. I need the Behemoths to spearhead our attack to free our trapped Army Group."

General Alan was slow in answering.

"That is an order," Sims said.

"Yes, sir," Alan said.

"What about Santa Cruz?" Levin asked.

"No!" the President said, turning on the small CIA Director. "I'm not ready for your grand solution. This is a soldier's war, not one for an atomic nightmare. Do you understand what nuclear war means? By the terms of the Non-Nuclear Use Treaty I signed in 2036, we scraped most of our remaining nuclear weapons. I also made a solemn vow never to use them first. We have far fewer now than our combined enemies. And we saw what happened in the Alaska War when we used them."

"Most of the world turned against us then," Levin said. "I understand that, sir. Maybe it was a mistake to use them then. Now, we don't have any choice. The world is breaking in and we have to stop them."

"Not the world, Director," Sims said. "The PAA has attacked us. So far, the South American Federation and the Germen Dominion have refrained. I don't want to use nuclear weapons and push them over the edge against us."

"But that's not the point here, sir," Levin said.

"I understand the point very well," Sims said. "If I unleash nuclear weapons, it may cause the Chinese to use nuclear weapons. They have many more of them than we do."

"It's a simple matter to make more," Levin said.

"No!" Sims said. "I am not about to unleash nuclear warfare and possibly end the world as we know it."

Levin frowned, and he glanced at General Alan. The Chairman of the Joint Chiefs minutely shook his head.

Anna noticed and she wondered what the interplay meant. It surprised her so few troops were in the Bay Area. They had rushed too many of them south, clearly. Yet if they hadn't…Southern California might already have fallen. On all accounts, they had to break out Army Group SoCal. Could the Behemoths achieve this miracle?

"Continue your brief," the President told the major.

She nodded, glancing at her computer scroll and bringing up another holo-image.

HIGHWAY 17, NORTHERN CALIFORNIA

Martha Rios's arms ached and fear twisted her stomach. She trudged along Highway 17, part of a mass exodus of people from Santa Cruz and the surrounding towns toward the Bay Area. Her daughter and ten-year-old son walked beside her. Each of them carried blankets and bottled water.

They had been marching for two days already, having fled the advancing Chinese. As far as she could see up the nearest hill, people marched. Behind her it was the same thing, masses, throngs of Americans trudging on foot like any third world refugee. Nearby, a man pushed a wheelbarrow, with an old Airedale sitting in it, letting its tongue loll as it panted. In the past, this would have been a throng of cars. Today, it was a massive jam of bodies, of people.

From time to time, a jet or helicopter flew overhead. Some of the people around her had binoculars. They looked up each time and reported a red star on each craft. Those were Chinese jets and helicopters.

"What if they start strafing us?" a man asked her.

"What?" Martha said.

"Shooting at us," the man said.

"They won't do that."

The man looked up as something loud, screaming and intensely brief passed over them. A vast groan lifted from the masses of people.

"What was that?" Martha's son Saul shouted.

"Shells," the man said.

"Are they firing at us?" Martha said.

The man craned his neck. The loud sound occurred again, and once more screaming shells made brief appearances overhead. "Look, those shells are headed west," he said. "It's American artillery."

"Who are they shooting at?" Martha asked. She shifted the groceries in her arms, held by brown paper bags. She needed a backpack. Many people here had those. She should have bought one a long time ago.

"I don't know where they're shooting exactly," the man said, "although logic would dictate it's somewhere directly behind us. The 'who they're firing at' is easy to answer: they're shooting at the Chinese."

Twenty minutes later appeared a more exact answer. Horrified screams occurred from the back of the horde. People there began to flee off-road and into the nearby woods.

"What's going on, mom?" Saul asked.

Martha shook her head and looked back. Thus, she saw Chinese Main Battle Tanks clank up the last hill behind them. Machine guns opened up and American civilians fell by the hundreds. Then loud shells screamed overhead, and this time, Martha saw their target: the same Chinese MBTs. None of the artillery appeared to hurt the enemy, as the Chinese tanks shot the shells out of the air.

"Mom, I'm scared," Saul said.

Martha blinked in horror, and she moaned along with thousands of other American refugees. The Chinese tanks roared down the hill, with their rattling, clanking treads. Some of the horde weren't fast enough to escape, and the tanks rolled over them, squashing people in an orgy of bloodshed.

Martha began screaming and she dropped her groceries and picked up her son. He was heavy, but she didn't care. She ran for the woods to escape the metal monsters that simply crushed people like so many ants. The Chinese were here and they were massacring everyone.

PRCN *SUNG*

Admiral Ling allowed himself a congratulatory smile. He sat in the command center, watching as the naval infantry's advanced armor crushed a mobile American artillery company along Highway 17.

Already, his carriers sped away from the American coast, no longer staying within forty kilometers of shore. It was time to get into the real ocean as naval doctrine directed. Many of *Sung's* UCAVs flew out of the Santa Cruz and surrounding airports. The amphibious assault had been a startling success. Marshal Nung had been correct in his pre-battle assessment. The Americans had stripped this area and likely sent the soldiers as reinforcements to the raging southern battlefields. Now, the Chinese Navy was on the verge of capturing the Bay Area. Once they secured the vast urban region, they would begin the critical drive into Central California.

The remaining troopships waited off Santa Cruz to unload tanks, artillery, mountains of supplies and yet more naval infantry. Soon, one hundred and fifty thousand troops would be ashore, conquering faster and farther than he had accomplished in South Central Alaska seven years ago. This was a great and glorious day. He was glad that he had accepted the assignment.

It was thirteen days already since the beginning of the grand assault into California and two days since the first Chinese naval infantry officer had set foot on American soil.

Ling reached into his uniform and extracted a thin flask from an inner pocket. He deftly unscrewed the cap with his fingers as he held onto the container. Then he sipped the contents, a trickle of *baijiu*. The white liquor burned against his throat going down. Oh, but that felt good.

"To the Chinese Navy," Admiral Ling declared.

Officers glanced at him, and for once, they grinned with delight in his presence.

"This has been a glorious day," Ling said.

Officers nodded. A few even nudged each other.

The Admiral took another sip and offered the flask to Commodore Wu. The short man accepted and sipped lightly, vainly trying not to screw up his face in distaste.

"We sank two Virginia-class submarines trying to penetrate our defenses," Ling said. "The Americans cannot spare many of those."

"No, Admiral."

"I, on the other hand, have not lost a troopship."

Commodore Wu nodded.

"Guarding those troopships cost us four destroyers and a cruiser," Ling said. "Our Blue Water Nay has taken a cut but it is more than ready for its next assignment."

Once more, Wu nodded.

"Perhaps I have allowed the Navy to lose too many mine-sweepers, but that came at the order of the Leader himself."

"Speed will neutralize the Americans," the Commodore quoted.

"For a land-fighting man, Marshal Nung is perhaps the greatest Chinese commander we have," Ling said.

Commodore Wu appeared surprised at this praise for a competing service.

"I salute him," Ling said. "Marshal Nung predicted that what is occurring would happen. At first, upon hearing his bold plan, I had my doubts. Now, I do not doubt. Our carriers are safe, the troopships have already begun deploying their masses and the advance armor bores into the American positions, meaning that soon the entire delta region will belong to us. Then California falls and the glory will accrue to the Navy where it has always belonged."

"Victory tastes sweet, sir."

Admiral Ling nodded, turning his head, taking in the officers and the command center screens. He would keep today's eye-recorded video for the rest of his life. The carriers were safe and the troopships were landing well ahead of schedule. The Americans had missed their chance of stopping the greatest Chinese amphibious assault in history. Now it was too late.

WASHINGTON, D.C.

275

It was a grave meeting in Underground Bunker Number Five. Anna listened as the major explained the disaster in minute detail. The critical element had been speed, gained by the Chinese by accepting tremendous losses in minesweepers. Most of the best formations of the Northern California Command were already deployed in SoCal. That meant there had been little to stop the Chinese once they reached the Monterey Bay shore. Small U.S. formations still plugged the gap between Santa Cruz and the Bay Area, but they wouldn't last long. Chinese reinforcements already poured in and they would reach the battlefield sooner than entrained forces from Texas would pass through the Rocky Mountains.

"Mr. President," Director Levin said, interrupting the major. "I would like to speak, sir."

Sims had been staring into space as the major spoke. He now blinked several times and swiveled his head. As he did, the President seemed to return to them instead of being lost in whatever haze he had escaped into these past few minutes.

"You said something?" Sims asked.

"Mr. President," Levin said, "I believe we have reached a critical impasse. The Chinese have gained Santa Cruz port, an unforeseen windfall for them. They have exploited it brilliantly and now threaten the entire state."

Levin turned to Anna.

She didn't want to support him in this, but he wasn't asking for her opinion, just what she had uncovered. "We believe Admiral Ling commands the invasion fleet," she said.

"Admiral Ling fought against me in Alaska," Sims said.

"Yes, sir," Anna answered.

The President scowled, causing deep lines to appear in his forehead. "I beat him in the end. Does he think this is a rematch?"

"Likely," Levin said. "It is my opinion that he begged for this chance to square off against you, sir."

Anna glanced at the CIA Director. She'd never told Levin that or even hinted at such a thing. In fact, it was probably the opposite. In her opinion, the Admiral was a reluctant warrior. Dare she speak up and say so, undercutting her boss? It would likely lose her this cherished post. Yet if she remained quiet, an even greater disaster might loom over them.

"Admiral Ling wanted to face me, did he?" Sims said.

"He wished for a rematch," Levin said. "He knows you're the President and now he wishes to get revenge."

Sims looked away. Soon he turned to Anna and asked, "Is that true: Ling wants a rematch?"

"I'm sure he knows who our Commander-in-Chief is," Anna said.

Before she could say more, Levin slapped the table. "There you have it, Mr. President. If that wasn't bad enough, old Admiral Ling has committed atrocities just as he did in Alaska. Victory at any costs has always been his motto. Can you imagine what will happen once he breaks into a major metropolitan area like San Francisco? Sir, we must use whatever means necessary to stop the Chinese."

"We're doing everything we can," Sims said.

Director Levin turned to the Chairman of the Joint Chiefs.

"Well, Mr. President," General Alan said, "we haven't done *everything* we can, not yet."

The transformation to the President amazed Anna. His eyes hardened and his shoulders straightened. "What are you talking about?"

General Alan hesitated.

Levin spoke up. "Mr. President, we have a spy deep in the Chinese military. What we're suggesting might well expose the spy. Yet for one operation, we can likely gain their IFF encryption key."

Anna tapped her scroll and typed "IFF." Ah, it meant, "Identify Friend or Foe." She speed-read the text. It was a command and control feature—an interrogation system—to identify aircraft, vehicles, soldiers and sometimes missiles as friendly. The system could not identify someone as hostile, just friendly if the IFF transponder returned a coded reply correctly once a beam had interrogated it. The military used IFF systems so they knew which vehicles, planes and sometimes missiles belonged to them and which they needed verbal or visual recognition. Ah, sometimes, friendly aircraft failed to respond correctly because of battle damage, equipment failure, loss of

277

the encryption keys or the wrong encryption keys. Terrain-hugging missiles and aircraft often had trouble responding to line-of-sight microwave IFF systems.

"What does any of that mean to us?" Sims asked.

"That if we're clever, sir," Levin said, "we can sneak several missiles among the Chinese."

"Ballistic missiles?" Sims asked.

"No, sir," Levin said, "cruise missiles."

The President drummed his fingers on the conference table. "I take it these are nuclear-tipped cruise missiles."

"Yes, sir."

"By the terms of the Non-Nuclear Use Treaty, we no longer deploy battlefield nuclear weapons," Sims said. "It would take time to ready nuclear-tipped cruise missiles and bring them near enough so they had a chance of landing among the enemy."

"I realize that, Mr. President," Levin said.

"Is this your plan?" Sims asked General Alan.

"Not altogether, sir," Alan said, "although I have approved of what the Director is suggesting."

"It sounds to me that there's more to your plan," Sims said, "something you haven't told me yet."

The CIA Director and the Chairman of the Joint Chiefs traded glances.

"The spy is my doing," Levin said. "There is also a specially constructed submersible belonging to the US Navy. The commander of the submersible is a deep-dweller and he has sat out the battle, inching closer to the Chinese these past two days. He possesses three cruise missiles, sir, each of them with a nuclear warhead. It is a suicide mission, of that there is no doubt. The submersible is fragile, constructed out of carbon fiber."

"Meaning it's practically invisible to enemy sonar," General Alan said.

"The drug cartels used to use earlier models to smuggle their product into the U.S.," Levin explained. "Ours is a far more advanced model."

"Keep talking," the President said.

278

"There's little more to say, sir," Levin said. "The captain brings his submersible near the surface as we launch a heavy, land-based missile assault against the Chinese position. As we've seen in Southern California, they will counter-fire. Some of their missiles will surely be launched from ships offshore dedicated to that task. We know that's Chinese naval doctrine. As the Chinese counter-fire, our captain targets his cruise missiles. Because of the spy, those cruise missiles will carry the latest Chinese IFF encryption key. That means the Chinese will leave the missiles alone. If a few officers wonder about them, they'll think of the missiles as more counter-fire. Once the cruise missiles strike—"

"What do you envision as their target?" Sims asked.

"Clearly, Mr. President," Levin said, "the target should be Santa Cruz port and the waiting troopships. Almost the entire Chinese naval infantry allotment is out there for the taking, but it will need a nuclear attack to destroy them."

"Target an American city?" the President asked coldly.

"This is war, sir. Sometimes, there are no good solutions but only those that will work."

"No!" Sims said. "It is diabolical and I refuse to listen to any more of this."

"Begging your pardon, Mr. President," Alan said, "I don't believe we have any other choice. Believe me, if we fail to halt the Chinese, they will continue advancing and will end up destroying far more American cities than we're planning to now. We're trading one city at this time to save hundreds of others later."

"And what will the Chinese do in response to our nuclear attack?" Sims asked. "Ms. Chen, what do you think?"

Anna could feel the hostile gazes drilling her. What could she say? If she agreed, she might be helping to start nuclear annihilation. If she disagreed, they would say she didn't want to see Chinese soldiers die.

"Maybe we could target the Chinese carriers," she said, temporizing.

"We don't know where those are," General Alan said frostily. "And the Chinese are much more alert to any attacks

279

committed against their precious carriers than against anything else."

It was time to speak her mind. "Sir," Anna said, "I loathe the idea of using nuclear weapons. I am utterly opposed to the idea. It might be the end of everything if we go nuclear in so blatant a fashion."

"We will be striking one of our own cities," Levin said. "How can the Chinese fault us for that? They have already helped terrorists use a nuclear weapon on us. They are in no position to act as our moral superiors."

"We must hit the Chinese now, sir," General Alan said. "If we pass this opportunity by, it could be the end of California. We might have to write off Army Group SoCal."

Sims shook his head. "We cannot afford its loss."

"Then we have no option in Santa Cruz," Alan said.

"Our reinforcements—"

"Likely won't make it fast enough, sir," Alan said. "I'm sorry, but I truly believe this is the only option. We should be thankful we have it. Now we must exploit it while the opportunity exists."

Sims turned away. Once more, he shook his head. "I... I don't know what to do. I gave my solemn word on this."

"Let us do it, sir," Levin said.

Sims stared at the white-haired CIA Director.

Anna's heart went out to the President. It was such a terrible burden. If they failed here, would it be the end of everything a few years down the line?

"Do it," Sims whispered. "Launch your secret plan. We cannot let the Chinese pour troops through the delta region."

USS *MERRIMAC*

Captain John Winthrop sat straight in his command chair. It hurt the small of his back to do it. Ever since receiving his orders, his back muscles had begun to cramp. But he'd be damned if he would slouch.

He had a crew of three, each of them a technician helping to keep the little carbon fiber sub intact. For the past three weeks, the small submarine had waited on the bottom of the ocean. For the past two days, it had crept toward Monterey Bay. Now it was in position and the latest buoy sent to the surface had relayed the message.

Captain Winthrop stared at the panels and screens without seeing them. He had volunteered for this assignment, so had each of his three crewmembers.

They had three cruise missiles, old Tomahawk cruise missiles ready in the launch tubes. The old United States Navy was gone, but not the old spirit of attack.

"Six minutes and counting, Captain."

Winthrop acknowledged the words by a simple nod. Soon, now, *Merrimac* would surface and fire its cargo. If they were lucky, they would submerge again into a watery oblivion and crawl away on the ocean floor. He dearly hoped they could do that. He didn't want to die.

I'm not going to die. We're going to do this and slip away. You think you Chinese bastards can blow up Livermore and get away with it. Never!

Captain Winthrop's father had died in the terrorist attack of 2037 on Silicon Valley in California. Ever since that day, Winthrop had burned for revenge against the Chinese. He wanted them to taste their own medicine. If he had to die to do his part, to stand on the ramparts as the Chinese tried to take down America—*then let's get started.*

"Three minutes and counting, Captain."

Is it three minutes until the end of my life? Would it be three minutes and a little extra until he saw his dad again? *I hope you're proud of me, Dad.*

"Two minutes and counting, Captain."

"Do you have to do that?" Warrant Officer Stevens asked.

Captain Winthrop stood up and took a step to Stevens, putting a hand on the man's shoulder and patting it several times.

Stevens looked up at him. The warrant officer was nervous, with a sheen of perspiration on his face. "I'm okay, sir."

"America rose up to greatness because enough people loved their country to die for her," Winthrop said. "I love America and I'm going to fight to keep her ours."

281

"Aye, aye, Captain," Stevens whispered. If anything, he looked more scared, not less.

"We're doing it, mister. We're doing our duty."

"Thirty seconds and counting, Captain."

For a moment, Captain Winthrop's eyes blurred. They cleared almost right away. He moved back to his chair and sat down.

"Ten seconds and counting, Captain."

"You're good sailors, gentlemen. It has been a thorough pleasure serving with you."

"Three…two…one…"

"Bring us topside, Ensign," Captain Winthrop said.

The USS *Merrimac* shuddered as it expelled water from the ballast tanks. Almost immediately, the carbon fiber submersible shot for the surface. Once they reached their destination, the old Tomahawks would fly.

SANTA CRUZ, CALIFORNIA

It was dark, although lights shined in Santa Cruz. Big Chinese troopships unloaded day and night. Some naval infantry rested in vacated homes, others already marched for the front. A mountain of supplies had gathered on the port's quays and docks. Trucks ground their gears as they started the journey for hungry soldiers at the front.

Many of the troopships still brimmed with personnel, awaiting their opportunity to dock.

In the midst of this activity, an alert finally reached the port commander. The Americans were attacking with missiles, long-range artillery, everything they could use.

Three minutes later, the lights began to go out in Santa Cruz. Even before that, counter-missiles sought out the American launch sites. Missiles also lofted from Chinese cruisers, while farther out at sea, the carriers' UCAVs catapulted into the air.

Meanwhile, two Tomahawk cruise missiles closed in on Santa Cruz and the Chinese ships offshore.

The Tomahawk was an old-style cruise missile, first introduced in 1970. Since then it had undergone many modifications. It was a medium-to-long-range, low-altitude missile, subsonic and jet powered. With a booster, it weighed 3500 pounds and was twenty feet, six inches long. Instead of the conventional 1000-pound munitions, each of these carried a W80 nuclear device.

Only two Tomahawks roared over the water. The third cruise missile had gone off course and plunged into the water. So far, the third, off-course missile had not exploded.

The two Tomahawks automatically provided the Chinese IFF signals. The other American missiles had NOT used the code. The thought was it would make the nuclear weapons a greater surprise and possibility they could do this without the Chinese ever knowing they had used the IFF code. In that way, they might be able to do it again. This time, the encryption key worked. The Tomahawks roared over the water, using data from multiple sensors.

Ten seconds left, and the Tomahawks bored in toward the city. At five seconds, the cruise missiles changed the direction of their flight and began to gain altitude. For the full impact of their nuclear cargo, the missiles needed height. As the troopships waited, as the last city light winked out, the Tomahawks reached target destination for a perfect airburst.

The first one ignited its W80 warhead over the port. An immense flash occurred and blast winds. Intense thermal radiation followed. The other W80 warhead created a sun-like flare of brilliance farther back and at precisely the same instant.

The twin attacks vaporized the nearest troopships and killed the naval infantry in them. They were the lucky ones who died right away instead of lingering for days with radiation poisoning. Other troopships farther away began to sink from blast and atmospheric shock damage.

Closer to Santa Cruz, a nuclear warhead tore apart docks and created an instant firestorm, devouring mountains of supplies. Next, buildings were flattened as if a mountain-sized giant had stepped on them, and greater fires started.

Most of the Chinese naval infantry resting in the city died immediately. The few who survived would wish they hadn't in the next few hours and days.

The attack reaped a dreadful harvest of Pan Asian Alliance soldiers and it changed the course of the Battle for California.

HIGHWAY 17, CALIFORNIA

Martha woke up as her son Saul screamed in horror. "Mama, mama, I can't see! I can't see! I'm blind!"

He had been awake because he had been too hungry to sleep. He'd looked at the nuclear explosion that lit the night from Santa Cruz. The intense light had been too much for his young orbs and he was blinded for life.

Among the refugees, many screamed similar words. Others saw the fireball rising into the night sky. It created a stampede of refugees, bringing even more horror.

USS *MERRIMAC*

For the next several hours after the annihilation of Santa Cruz, Chinese helicopters from the supercarrier *Sung* dropped depth charges, beginning at the cruise missiles' launch position.

Captain John Winthrop used the bottom of the sea to crawl away. The *Merrimac* shuddered, the lights flickered on and off and endless shocks made the men hunch and pray. Maybe it was a miracle. Maybe the Captain was lucky or maybe the carbon fiber boat was just too damn hard to spot. In the end, the fragile submersible escaped Chinese vengeance to fight another day.

-10-
Breakout

TEMECULA, CALIFORNIA

Stan sat at a flimsy card table with his crew, beside their Behemoth tank. A huge anti-radar camouflage net flapped gently overhead to hide it from Chinese surveillance. Several sparrows rode out the motion as if they were swimmers at sea.

Stan drank a Budweiser with Jose. Nearby, a small dog barked at them from behind a white-picket fence. An old lady stood on the porch of the house, staring at the three-hundred ton monster. MPs had vetted her earlier. Her husband had fought in Iraq decades ago. She was a loyal American and had brought the tankers milk, cookies and Budweisers.

Jose was thinner now, with hollow-looking eyes. He guzzled his Budweiser with a loud sigh before wiping his lips with the back of his hand.

Before this, the Behemoth Regiment had guarded Palm Springs for almost a week. When Jose wasn't in the tank on patrol, he was working in it, helping to keep the Behemoth running. Then movement orders had come day two days ago, a day before the nuclear attack on Santa Cruz. It had been hectic after that, with the Behemoths loaded onto the massive carriers and brought to Temecula under the greatest secrecy. A regular tank division now held the pass at Palm Springs, with heavy Militia and artillery support.

"Oh-oh," Jose said.

"What's wrong?" Stan hated to hear those words.

Jose pointed with the long neck of his beer bottle. "Here comes the Colonel. I wonder what we did wrong this time."

Stan craned his neck, twisting around. Sure enough, Colonel Wilson headed straight for them with his long stride. The man's uniform was perfect as always. Dust, sand, grime, oil, it didn't matter. He was immaculate. Stan and Wilson had been staying out of each other's way. Stan preferred it that way, but he knew it couldn't last.

Putting the lip of the bottle to his mouth, Stan took a long swallow. He was dog-tired. They all were. Too much rested on their giant tanks. For once, America had the superior equipment. The trouble was there were only a handful of Behemoths to go around. Truthfully, they needed about two or three hundred, not the meager fifteen.

"Here we go," Stan whispered. He put the bottle on the card table and stood up.

"Don't take any of his crap," Jose said.

Stan shook his head. "We're all on the same side. Despite what we feel, you and I need to show him respect."

"Why? He never shows us respect."

"Look around you, my friend. The why is very easy to answer. We're America's last hope and we have to stand together."

"Why don't you tell him that?"

"Maybe I will," Stan said. He waited, and he turned to face the Colonel.

Wilson walked up briskly, and said, "I need to talk to you."

"Would you like to sit down, sir? Jose, are there any more beers?"

Wilson shook his head. "No. I don't drink."

Stan kept a grimace off his face. He should have known.

"I'd like to speak with you alone, Captain."

"Yes, sir."

Wilson stood there for a moment. It seemed he didn't know what to do. He glanced at the little barking dog behind the picket fence. He shook his head and then pointed down the opposite street.

"That way, if you please," the Colonel said.

Stan frowned. This wasn't like the man. Usually, he just rapped out what he wanted to say and left, or he sent Stan on his way. What was this about?

Stan followed Wilson. They walked in silence, passing an odd mixture of perfect homes and others shredded from Chinese bombs. Suddenly, the Colonel spun around and he glared at Stan.

"We've had our differences," Wilson blurted.

"Yes, sir, I'd say that's true."

"Damnit, soldier, I don't want—" Wilson cut himself off and glared at the street.

Stan raised an eyebrow.

Wilson looked back up. "I've spoken with General Larson. We're going to lead the assault all the way down to Escondido if we have to."

"We, sir?"

"The Behemoth tanks, man. Surely, you must know what I'm talking about."

Stan shook his head.

Wilson glared at him, and he seemed to become angrier the longer he looked at Stan. At last, in seeming exasperation, the Colonel threw his hands into the air.

"I can't do it," Wilson said.

"What is that, sir?"

"You're making this too difficult for me."

"Colonel, I have no idea what you're talking about."

Wilson blew out his cheeks, turned around, took three steps away and then spun back to face Stan. "You're a Medal of Honor recipient."

"Yes?"

"You've faced the Chinese before and you've beaten them."

"Well, that's not exactly what happened, sir. What I did—"

"You outsmarted them."

"I suppose that's one way to look at it."

"Captain, what General Larson is demanding—no, this doesn't originate with him. It's from much higher up the chain of command. In any case, using our Behemoths to lead the assault down to Escondido is the wrong way to use our tanks. They're good at long-ranged combat. The force cannons, it's their specialty picking off the enemy before they're anywhere near the range of their weapons."

"I agree with you."

"Now we're supposed to lead the charge into rugged terrain, to try to break through to our trapped Army Group." Wilson shook his head. "It's suicide for us and I don't know what to do."

"Meaning what exactly, sir? I'm not sure I follow you."

"You're a bastard, Captain Higgins. I'm trying to apologize to you, damnit."

Stan blinked in wonderment. "Apologize to me, sir?"

"Isn't that what I just said?"

"Yes, you did, sir." *I never expected this.*

"You're the combat expert among us. There's never been any doubt about that."

"Ah…you're a wizard on the technical aspect of the tanks, sir."

"That's not what we're talking about here. Captain, the Chinese are beating us. Look at what happened up north in Santa Cruz. We used nukes in an attempt to balance the situation. We actually annihilated one of our own cities. It's unimaginable."

"The Chinese used electromagnetic pulse missiles on us, sir. I'd say we're striking them back tit-for-tat."

Wilson shook his head. "None of that matters to us here. I need a tactical solution that will save our tanks and give the chain of command what it's asking from us. I don't like you, Captain. But I can't worry about that anymore. The Chinese have invaded our country. I don't always get the choice of who stands beside me. Well, you stood against them before and beat them. I would be a fool to waste that asset in my command. I want your battle cunning, Higgins. More than that, your country needs your brilliance and insight once more. Will you help me?"

Stan turned away. "I don't know that I have anything particularly brilliant to add, sir."

"Then you'd better start thinking. You'd better give me a tactical solution to using our Behemoths in rugged terrain and in an urban environment. We have a day to prepare. Time is running out. Army Group SoCal is dying on the vine. They no longer have the power to dig out of their encirclement."

"You're right, sir."

"Use the historical acumen stored in that undisciplined brain of yours. Give me something to work with."

Stan faced the Colonel. "I'll try my best, sir."

"No, Captain Higgins. I don't care anything about *trying*. I want success."

Stan nodded. He could live by that philosophy.

"Do we understand one another?" Wilson asked.

"We do, sir, and thank you."

Wilson nodded the barest fraction. "That will be all, Captain. Carry on."

Stan turned around and headed back for the Behemoth, his mind awhirl with ideas.

SAN YSIDRO, CALIFORNIA

Marshal Nung buttoned his uniform. He had new brass buttons, bigger than normal. It took a good shove with his thumb to force them through the cloth slots. This was the best he'd felt since the unfortunate mixture of tranks and amphetamines.

He stood before a mirror, studying his features. He didn't like the splotches on his face, as they told their own story. A man like Kao would have probably used makeup to hide the discolorations, but he wasn't Kao. He would face life with his warts and all, and he would conquer by superior willpower and aggressiveness. An army was only as good as its commander. It was an old lesson of war. His army was winning, although a tally sheet of casualties might not show it right now.

There was a knock on the door and an aide popped his head inside. "The conference starts in two minutes, sir."

"I'll be there," Nung said.

The aide disappeared as the door closed.

Chairman Jian Hong—the Leader—wished to speak with him, together with Marshal Kao of the Ruling Committee. It was going to be a three-way conference call. The nuclear assault in Santa Cruz had shaken the Ruling Committee. It was the Navy's fault. Anyone with half a strategical brain could see that. The Navy had badly erred there and reaped a bitter rebuke from the enemy. Correction: the Naval Commander had made a gross error and he had paid a grim penalty. The trouble was that Admiral Ling had also made China pay.

Nung spun on his heel. Dizziness occurred and he lowered his head, taking several calming breaths. When the dizziness passed, he marched for the door, strode down the hall and came to the comm-room.

This was an advance outpost and more communications equipment was on its way. Nung planned to turn this into his new, First Front Headquarters.

"There's bottled water and food behind you, sir."

Nung nodded in acknowledgement as he sat down before the screen. An aide handed him his military cap. Nung put it on and the aide adjusted it.

"Seven seconds, sir."

Nung stared at the screen. What did the Leader want to tell him in the presence of Marshal Kao? It wouldn't be anything good, of that he had no doubt. He didn't have long to wait to find out.

The screen came alive and Nung found himself looking at the Leader on the left of a split-screen and Marshal Kao on the right. Jian Hong was puffy-faced with bags under his eyes. It indicated worry. Aesthetic Marshal Kao had a pinched look, which could mean many different things.

"Gentleman," the Leader said. "It is good of you to meet with me. You are well, Marshal Nung?"

There was more to the question, Nung was certain. Yes, he noticed the tiny twitch of eye movement in Kao, as if the man yearned to speak up.

"I am tired in a good sense," Nung said, "tired like a worker hard at his task but brimming with the energy to complete the work he has begun."

"There you are, Marshal." The Leader appeared to address the words to Kao.

Nung decided it would be wisest to let the matter drop. "And you two gentlemen are doing well, I hope?"

"Yes," Kao said.

The Leader frowned. "I must admit to a sense of unease. Predictions were made in my presence and yet reality has shown me a different face. I continue to attempt to reconcile the two."

"Leader, if I may interject a point," Kao said.

"Before you do, I would like Marshal Nung to understand the nature of the conference call. Marshal," the Leader told Nung. "The battle in California was supposed to be a swift affair, which would allow us to gobble up a profitable state and strengthen our overall strategic position versus the Americans."

"Leader," Nung said, "that is exactly what is occurring even as we speak."

"Respectfully," Kao said, "I would beg to differ with your assessment."

"You are free to do so," Nung said. "But I would like to point out that we are on the verge of a climatic victory."

"You're speaking about the capture of California?" the Leader asked.

"The state will fall to us like dominos," Nung said. "The first piece that will begin the process is the American Army Group of an original six hundred thousand soldiers. We have cut them off from Los Angeles and have begun devouring this Army Group so it is already smaller and vastly weaker than on the opening day of war."

"You have told me this before," the Leader said. "Yet we have not even captured any of the outlying suburbs of Los Angeles. To have truly encircled the Americans, your tanks were supposed to have driven through Palm Springs, captured Los Angeles and sealed everyone from the Grapevine Pass."

"Little is certain in war, Leader," Nung said. "The Americans surprised us with their giant tanks. Yet I have used the Tank Army that would have captured Los Angeles and whittled away more of the trapped Army Group. It is only a matter of days now before the entire enemy Army Group ceases to exist as a military obstacle."

"You have fought a fierce campaign," Kao said. "No one can drive soldiers to battle like you. Yet I would be remiss if I did not point out that the Americans are reinforcing the state in greater numbers than you had anticipated. In the end, if you destroy Army Group SoCal but the Americans place greater numbers of soldiers there, you will have failed to capture California."

"Allow me to disagree with your assessment in an important particular," Nung said. "The Americans have entrained some reinforcements. I predicted they would do as much. Nevertheless, they have not sent anything approaching an entire new Army Group. Perhaps they would if we gave them the time. Once I capture Los Angeles, I will use my White Tigers to seal the Sierra Nevada passes." Nung cleared his throat. "Leader, Marshal Kao, I understand your concerns. War is a messy business with its difficulties. The incident in the north, in Santa Cruz—"

"It was more than an *incident*," the Leader said heatedly. "The Americans used nuclear weapons against Chinese troops. We must retaliate or they will think they can do such a thing again with impunity. This cannot stand."

"You have a valid point, sir," Nung said.

Kao's eyes widened, probably in surprise.

Nung chuckled inwardly. It was Chinese military doctrine to stay well away from nuclear weapons. The Americans had just shown that there was a time and place to use them. A wise commander would consider the ramifications of the nuclear assault with care.

"Go on," the Leader said.

"If it comes down to it, sir," Nung said, "I suggest we use nuclear weapons to render the Sierra Nevada passes unusable."

"Our ICBMs would never make it past the American strategic lasers," Kao said sharply.

"I agree," Nung said. "That is why I believe White Tiger Commandos would need to carry the nuclear weapons with them. They would set the weapons like gigantic mines in the passes, ready to explode at the best possible opportunity."

The Leader's eyes shone as he nodded. "Yes, yes, I like it. We will pay them back in the same coin they have paid us. When they move mass troops through the passes, we annihilate them."

"Exactly, Leader," Nung said.

"We do not want to start a nuclear holocaust," Kao said. "I think we should reconsider this idea."

"Bah!" the Leader said. "*We're* starting nothing. The Americans used the nuclear weapons first. They have always used them first, and they signed an accord with us saying they would never use them. Now it is time to teach the Americans a lesson. They cannot continue to use such weapons against the Asian peoples. I will not stand for it."

"We will use them in accord with my strategy of a swift assault," Nung said.

"Leader," Kao said, "could we address the central issue?"

Jian Hong became thoughtful, with his eyes half-lidded. "Proceed as you wish, but I expect you will find that Marshal Nung has an excellent explanation for what occurs."

"Nung is a gifted speaker," Kao said. "He has also proven to be an excellent commander of small formations. The Siberian and Alaskan Wars show that. The current bloodbath seems to be something altogether different."

"You intrigue me," Nung told Kao. "Please, let me hear your concerns."

"In a nutshell," Kao said, "China has lost far too many soldiers these past weeks for the present gains."

Nung bowed his head, and this time his eyes were bright as he began to speak. "If the war stopped this instant, I would agree with you. My operational method is simple and therefore elegant. Speed is its essence. That does not necessarily mean speed along the highway. I have increased the tempo of battle in California by attacking night and day, by rotating formations and never giving the Americans a rest. It also means headlong attack at times and those attacks are in an urban environment, often considered the worst place for swift advances. That means heavy losses at times among our soldiers. I have tried to ensure that those losses are sustained primarily by penal units and the special infantry."

"That has not always been the case," Kao said.

"You are correct. We have sustained heavy losses, both in men and materiel. What I have done is bring the Americans to the brink of defeat. Once the remnant of Army Group SoCal enters the prison camps, California and the entire West Coast will be plucked like a ripe peach. We will not rest, but endlessly assault the enemy until he collapses from exhaustion."

"What if we collapse first?" Kao asked.

"No. We are the greater power, have better soldiers and the superior technology."

"The American Behemoth tanks are proof of this, yes?" Kao asked.

"The nuclear strike in Santa Cruz is proof of this," Nung said. "The Americans had to resort to it because they lacked enough soldiers. It is clear they are exhausted. Several more headlong assaults—"

"I would like to point out that we have not merely sustained *heavy* losses, but debilitating losses," Kao said. "You need to use a more methodical approach now. In a vast urban and mountainous environment, you must proceed with a siege mentality instead of trying to press as if you're a tank commander on the steppes of Siberia."

They always return to that, don't they? They are envious of my past feats. Nung smiled grimly. "Forgive me, please, Marshal Kao, but I come to a different conclusion. Now is the moment to reap the rewards of our continuous attack. It is a sin to give up at the goal line. That is where we are, and you must have the courage to finish what we started."

"Yes!" the Leader said. "Finish this fight, Marshal Nung. Defeat the Americans as quickly as you can. I do not want any more Santa Cruzes. We must capture Los Angeles and then California. Then you must rest your troops as we shift the focus to Texas and New Mexico and mass supplies there for the second strike."

Nung bowed his head. He had won again, even though it was obvious that Kao intrigued against him. But the Leader was wrong in a critical area. He would not stop with California's capture. He wanted the entire West Coast.

As long as I'm commanding the First Front, we will attack until victory is mine.

"Do you have anything else to add, Marshal Kao?" the Leader asked.

Kao must have understood which way the wind blew. He shook his head and the conference soon ended.

POWAY, CALIFORNIA

Paul Kavanagh ducked behind a concrete wall. Seconds later a powerful explosion shook the area. Debris rained and more enemy shells landed. A titanic *clang* told Paul the M1A3 tank helping them hold this street was no more.

He glanced back and could see the separated turret laying sideways, the bent cannon thrust part way into a burning shoe store.

"Chinese UCAV," Romo said.

Paul looked up and noticed where Romo pointed. Yeah, he saw it, a slow-flying prop job. It had another Annihilator missile under a wing like the one that had just killed the Abrams. It also had a long cannon—it must be a vehicle-hunting drone. Even as he watched, the cannon chugged, and a Stryker hiding from the Chinese Marauders down the street sagged as tires deflated and shells punched holes in the skin.

Paul was part of the rearguard in Poway, fighting with a platoon of the 23rd Infantry Division. The platoon was down to sixteen soldiers, including Paul and Romo. They didn't have any Blowdart shoulder-launched missiles to take down the enemy aircraft. They'd used the last one days ago.

"Ready?" Paul asked.

"The drone is too far and likely flying too fast for us," Romo said.

"That isn't what I asked. Are you ready?"

Romo glanced at Paul. They were both covered with grime, with the dirt worked deep into their skin. Each had a patchy uniform and badly dinged and used Kevlar armor. Paul wore a bandage on his cheek, while Romo had a bigger one on his neck. Paul had sewn the neck wound closed three days ago and it was infected. The assassin was too proud to complain. Each of them had the hollow stare of a soldier who had seen too much combat.

"Amigo, I was born ready," Romo said.

"Glad to hear it. Let's take down the S.O.B."

The UCAV dipped toward them, its cannon chugging. A Bradley Fighting Vehicle barely avoided destruction by backing up fast. Huge chunks of pavement geysered upward and sprayed the pieces in all directions like a granite shower.

Paul grunted as he grabbed the .50 caliber Browning. Romo did likewise. They hefted the machine gun, putting its tripod onto the concrete wall. Paul slid around Romo and clutched the butterfly controls. Romo leaned heavily against the tripod. He'd already put plugs in his ears.

Swiveling the machine gun, Paul used the laser rangefinder. It was an upgraded Browning. The ballistic computer flashed the coordinates. Paul adjusted and he used his thumbs, pressing the buttons. The heavy machine gun was loud, and it shook. Red tracers helped Paul make minute corrections. As a Bradley Fighting Vehicle blew up from the UCAV's cannon, .50 caliber bullets riddled the drone. The Chinese craft nosedived, and seconds later, it hit the ground, exploding out of sight.

Paul released his grip and slapped Romo on the back. The two of them lifted the big machine gun, taking it down off the wall. Both men ran crouched over, hidden from the enemy. Seconds later, Chinese shaped-charge grenades hit the wall where they'd just been, demolishing it.

That was one of the rules. You couldn't stay in the same spot long. Anyone who didn't learn that was already dead or much luckier than he had a right to be.

"Here!" Paul shouted.

Romo grounded the tripod and slid the hot barrel through a hole in the concrete, wearing gloves. One time, when the barrel had glowed with heat, Romo had unzipped his fly and urinated on it. Now, he readied more ammo, giving Paul the thumbs up.

Paul lay on gravel, squinting down the sights. He was deep down exhausted. It was the kind of tired where you felt it in your bones. He wanted a hot bath and to sleep for days. Romo and he had been on the run for too long. They had fought too many battles and hiked over too many mountains to make it here into this particular pocket.

Army Group SoCal wasn't one big united entity anymore, but just fractured parts holding out in different southern cities and hills. As far as Paul knew, this pocket was the farthest northward. It was the closet to LA. The trouble was that he and Romo were the rearguard. If a miracle occurred and somehow the U.S. Army in LA fought through to them, they would have to stand guard, buying time for the others.

"Movement," Romo said.

"Ready."

Romo picked up a Chinese RPG. That was how they operated these days. They scoured battlefields, looking for enemy equipment. Sometimes an American UAV dropped supplies, but that didn't happen often. The Chinese were doing their best to destroy every vestige of Army Group SoCal, and they were doing a good job of it, too.

"There," Romo said, pointing.

Paul saw them. Chinese soldiers in dinylon battle armor raced into view as they sprinted for cover. The lead man wore a black visor with a little antenna jutting up from it. These weren't penal soldiers or the dreaded special infantry. These were regular fighting men. They were the kind that wanted to survive combat.

As if on cue, three Marauder drones appeared down the street. Their cannons roared one right after the other. Shells whistled and blasted sections of the concrete wall.

"Not yet," Paul said. He didn't speak to tell Romo what to do. The assassin knew better than he did the moment to strike. Paul spoke out of habit, out of an inner need.

The Marauders' treads churned rubble. The light tank drones with their forest of antenna clanked toward them. The big cannons looked pitted around the mouths from too much firing. Now those cannons fired again, shaking the SUV-sized tanks. The shells made a dreadful noise, smashing into the concrete wall and into buildings, making everything shake.

On their bellies, Chinese soldiers crawled after the drones, working to get closer to the hidden Americans.

A sound crackled in Paul's ear. It was their platoon leader. Actually, it was their company captain, but there wasn't any company any more, just this skeleton of a platoon of sixteen sorry soldiers. The good thing was that these were the toughest, shrewdest and luckiest sixteen. It's why they were still alive and why the rest of the company was dead meat. Still, the sixteen survivors were bone-weary and just wanted to go home.

The three tank-drones repeated their performance and the Chinese infantry crawled that much closer. Paul counted twenty of them and figured there was another forty soldiers hidden around here somewhere. It was a Chinese infestation.

"Bunch of cockroaches," Paul muttered.

"That's close enough," the captain said into Paul's ear via the implant. "Let her rip, gents."

From his belly, Romo poked the RPG through a hole in the concrete. Enemy bullets flew at him. The Chinese soldiers must have been waiting for this. The slugs peppered the wall. Cool as you please Romo continued to sight.

Paul pressed the trigger of his .50 cal. His big bullets struck the nearest drone with hammering clangs. He tried to shoot out the camera ports. Blinding these tanks made everything easier.

Now Romo fired. There was a whoosh. The shaped-charge grenade flew and struck the Marauder drone, knocking off one of the treads.

"No kill on the cannon," Paul said, as Romo pulled back beside him.

The drone fired, the shell screaming. It blew up more of the wall and this time it was uncomfortably near.

Paul pressed the butterfly triggers, and he began counting the number of Chinese he killed.

The implant crackled in his ear, "What are you doing? Pull back, soldier. We don't want any more heroes. We can't afford it."

"Let's go," Paul said.

With robotic skill, he and Romo went to work taking down the machinegun. Seconds later, they ran, lugging the .50 caliber between them. The other Americans also retreated. That was the secret to the fight. You didn't stay in one spot long. You traded space for time. You set up in a new ambush site and made the Chinese start the process all over again. It meant the pocket was always shrinking. Theirs wasn't going to last long, but while it did last, Paul planned on taking down as many of the enemy as he could.

AVOCADO HIGHWAY, CALIFORNIA

Early in the morning of the next day, all fifteen operational Behemoths were on the move, hauled on their massive carriers.

Stan sat in the cab of his carrier, staring at the mountains around them. He'd been working out ideas on his iPad. This was a gamble, and as far as he could see, it was time to use the Behemoths as a closed fist. They had to smash through the Chinese line hard and fast. It needed to be a stunning blow. Since it was a gamble, and since time would be at a premium, why not risk everything right away?

M1A3 tanks ranged ahead, together with anti-air tac-lasers and Humvee Avengers with Blowdart missiles. Behind the Behemoths and the rest of the attacking force were hundreds of heavy trucks and haulers. They brimmed with supplies, and if everything went right, they would haul out weary soldiers of Army Group SoCal on their return to Temecula.

The carriers traveled for a time at fifteen mph. At mid-morning, the radio crackled. The lead elements of the breakthrough assault had reached the enemy.

In the cab of the carrier, Stan and Jose traded glances. Several seconds later, the radio squawked. Stan answered.

"What do you think?" Colonel Wilson asked.

"We're not close enough yet," Stan said. "Let's wait to unload."

"And if the Chinese send jets at us?"

"I don't think they're going to do that just yet, sir. Give it another half hour and then we unload."

"That's cutting it awful close, Captain."

"Sir, this is a gamble, and—"

"You explained it to me earlier. Place everything on the bet, holding nothing back. All right, I asked for your advice and you're the hero of Alaska."

"That doesn't make me right," Stan said.

"No, but it means you might actually know what you're talking about. We'll do this your way, Captain."

The words should have made Stan feel good. Instead, they tightened his gut. Is this what it felt like being a commander? Then he wanted nothing to do with the job. It was one thing risking your life on the line of battle. It was quite another sending other men to die for your ideas.

"Are you a praying man, Colonel?" Stan asked.

"I've been to church."

"Well, sir, if I were you, I'd start praying pretty heavily right about now. We're going to need all the help we can get."

SAN YSIDRO, CALIFORNIA

Marshal Nung yawned as he entered the commander center. This was more like it. The technicians had been busy all last night. Now it looked like the regular command center back in Mexico. Everyone was here now, too. That included General Pi and Marshal Gang.

Moving to the computer table in the center of the chamber, Nung nodded to the larger Marshal Gang. The man looked at him stonily before grunting an acknowledgement. Nung acted better than he felt. He was sure Gang sent daily reports back to China to Marshal Kao. Well, everyone had his or her afflictions. Old-woman marshals were one of his.

"Put up situational map on the screen," Nung said. The tac-officer obeyed and Nung surveyed the situation. Something caught his eye up there to the north.

"What's this?" he asked, tapping the table along I-15 between Escondido and Temecula.

"I'll find out, sir," General Pi said. The officer spoke into his wrist microphone. Several minutes later, he said, "It appears the Americans are probing there, sir."

"Probing?" Nung asked.

"There are reports of Abrams tanks, sir."

Nung frowned. "Do we have a visual of what's going on?"

"Negative," the tac-officer said.

"I want a drone out there," Nung said.

"Yes, sir."

"Is something wrong, sir?" Pi asked.

"We're eating the Americans," Nung said, "devouring them as I had anticipated from the start. Finally, some of the trapped formations have begun to surrender. Yet I fear we might not have made the net strong enough in this area. We've taught them that driving down the coastal route simply makes them targets for our sea-borne hovers and missile cruisers. There's something different about this attempt here."

"Are you sure, sir?" Pi asked. "We've driven off every attempt they've made to break through to the trapped army. I think they no longer have enough soldiers to make any more attempts."

"You are wrong," Nung said. "The Americans don't have enough soldiers *not* to try. Now get me those visuals, even if you have to send a wing of fighters to get it."

AVOCADO HIGHWAY, CALIFORNIA

For this operation, Stan was privy to more information than usual. It came through Colonel Wilson. The Behemoth Regiment had become the most important formation in all of California. That meant General Larson often spoke to Wilson. Wilson in turn had made Stan his right-hand advisor.

Fifteen Behemoth monsters clanked south along I-15. They were like fifteen, slow-motion semis, but with long cannons and squealing treads. Each tank proudly flew the Stars and Stripes and each approached the increasingly heated battle.

"We've lost eleven Abrams so far," Wilson radioed.

Stan sat in his commander's seat in the Behemoth. The trouble was the terrain. Here it definitely favored the defender. And in this instance, Chinese troops had infiltrated between Temecula and Escondido and grown stronger through helicopter reinforcements.

Stan spoke into the receiver. "I suggest you tell General Larson that he should accept the losses of all his Abrams in order to smash through the Chinese line. If we don't break

301

through into the pocket today, we can kiss California goodbye."

"Those are harsh words, Captain."

"Yes, sir, but the truth is we're going to need more soldiers in order to defend Los Angeles. That means a few lost tanks here won't matter in the end. All that matters is getting the trapped men free and ready to face tomorrow. This is our Dunkirk, sir."

"Dunkirk, I've heard that name before," Wilson said.

"You should. It's a story of great valor and cunning. In 1940, the German panzers had slipped through the Ardennes, shattered the French and trapped the British Army on the coast. The British retreated to Dunkirk, and it was only a matter of time before the panzers came in to finish the job. Hitler took too long, however, interfering with his generals. That gave the British time to send every ship afloat to Dunkirk, where they ferried over 300,000 soldiers back to England. It saved the British, sir, because without those troops they wouldn't have been able to hold out against a German cross-Channel invasion."

"And you think this is our Dunkirk?" Wilson asked.

"I think so, sir. We need to ferry out our soldiers to fight again another day."

"Yes, it's what I'll tell the General. A few Abrams don't matter now."

"In truth, our Behemoths don't matter either," Stan said. "We have to break through and free these soldiers, sacrificing whatever we have to in order to do it."

"I hope it doesn't come to that," Wilson said.

"Those are my sentiments exactly, sir."

SAN DIEGO, CALIFORNIA

Flight Lieutenant Harris found it hard to concentrate. He could hear Chinese artillery shells landing near the bunker. That shook the equipment in here and made plaster fall from the ceiling. PAA forces had steadily infiltrated San Diego and pushed back the American perimeter.

It was the confounded hovers. The Chinese controlled the ocean, reinforcing at will along the coast and attacking anywhere there that they wanted.

"Lieutenant," a voice said in his ear.

Harris wore drone-gear as he piloted what would likely be his last V-10 UCAV. He was part of an air wing over I-15. They were covering the great escape, or what they hoped would be the great escape of the trapped American troops. Unfortunately, no one was coming for them here in San Diego. It was too far behind enemy lines. The terrible part was that they weren't the only cut-off and trapped city. All over San Diego County the situation was the same. The Chinese had shattered the integrity of Army Group SoCal and now squeezed each pocket tighter and tighter.

"Look to your left," the air-controller said.

"Sorry," Harris said. He had to forget about his own troubles. He had a job to do. He concentrated on flying his V-10. He ignored the shudder around him and the piece of plaster that fell near his feet. Instead, concentrating, he peered through the VR goggles and saw that the sky over I-15 swarmed with Chinese drones and jet fighters.

Clenching his teeth, Flight Lieutenant Harris decided this was going to be the only payback he would get. Soon, he would be dead or he would be a prisoner. Would they ship him south into Mexico, or would they transport him across the Pacific to China? Either way, he would never come home. He was certain of that.

"Let's do this," he whispered.

Several J-25s bored toward them. Higher up were recon drones. Battle ops called for no enemy recon vehicles. They were trying to keep the Chinese blind about what was going on along the highway.

The threat receiver growled in his ear. Harris expelled chaff, executed a hard-G maneuver and brought his small V-10 into position. He had lock-on, and he launched two Sun-stingers. Then he decided—

In his operator's seat, Harris shook from side-to-side. He had no idea what was going on. Then someone tore off his VR goggles. A panicked MP with blood running down his face stood before him.

"What are you doing?" Harris asked.

"Chinese soldiers have blown the bunker entrance," the MP said. "Take this." The man shoved an assault rifle into his hands. Then the man fell backward, and try as he might, the MP couldn't get back up.

Harris stared at the dying man and then at the ugly thing in his hands. Feeling as if he was in a nightmare, he called the air-controller. "I have to sign off. Someone else needs to control my drone."

The air-controller acknowledged.

Standing, ripping off the leads attached to him, Harris brought up the assault rifle and moved toward the sound of gunfire. The Chinese were in the bunker. What did that mean?

Blinking, Harris realized what it meant. *I'm going to end up in a Chinese POW camp. They're going to starve me to death and practice horrible experiments on me like the Japanese did to some of our soldiers in World War II.*

A well of fear constricted his chest. His eyes bulged, and Flight Lieutenant Harris began to shake. This wasn't anything like flying drones. This wasn't like a first-person shooter computer game, either. This was for real.

You can't become a prisoner.

Another MP ahead of him turned the corner and fired his weapon behind him. Armor-piercing bullets ripped through the corner and blew the MP backward.

With a howl of anguish, Harris ran to the same corner, stepping over the MP. He saw two armored Chinese soldiers. He lifted the assault rifle and emptied the magazine at them. He shot the floor first, then one of the enemy and finally the ceiling. It was crazy, the assault rifle shook like mad as he fired, causing the barrel to rise. He must have gotten lucky, because one of the Chinese lay on the floor with a gaping wound in his face. The other one aimed his assault weapon.

Grinding his teeth together, Harris yanked out the magazine and started to put in another one. But he was not ground-combat trained and he had forgotten to duck back out of sight. As he slapped the magazine into the slot, the Chinese soldier fired a three-round burst, two of them catching Harris in the chest. He staggered backward and crashed to the floor. He found it hard to breathe, hard to see.

What's happening?

Boots appeared before his eyes. A soldier spoke Chinese. Then a barrel appeared before Harris's face. He heard a click, and then Flight Lieutenant Harris didn't hear anything at all, ever.

SAN YSIDRO, CALIFORNIA

"Those are the giant tanks," Nung said. He stared at the computer table, at images recorded from the air-battle over I-15. Beside a giant tank, a passing Humvee looked like a child's toy.

"If the giant tanks are here," Pi said, "it means they are no longer guarding Palm Springs."

Nung looked up. This was an excellent point. "Alert the general of the Tank Army outside Palm Springs. I want his advance units to make an immediate assault upon the city."

"Palm Springs is surely heavily guarded by others," Pi said.

"Yes, surely," Nung agreed.

Marshal Gang muttered under his breath as he strode to the computer table. "I would make an observation."

"You are free to do so," Nung said.

"The Americans have entrenched themselves in Palm Springs," Gang said. "A frontal attack now would mean heavy losses to our T-66s. A methodical assault with intense artillery preparation is the correct procedure."

"For assaulting an entrenched enemy, you are correct," Nung said.

Gang raised his eyebrows, likely in surprise. "Is this not what they are?"

"I see the broader picture," Nung said, "because I have a grand strategical goal. Everything I do is based upon that goal. The Americans have one technologically advanced weapons system over us: the giant tanks with their electromagnetic cannons. They stopped us at Palm Springs. Now they are gone, fighting down here near Escondido. We must immediately

305

launch an attack at Palm Springs, because that will shake the morale of the enemy commander more than anything else we can do."

"I do not follow your logic," Gang said.

It was so obvious that Nung was surprised at Gang. "The enemy has taken a risk. The giant tanks blocked us at Palm Springs because their extreme range and powerful gun trumped our superior numbers. Now the enemy tanks no longer have the better range because the terrain they are in blocks such long-distance firing. Instead, for close tank combat, we have the advantage with our triple-turreted armor. While I do agree that our Tank Army will take heavy losses as it assaults Palm Springs, it will also put tremendous pressure on the American commander. Even if he can break through down here near Escondido, it won't matter if I can succeed in Palm Springs. The Tank Army will race through the pass and assault San Bernardino. We will cut off Temecula—cut off this entire region down here—from Los Angeles. That means Army Group SoCal remains trapped and these new formations sent to rescue them will be caught in the giant net with them."

"This will only come at a heavy cost in men and materiel," Gang said. "Why not win Palm Springs through a properly planned and executed assault?"

"I just explained that to you," Nung said in exasperation. "Don't you understand anything? Have you learned nothing while in my presence? You have watched and reported on my health; why not report to Kao on the excellence of my operational grasp? Speed is the essence as we outmaneuver the Americans. Now is the time to rush Los Angeles as the enemy commander expends his best formations driving into our net. By the time he turns around and rushes those formations back to Los Angeles, it will be too late."

Gang was stony-faced, with his shoulders hunched. "How do we defeat the giant tanks? What is your excellent plan for them?"

"They are in rough terrain, as you can see. The terrain negates their range advantage because their line of sight is blocked, not allowing them their six to seven-mile shots. Even better, they have given me the perfect target."

306

"I do not understand."

Nung smiled craftily. "I saved a Blue Swan missile for a critical moment such as this. The missile will EMP the giant tanks, rendering them useless. Then we will rush helicopter-borne infantry around them and delay the Americans from retreating or turning around and racing for Palm Springs. Gentlemen, I predict that the Battle for California will be won right here."

AVOCADO HIGHWAY, CALIFORNIA

Stan sat in his Behemoth as they rumbled to the attack. He watched his screens, with intelligence provided by UAVs, his tank-cameras and scouting infantry.

The Chinese waited up on the rocky hills surrounding the highway. Burning and destroyed Abrams littered the concrete road. With the squeal of metal, Stan's Behemoth shoved the hulk of an M1A3 to the side and continued its advance.

The three-hundred-ton monsters were a sight, majestic creations, clanking and squealing south. There were twelve of them. Three had stalled due to engine failure. Three Behemoth-haulers had rushed forward to retrieve them, but that meant nothing here on the battlefield.

Chinese Main Battle Tanks were at the top of the rocky hills. The MBTs had been in hull-down positions earlier. Now they waited out of sight, hidden from the Behemoths. Unfortunately for them, they were visible to the recon drones buzzing overhead.

"Get ready," Stan said. "Three MBTs are moving up to make their attack."

On the screen and seen from the UAV's angle, Stan watched the Chinese tanks clank the short distance to the mountaintop. Soon, their cannons poked over the hill, targeting them. Each cannon belched fire and shot a sabot round.

The tactic had worked against the M1A3s, as the evidence on the road proved. The Chinese shells screamed down. Stan's Behemoth—like all the others—had an advanced Artificial Intelligence. It tracked the shells and automatically targeted

307

them with the 30mm cannons. To insure the enemy shells never hit, beehive flechette launchers blasted. This time it worked, as none of the enemy shells reached the Behemoth's incredibly thick armor.

"Have you computed their position?" Stan shouted.

"Roger," Jose said, with his forehead pressed against the targeting scope.

Stan glanced at the intel-screen. The Chinese had played it smart. Their crews were apparently highly-trained professionals. As soon as they'd fired, the three MBTs had ducked back down behind the rocky hill. Against normal munitions, the rock and earth would have protected them. The force cannons were anything but normal.

"Fire!" Stan shouted, unable to give the command it in a quiet voice.

Jose pressed the switch. Power flowed through the force cannon. The Behemoth shook as the penetrator round ejected at a terrific velocity.

The depleted uranium rod zoomed with unerring accuracy. It smashed through rock and dirt and scored a direct hit against the Chinese MBT on the other side. The round burned through the armor and BB-sized molten pellets ignited everything inside the tank. The MBT exploded.

The other Behemoths did likewise, and the enemy tanks up on the hills burned or exploded. The sheer power of the force cannons was too much to resist.

"We've broken through," Colonel Wilson shouted over the radio.

The twelve Behemoths led the assault down I-15. They were nearing the trapped Americans. As of right now, it looked as if the gamble was going to pay off.

VISTA, CALIFORNIA

Forty-seven minutes after Stan's Behemoth destroyed a Chinese MBT, a Blue Swan carrier pulled off the road. It pulled into the Vista Mall parking area and came to a stop.

Technicians jumped out of the cab as the launcher bed began to rise.

"Do you have the coordinates?" the major in charge of the missile asked his chief technician.

"Yes, sir," the tech said, lifting his Graceful Swan netbook.

"How long until you're ready to fire?" the major asked.

"Twelve minutes at the most, sir."

"Make sure you avoid all errors. This missile must fly directly to target and in as little time as possible."

"It will fly, sir. I stake my reputation on it."

"No," the major said, a hard-faced man. "You are staking your life on its success."

The technician blanched as he backed away and hurried to his team.

SAN YSIDRO, CALIFORNIA

Nung paced in the command center as he carefully set his soft-soled shoes on the floor, listening to their nearly inconspicuous squelch. He could not help himself as nervousness seethed through his body. Information about the giant tanks was beginning to concern him. The Americans had truly developed a marvel with the tank. They were slow as armor vehicles went, but nothing appeared to be able to stop them.

I was wise to save a Blue Swan missile. Yes, the Americans have a marvel, but we Chinese have the greater technological tool.

"Sir," General Pi said. "The Blue Swan missile is ready to launch."

Nung turned and marched to the computer table. "In case the Americans have a trick left, we will precede the Blue Swan attack with a mass of cruise missiles swarming the enemy."

"Yes, sir."

"Are the helicopter-carriers ready?" Nung asked.

"They are filled with White Tiger Commandos. The cargo helicopters are lifting Marauder tank and several mortar-jeeps.

309

At your word, they will swing behind the Americans and seal them in the trap."

"Good." Nung waited a moment, savoring this. He glanced at Gang in his corner. How the marshal must hate this. Nung turned to General Pi, and he let a fierce grin stretch his lips. "Let the attack begin now, and give me those giant tanks."

VISTA, CALIFORNIA

The Blue Swan missile stood ready. Cables snaked from it to the control panel. The technicians in their white coats spoke among themselves while the major watched.

The major stiffened as he stood at the comm-table, hearing General Pi personally give the order. The major took three steps toward the technicians, shouting, "Is the missile ready?"

"It is ready," the chief tech said.

"Put in these coordinates," the major said, pressing a button on his console.

The techs made adjustments and then signaled that they were set.

"Fire!" the major shouted.

The chief tech tapped a screen.

The Blue Swan ignited on its launch pad as smoke billowed densely. The EMP missile lofted slowly at first and then quickly gained speed. It roared as flames flickered from its exhaust port. Then it shot toward the highway where the Behemoths smashed everything in their path.

AVOCADO HIGHWAY, CALIFORNIA

"How much farther until we reach Escondido?" Jose asked from his gunner's seat.

"A little less than a mile," Stan said.

There were nine Behemoths left. None had dropped out due to battle damage. For each, it was equipment failure, usually in the treads or the engine. The stalled Behemoths were already on their carriers and headed back toward Temecula.

Behind the advancing Behemoths and Abrams, Bradleys and Strykers followed the heavy trucks and haulers. From a recon UAV, the mass looked like a giant mechanical snake slithering toward the trapped pocket.

"Captain," Colonel Wilson radioed. The man sounded worried.

"What is it, sir?" Stan asked.

"Get ready! The Chinese are sending cruise missiles!"

"Are they nukes, sir?" asked Stan.

"That is unknown, but they're coming fast. You have a minute or two left."

"Are the tac-lasers ready, sir?"

"Captain, they're going to swamp us!"

"No," Stan said, knowing Wilson knew better. "We've been waiting for this, remember? It's time to employ our special tactic and teach the Chinese another reason why they shouldn't mess with the Behemoths."

"But if they're using nuclear weapons—"

"Let's fight, sir, and worry about the results later."

"I hope this works, Higgins. Colonel Wilson, out."

"Yeah, me too," Stan whispered. "Jose!"

"Right here, Professor."

"Raise the cannon. It's time to see just how good these Behemoths really are."

On I-15, a little less than half a mile from the forward line of the trapped Americans, the nine Behemoth tanks raised their force cannons. The ejected shells flew many times faster than a rifle bullet, and the shells could fly in a relatively flat trajectory.

The Behemoth AIs linked with the tac-laser defensive net, and several extra UAVs were already sending data. All the while, the Chinese cruise missiles bored in on the Behemoths.

Ninety-eight seconds later the mayhem began. Cruise missiles approached and laser beams flashed. Flak fired and chain-guns chugged. Even more impressively, the force cannons shot cruise missiles out of the sky from long range, well before the missiles detonated their warheads.

One enemy missile acted much differently than the others, and it came last in the attack. This missile did not try to hug the ground as it approached the Behemoths. Instead, it flew upward to increase the range of its EMP strike.

Inside Stan's Behemoth, he said, "Look at that, Jose. It's going for an airburst. The missile must be a nuke. Take it out."

The giant cannon swiveled. The AI fired a targeting laser and computed the missile's height, speed and future position several seconds from now. Automatically, the AI fired the force cannon and the Behemoth shuddered as the round sped skyward.

Meanwhile, the Blue Swan reached its desired position. Within it, the computer triggered the firing mechanism. The first explosion occurred which would initiate the EMP burst.

At that moment, the Behemoth's round smashed the Blue Swan missile. Instead of creating an EMP blast, the missile disintegrated in the air, the pieces raining down as useless junk.

As quickly as the missile attack had begun it was over. Several cruise missiles had reached their targets, but the rest were destroyed. The cost was several burning tac-lasers and chain-gun platforms with their accompanying crews, but not one Behemoth was lost.

In their slow and relentless rumble, the nine giant tanks continued toward Escondido.

SAN YSIDRO, CALIFORNIA

Marshal Nung stared at the computer table, blinking in astonishment. "Did you witness that?" he whispered. "The tank destroyed our missile."

"What now?" Gang asked.

Nung looked up. It felt as if his eyes were on fire. He struck the computer table. "Nothing changes."

"Everything changes," Gang said. "You have failed to halt their breakthrough."

"Ah, I see. One failure shatters your resolve—how truly pitiful."

Marshal Gang stiffened, while those in the command chamber at their various stations showed shock and surprise at the insult.

Nung looked away. He must control his temper and tongue no matter what the provocation. He could not speak this way to a fellow marshal. Word of it would filter back to the Ruling Committee and they might see it as him cracking under the strain of command. Even so, it was impossible that he apologize to Gang, to this tool of his enemies.

Nung shook his head and he faced the others. "In war, many attacks fail. The one that succeeds is the critical assault. This setback has done nothing to alter my will or change the ultimate fate of the Americans."

"Have I heard you correctly?" Gang asked. "Formerly, you said that trapping the Americans was the linchpin to your plan as you starved the enemy of needed troops. Now, with the failure of the Blue Swan missile, the enemy has broken through to Army Group SoCal. He will be able to reinforce his defenses with these badly needed soldiers."

Nung massaged his forehead, struggling to maintain his decorum. "In an instance like this, precision is vital in deed and word. The Americans have only broken through to this northernmost pocket; they have not broken through to the entire Army Group SoCal."

"Perhaps that is so," Gang said, "but this is the largest of the trapped pockets."

Nung studied the computer table, the operational map. The lights on the side were all blue, indicting everything worked properly. In his thoughts, he put aside Gang and his words and concentrated on the military and strategic situation. After a time, he began to speak. "With these giant tanks, the Americans have broken through. That is true. But it will be another matter entirely to escape with these soldiers into Los Angeles."

"You are the eternal optimist," Gang said. "It is one of your military gifts. Yet I would suggest that you are underestimating the importance of this attack. I fear it might begin a chain-reaction of assaults against the other beleaguered forces, the other pockets, as you call them?"

Nung raised an eyebrow. The suggestion was preposterous. It was mere rhetoric, wind. He had no time for Ruling Committee gadflies, even if Gang was the second-most senior marshal in Greater China after Kao. He had a campaign to win. This was a setback, nothing more. With the giant tanks down here in Escondido, it meant they no longer helped guard Palm Springs. He would have to make the Americans pay for that. In fact, looking at the operational map…yes, he knew what to do. This reminded him of Siberia, of the drive to Yakutsk. Once more, he must outflank the enemy.

"We must call Marshal Kao," Gang said.

Nung looked up in surprise. He was forming a plan and had already forgotten about Gang. "If you will excuse me, Marshal, I have no more time for handwringing. The Americans have handed us a rare opportunity. We must snatch it while there is still time. Yes, they have stolen a march on us. It was clever of them and it was bold. Now, I plan to use their boldness against them like a Shaolin priest practicing kung fu on a pirate."

Gang opened his mouth, and hesitated. He glanced around the room. Perhaps he saw the command personnel eagerly waiting for Nung to unfold his new insight.

"As you wish, Marshal," Gang said. He retired to his corner, sitting, watching and waiting.

The man is a vulture, hungering for me to show weakness. Nung shook his head. *I cannot falter now. I must outmaneuver the enemy and change this disaster into an even greater victory.*

"What are your orders, sir?" Pi asked.

Nung continued to study the operational map. He must outmaneuver the Americans, but he must not make hasty decisions. This was a moment for careful reflection. He waved General Pi to silence. Then Nung put his fingertip on the computer table as he concentrated. The Americans had lunged into Escondido, using the giant tanks to bolster the assault. It indicated they used their best—their most offensive— formations to make the assault. That meant they had thinned out these formations from elsewhere. The problem was some of the other trapped American formations farther south of Escondido. According to reports, some of the pockets were on the verge of collapse. The others would last several more days, maybe even a week. Those pockets tied down Chinese formations needed for the assault on Los Angeles. Perhaps it was time to screen some of the pockets and gather greater hitting power to continue the lunge for the sprawling American city and the Grapevine Pass behind it. If he could trap all of Los Angeles in a gigantic pocket...

Nung leaned over the table, tracing the coastal route along Highway 5 from Mexico to Los Angeles. He nodded and stepped around the table. He tapped Palm Springs, and he eyed Temecula and then followed the route to Corona. Yes, it was becoming clear what he needed to do. The trick would be to slow the escape of these soldiers from the Escondido Pocket in order to give him time for the Tank Army waiting south beyond Palm Springs.

Nung straightened and regarded General Pi. "You must put me through to the Tank Army General. It is time to light a fire under him and reignite the original assault against Palm Springs."

"Yes, sir," Pi said.

Once more, Nung studied the computer table. He moved around it again and stabbed a finger along I-15. "Here," he said. "This is where we are going to send the helicopter-borne troops."

"There, sir?" Pi asked, sounding surprised.

"They will not survive their attack, I realize this. And we must work out a tactical plan to put them down there so they last as long as possible. They must buy us time while the Tank Army takes Palm Springs and then smashes through the pass to San Bernardino and beyond."

"Sir?" Pi asked.

"It will become a race. If we win, once more we will cut off these freed soldiers and we will capture the attacking American forces and the giant tanks along with them. Yes, if we win this race, we will win the battle in Southern California and ready ourselves for capturing everything."

-11-
Drive on Los Angeles

WASHINGTON, D.C.

In an emergency session of the War Council, Anna sat down beside Dr. Levin. The CIA Director glanced at her and then ignored her presence.

Since the nuclear attack in Santa Cruz, the atmosphere in Underground Bunker Number Five had turned more unrelentingly grim. The success of the assault should have lightened their hearts, but it hadn't.

We can feel the evil of what we've done. We have unleashed the terrible genie, and now we wait for him to turn on us. The Chinese will use nuclear weapons soon. They have refrained from it too long to resist the urge this time.

The President entered the chamber looking more worn than ever. The past few days had aged him. The good news warred against the bad, and everything hung on a knife's edge as the Chinese battled through the San Gorgonio Pass between the San Bernardino Mountains on the north and the San Jacinto Mountains on the south. If they broke through, they would be in Greater San Bernardino. Given their past actions, the Chinese might be tempted to race to Corona and block the soldiers escaping out of the Escondido Pocket through Temecula.

That was the chief worry and the reason for the meeting. Yet in the northern half of California, the Chinese assault continued despite staggering losses to the nuclear-tipped cruise missiles. The enemy was on the verge of breaking through into the Bay Area.

They had spoken about the Bay Area last meeting. The consensus in the White House bunker was that after the Tomahawk attack, the Chinese had too few naval infantry left to carry the day in San Francisco and San Jose. What the enemy did have was air superiority and the ability to shift his few troops like a chess master.

On the American side, reinforcements kept trickling in, enough so a form of stalemate had occurred. The trouble was that those soldiers were a drain. SoCal Command desperately needed every grunt it could get to hold the coming battle for LA.

"General Alan," the President said. "It's time for a new assessment of the situation in Greater Los Angeles."

The General of the Joint Chiefs stood up. The strain showed in his cheeks, how lean they had become. He looked as if he'd been fasting for a week, his motions now lethargic and his face lacking its natural animation.

"Mr. President, the situation has become fluid and threatens to become even worse. The first soldiers from the Escondido Pocket have reached Temecula. According to estimates, there are nearly one hundred and eighty-four thousand Americans in or around Escondido and Poway."

"So few?" Sims asked. "I had hoped for more."

"Well, sir—"

"Army Group SoCal originally contained six hundred thousand soldiers."

"Yes sir, but if you'll consider—"

"Are you telling me that we're attempting to free one hundred and eighty thousand Americans out of an original six hundred thousand?"

"The Chinese have sustained heavy losses as well, sir," General Alan said. "We believe they may have nearly one million casualties. That's dead and wounded, sir."

President Sims snorted. "Those estimates sound much too high to me. If you say one million, I doubt it's even five hundred thousand." He scowled. "It's impossible *we've* lost so men in so short a time."

"I assure you our estimates on the enemy are accurate, sir."

"I'm not worried about the enemy, but about us! How can we have lost so many soldiers?"

"Ah...there are several ways to look at this, sir. In World War I, in 1916, the British once took 60,000 casualties in one day of the Battle of Somme, 20,000 of whom were killed. I remember reading that sixty percent of the officers involved died on the first day. We haven't lost that many soldiers in a single day's fighting, Mr. President. But—"

"I'm not interested in World War I," Sims said, as he waved his hand as if to erase the words. "How is it possible we have so few troops left?"

"They're trapped, sir. As you know, the Chinese have surrounded masses of our troops all over southern California. And we have taken appalling losses. Modern war is brutal."

"Yes, but one hundred and eighty thousand soldiers out of the original six hundred thousand—I thought we were going to rescue more of our men."

"By my estimates, sir, there are another two hundred thousand Americans in five different pockets."

"Can we reach them from Escondido?" Sims asked.

Anna blinked in surprise. What was she hearing from the President? He used to be a commanding general. He should know these things. He should be giving orders, not asking questions of General Alan. How much sleep had the President been getting? He looked exhausted. She wondered about his mental health.

"Sir," Alan said, "I'm afraid we might not get the one hundred and eighty thousand into LA. That's why we've called the meeting."

"...Yes," Sims said, rubbing his temples. "That's right. Please, continue, General."

"Thank you, sir. Well, we've finally discovered one of the secrets to their continuous assaults. Before I tell you about that I want to reiterate that the Chinese switch formations

318

constantly. They retire the fatigued formation and bring up another to continue the attack. It's true that other armies have done this in the past. The Chinese appear to have made it an art. They are well trained in this particular maneuver."

From an aide, Sims accepted a pill and a glass of water. He popped the pill and drank. Then he returned his attention to the General of the Joint Chiefs.

"The Chinese have been ruthless in their use of penal battalions," Alan was saying, "accepting staggering casualties. I stand by the nearly one million enemy casualties, sir. Our soldiers have fought heroically. In any case, the Chinese also have these special infantry. That is the new thing we've learned, sir: the feature that makes the formations so special." The General glanced at Anna. "Surprisingly, the CIA discovered their specialty, as it were." Alan nodded to her.

"With your permission," Anna said to Levin.

"You do not need his permission to speak here," Sims said. "You already have mine."

"Yes, Mr. President," Anna said. Out of the corner of her eye, she saw Levin scowl. But she couldn't worry about that now. She cleared her throat and concentrated on Sims. "There were certain features about the special infantry that have troubled me for some time now. I checked the records and—"

"Summarize the information please, Ms. Chen," Sims said.

"Yes sir. It appears the Chinese created the special infantry formations with the idea of accepting fifty to sixty percent casualty rates as a matter of course. Perhaps they studied General Alan's Battle of the Somme."

No one smiled.

"Ah…" Anna said, "I believe the Chinese have studied the problem of modern war in detail. I'm speaking about the lethality of it. They appear to have come to certain conclusions quite different to anything we would have decided. I mean, of course, the acceptance of mind-numbing losses.

"Now, as few soldiers would care to join such an organization or perform with any zeal in it, the Chinese refined the needed motivations. Normally, to stir their soldiers, militaries make appeals to glory, to patriotism or to duty in order to energize regular fighters. On the other hand, we

319

believe the special infantry respond to post-hypnotic suggestions and drugs. The process appears to have created a suitably compliant soldier—a zombie if you will—more than willing to expend his life in pursuit of the attack."

"What you're saying—that's evil," Sims said.

"And grossly wasteful of lives," General Alan added.

"Nevertheless," Anna said, "the special infantry exists and we have the evidence of their actions. The Chinese have used them to break stubborn resistance and to do it *fast*. There seems to be an emphasis on speed in this campaign. I have complied data of special infantry use in other conflicts..." Anna saw the President scowl. "Umm...well sir, let me distill the reports to this: the special infantry has never exceeded two percent of any Chinese army in any situation until now."

"You're saying there is a different percentage in Southern California?"

"Yes, Mr. President. It appears to fluctuate between four to seven percent. We believe more special infantry lands from China every day. Naturally, such formations do not last long."

"And you're telling me that this is what happened in Palm Springs?" Sims asked.

Anna glanced at General Alan.

The slim general motioned to his aide, the major. She switched on the holo-video in the center of the table and began to explain what they viewed.

It began as a classic attack with heavy artillery fire and then T-66s on overwatch as they advanced in three-tank platoons toward the outskirts of Palm Springs. From above, Chinese UCAVs bored toward the city. American tac-lasers beamed, taking down a dreadful number, while SAMs rose to engage the aircraft. Then air-to-ground missiles fired from Chinese standoff bombers arrived. It was like many of the other battles, a furnace of destruction. Finally, the Chinese reached the urban areas.

The major used zoom, showing them Chinese ground assaults. It showed wave after wave of special infantry doggedly charging the entrenched defenders who used heavy machine guns and mortars. Thousands of enemy soldiers died, yet still they advanced, still they attacked. Meanwhile, the T-66s crept into position.

"This is horrifying," Sims whispered. "It's a butcher's yard."

Now a new tank assault began, sometimes churning over the dead bodies of special infantrymen. The weight of the attack was too much for the outnumbered defenders. The Chinese entered Palm Springs and a savage street-by-street battle for the city began as other T-66s circled the city.

"They just keep coming," Sims said. "We're destroying so many. How can the Chinese afford the losses?"

"That is the question," General Alan said. "We're killing more of them than they kill of us, but they keep pushing us back. Now the Chinese are halfway through the I-10 corridor of San Gorgonio Pass. We're fighting every inch of the way and it's a deathtrap for their tanks. The width of the pass is one to two miles. The Chinese are using heavy air support, massive artillery bombardments and hordes of attacking special infantry. Even so, we're killing them at five-to-one ratios, sometimes even ten to one, but they always have more hardware, more tanks, aircraft, artillery and bodies."

"We have to accelerate the retreat along I-15," Sims said. "We need those soldiers."

"Yes, Mr. President."

"What do you need from me?" Sims asked.

"Sir, I believe that *all* the California-bound reinforcements must head to Los Angeles. We have to let NorCal Command cope with the situation in the Bay Area as it is. The battle in the southlands is the critical conflict now."

"And if the Chinese capture the Bay Area?"

"We're raising new Militia units there even now, sir, just as we're doing in Greater Los Angeles. In the south, the Chinese have three times, maybe more, the number of soldiers we do. In the Bay Area, I believe we have more men. The Chinese might win local victories there, but I do not believe they can capture the entire Bay Area fast enough to matter, not unless they receive reinforcements."

"Which the Chinese might very well receive if they capture the ports of San Francisco or Oakland," Sims said.

"True. We have to decide on priorities, sir, on which situation is more pressing."

"It will become very pressing if the Chinese land another one hundred thousand soldiers in San Francisco or two hundred thousand."

"Our submarines are lurking there, sir, in greater number than previously. If needed, we can sacrifice them in order to destroy enemy troopships."

The President drummed his fingers on the table as he scowled at the holo-vid. Taking a deep breath, he said, "Send all the reinforcements south to Los Angeles. The Chinese are making their play there, so that is where we have to stop them."

POWAY, CALIFORIA

The extended battle in the Californian city had turned it into a mass of rubble as far as the eye could see. Chinese artillery had pulverized Poway for days. Tanks moved like ancient dinosaurs, shoving aside concrete and twisted steel girders. Shaped-charge grenades, armor-piercing mortar rounds and heavy machine gun fire hammered at the armored creatures. Sometimes, pterodactyl-like UCAVs swooped over the grim terrain. Missiles launched from under their wings, burning red and striking with tremendous clouds of smoke. In the end, the dinosaurs always died to the small mammalian creatures that lived like rats in the rubble, popping up to shoot and scoot elsewhere.

Grime and dust coated Paul Kavanagh. He lay on pulverized gravel and concrete. He wore heavy body armor and had several small computers attached to his suit. They had been flown in special delivery. The computers fed him a constant stream of data. He fed higher command with surveillance information. Romo was nearby, crawling ahead to take out a Chinese sentry.

Paul stiffened as he heard a gurgle of sound. A moment later, one of his computers beeped quietly. Staying on his belly like a snake, Paul slithered forward, following a signal. Soon he reached Romo. The assassin lacked any body armor, but wore a camouflage suit. The corpse on the ground still grabbed at the piano-wire-like garrote that had constricted his throat and breathing. Blood trickled past the wire.

Romo motioned south toward the next Chinese position. Paul nodded, and the two of them began to crawl.

The Chinese had hit Poway with everything. Likely that would continue. The special infantry had been here. Those soldiers never stopped until they were dead. Now bloated corpses littered the battlefield so a foul-smelling miasma floated over the rubble.

Paul used his elbows to pull himself forward. He and Romo were part of the rearguard in Poway. They had to keep the Chinese at bay, lest the enemy motor after the escaping soldiers. They kept hearing news of other places, but didn't care anymore. This rubble moonscape was all that mattered to them.

Paul and Romo had been on this particular mission for a full twenty-four hours. Like moles, like rats, they had moved past many Chinese outposts and concentration points. Now they approached the southern portion of Poway, a place they had escaped days ago—in what seemed like another lifetime.

The Chinese ruled the skies. The Americans in Poway lacked UCAVs, fighters, bombers, anything that flew. Tac-lasers, SAMs and linked tank defense-nets were the only way to halt the Chinese from flying wherever they wanted. Word had come to them that more American air was transferring to SoCal, but that would take time.

Word had also come down that the Americans in Escondido were all out of time. It was escape today or they would never have another chance to do so. The Chinese had made it through San Gorgonio Pass and were pushing into Greater San Bernardino.

"There," Romo whispered.

Paul crawled beside his blood brother. They were commandos. Thus, this mission had fallen to them.

"Do you see?" Romo whispered.

Paul pulled out special binoculars. They were linked to his computers and they allowed battalion HQ to see what he saw. What he saw just now was an assembly area for more…

"Special infantry," Paul whispered. He loathed the zombie troopers. It appeared that the Chinese gathered their men for what would likely be another attempt to drive the Americans out of Poway.

"Receiving," an operator whispered in Paul's ear through his implant.

"Activating laser," Paul whispered in his throat microphone. He already held a laser designator and aimed it in the middle of the assembly area.

He didn't have long to wait. Thirty-four seconds later, the beginning of a highly accurate American mortar bombardment hit the assembly area. Shrapnel exploded and mowed down enemy combatants.

"That's it," the operator told Paul through his ear-implant. "The Colonel says he wants you two back at HQ."

"Negative," Paul said. "We're out here now. We might as well stay and feed you more information as it comes."

"I'm relaying that. Oh."

"What is it?" Paul asked.

"Ah…the Colonel has been listening to your transmission," the operator said. "He told me to tell you that you're not suicide soldiers. You're Americans. You're to get back here as quickly as you can. That's an order."

Paul and Romo traded glances. They both knew Poway would be their grave. The Chinese simply had too much.

Disengaging his throat microphone, Paul asked, "Well? What do you think? Do we go or stay? As far as I'm concerned, I'm sick of crawling."

Romo took his time answering. Finally, he said, "It would be a shame to give up now, not after all we've been through. Let us return to our line."

Paul stared at the special infantry groaning on the gory assembly area. A few tried to crawl away. American mortar shells continued to rain death. He wasn't dead yet, but the rearguard wasn't going to last forever against the Chinese. He was so tired, just sick of crawling, shooting, watching people die. Yet…he'd never given up before. Was this the place to call it quits? If he did, he would never see his family.

You're never going to see them away. The Chinese have as good as killed you.

Paul scowled. That sounded like quitter thinking. He'd never been a quitter before, why start now just because things looked bleak. Yeah, he might never see his wife again, but at least he was going to try until the very end.

"What the hell," he said. "Let's go back and stick it out until they put a bullet through our brains."

As he said that, a bitter well of determination rose up. Yeah, he was sick of fighting and he was weary. It just never ended. But he was going to see his wife again and see Mike. If he gave up, some Chinese soldier would rape Cheri and shoot his son.

Not while I'm alive, damnit. "You ready?" he asked Romo.

The assassin looked at him with his dead eyes. There was a flicker in the center of them, something dark and deadly.

"Si," Romo whispered. He shouldered his assault rifle and began to crawl through the rubble back toward the American lines.

RIVERSIDE, CALIFORNIA

With the others of the Eagle Team, Fighter Rank Zhu huddled around First Rank Tian. The thick-necked First Rank showed them a computer scroll and outlined the plan.

The White Tiger commandos stood outside a Safeway grocery store. Behind them in the street, artillery thundered with each salvo, the shells screaming overhead. They bombarded the Americans in another part of Riverside. T-66s waited in the parking lot, black-uniformed tankers sitting on their monsters, smoking looted American cigarettes.

"The enemy has stiffened here," the First Rank said, tapping the scroll.

Like the others, Zhu nodded. They no longer referred to him as the rookie. He had become one of them through the blizzard of endless combat. Their flight equipment was piled to the side, waiting for the next mission to begin.

"The Americans believe these buildings will act like bunkers," Tian explained. "We will show them otherwise."

In the past, Zhu might have grinned. He'd wanted to show the others he was good enough. He was too tired these days to worry about such a thing. They had made six...no, seven combat drops since the beginning of the campaign. Many of the commandos were dead. In fact, so many had died in the battle through San Gorgonio Pass that three-quarters of their squad were originally members of other squads. The Eagle Teams had paid a bitter price in blood helping to pry open the pass.

"Zhu, are you listening?" Tian asked.

"Yes, First Rank."

"No more stims for you," Tian said.

The others chuckled, even though it wasn't funny. One of the Chinese secrets to continual assaults was good stims that didn't turn the user silly, at least not until four days of continuous use.

Zhu had been on stims for three days already. They all had. Otherwise, they would have fallen asleep on the spot. Soon now, they would have no choice but to lie down and sleep, or risk using stims and accept the consequences.

"Are there any questions?" Tian asked the group.

Zhu began to scratch his face, letting his nails dig into the skin.

"Fighter Rank!" Tian said.

Zhu dropped his hand, and he discovered that several of his fingernails had become bloody. What was wrong with him?

"How many stims did you take this morning?" Tian asked.

Zhu shook his head. He couldn't remember.

"Stay close to me, Fighter Rank." Tian seemed embarrassed saying it.

"Yes, First Rank." Zhu wondered what would make the First Rank embarrassed. It was strange.

"Gear up," Tian said. "It is almost time to begin."

Zhu bandaged his face first. Then he began to don his jetpack and other equipment. It took time. Meanwhile, First Rank Tian inspected each of the commandos.

As Tian slapped Zhu's jetpack and tested one of the straps on his chest, the First Rank said softly, "You must be more careful, Fighter Rank."

"First Rank?"

Tian tugged a strap harder than necessary. "Too many died in San Gorgonio Pass. It was a bloodbath."

"But we won," Zhu said.

Tian released the strap and scowled at him. "Don't be a hero, Zhu. That is an order."

"Have I done something wrong?"

"You skinny fool," Tian hissed. "I'm sick of seeing my friends die. When you joined us you were so wet behind the ears it was painful. Then you became a real tiger in combat, a White Tiger." Tian shook his head. "Who would have believed it? The others are dead now but for us two. I won't die here. My mother read my horoscope before I left China. I will survive, and it will be a sorrow to me. Now I'm beginning to understand what she meant. I do not want you on my conscience, Fighter Rank."

"Yes, First Rank."

A ghost of a smile appeared on Tian's face. "You still don't understand. You are a fool, Zhu, and you're skinny and it makes no sense you should survive where the others have died. How have you managed this miracle?"

"I don't shirk my duty."

Tian looked away. "No. You have a death wish. Because of that, Yan Luo laughs at you just like the rest of us used to do."

"That is not true. I do not want to die."

"No?"

"I want to live, but I want to fight well even more."

Tian slapped him on the shoulder. "You have believed everything the instructors told you, Fighter Rank. It is a marvel. During this flight, I want you to stay close to me. Do you understand?"

"Yes, First Rank."

"You are to guard my back. That is an order."

"Guard you?" Zhu asked.

"I have too much to worry about and oversee during a fight. To have to guard myself every minute of the fight while I'm doing it, no, I'm not a wonder child."

Zhu stood straighter. "Ah, I understand. Yes, I will guard your back, First Rank."

"I'm counting on that," Tian said with a nod. "Now, hurry to your helo. We're about to lift-off."

***

Fourteen minutes later, the air taxis lifted with the Eagle Team members in place on the poles. Behind them, Gunhawks lofted to provide fire support.

Zhu watched entranced. This never failed to awe him. As the rotors turned faster, the ground dropped away and the city soon looked like a toy set. Radio chatter played in his headphones. Artillery opened up and a company of special infantry attacked the American line.

"Proceed to your grid coordinates."

"Roger," the air taxi pilot said.

Zhu's gut lurched as his helo headed back down into the battle. Around him, other helicopters zoomed for the large buildings a block behind the main enemy defenses. The American infantry had found large buildings to fortify. Clearing them in the old-fashioned way took time and blood or it took the buildings' destruction through artillery or tank fire.

"Now!" Tian said.

Zhu released his handlebars and jumped hard. He activated his jetpack and thrust away from the deadly blades. Then he dropped with his fellow Eagle Team soldiers. The top of a seven-story building rushed up. The tactical plan was simple. Grab several large buildings behind enemy lines: let the Americans know they had been cut off and trapped. First, they were going to have to secure this building.

"Fighter Rank, you're too far ahead," Tian said through the headphones. "Slow your descent and wait for me to land."

"Yes, First Rank." Zhu applied thrust. As his jetpack hissed, the heavy straps pulled at his shoulders. Others dropped faster now, and they landed on top of the building. Immediately, the commandos shed their jetpacks and raced for the stairwell.

The Army wanted Riverside fast, and using the White Tiger Eagle Teams was one of the secrets to getting it as soon as they wanted it.

Then the roof of the building rushed up, and Zhu touched down. He yanked his straps and the jetpack fell away with a clatter of noise. Grabbing his assault rifle, Zhu checked his impulse to follow the others already pouring down into the building. He must guard the First Rank's back.

A moment later, a bulky trooper landed beside him. The White Tiger shed his pack and flipped up his visor. It was Tian. He shouted orders into his throat microphone, constantly checked the computer scrolls attached to him and he strode toward the stairwell.

"Cover my back," he ordered Zhu.

Zhu raced into position, with his assault rifle ready. If the Americans came for Tian, they would first have to get past him. What a great honor the First Rank gave him. Zhu swore a silent oath then that before Tian died, he would die first protecting him.

White Tigers forever! In his mind, Zhu was finally and truly one of China's greatest elite soldiers. This position of honor from First Rank Tian proved it.

MURRIETA, CALIFORNIA

Stan was near the junction of I-15 and I-215. Five of the Behemoths were slated to head up I-215 to Perris and Riverside beyond. According to Colonel Wilson, SoCal Command had decided to split the regiment. They needed something to stop the Chinese advance. The enemy was chewing through Riverside too fast. The Behemoths were to give the Chinese something to think about and would provide anti-air protection for the last-ditch defenders.

"That's a mistake, sir," Stan said over the radio to Wilson. Each of them waited in their carrier-cab. Stan's tank had engine trouble again. Because of that, his tank would soon begin the slow journey to Corona.

"It's out of my hands," Wilson told him.

Stan studied his netbook. "Our Behemoths operate better when used all together like a closed fist. You need to explain that to General Larson, sir. We can't allow the Chinese to nibble one of our greatest tactical assets away, namely, these super-tanks."

"This is war, Captain. Sometimes there are no good choices."

Stan almost replied to that. Then he thought more carefully. Wilson was right and it showed him the Colonel had changed. Wilson wasn't Mr. Martinet anymore. Battle had transformed his outlook to something more rational.

"Yes sir, you're right," Stan told him. "It's just..."

"I don't like the order, either. I'm not sure we'll see those men again in this world."

Stan swallowed hard. He'd been training with the Behemoth crews for some time. What an awful thing. The others had kept their tanks running and because of that, the Army had likely signed those men's death warrants by sending them against the Chinese in Riverside.

"We're leaving," Jose said, climbing into the cab. The cushions compressed beneath his weight, making crinkling noises.

Soon, Stan heard the carrier's engine rumble. With a lurch, they began the slow, fifteen mph crawl for Corona. Beside them on the highway, Americans marched and others rode bicycles. The Chinese were coming, and SoCal Command was rushing this remnant of Army Group SoCal to Los Angeles.

Good luck, Stan thought toward the handful of Behemoths off to engage the Chinese Tank Army.

"Who's going to lead them, sir?"

"I am," Wilson said.

Stan sat blinking in the cab. "You, sir, you're leading the charge?"

"My tank is still in top running condition. It has always been the best-maintained Behemoth in the regiment."

"But sir..."

"By the way, Higgins, I spoke to General Larson. On my recommendation, he has promoted you to major. *Major* Higgins, you have command of the regiment until I return. I want you to keep those tanks alive and I want you to stop the Chinese from taking our cities away."

"Sir...I..."

"You know more about tank combat than the rest of us, Major. You take care of the regiment."

"Yes sir. I will. I...wish you Godspeed, sir. You'd better come back to us."

There was a raspy laugh. "You're a good man, Major. I respect you."

"I respect you as well, sir."

"Thank you, Major. I know in the past I may have been a—"

"Please, Colonel. You can tell me when you get back."

"Uh...yes, I suppose those sorts of things are best said face-to-face, aren't they?"

"That's right, sir."

"Good-bye, Major."

"Good-bye, Colonel Wilson. Give them hell."

BEIJING, PRC

Jian Hong stood outside the main, open-air polar bear cage of his extended zoo. It consisted of a giant pit, with rocks and a pool. A large concrete ditch fronted that and up here was the iron rail where Jian rested his hands.

The large mother bear swam in the water of the pool with her two cubs. They looked like giant swimming dogs.

"The breeders say she is my best mother," Jian told the Police Minster.

Xiao Yang, the Police Minister, was lean and wore a black uniform. He wore thick glasses and possessed strangely staring eyes. With his hands behind his back, he craned his neck, as if it was impossible for him to see the bears otherwise.

Jian tightened his grip on the black-painted rail. He sighed before glancing around. Tall Lion Guardsmen stood by the baboon enclosure. Since the last assassination attempt, he had doubled the number of his security personnel. It always comforted him seeing them.

"Why are you here, old friend?" Jian asked quietly. "I know you do not care for animals."

"You have excellent polar bears, Leader."

"Please," Jian said. "You do not need to pretend." He smiled as he said it. Xiao didn't need to pretend, but if the Minister of Police feared Jian, that showed *he* wielded true power. The fact of Xiao's fawning made him feel good. It still surprised Jian how far and how fast he had climbed. It was because he had dared to strike at precisely the right moment.

"Despite my lack of understanding concerning your pets," Xiao said, "the bears still seem healthy to me. It is my policy to attempt to see a situation as it is, not as others would have me believe it to be."

"You are being cryptic, old friend. There is no need for that between the two of us."

The Police Minister's tongue appeared as it wetted his lips. They were always wet looking, his lips. It was rather repugnant now that Jian thought of it. The man was repugnant, but he had his uses and he ran the police with an iron hand. Fortunately, the man was transparent, at least to someone with Jian's perceptiveness. It meant Jian could trust Xiao, at least to a point.

After Foreign Minister Deng, Xiao was the most dangerous man in China, making him the third most deadly. Clearly, as Leader, Jian knew himself to be more dangerous than any of the others. Hadn't he risen to the very top? "Risen" was perhaps the wrong word. He had climbed over the dead and grasping to reach the pinnacle of power on Earth.

Jian would do *anything* he needed in order to keep power. That included shooting old friends if the time ever came.

For a while, Jian watched the polar bears. At last, he turned to the patiently waiting Xiao. The man had no time or instinct for appreciating such beautiful animals as these. It showed that he lacked spirituality. Xiao's patience, however, was another sign of Jian's power. It also showed him that the Police Minister truly was dangerous. Patience was a priceless gift if wielded skillfully.

"Would you like one of the cubs?" Jian asked.

Xiao bowed at the waist. "You honor me, Leader. I would be delighted."

Jian laughed. "You do not want a polar bear cub."

"Even so, Leader, I would gladly accept one."

"And if it died from inattention and a lack of love?"

"I would execute the zookeeper who would have failed me," Xiao said.

"Hmm," Jian said. "Tell me, why are you here today? Does it concern California?"

"Yes Leader."

"Are you going to tell me that the others on the Ruling Committee are worried about the mounting casualties?"

"Yes Leader."

"Ah, I see. Then you may now consider me told."

"Leader...if you would allow me to speak further on the matter...I would greatly appreciate it."

Jian watched the mother bear climb out of the pool and shake herself like a dog. "Very well," he said, "what is your warning?"

"I have inspected the numbers, Leader."

"Do you mean the casualty lists?"

"Yes Leader."

"They are exorbitant. Is that what you want to say?"

"I believe Deng and his clique expected heavy losses," Xiao said. "I think they also expected a larger area of conquest in exchange for the blood of Chinese soldiery."

"I have spoken to Marshal Nung. He has assured me that the heavy losses will bring us exceptional victory. We must have patience in order to realize complete victory."

"I understand that you support Marshal Nung, Leader, but..."

Jian released the rail and tore his gaze from his beloved polar bears. He studied Xiao. The Police Minister looked at him as a giant goldfish might. The thick glasses were like peering through an aquarium.

"But what, Police Minister?" Jian asked in a silky voice.

Xiao hesitated before saying, "Leader, it appears as if the assaults have bogged down."

"This is *your* assessment?"

"No Leader. Marshal Kao told me—"

Jian raised his right hand, halting Xiao's words. "Let me explain something to do you. Marshal Kao despises Marshal Nung."

"I am aware of that."

"I will tell you something more. There is no one in China like Marshal Nung. He hastens to the attack while others careful weigh options. He takes an army and grinds the enemy down with it, destroying them so he can achieve victory."

"He is chewing through his own army as well, Leader."

"I grant you that," Jian said. "Yes, he is not afraid to spill blood. Even so, we have far more soldiers and more equipment than the Americans do. Nung has nearly obliterated an entire American Army Group in some of the toughest defensive terrain in the country. What is more, he is on the verge of smashing through Los Angeles. Once he breaks through into Bakersfield, I believe he will give us the entire state and perhaps the whole West Coast. It will be a bitter and devastating blow to the enemy. My analysts tell me it will shatter American resolve. Perhaps you don't believe that. But it is a historical fact and rather well known that the Americans loathe losing men. They do not have the stomach for sustained combat that brings death to hundreds of thousands of their own soldiers."

"That has been true in the past during their foreign adventures into other countries," Xiao said. "Will that hold true as they defend their homeland?"

"Americans are Americans."

"Ah, yes," Xiao said. "That is succinctly put, Leader. Yet if I may be so bold, I would like to tell you about Marshal Kao's charts. It outlines—"

Jian began shaking his head. "I have seen Kao's precious charts. I have also witnessed Nung's continued advance and the tens of thousands of Americans marching into captivity. Perhaps I will even keep some here next to my polar bears."

Xiao chuckled politely, a false noise like a sitcom's laugh track.

"The fact is," Jian said, "that Marshal Nung will soon capture Corona. Ah, you no doubt didn't believe I followed the situation as carefully as that, but I attend a daily briefing on the battle. Our Nung will bottle the Americans that the giant tanks freed from the Escondido Pocket."

"And if he fails in that, Leader?"

Jian looked away. He didn't care for the Police Minister's insistence in this. "As long as Marshal Nung advances, I will support him. The man has an iron will when it comes to devising ways of outmaneuvering the enemy."

"Yes, I see. If I may ask one more question, Leader?"

"Speak," Jian said, letting a hint of annoyance enter his voice.

Xiao hesitated once more before saying, "What if Marshal Nung destroys the sword you've given him as he dashes it against a rock-like defense?"

"Hmm...that was well said. Yes, I must consider such a possibility, shouldn't I? Are you suggesting we halt the offensive?"

"No," Xiao replied. "But I urge you to give Marshal Kao's analysis greater weight. Perhaps Nung is correct and the Americans are on the verge of collapse. We have killed and captured the majority of them in Southern California. If he captures the state and if he carves out the entire Western Coast, then he would be a hero of the people. But if he destroys the sword you've given him, Leader, he will have become a veritable devil to our great cause."

Jian thought about that as he watched one of the cubs nursing. Could Kao be right? Nung was such a fighter, a real fire-eater. The man had told the Ruling Committee in advance that his armies would sustain heavy casualties during this battle. Hadn't the others been listening? This...situation wasn't a surprise. Well, maybe the broad extent of the losses was rather grim. But China possessed young men in abundance, eager to win marriage permits. Joining the military was one of the quickest ways to do so. There were always more hungry young men to feed the furnace of war.

Jian faced the lip-wetting Xiao. Truly, that was a disgusting habit. "Police Minister, Marshal Nung fights, and China needs a fighter, as North American cannot be conquered any other

335

way. As long as he advances, I will support him. Now, if you will excuse me?"

Xiao bowed at the waist and he bowed deeply. "Thank you for your time, Leader."

"No, I thank you for your forthrightness, old friend. Now, I bid you a good day."

INTERSTATE 215, CALIFORNIA

Colonel Wilson stood in the top hatch of his Behemoth. The monster clattered and clanked at twenty-five mph. It tore up the freeway, spewing concrete chunks behind the treads.

A few Strykers acted as scouts, roaming ahead on the freeway. Thirteen M1A3 Abrams roared behind the Strykers but ahead of the Behemoths. Behind Wilson's five experimental tanks followed Bradley Fighting Vehicles. These also carried extra ammo and battery supplies for the Behemoth tanks. Interspaced among the heavier vehicles were Humvee Avengers carrying Blowdart anti-air missiles.

This was a suicide run, a desperation gambit by SoCal Command to halt the Chinese assault toward Corona—at least for a little while. The formation came up from the south toward Riverside, if nothing else, to destroy the Chinese supply line feeding the assault units heading toward Corona.

America needed time to get the soldiers out of Escondido and Temecula. Then command needed time to set the men into strong defensive positions in Greater Los Angeles and rearm them with supplies rushed west through the Sierra Nevada passes.

The Chinese had to know the Behemoths were coming. Wilson was surprised that so far the enemy hadn't—

He put a hand on his headphone. "Sir," his comm-officer inside the Behemoth told him. "I have word from SoCal Command. Chinese aircraft are on their way."

Wilson slid down from the hatch, closing it with a clang. The Avengers were useful, but they weren't tac-lasers and couldn't handle a truly concentrated air attack. No. Today, as Captain—as Major Higgins had shown earlier, the Behemoths would have to provide the chief anti-air defense with their amazing electromagnetic cannons.

Wilson strapped himself into his commander's seat. He was surrounded by screens and knew the Behemoth to be the most advanced tank the world had ever seen. Science fiction novels had predicted tanks like this. His father used to read to him. He remembered the Bolo stories by Keith Laumer. These tanks weren't sentient like those in the series, but the internal AI gave them yet another edge over the Chinese.

Wilson had listened to Higgins before telling the other officers about the superior Chinese equipment during the Alaskan War. This time, it was different. Yet now they were throwing away these marvelous tanks in a seemingly futile effort.

"Sir," the comm-officer said. "The Chinese appear to be using drones. And it looks as if they have stand-off bombers behind them."

Wilson nodded. The American Air Force had taken a terrible beating in the earliest phase of the war. It was unconscionable the U.S. lacked air superiority over its own land. Yet such was the case here. The Chinese, Japanese and Korean factories simply poured out too much materiel. It was the reverse of World War II, where America had swamped the Axis Powers through abundant supplies, materiel and hard fighting by tough soldiers.

"Link the defensive net," Wilson ordered.

"Yes sir."

The Behemoths slowed, and the Humvee Avengers circled the big tanks. The engine revved and the huge monster began to shake with power.

Four minutes later, the attack began as Chinese UCAVs roared at treetop level, with their main cannons chugging shells and other drones firing air-to-ground missiles.

The nearest Avengers fired as Blowdart after Blowdart hissed out of the tubes and rocketed at the enemy.

"I'm switching over air command to the AI, sir."

Wilson rubbed his mouth nervously. It was a strange feeling giving the Behemoth control on the weapon systems.

He had never gotten used to that. It made him feel like a mouse inside a steel trap.

"Yes, switch over command," Wilson said.

The turret swiveled, the cannon adjusted and the *SLAM* of the shell leaving the gun made the three-hundred ton monster shudder.

Wilson watched on his screens. It was incredible. The drones bored in, chugging shells at them. The Behemoth 30mm cannons fired defensively and the flechette launchers filled the air with clouds of metal.

A heavier air-to-ground missile appeared. It must have come from a standoff bomber. Yes, the drones were a shield for the more dangerous aircraft: how very elementary and yet clever of the enemy. An M1A3 exploded, rocking the seventy-ton vehicle as both sets of treads peeled away. The Bradleys joined the Avengers and fired anti-air missiles.

Wilson clenched his jaws so tightly that the muscles hinging them throbbed with the effort. A drone disintegrated, pieces of it raining like hail. Then three more blew up.

Inside the tank, the turret swiveled fast with its electric motors. The cannon adjusted yet again and the great tank repeatedly shuddered. Like duck hunters gone wild, the five Behemoths blew down the drones. In some cases, they reached out twenty miles and destroyed fleeing bombers.

"Five Abrams are gone," the comm-officer informed him.

"Keep advancing," Wilson said. "We're not going to stop the Chinese if we stand still."

"Cruise missiles!" the comm-officer shouted.

"It's all up to the AIs now," Wilson said, speaking much more calmly than he felt.

The engine revved, thrumming so his bones shook, and Wilson wondered if that had occurred because the AI had willed it so. How long would it take before such tanks dispensed with their human crews and highly advanced artificial intelligences did the job?

Rubbing his sore jaw, Colonel Wilson watched the screens as if they showed the Super Bowl with his favorite team, the quarterback daring to sprint for the end zone, with the opponent's most brutal safety heading straight at him.

338

"Hit!" the comm-officer shouted.

On a screen, Wilson watched a cruise missile explode, the fiery parts raining on a grove of nearby peach trees.

Eleven seconds later, Wilson groaned as he watched another Abrams blow up. Farther away, Strykers became burning hulks. The cruise missiles were so damned fast and agile against the Blowdart missiles. Fortunately, the Behemoth's AI and the electromagnetic cannon were too good for them.

"How many more cruise missiles do they have?" Wilson asked.

The comm-officer was slow in answering. Checking his screens, Wilson couldn't see that there were any more.

"SoCal Command just called, sir. It sounds as if that's it for the moment."

As he hunched over the screens, Wilson blinked furiously. Had they really survived the combined air and cruise missile assault? These tanks were amazing. It was incredible. "How…how are we doing on shells?"

"Our tank is down to forty percent ammo supply, sir."

"Are the other Behemoths in a similar predicament?"

"I'm sure they are, sir."

"Then we're calling a halt, a short one. Some of those Bradleys survived. I want them to load us up to the gills. Then we're continuing the advance to Riverside. I can't believe it. These tanks work even better than I'd expected."

"That's good for us, sir."

"Indeed," Wilson said. "Now let's get moving."

SAN YSIDRO, CALIFORNIA

Marshal Nung scowled at General Pi. They both stood around the computer table, witnessing the giant tanks shrugging off a combined air-cruise missile attack.

"What are your orders, Marshal," Pi asked.

"We destroyed most of their attendants," Nung muttered. He meant the Abrams, Strykers and some of the Bradleys. The giant tanks were beginning to feel invincible to him. How many of those tanks did the Americans have that they could just throw these away in a suicidal fury? Yet was it a suicidal attack? Clearly, the Americans attempted to thwart his advance toward Corona. What was the right move? Should he let the T-66s race ahead, or should he order them to turn south and destroy these five giant tanks.

"Sir?" General Pi asked.

"I dare not let the American soldiers run free into Los Angeles," Nung said.

"Many have already left Corona, sir, heading for Fullerton, Anaheim and Pomona in the north."

"I understand that." Nung frowned for a time before saying, "Los Angeles is a heavily urbanized environment. I had hoped to destroy the American army before having to wade through the great city."

"Begging your pardon, Marshal?"

"Yes, yes, give me your wisdom."

"I do not believe we can allow the American tanks to run amok among our supply vehicles. Those tanks—"

Nung hung his head, and he shook it. He hated to give the order. He loathed the idea of turning back. He had never done such a thing in Siberia and during the Alaskan Campaign with the swift run across the Arctic ice…

"They are slow tanks," Nung said.

"They're fast enough if we cannot destroy them, sir."

Nung slammed a fist onto the computer table. "Turn the T-66s. We must destroy these tanks first. Then we will race to Corona."

"As you command, Marshal," General Pi said, motioning to the chief communications officer.

RIVERSIDE, CALIFORNIA

Colonel Wilson fingered the microphone as he sat in the commander's chair inside his Behemoth. He neared Riverside after enduring several air assaults and cruise missile attacks. Most of the accompanying vehicles were burning wrecks. Each of the five Behemoths had survived. They kept heading north toward the main enemy concentration near Riverside.

Several computer screens surrounded Wilson, giving him visuals outside and images from an Air Force recon UAV that sneaked onto the battlefield. The U.S. drone wouldn't last long, but while he could, Wilson studied the situation from an aerial view.

The Chinese had burst through Riverside. Chinese triple-turreted tanks and IFVs charged toward Corona. Now, some of those T-66s had turned back, likely to engage his Behemoths.

He had to keep buying the U.S. Army time. Most of the troops freed from Escondido carried personal weapons and little else. That meant most of the heavy equipment remained in the pocket. The soldiers didn't have the weaponry needed to face T-66s, not yet, anyway.

Wilson opened communications with the other four Behemoths. "Men, we're too slow to run away. Otherwise, I might suggest it now that we have the T-66s turned around." He closed communications because suddenly his throat was too dry to speak. He tried swallowing several times and finally twisted open one of the bottled waters. He sipped several times.

Let's try this again.

Clicking on the microphone, he said, "Sorry for the interruption. Men, it has been an honor serving with you. We helped create the greatest tank ever made. We've also shown the Chinese a thing or two I'm sure they hadn't expected. Now, I don't know about the rest of you, but there is not another, a finer company of men, of soldiers, that I would rather die with."

There. He'd said it. They were going to die. There was no turning back with these slow monsters. Thus…thus…Wilson took another swallow of water.

"I have an idea, gentlemen. I mean to teach the Chinese a lesson that they will never forget. I mean to show them what Americans can do when they are good and pissed. I'm going to walk among their best tanks and proceed to kick their sorry asses from here to kingdom come. I'm going to use these Behemoths as they were meant to be used, and that is to ram my fist down their collective throats and make them gag."

Wilson frowned. That sounded like a speech. He had been making those all his life. He couldn't stop that even here at the gate to death. Well, maybe that was all right. He had been giving speeches and acting like a prick for far too long. Now he could redeem everything by fighting bravely and with deadly force.

"General Larson believed we had to defend Los Angeles by attacking here. Sometimes, gentlemen, life or God, I'm not sure which, hands you a shit job. We have such a job this time. We signed up as soldiers, and that means that sometimes you have to put your body in harm's way. Well, I love my country. These aggressors are here to steal it out from under me. That means I'm going to fight until I'm dead or until I've driven them into the sea. I'm sorry for talking so much. I'm sorry for many things. I suppose I mean to make up for everything rotten I've done by laying down my life. 'Greater love has no man than this: that he lay down his life for his friends.' That's from the Bible, gentlemen, the very words of God. We're going to lay down our lives in the next half-hour. Let's make sure we do it in such a way that we save our brothers so they can drive the Chinese into the sea."

Wilson set down the microphone as a strange calm settled over him. He felt like a still lake on a perfect day, the sun a delight on the skin. One by one, his tank commanders called in, agreeing with him.

Afterward, near the city of Riverside, began the death ride of the Behemoths into the heart of the Chinese advance.

It began as long-range howitzers rained down a sheet of steel against them. The Chinese had seen their advance and likely they knew their route. Normally, that should have been enough to set up a perfect ambush. It didn't work out that way this time. The howitzers attempted to pummel the Behemoths, but most of the shells never made it through the tank defenses. Those that did rained on reinforced armor. The Behemoths, unlike most modern tanks, had put as heavy armor on top as they did in front. It made for an extra-heavy and tall tank, but with this engine, it didn't matter.

Drone hovers appeared, firing as they raced like greyhounds toward the Behemoths. If they could get close enough, the experimental tanks would be unable to use their defensive fire effectively. Behind the hovers came Marauder light tanks. For several minutes, confusion reigned. The Chinese vehicles and howitzers spewed mass fire against the five American giants.

Wilson winced each time an enemy sabot round made it through the blizzard of defensive fire and hit the tank. Each round *clanged* like a hammer, ringing in the Colonel's ears. But none of the lighter cannons had the force to break through the special armor.

In return the five Behemoths reaped a swathing harvest of enemy vehicles. Hovers exploded, flipping over and burning. One flew into the air, spun and landed so the cannon bored into the earth like a drill, until it snapped and the vehicle crashed again, this time onto its side. A light tank burst into flame. A crewmember opened a hatch and tried to escape. The hatch banged onto him, trapping the man. He opened his mouth, screaming surely. His hands covered his face, but the flames melted those and soon the man sagged, dead.

It was grim. It was war, and the Behemoth was a demon in its element of destruction.

"I'm seeing the howitzers, sir, in the long-range scope."

"Give the AI its head," Wilson ordered.

The turret swiveled, a targeting laser sighted and the tank shuddered as the cannon spewed a shell. Two miles away, a howitzer blew into separate pieces.

The other howitzers continued banging away, sending their shells in a ballistic trajectory. The Behemoths fired their penetrators in a nearly straight line and many times faster than the enemy munitions.

Chinese infantry began to appear from ditches, doorways and on rooftops. They popped off RPGs. Those had no effect on the Behemoths, but they kept trying. Too many failed to run away in time and died to flechettes shredding them into gory ruin.

A mile and a half later, the first T-66s entered the fray. They were eighteen of the advanced Chinese tanks in the first wave. None survived, although they knocked a tread off a Behemoth.

"What are your orders, sir?" the crippled Behemoth commander asked.

"Tell me this," Wilson said. "Can you bail out and run back to our lines?"

"We would never make it, sir."

"I agree."

"So…"

"So you remain where you are, commander," Wilson said. "Your cannon has greater reach than any other vehicle on the battlefield does. You've just become our artillery support, in a manner of speaking."

"Yes, Colonel, I understand. Good luck, sir."

"We do this for America, commander."

"And for our families, sir."

"Yes," Wilson said. "They are the heart of our country."

Because the first wave of T-66s failed to halt them, the Behemoths advanced. A new American recon drone appeared overhead after a Chinese SAM had destroyed the first one. This UAV provided them targeting coordinates on hundreds of big Chinese supply trucks in the distance.

"Fire at will," Wilson ordered.

In a matter of three and a half minutes, one hundred and sixteen haulers exploded and began to burn. Very few escaped.

"I'm low on ammunition, Colonel," one Behemoth commander radioed.

"There's no help for it now," Wilson said. "We keep advancing. Choose your targets carefully. If nothing else, you can provide us with protective fire."

The four Behemoths, three surviving Bradleys and two brave and lucky Humvees reached the outskirts of Riverside. The final battle began with another cruise missile attack, followed by a thousand special infantry, fifty light tanks and two hundred and forty-one T-66s. It was an inferno of destruction, with nearly one hundred percent Chinese losses.

Then the first Behemoth finally died as four T-66 shells made it through the defensive fire and together hammered through the amazingly thick armor.

A new air assault destroyed a second Behemoth, this one to the rear of the formation. That left three experimental tanks, then two and finally Colonel Wilson was alone with his crew among a sea of burning Chinese vehicles.

Wilson viewed the screens. He had never seen a battlefield like this. Over two hundred and twenty triple-turreted tanks burned or lay on their sides, destroyed. The Behemoths had become a plague to the Chinese tanks.

Now three more big enemy tanks clanked into view.

"Sir!" the comm-officer shouted.

The Behemoth turret swiveled. The giant tank shuddered, and they destroyed yet another enemy tank. Then the world ended for Colonel Wilson as the enemy cannons blew past the defensive fire and opened holes in the battered armor. The huge engine exploded. The world turned white and Colonel Wilson became simply the latest Killed in Action in the defense of his homeland.

POWAY, CALIFORNIA

Three days after the original breakthrough of the Behemoths into the Escondido Pocket, Paul clutched the butterfly controls of a Browning .50 caliber. He shared a foxhole with Romo outside of Poway. Clouds hid the sun. The Chinese were stirring in the rubble of the destroyed city, likely getting ready for yet another attack. To Kavanagh it seemed as if the enemy never slept.

All during the exodus of the trapped Americans through Escondido and I-15, the Chinese had fought their way through Poway, trying to rush the rearguard, to shatter them and collapse the pocket.

Paul's eyes felt gritty and he yawned. He'd been fighting nonstop for days and he just wanted to sleep. He feared that if he did, he wouldn't wake up in this world. He'd been thinking a lot about his family lately. He realized now that he would never get to see them again, but at least he had done his part to make sure LA didn't fall to the Chinese.

"How many did you say again?" he asked Romo.

The assassin sat in the bottom of the foxhole as he clutched extra ammo. He had been to battalion HQ and come back with news.

Romo lifted his chin off his chest. "What did you say?"

"How many of us have made it out of the cauldron so far?"

"I don't know. I can't remember."

Paul shrugged, wondering when the Chinese were going to attack. He was bone-tired.

The Chinese had dropped leaflets, showing long lines of American soldiers marching into captivity. The Chinese were busy mopping up the remnants of the once proud Army Group SoCal. Soon, now, everything would hit Los Angeles. First they would first sweep away the rearguard here in Poway and eat up what was left of the Escondido Pocket.

It was just a matter of time before the Chinese juggernaut hit them. The truth, the Americans who had had held out for weeks south of here had given the Chinese something to do. American stubbornness had given the men here time to reach Los Angeles.

The Chinese in Poway...Paul rubbed his eyes. He'd almost fallen asleep. It had been a long trek since Mexico, since the commando assault on the Blue Swan site. Now—

"Brother," Romo said, shaking his shoulder. "Wake up."

"Huh?" Paul lifted his head from where it had dropped onto his crossed arms. He'd fallen asleep after all, standing upright in the foxhole. His mouth tasted like old coffee grinds, and he smacked his lips. Then resolve filled him as he remembered where he was. He gripped the Browning and swiveled it—

"Did you hear me?" Romo asked.

"The Chinese aren't attacking yet," Paul said, scowling as he studied the enemy. Couldn't Romo let him get a little shuteye? The lousy assassin—

"Forget about the Chinese," Romo said. "The Colonel wants us back in Battalion HQ."

Paul glanced at Romo. "What are you talking about?"

"You've been given orders to go to Battalion HQ. You were asleep when it came."

"Why are we supposed to go back there?" Paul asked.

"Let's go see."

With his index finger, Paul dug grit out of his right eye. He nodded and grunted as he heaved up out of the foxhole. They crawled to a trench and then hurried back toward the rear.

Battalion HQ was a sandbagged position with logs over a very large hole and with lots of dirt over the logs. Back a ways, a small black helicopter waited beside three tough-looking soldiers in body armor.

"Hold it," an MP said, coming out of the shadows of the HQ.

"We're supposed to report," Romo said.

"Who told you that?" the MP asked.

"This is Paul Kavanagh, Gunnery Sergeant Paul Kavanagh of Marine Recon."

"Oh," the MP said. "Then you'd better head over there, you lousy bastard," he told Paul. "Hurry your butt, you lucky S.O.B."

"What's going on?" Paul whispered, as Romo pulled him away from the MP, out of the trench and headed for the helo.

The assassin shrugged.

At their approach, the three tough-looking soldiers raised their weapons. By their insignia, they were Green Berets.

"This is Paul Kavanagh," Romo said.

The meanest-looking of the three squinted at Paul. "You don't look like much to me."

Paul just stared at the man. He had a nametag, if you could believe it. It said Donovan.

"All right then," Donovan said. "Let's go."

Paul shook his head. "What are you talking about?"

"You're leaving this shithole," Donovan said.

Scowling, Paul asked, "Why?"

"He asks why?" Donovan told the other two. One of them shrugged. "I'm guessing you know a General Ochoa," Donovan told Paul.

"The General Ochoa of SOCOM?" Paul asked.

"That's right."

"Okay? Yeah, I know him. What about it?"

"General Ochoa must figure you're something special," Donovan said. "Otherwise, he wouldn't have sent us to fly in and pick you up. You're going to LA."

347

Paul stared at the man.

"Did you hear me?" Donovan asked.

"Yeah," Paul said. He heard; he just couldn't believe it. "Come on," he told Romo. "Let's board the helicopter."

"Sorry," Donovan said, putting a hand up near Romo's chest. "He's not coming. I only have orders to take Paul Kavanagh."

Paul stood as if struck. He began to shake his head.

"Do not be foolish," Romo told him. "Get out alive while you can."

"No."

"Do we have to drag you out?" Donovan asked.

Paul stepped away from the three SOF soldiers and drew his sidearm, aiming it at Donovan. "I'm staying unless you take my blood brother with me."

"Your what?" Donovan asked.

"You heard me," Paul said.

Donovan studied Paul and finally backed away. He went to the helicopter and climbed in.

"You are mad," Romo said. "I would leave you if they offered this to me."

"No you wouldn't," Paul said.

Instead of arguing, Romo looked away.

Donovan jumped down from the helo. He looked bemused as he approached. "Well, well, well, it seems like General Ochoa is in a good mood today. You can bring your little buddy with you. Come on then. Let's get going while the corridor is still open. It won't last forever."

Paul holstered his gun and strode past Donovan and the other two SOF soldiers to climb into the back of the helo. Romo followed. As they buckled in, the three Green Berets entered and the rotors sped up. They lifted, and Paul felt a sense of déjà vu. This was weird. He was going to live and he might even see his wife again, see his son.

The helicopter kept low, a mere fifty feet above the earth. Assist jets kicked in and the little machine zoomed fast, soon flying over Escondido. In minutes, it shot over a long marching column of American soldiers heading for Temecula. They were on I-15, the last open corridor to freedom and Los Angeles.

Paul was glad to leave, but he couldn't help but think of the soldiers outside of Poway holding the line while others marched away to continue the fight. It wasn't just. It wasn't fair. It was war, and she was a mean-faced witch.

-12-
The Battle for Los Angeles

WASHINGTON, D.C.

It was a somber meeting in the underground bunker. The briefing major spoke in a monotone, making Anna wonder if the woman used drugs. Beside her, Levin doodled listlessly. While the President, he watched the proceedings like a man awaiting his death sentence.

There should have been some delight, Anna felt, because the majority of the soldiers from the Escondido Pocket had reached Corona before the Chinese. The soldiers had split in different directions. One third of them had gone to Pomona in the north. The rest had traveled to Fullerton and Anaheim in the west. The sacrifice of the Behemoths had brought about the needed miracle.

Anna believed the somberness was because the situation was still grim and the enemy almost as unrelenting as before. The Chinese simply refused to slow down.

According to the major, in a normal battle the Chinese would have accepted this victory to rest and resupply their troops before they started the next round. Intelligence showed that the Chinese were exhausted just like the Americans. Instead of following their usual doctrine, the Chinese kept pushing. They had swept through the defenses at Corona, rushing after the escaped soldiers until the battle-lines now reached Fullerton and Anaheim and Pomona. Just as bad, with so many of the formerly trapped Americans entering POW camps, the Chinese advance up the coast had picked up speed again, reaching Costa Mesa and Huntington Beach.

General Alan of the Joint Chiefs motioned to the major. As she sat down, he stood up.

"Mr. President, I suggest we speak frankly."

"Of course," Sims said.

General Alan tapped the table before saying, "As I'm sure you are aware, sir, there is a grave psychological effect on a soldier when he is constantly retreating. His belief in holding his position weakens each time the enemy drives him back. Our soldiers have retreated across Southern California from the border fortifications to Los Angeles. They are shocked. They are tired and now they have lost most of their heavy equipment. The Chinese have more numbers, more equipment and in most cases, better tech."

"Are you saying we cannot win?" Sims asked.

Anna noticed the President asked that with an edge to his voice.

"No, Mr. President, I am not saying we cannot win. I am saying that we have reached the crisis point. I'm sure the Chinese have problems. Nevertheless this accelerated attack with their acceptance of sustained casualties has produced results for them, if at a very bloody cost. In the end, who pays the highest butcher's bill doesn't determine victory, but who wins the political contest does. The Vietnamese took vastly more losses than we did back in the 1960s and 70s, yet they won the political battle because the Communists remained in power there. We have hurt the Chinese, sir, but at this point, they are winning the battle."

"Don't you think I know that?" Sims asked, with his voice harsh with a burr as if he'd shouted a long time.

"We are speaking frankly, sir. We are facing the grim reality of defeat. The majority of our troops in Los Angeles lack heavy equipment. We are shipping them more, but the trains need time. The trucks need time. The soldiers also need time to regain confidence in themselves."

"They're all out of time," Sims said.

351

"Understood, sir," Alan said. "I suggest, therefore, that we use our submarines more boldly. Of paramount importance would be the sinking of Special Infantry transports. We cannot let the Chinese practice anymore of their SI wave assaults against us."

"Can we distinguish those transports from others while they are en route?" Sims asked.

"Director?" General Alan asked.

Dr. Levin nodded slowly. "Possibly," he said.

"Are you referring to your spy-ring in Beijing?" Sims asked.

"Yes, Mr. President."

"Then I agree to this bolder use of our submarines," Sims said. "Now, what else can we do?"

"Our soldiers can start holding their ground," Alan said. "We are now in one of the most extensive urban environments in the world. Such territory makes for excellent defensive terrain. There is little likelihood of the Chinese cutting our supply lines here, as the critical one runs through the Grapevine to Bakersfield and through Central California and then to the Sierra Nevada passes."

"They need to hold," Sims said, "but we need to buy our soldiers time, even if it's only an extra day."

"Why not rush mass reinforcements to Los Angeles?" Levin asked. "We have more troops, many more."

"We could do that," General Alan admitted. "But we would do so at a grave risk elsewhere, and in more critically strategic locations. That is what I mean about speaking frankly. We must look at the strategic picture. This attack into California is simply the opening assault against North America. My DIA analysts suggest that counting the naval assault, two million PAA soldiers have driven into the state. That leaves over nine million more for us to deal with. The Germans are heavily reinforcing Cuba, which indicates they are getting ready to move against us. The South American Federation and the rest of the PAA forces are, in our estimation, operationally ready to invade Texas and New Mexico with a mass assault that will make the Californian attack pale in comparison."

General Alan glanced around the table. "Until the enemy commits himself, we must carefully weigh the reinforcements we send to Los Angeles. If we entrain too many, we could weaken ourselves elsewhere at too great a cost."

"We cannot afford to lose California," Sims said.

"I agree, Mr. President. But neither can we afford to save California and lose Texas, which would be a much deadlier blow to our defenses. In the worst case, we could set up new defenses in the Sierra Nevada Mountains. But to lose Texas…it would open up the underbelly of America to the aggressors."

The silence grew as General Alan stopped talking. The importance of his words stamped themselves onto Anna.

President Sims seemed to age before them as his shoulders drooped. Finally, he cleared his throat and said in a soft voice, "Then it's up to the soldiers in Los Angeles to hold on until new heavy equipment can beef up their formations."

"It's up to the soldiers on the ground to hold," General Alan agreed. "If they can, they could turn the Chinese drive into a prohibitive siege for the enemy."

The President stared at his hands. After a time, he said. "I admit to finding myself dumbfounded at Chinese aggressiveness and to their adroit maneuverability in the Southern Californian environment."

"Begging your pardon, sir…" General Alan said.

"Go ahead, speak your mind," Sims said.

"Respectfully, sir, I would hardly call what we've seen high maneuverability on their part. Except for the original tank drive past the Salton Sea, it has been more like endless grinding battles of attrition."

"No," Sims said, "I don't see it that way. The Blue Swam missile assault nearly collapsed our entire SoCal Fortifications. Using the partial success of the EMP missiles, the Chinese have used grinding attritional battles to break through in critical areas and then they proceeded to surround our shattered Army Group. We've witnessed slow-motion maneuvering in an environment that usually brings month-long sieges. When you think about, it is very original in concept and execution, much like their drive across the Arctic ice seven years ago."

General Alan shrugged and turned to whisper to the major, his aide.

"Are the Chinese historically known for such military innovation?" Sims asked.

With a start, Anna realized he addressed her. "Uh...I'm uncertain, Mr. President. In the past, my analysis concentrated on the political aspects, not the military."

"It's something to think about," Sims said.

"Mr. President," General Alan said, "if you'll consider this..."

Anna cocked her head as she thought about what the President had just asked her. It was a chance comment perhaps, but something about it nagged at her.

I have to study this.

She took out her smart phone and turned on the recorder, telling herself to look into this first thing tomorrow morning.

SAN YSIDRO, CALIFORNIA

Marshal Nung sat back at his desk. He rubbed his orbs until purple spots appeared before them. They were tired from reading endless reports.

He had been studying the American air commitment with a careful eye. During the first days of the campaign they had burned up a large portion of their air forces. Because of the commando attacks on the Blue Swan launching sites, it had won the Americans much. In his estimation, it had been a worthy exchange for the enemy. Still, U.S. air power had been steadily dwindling throughout the campaign.

Now he had reached the critical phase of the Battle for California. So much had gone wrong, a common problem in war. No plan survived contact with the enemy. He hadn't expected the casualties to reach such an excessively bloody point so quickly. Yet they had. It was a fact. He couldn't change that so there was no use worrying about it.

The key elements were easy to see. The Blue Swan missiles hadn't worked as thoroughly as he'd hoped. Still, they had torn holes in the SoCal Fortifications. The missiles had given him his great chance. Another element had been the giant American tanks. They had thwarted him at Palm Springs. They had also freed a pocket and slowed his advanced into Los Angeles.

Now it was time to commit the final reserves. He had many fresh divisions left and it would take a day or two to deploy them at the front. They would have to grind through the defenses in the great urban sprawl that was Los Angeles.

Another bitter pill had been the failure of the Navy to capture the Bay Area and drive through the delta into Central California. The naval infantry was bogged down now in the Bay Area, crawling toward San Francisco. They tied down some U.S. formations, but they did not threaten the state with sudden capture. The nuclear missiles there had won the Americans a great reprieve.

It was time to return them the favor. It was time to beseech the Leader and gain approval to use nuclear weapons against the U.S. He would not use them on American cities nor would he use them on American formations. He would not give China a nuclear black eye. But with nuclear weapons he would cut off the Los Angeles troops from reinforcements.

Marshal Nung sighed, rubbed his eyes and picked up his e-reader. He had a few more reports to digest. Then he needed to speak to the Leader. He could no longer spare the Eagle Team troops. He was going to need every one of them to outmaneuver the enemy in Los Angeles.

The answer was there, in the heavy American losses in air assets. Nung hadn't expected the enemy to use his air so freely and let it dwindle to almost nothing. That was the opening he needed for something new.

Nung began reading again, clicking his e-reader, and soon he smiled. This could work. This would ensure that the Americans holding Los Angeles would wither on the vine. The battle had been costlier than expected, but it was still possible to win the entire state with the troops he had remaining. What he needed to do was gain the Leader's permission and then begin the last leg of the Southern Californian assault with his last fresh formations.

BEIJING, PRC

"Yes," Jian Hong said. He spoke via a computer screen to Marshal Nung. The entire Ruling Committee attended, listening to the exchange. Nung had been most persuasive regarding the need for nuclear weapons.

Naturally, Marshal Kao and Foreign Minister Deng had disagreed. Jian had sat back and let Nung argue with them. Kao and Deng feared nuclear escalation, or so they said. Jian was beginning to wonder if those two feared nuclear usage because they secretly wished for the California attack to fail. Well, he would put an end to this right now.

Jian sat stiffly in his chair as the old Chairman used to do in these situations. He said, "It is time to teach the Americans that they are not the only ones who can unleash nuclear fire." Jian directed his words to Nung but wanted Kao and Deng to understand why he was giving the order. "You have my go-ahead, Marshal Nung. Teach the Americans a most bitter lesson."

DONNER PASS, CALIFORNIA

Captain Lee of the Chinese Air Force glanced out of his Ghost aircraft canopy. Stars twinkled overhead, while pines carpeted the nearby mountainside. In the distance loomed giant peaks.

He went from south to north along the Sierra Nevada Range along with six other pilots in their ultra-stealthy bombers.

Thirteen paved roads crossed the mountain range east to west into California. Due to glaciation, most of the passes proved treacherous even in summer. By fall, they were snowed in except for the Donner and Beckwourth Passes. Snowplows working day and night kept the two passes open. The Central Pacific railroad used the Donner Pass, while the Western Pacific used Beckwourth.

Marshal Nung wanted both the Donner and Beckwourth Passes unusable, particularly the rail lines running through them. In the past twenty years, with the continually rising cost of gasoline, railroads had taken on greater importance in America.

To that end these seven upgraded and highly-modified Ghosts S-13E3s had slipped past American radar guarding the Greater Los Angeles area.

During the Alaskan War the original Ghosts had been the latest in ultra-stealthy tech. These seven used technologies perfected since that conflict. These Ghosts were also bigger and had greater range than those used in Alaska. They used air-to-ground missiles that the pilots would fire from a safe distance.

Captain Lee took his Ghost lower. He led the attack, and he was nervous. This was a great honor and it was a dangerous task. Each of his missiles carried a nuclear warhead. China was finally going to retaliate for the treacherous nuclear attack in Santa Cruz.

Under most conditions, High Command would have sent drones for such a mission. But secrecy was critical, and drones needed radio guidance, which the Americans might have been able to trace.

Chinese stealth technology was advanced, but there were rumors that the Americans had perfected a new surveillance system. Captain Lee had heard the rumors from his wife who worked in Intelligence. According to her, that's why China had helped terrorists explode a nuclear device in Silicon Valley.

China's leaders wanted to keep its technical edge over the Americas. Once, America had possessed the best tech. They used to be an innovative people and China's leaders didn't want to allow the enemy to climb back up the tech tree.

Captain Lee grinned. It was a good thing, too, good for him, this technological edge. Otherwise he would be in even more danger flying this boldly and deeply into enemy territory. All he needed was another sixteen minutes and he could launch the missiles. He was here to teach the Americans a bitter and deadly lesson.

CHEYENNE MOUNTAIN, COLORADO

In NORAD Command, an air control officer frowned at the strange images on his screen. Finally, he signaled the colonel, motioning him near.

"Sir, I'm sorry to trouble you, but I don't understand these signals." The air control officer tapped his screen.

The colonel frowned as he leaned down to study the images. His aftershave was strong and enveloped both men.

"This is the Sierra Nevada Range, sir," the air control officer said with a hand before his mouth.

"Show me the pattern since you first spotted these."

The air-control officer held his breath and manipulated his screen as ordered.

The colonel straightened. "Are there any Reflex interceptors in range?"

"Yes, sir."

"Alert them and burn whatever they are."

The air control officer twisted around in his chair to look up at the colonel. "What if they're our planes, sir?"

The colonel didn't look at the air-control officer, as he was too busy staring at the faint, intermittent images on the screen. "God help us if they are, but I doubt those are our planes. They have no IFF. Order the Reflexes to intercept them and burn them now!"

FRESNO, CALIFORNIA

As the stars slowly wheeled across the heavens, minutely shifting their patterns, Major Romanov's Reflex interceptor picked up speed and began climbing. Romanov belonged to a trio of aircraft. The three planes had been cruising, part of the North American Defense Net. Twenty-two such craft were up at all times around the continental U.S.

Each interceptor was larger than a Galaxy cargo plane. Each carried an ultra-hardened mirror on the bottom of the aircraft, the *reflex* of the strategic battle system.

Giant Anti-Ballistic Missile (ABM) stations ringed the country. Their task was to stab the heavens with a powerful laser and burn down incoming warheads. These stations made an ICBM exchange between the North American Alliance and China nearly impossible. In 2038, President Sims had used the strategic ABMs to destroy every enemy satellite the lasers could reach. No one was going to monitor the U.S. or use space mirrors to fire enemy lasers down into America if he could help it.

Instead of ICBMs, the danger now came from slippery cruise missiles and low-level stealth bomber attacks. The strategic ABMs could not hit those unless they were in direct line of sight to the particular station. The Reflex interceptor changed the equation, as the ABM station could bounce the laser off the plane's mirror and hit a low-flying target. The trick was making precise calculations and getting the Reflex high enough and in exactly the right position.

The huge planes lumbered higher and higher, afterburners giving them speed. Romanov glanced outside and saw a huge wing wobble the slightest bit. The red light on the end always comforted him and he didn't know why. In time, as the NORAD colonel cursed at the Reflex pilots to hurry, the planes moved into their positions.

Three distant AWACS now monitored the Chinese Ghosts. NORAD had ordered recon drones toward the first faint images. Now the air control officer could see the enemy aircraft much more clearly.

"We have target acquisition," Major Romanov said in the first Reflex interceptor.

"Fire," the NORAD colonel ordered.

The strategic ABM station in Fresno aimed its giant laser at Romanov's mirror and fired its pulse. The powerful beam flashed upward. Like a banking billiard ball, the ray struck the airborne mirror and sped toward the Sierra Nevada Mountains. The first pulse stabbed into the darkness and burned down a Chinese Ghost, shearing off the rear third of the bomber.

A cheer erupted in Romanov's headphones from NORAD Command. It made him grin.

Another pulse-beam from the Fresno station struck his reflex mirror. It bounced and traveled at the speed of light and missed the targeted bomber by seventeen inches.

Major Romanov heard groans in his headphones. Then a warning light flashed on his control panel. He flipped a switch, studying the readings. The mirror had taken damage, too much according to this. With each accumulated pulse-strike, the odds would increase of a burn-through against the plane.

"This is Echo Three," Romanov said. "My mirror had degraded three percent beyond the safety limit." Time seemed to stretch as Romanov awaited orders.

"Keep on standby," the NORAD colonel said. "We may need you before this is over."

The Fresno ABM station held its fire. Major Romanov banked his giant plane and took it out of position, lowering his altitude. They might need him before the night was through. That meant they might bounce the laser off his degraded mirror, possibly destroying his craft.

I might die.

It was a fearful thought, one he hadn't envisioned while taxiing down the extra-long runway early this evening. He might die, but he was here to fight for his country.

The damned Chinese, why are they invading our country anyway?

The second Reflex interceptor moved up into position. Two and a quarter minutes later, the Fresno station fired its laser. The beam bounced off the new plane. This time, the pulse-laser struck true and burned down its second Ghost bomber, igniting the craft's fuel and causing a spectacular midair explosion.

DONNER PASS, CALIFORNIA

Captain Lee watched in horror as stealth bomber after stealth bomber perished to the great beam firing down from the heavens.

The Americans tech was better than the country had a right to possess. This was terrifying.

He increased speed and spilled chaff. He fired two decoy missiles. Each emitted strong signals. Somehow, the Americans could see them and he had to confuse the enemy.

Captain Lee gritted his teeth, willing his bomber to go faster. If he was going to die, he wanted to deliver his cargo. He needed another three minutes. He turned control over to the aircraft's AI by pressing a button. The Ghost would jink now, maneuvering in a hopefully unpredictable manner. If the Americans used space lasers, as they must be since the beam slashed downward from above, those took time to beam to target. In that delay from sighting and firing was his slender hope.

The next few minutes of violent maneuvering brought vomit acid burning to the back of Captain Lee's throat. The terrible laser destroyed most of the stealth bombers until only his plane survived. Twice more the laser struck, missing his plane by centimeters.

Now he had reached the maximum range of his missiles to the two targets. Captain Lee's fingers moved fast, arming the missiles as the AI jinked again. The great beam flashed a third time, and once more, the Americans missed his plane.

Captain Lee laughed in nervous desperation. "Launching," he whispered.

The first missile detached, causing the Ghost to wobble. Then a great flame appeared, and the nuclear-tipped missile flashed toward the Donner Pass.

Captain Lee detached his second missile, and the Ghost wobbled once more. At that moment the great beam bouncing off a Reflex interceptor found the captain's plane. It burned through the canopy, instantly killing Lee and cutting the Ghost in two.

As the Chinese Air Force captain died, his second missile ignited, rocketing toward the distant target of Beckwourth Pass.

CHEYENNE MOUNTAIN, COLORADO

"Those are missiles, sir," the air controller whispered.

"Burn them. Burn them now."

"Do you know what they are, sir?"

"I don't give a *damn* what they are. I want them taken out before they hit."

361

FRESNO, CALIFORNIA

Major Romanov's throat had turned dry. NORAD gave the order and he took his plane back up.

He was glad his hands didn't shake. The other two interceptors headed back to base in Fresno. Their mirrors had degraded too much. The mirrors wouldn't reflect with a reasonable chance of accuracy. The calibrations needed due to distance were far too fine.

Romanov blinked and brought his aircraft into perfect alignment. The stars were bright up here and there were no clouds, just him and endless solitude. He radioed NORAD. They were going to use his mirror now. If the beam burned too strongly or if mirror had too many microscopic flaws—

As he held his position, Major Romanov began to pray, something he hadn't done in years.

DONNER PASS, CALIFORNIA

The first Chinese air-to-ground missile hugged the terrain. It expelled chaff and radio-emitting decoys. Twice a laser flashed by it, hitting the wrong target or missing by just enough.

Then the missile closed on its target. Its onboard computer adjusted the flight path, pitching the missile up. At precisely the height to give it maximum efficiency the nuclear warhead ignited. A fireball consumed the rail line and bridge and it tore into Donner Pass, causing rocks and boulders to fly and fall. A convoy was using the road, twenty huge transport trucks bringing M1A3 tanks to Los Angeles. The haulers and tanks crumpled and exploded in the fireball and blast, none of the drivers surviving. It was the first direct successful Chinese nuclear assault upon America.

FRESNO, CALIFORNIA

"What is the status of your mirror?" the NORAD colonel asked Major Romanov.

The major sat blinking in astonishment. The Chinese had exploded a nuke.

"I repeat—"

"It's operational," Romanov said.

"Say again."

"My mirror is operational. Go ahead, use it."

Romanov was lying. *They're using nukes on us.* He was lying, but he knew his duty. He was on the rampart defending his country. There was no one else to do this, just him.

"The laser is ready for firing," the Fresno station chief reported.

"Fire," the NORAD colonel said.

BECKWOURTH PASS, CALIFORNIA

The second Chinese air-to-ground missile streaked toward target. There was no more chaff in its container and it had deployed every decoy. In another fifty-eight seconds, it would reach ignition point.

Then the pulse-laser from Major Romanov's heavily degraded reflex mirror struck the Chinese missile. The missile exploded, but the nuclear warhead did not detonate. It tumbled earthward, unexploded, saving the Beckwourth Pass for America's use.

FRESNO, CALIFORNIA

"You're a brave man, Major Romanov," the NORAD colonel said. "I saw the degradation percentage regarding your mirror. It's a miracle your plane is still intact."

"Yes, sir," Romanov said. Sweat bathed his face and he was shaking. He couldn't believe he was still alive or that they'd destroyed the second missile.

"Return to base," the NORAD colonel said.

363

"Yes, sir," Romanov said. He peered out of the window at the stars above. "Thanks, God. I appreciate that." Then he banked the giant interceptor, heading back for Fresno.

LANGLEY, VIRGINIA

Anna Chen was back in her CIA cubicle the next morning, searching and compiling data on the Chinese command structure and on their marshals.

She'd received information about the nuclear strike last night, and it filled her with fear. The Chinese had overcome their inhibition against using the ultimate weapon. Now she wondered where it would lead. Massive nuclear usage…it could destroy the civilized world.

Yes, Director Levin had been correct in one sense. The American nuclear missiles had saved the situation in the Bay Area. But what would be the future cost? This attack on the Sierra Nevada Passes—nuclear employment would likely escalate now. It was the human pattern. Levin had won a battle but may have caused the loss of the war and the world.

Levin seldom spoke to her now and he no longer confided in her. Should she have backed him on his wish to use nuclear weapons?

"No," she whispered. She had to follow her conscience. She would be no good to anybody, least of all to herself, if she went against what she knew was right.

Anna sipped tea and continued to read. After several hours of intense study, it began to dawn on her that Marshal Nung was an outcast among the others in Chinese High Command. He seemed very Old Russian in his approach to military problems.

The Russians, as she had read today, used to have very inflexible ideas about how to run an offensive. They had learned bitter lessons from the Germans in two World Wars. The Second World War had been particularly savage for the country. Although Russia eventually won the conflict, they had taken staggering losses. The German method of combat, the blitzkrieg or lightning war, had awed the Russians, stamping it on their hearts and minds. Years later, in their military manuals for attacking Western Europe during the Cold War, the Russians had advocated a similar form of ceaseless assault. They had believed in the Axe Theory of combat: to pour troops into the most successful advances and to ignore whatever didn't work, discard whatever failed.

Marshal Nung appeared to have learned his earliest military lessons at the Moscow Academy. Ever since then, he had attempted to practice "lightning war." That appeared to be at odds with normal Chinese military doctrine.

What did that tell her?

Hmm. Marshal Nung had led the only truly successful attack during the Alaskan War. He had captured his target, even though he had taken brutal losses doing so. In the Siberian War, he had made the brilliant strike that brought Chinese victory.

He is their Russian. No, he is a German-practicing theorist of blitzkrieg, but with a Chinese disregard for materiel losses.

Anna sat back so her chair creaked. Her eyes were half-lidded. Probably better than anyone in America, she grasped what the political infighting was like on the Ruling Committee. Nung was Jian Hong's darling. The Leader backed the Marshal and together they had achieved what President Sims deemed as a military miracle. The originality for the California assault likely came from Marshal Nung.

Anna picked up her e-reader and studied wartime assassinations. Hmm, this was interesting. In 1943, in something called Operation Vengeance, America sent a squadron of P-38 Lightning fighters on a mission of assassination. The pilots were to target Admiral Yamamoto's plane, hoping to kill the man who had planned the attack on Pearl Harbor. The pilots succeeded, and according to this article, Admiral Yamamoto's death had damaged Japanese morale.

Anna continued reading, and she found out about the British commando attempt to assassinate the Desert Fox, General Rommel, in North Africa in 1941. It had been called Operation Flipper. It might have worked, too, but Rommel had gone to Rome to request replacements for supply ships sunk by the enemy. Thus, he was not in place when the commandos struck.

What would happen if they killed Marshal Nung? If nothing else, it might give the soldiers in Los Angeles time as the Chinese reorganized their command structure, or as the new commander took over.

Anna stood up, determined to take this to the President.

ANAHEIM, CALIFORNIA

As the political leaders and their aides spoke, argued and decided strategy, Captain Stan Higgins smoked a cigar as he leaned against his worn Behemoth tank. His eyes were red from a lack of sleep and his arms and legs felt jittery because of the stims he'd been taking to stay awake.

The promotion to major hadn't gone through, so he was back to being a captain again. Not that Stan cared one way or another. He knew he wasn't going to survive the war. He was going to die in LA. The odds were simply too heavily stacked against him.

Stan rolled the cigar in his fingers and thrust it back into his mouth. He liked the strong taste and the smoke helped keep him awake. It bothered him that General Larson had ignored his advice. Instead of keeping the battle-winning Behemoth Regiment intact, the General had split it into its component companies. The General had spread the companies throughout Anaheim. The city—part of Greater Los Angeles—was a wasteland of rubble and skeletal buildings. General Larson had told Stan his reasoning. He needed the Behemoths all along the line in order to stiffen the soldiers by bolstering morale. If they saw the tanks with them, they would likely stand their ground longer.

Stan inhaled on the cigar. Above, the sky was black from burning oil, rubber and a host of other inflammables. Los Angeles and Anaheim in particular was aflame.

Chinese artillery boomed in the distance. From offshore, enemy battleships sent titanic rounds hammering into everything. If one of those giant shells hit his tank directly, it would take out the Behemoth.

Stan exhaled cigar smoke. For two days now the Chinese had ground into Anaheim. Special Infantry wave assaults, penal battalions attacks, Eagle Team jetpack commandos, Marauder tanks, T-66s, IFVs, assault guns, mortars, mag grenades, RGPs, cannon shells—Stan rubbed his eyes. The Chinese assaults just never stopped. It was more than depressing. It was soul numbing.

The naval gunfire shells were landing closer now. Each strike shook the ground and caused rubble and concrete to geyser and rain. The chatter of enemy machine guns began. PAA soldiers shouted hoarsely. Bugle blasted and bullets whined.

"Professor," Jose shouted down from the tank's top hatch. "The General wants to talk to you."

Stan ground out his cigar and stuffed the unused part in his front pocket. Then he grasped the rungs on the side of the tank and climbed up. He was so damned tired that it was hard to think. Smoking the cigar was his one moment of peace in a world that had turned into a hectic and never-ending battle.

The Chinese never stopped. Of his three tanks, only his own worked now. Two M1A3s had dragged the stalled monsters deeper into Anaheim. They were the last ditch stronghold in case everything fell apart, which it looked like was happening and would only accelerate.

As Stan climbed up the tank, he paused and turned his head. Look over there, a hundred American teenagers ran for their lives, leaving their foxholes and rubble strongpoints. Most pitched aside their assault rifles. Stan looked left. A seven-story building collapsed. Through the dust he saw running American soldiers, although most of them kept their weapons.

The Chinese kept pushing them back, destroying everything and sending Eagle Teams commandos behind every defensive position. The enemy had gone berserk, pouring men and materiel at them.

The Chinese didn't have a limit. It was crazy. It was mad. And it was all too true.

Stan slid into the tank, plopping himself into the commander's seat. He flipped on a screen. General Larson glared at him in it. The man was tall, a real tactician, brilliant usually.

"Captain, you're the only thing that's stable in your part of Anaheim. The Chinese are pouring through our lines. You have to stop them."

"Yes, sir," Stan said. "You realize I only have one Behemoth running, right, sir?"

"Higgins!" the General shouted. "Stop the attack. I can't afford to have your line crumble into nothing. We're stretched everywhere right now and every line is shaky. You have to give me something solid. I need you to anchor your location down *hard*."

"With one tank, sir?" Stan asked. He was too tired. Otherwise, he probably wouldn't have talked this way.

"You have your orders, Captain. I expect you to do your duty."

The screen went blank.

"Well," Stan said into the quiet compartment. "You heard the General. We have the Behemoth and just about nothing else. Let's see what we can do."

"Better close the hatch, Professor," Jose said from below. "I don't want you to catch your death."

Stan reached up and closed the hatch with a clang. A moment later, the driver started the mighty engine. The tank shook. It didn't run as smoothly anymore. Too many things ran on a knife's edge.

"Battery power is at eighty percent," Jose said.

"It will have to do," Stan said. He'd switched on every screen, and he now studied the situation with a critical eye. Seven Marauder tanks were roaming the streets, heading for the American teenagers. The teenagers had been formed into a Militia company three days ago. Stan didn't blame the poor kids in the least. In fact, they reminded him of Jake. What had happened to the Bradleys that were supposed to help—

Oh, he saw the Bradleys on Screen 3. They were burning hulks or they were flipped upside down. Something had taken them out. Maybe the battleship shells had done it.

368

The Behemoth clanked toward the approaching Marauders two streets over. Stan used images from a video-cam from a soldier recording in the rubble. The tank's AI computed distance and trajectory.

"The cannon's ready, Professor," Jose called up.

"Do you see the Marauders," Stan asked.

"Roger."

"Take out the back tank first."

The Behemoth shuddered in a quick succession of shots. At least Jose and other mechanics had fixed the turret swivel. It moved like lightning, just as designed.

Stan watched on his screens. One after another, the Marauders exploded. Some of the Behemoth shells bored through rubble or buildings like a .44 Magnum through a cheap car. The last two Chinese light tanks reversed course and fled. It didn't help, and soon they were also burning hulks.

"Good work, Jose," Stan said. "Now let's head to grid seven-nine-nine."

Stan saw an Eagle Team in flight. They were swinging wide, but not widely enough. Using the 30mm guns, Stan took over control and sent several antipersonnel rounds screaming at them. The AI had set each shell's proximity fuse. He watched on Screen 1. The Chinese jetpack commandos fell like wasps hit by bug spray.

The AI took over in emergency defensive mode then. The tank revved, backed up, and the 30mms and flechette launchers chugged. Seconds later, battleship shells landed uncomfortably near. The Behemoth shook from their impact on the ground. If one of those hit them directly—

The turret swiveled as T-66s appeared in the distance and across the rubble. The Behemoth shuddered again, this time from its own cannon. The mighty engine whined from the strain and Jose shouted that battery power was down to fifty-three percent.

Like prehistoric dinosaurs, the Chinese triple-turreted tanks fought the mighty Behemoth. It was mayhem, flying shells and defensive fire. Twice, a T-66 shell slammed against them, deflected by its immense thickness.

369

Stan's ears rang from the noise and none of them could hear what the other man was saying. It didn't matter at this point. They knew the routine. Seven enemy tanks burned, flipped or stood as useless scrap metal.

Stan slid from his seat and tapped the driver's shoulder. He motioned, *back her up fast*.

The Behemoth retreated, and barely in time. A mass artillery hurricane fell where the tank had been. Seconds later, battleship shells crashed. They caused rubble and cement to geyser like titanic whale blowholes spewing water.

Stan took the Behemoth out of easy enemy view. Then, by hand signal, he motioned for the driver to head down a side street. The massive tank rumbled and crushed everything in its path.

"Can you hear me?" Stan shouted.

"A little, Captain," the driver said.

Stan climbed back up to the commander's seat. In a screen, he saw advancing Chinese infantry. Because of the hurricane artillery barrage, he didn't think they heard the tank. That didn't happen too often, but when it did—

"Now," Stan said.

The driver drove the Behemoth into the back of a standing building. Moments later, the giant tank burst out of the front. Before them were over two hundred Chinese infantry. Some stood waiting, maybe for the artillery bombardment to end. A lot of them sat on packs as they snacked and drank bottled water. The soldiers scrambled to their feet and grabbed their weapons. It didn't matter. In less than two seconds, thousands of flechettes made a gory ruin of the enemy. Body armor didn't help them today.

"Keep going!" Stan shouted. "Let's see if we can catch something behind the buildings of seven-nine-eight."

The Behemoth raced to the buildings when five drones darted in from the sky like rocketing hawks. The enemy aircraft fired their main guns. The shells struck with resounding clangs, making a terrible din within the tank, but they did nothing permanent against the Behemoth's heavy armor. In turn, the tank's AI shot the drones out of the air.

The Behemoth turned the corner. At point blank range, enemy troops raced back into open IFVs. Some of the Chinese sprinted away. Others opened fire on the tank. Their puny guns—IFVs and soldiers alike—could do nothing against the American marvel. In return, Stan and his crew destroyed everything.

"It's time to fall back," Stan said. "Turn over air and missile defense to the AI."

It was good thing he did that. Chinese artillery rained. Several times, shell fragments clanged against them. Then battlefield missiles targeted them. The AI shot them down, although several nearby blasts rocked the Behemoth.

"We're low on ammo," Jose said.

Stan checked battery power. Look at that. One of the main batteries had decided it could hold juice after all. They were back up to sixty-one percent.

"Well done, Captain Higgins," General Larson said, appearing on screen 5. "It looks as if you've stemmed the local assault."

"If I had all the Behemoths together—" Stan began.

Onscreen, General Larson held up a hand. "What do you think is going on, Captain? We're holding on with nothing to spare. Your Behemoth and others in the line are doing miracles. It's why we're holding on in Anaheim. We aren't attacking anymore. We're simply buying our country time and hopefully bleeding the Chinese beyond anything they expected."

"Yes, sir," Stan said. He could have added that one of these times the Chinese were going to get lucky. Actually, the enemy didn't even need to get lucky. The odds would finally catch up with each Behemoth.

But what did it matter saying that? Everyone knew the odds. At least for another hour this portion of the line in Anaheim still held. It would give command time to reorganize. Maybe it would give the teenagers time to stop and catch their breath. Maybe it would even give the Militia enough time so their nerve returned and they went back to holding their part of the defense.

Like a deadly Great White Shark, the Virginia-class fast attack submarine glided through the deep. It was in the main shipping lane between Chinese-controlled Hawaii and the U.S. Pacific Coast.

It sped from its grisly handiwork, the sinking of a Chinese SI transport, with thousands of dead and dying Chinese soldiers in the water. With critical intelligence received twenty-eight hours ago, the *South Dakota* had moved into range, then crept into position and Captain Leroy Clay had proceeded to hunt.

Two modified Mark 48 torpedoes had left the tubes and demolished the large cargo vessel. Now the submarine glided away, heading deeper, sinking through a cold-water layer, called a thermocline.

The sonar men listened. The rest of the crew waited in terrible anticipation and Captain Clay stared into space. He was a six-foot-six black man, often having to hunch as he moved through the submarine.

There, the sounds of distant, underwater explosions told the story.

"They're hunting us now," Captain Clay said.

"They're well out of range, Captain," the chief sonar-man said.

"And we're going to keep it that way," Clay said. "Conn, take us deeper. I want the cold water layer hiding us."

"Aye, aye, Captain."

For the next thirty-seven minutes they played the old cat-and-mouse game first begun in World War I between the British and Germans. The submariners endured the hammering thuds against the skin of their vessel. None of the depth charges—giant grenades really—were near enough to cause concussion damage against the hull integrity of the fast attack submarine. This time the *South Dakota* was going to beat the Chinese, or they should have.

Forty-one minutes after the sinking of the SI transport, the rules changed in the deadly game at sea.

"I think they're leaving, Captain," the chief sonar-man said.

Clay nodded, and he continued to wait. It was perhaps his greatest virtues as a submarine captain.

Later, the sonar-man added, "I don't hear any enemy ships, sir."

"They can still use helicopters to drop the depth charges," Clay said.

The *South Dakota* continued with silent running. Fifty-three minutes after the transport's sinking, the sonar-man cocked his head. He might have heard—

A terrific and terrible underwater explosion occurred. This depth charge wasn't any closer than the previous ones had been. The difference was in its explosive power, fueled by a nuclear warhead. Then came another enormous explosion.

The first concussion shock slammed against the *South Dakota*, tilting the submarine and throwing officers and crew out of their chairs or positions and onto the deck. Before they had time to right themselves, the second shockwave struck, breaching the integrity of the hull, ripping it open like a bear smashing a can of beans.

Cold ocean saltwater poured into the submarine. Captain Leroy Clay looked up from where he lay on the deck. Water boiled and rushed toward him. He would have won. He had won, but the Chinese were changing the rules.

The water picked up the six-foot-six captain and hurled him against a bulkhead. It knocked him unconscious and then ocean water flooded the *South Dakota*. The crumpled war vessel sank like a stone, beaten to death by nuclear detonations.

WASHINGTON, D.C.

Ushered in by the secretary, Anna timidly stepped into the Oval Office. President Sims sat behind his desk, leaning back as he spoke to General Alan. The two of them seemed to be in an earnest conversation. Both men turned as the secretary and Anna entered.

"Ms. Chen," Sims said. "Good, I'm glad you're here. Perhaps you can help me convince the General I'm right."

373

The secretary quietly took her leave, closing the door behind her.

"Help, sir?" Anna asked.

Sims scowled as he said, "The Chinese Navy has begun to use nuclear depth charges against our submarines."

Anna closed her eyes as if she could shut out reality. If she couldn't see it, it wasn't real. Here it was—the escalation of nuclear weapons. This was exactly what she had feared. She opened her eyes, deciding to face fate head on.

"Using Levin's spy-ring in Beijing, our commanders were able to target several SI transports, but at a terrible cost to our dwindling submarine fleet." Sims shook his head. "We're running out of options. If the Chinese have begun using nuclear weapons at sea, we have no course but to do the same."

"Oh," Anna said.

General Alan became stone-faced.

"First the attack in Donner Pass, now this," Sims said. "It has to stop. We no longer have any choice."

"Uh...if you'll recall, sir," Anna said, "we used nuclear weapons first."

Sims's face thundered and he banged a fist on the desk. "I need to speak with Director Levin."

"Sir, if you would just—" Anna said.

"Not now," Sims said. "The Chinese are raining nuclear weapons—"

"Mr. President!" Anna said, speaking louder than she ever had to him.

Sims raised an eyebrow, glanced at General Alan and sat farther back in his chair.

"Sir," Anna said, speaking more softly and with greater deference. "You know surely that I understand the Chinese mindset."

"Dr. Levin made that clear to me, yes."

"I think if you take a step back a moment, you will see that they have carefully chosen how they use these nuclear weapons."

"Explain that," Sims said.

"The Chinese have not targeted cities and they have refrained from attacking land formations."

"It's simply a matter of time now before they do," Sims said.

"Sir, I would like to point out that we used nuclear weapons first. In the Alaskan War, we used nuclear torpedoes on two different occasions. Not once did the Chinese do similarly."

"Are you suggesting the Chinese are superior to us," General Alan asked in a biting tone.

What's wrong with him? Anna wondered. She and the Chairman of the Joint Chiefs were on the same page regarding nuclear weapons. Now his racial bigotry was interfering with his better judgment.

"I'm simply pointing out that Jian Hong must have been under tremendous pressure to retaliate against us," Anna said, "to allow his military to hurt us with nuclear weapons just as we've hurt them."

"Then you *are* saying they are morally superior to us," Alan said. "You're suggesting we forced them to use nuclear weapons."

"If that's true," Anna said, "then they forced us to use them. They attacked us. They're invading our country, which makes them the aggressors. Men—and women, too, for that matter—aren't always logical. In my opinion, we are not even rational beings, but rationalizing ones. We act on our emotions and then make up reasons—rational sounding reasons—for why we do X Y and Z."

"What are you suggesting with this mumbo-jumbo?" Sims asked.

"That further nuclear weapon usage will escalate into a possible world-wide holocaust."

"Our ABM stations will protect us from that," Sims said.

"We've seen three different instances now where the nuclear attack came from everything but an ICBM," Anna said. "Will the ABM stations protect us from other, imaginative nuclear weapon use?"

"Are you suggesting we drop our pants for the Chinese?" Sims asked. "That we let them nuke us at will?"

"No, sir," Anna said, her voice hardening. "I'm suggesting we beat the Chinese in Los Angeles and slow the speed of the enemy assault."

Sims sat blinking at her. "That's a swift change of topic."

"Yes, Mr. President."

"Very well," the President said, indicating a chair. "Make your case."

Anna sat down and proceeded to tell the President and the Chairman of the Joint Chiefs about Operation Flipper and Operation Vengeance in World War II. Each time, the raid had targeted an enemy commander.

"Are you suggesting we attempt to assassinate Chairman Jian Hong?" Sims asked. "I'm not sure I like the idea of starting an assassin's war between heads of state."

"Mr. President," Anna said, "I have evidence that shows the critical nature of Marshal Shin Nung's presence in the current conflict."

"Let's hear it," Sims said.

Anna told him what she had learned about Nung and his previous exploits in Alaska and Siberia.

"Let me see if I get this straight," Sims said. "You believe the speed and ferocity of the present attack is due to Marshal Nung?"

"That's exactly what I'm saying, yes sir," Anna said.

The President turned to General Alan. "What are your thoughts on this?"

Alan stared at Anna. Slowly, he began to nod. "It's an interesting concept, certainly. How do you suggest we exploit this information?"

"In a similar manner as we solved the Blue Swan missile crises," Anna said. "Maybe we should contact General Ochoa of SOCOM."

"Send our commandos in one more time?" Alan asked. "It would be their death sentence. Frankly, I doubt they would get anywhere near Marshal Nung."

"I'm not saying it's a good chance," Anna said. "I'm just giving you another option, a way to help our beleaguered troops in Los Angeles. If you took away the guiding hand, it might slow down the pace of the enemy assault. That could possibly be the margin—"

"Yes!" the President said, slapping his hand hard against the desk. "I like it. It's bold, and it's something other than just waiting to lose. In the end, in some fashion, we have to go over to the assault to win. I know it will risk the lives of these brave men, but that's better, I think every one of them would agree, than waiting to die in their foxholes."

"Should I look into this?" General Alan asked.

"No," Sims said, picking up his phone. "I'm going to talk to General Ochoa and get the ball rolling right now."

-13-
The Raid

LOS ANGELES, CALIFORNIA

As the battles raged on the front lines in Costa Mesa, Huntington Beach, Fullerton, Anaheim and Pomona, Paul Kavanagh soaked in a hot bath. He was in the northern edge of Los Angeles, in a Best Western Hotel.

Romo and he had arrived last night, and slept like the dead. In the middle of the morning, Paul soaked in the steaming water. His body ached and his soul was numb. After a time, he let some water out and turned on the faucet, adding more hot liquid. This felt good.

With the back of his head resting on the bathtub's porcelain, he began to think about Sheri and Mike. There were close now, a short drive north to Newhall. Was it time to go AWOL and see them?

I've done my part. The military can't reasonably expect any more from me.

It was time to take his family to Colorado. From what he'd seen, China was going to capture Los Angeles. There just didn't seem to be any way of stopping the enemy. For sure, he didn't want his family to end their days in a PAA labor camp.

"Amigo!" Romo shouted through the door as he banged on it. "Are you about done in there?"

"Are you waiting to get in?" Paul asked.

"Me? No. There are some men out here who wish to speak with you."

Paul blinked lazily and slid down, letting the hot water soak his face. Several seconds later, he surfaced, and he was frowning.

They'd made it, Romo and him. Had the assassin contacted Colonel Valdez? They were blood brothers, right? But did that hold now that they were safely behind American lines?

With a groan, Paul emerged from the bath, with water dripping from him. He was sore everywhere, and there were a dozen black bruises on his skin. The worst was a fist-sized mark in the middle of his left thigh. He stepped out of the tub, wrapped a towel around his waist and lifted a thicker towel. He had a pistol hidden on a stand, with a bullet already chambered.

Taking the gun, Paul put his ear against the door. He couldn't tell who was out there, if anyone. Quickly, he opened the door, with his gun aimed—

Sergeant Donovan of the SOF sat in a chair. The man raised his eyebrows. "Expecting trouble?" the Green Beret asked.

Paul lowered the gun. "I've been in combat mode for a while."

"Sure," Donovan said. "Hey, Romo, you can listen to this, too. General Ochoa would like to speak with both of you."

Romo looked up from where he dealt cards onto a table. He turned toward them, and his dark eyes flickered as he took in Paul's gun.

"What's this concerning?" Paul asked.

"You'll find out soon enough," Donovan said.

"And if we don't feel like going with you?"

Donovan grinned. "Orders, Sergeant. Why make life tough for any of us?"

"Yeah," Paul said. "I see what you're saying. General Ochoa is already going to do that for us, isn't he?"

"Maybe," Donovan said. "Maybe he wants to talk to you about some medals."

"Yeah, sure. Give me a minute. Let me get dressed."

Donovan grunted as he stood and stepped outside onto the balcony.

379

"I keep my word," Romo said, as Paul headed for the bathroom.

Paul glanced at his blood brother, Colonel Valdez's best assassin. Romo didn't miss much. Since there was nothing he could say, Paul nodded, entered the bathroom and shut the door behind him.

***

Twenty-three minutes later, Paul, Romo and Donovan strode down an underground corridor. MPs stood outside a door. The smaller one opened the door, keeping hold of the knob as the three men filed inside.

There was a table with a computer screen on it, a bar with bottled drinks and four empty chairs.

"Are you staying?" Paul asked Donovan.

For an answer, the Green Beret sat down and opened a Gatorade.

Paul rubbed his eyes. This felt like déjà vu. Man, he was old, too old for any more of this. Let the young have their shot at being a hero. He was sick and tired of desperate action. Had he ever craved this sort of thing? Yeah, he'd been young and full of piss and vinegar once. He had fallen for the catchy slogans and loved being in prime condition. Now…now he just wanted to go home. He wanted to sit on his sofa and watch TV, maybe go outside sometimes and weed his vegetable garden. Everyone kept one these days.

The screen came to life. It showed a haggard-looking General Ochoa, with a large American flag behind him. His dark eyes seemed to bore into each of them.

"I'm going to be brief," General Ochoa said. "The President has spoken with me, and he believes we can slow down the relentless Chinese advance."

"Does it involve us doing something harebrained?" Paul asked.

Ochoa gaze slid away from Paul's for a moment. "You're the three best commandos I have in the theater of operations. You know my beliefs about using the best and this is going to be the most important commando raid so far."

"More important than the Blue Swan fiasco?" asked Paul.

"Son," Ochoa said, staring him in the eye. "I've had just about enough of your quips. You're in SOCOM and you're under my orders. The President believes and I concur with him that this next mission is vital to the integrity of our country."

Paul struggled to rein in the compulsion to get up and walk away. What would Ochoa do? Likely, the general would order the MPs to throw him in the brig. Did it matter what he had done before? Not enough that it would sway Ochoa, the man was pure hard-nose, all business.

Ochoa's pause seemed longer than necessary. Finally, he said, "You three are going to lead a raid on Marshal Nung's Headquarters."

"That sounds important," Paul said. "Who is he anyway?"

"Marshal Nung is the enemy First Front commander, the Chinese officer running the California Invasion. His HQ is in San Ysidro, where the Ninth Division used to be. I believe you were there not that long ago, bodyguarding Colonel Norman."

Paul stared up at the ceiling. This was worse than he'd expected.

"I know this will be a dangerous mission," Ochoa said. "And we don't have much time to prepare. Fortunately, Colonel Valdez has agreed to help us from Mexico."

Paul glanced at Romo. The assassin shook his head in the way that meant he didn't know anything about this. Paul regarded Ochoa. In his experience, the General never forgot anything, and that would include Valdez wanting his death.

"Uh, I have a problem with that," Paul said. "Last I heard, Valdez still lusts for my head. Seems stupid of me to walk into Mexico and give it to him."

"Colonel Valdez will have to wait for your overvalued head," Ochoa said. "Right now, I have need of you."

"And you've no doubt already told him that. Is that what you're trying to hint to me...sir?"

Ochoa turned his Aztec death-stare onto Paul. "Gunnery Sergeant, I've studied your profile on more than one occasion. You have trouble with authority. So far, I haven't needed to reprimand you for insubordinate attitudes. Do I need to summon the MPs to take you to the brig?"

"Yes sir, I think that would be a good idea. I don't mean any offense, but I don't relish having you send me to my death."

"Listen here, Kavanagh. The country is at war with the most powerful alliance in history. The PAA, SAF and the GD, along with the Iranian Hegemony, are all lining up against us. The bigger war is going to start soon. We need to end this conflict or stabilize it as soon as possible."

"You think killing this Nung will do that?" Paul asked.

"The President believes it, or his advisors have convinced him of it."

"What do you believe, sir? I mean really?"

Ochoa's features became flinty. The General opened his mouth, only to close it. Finally, in a quiet voice, he began to speak:

"Colonel Valdez has agreed to abide by my conditions. I've told him your importance to the mission. You're a killer, although you're a hell of an insubordinate soldier. How you and Romo made it back to our lines is beyond me. But that the two of you did only proves my theory. Marshal Nung is supposed to be one of those rare, operationally-gifted commanders. He knows how to win battles. From my information, the rest of the Chinese High Command dislikes him and his methods. We're hoping that killing him…well, we're hoping it will bring about a change in Chinese operations."

"Sounds like a slim hope," Paul said.

"Yes, I suppose it is. The sad truth is we're down to that. We're going to need some old-fashioned skullduggery and luck to slip you into First Front Headquarters. I don't think we can fly you straight in this time. That's why you're going to have to take the long way through Mexico. And that's why we need Colonel Valdez's help."

"Okay. I see what you're saying. Now what do you have planned for getting us back out once we've completed the mission?"

Ochoa shook his head. "This is a one-way mission, gentlemen. Unless you can fight your way back like you did before, or unless you can convince Colonel Valdez to help you escape."

Paul closed his eyes. This was it: a suicide mission. If he could talk Valdez into helping him escape…right! It would be out of the fire and into the cannibal's cooking pot.

Beside him, Romo leaned near, whispering, "If we make it in, I think we could slip back out into Mexico."

"Yeah, and into your Colonel's hands," Paul whispered.

"What is he saying?" Ochoa asked.

Paul studied the general. The truth was U.S. High Command would never let Cheri, Mike and him relocate to Colorado. If he went AWOL trying that—it was starting to look as if he had one chance to save his wife from Chinese occupation. It was this harebrained commando raid. *He Who Dares, Wins*, or some other B.S. like that.

Paul shook his head so his neck bones cracked. "Sir, I'll do this if you promise to relocate my wife and son to Colorado."

"Where are they now?"

"LA."

"Can you be more specific?"

Paul gave him the address.

"I give you my word," Ochoa said. "We'll move them tomorrow."

"Thank you, sir. When do we leave for this mission?"

Ochoa hesitated before saying, "Tonight."

SAN ANTONIO, TEXAS

Colonel Valdez slammed his beer onto the desk, causing amber-colored liquid to slosh over the rim and stain the papers below. He was in a former bank vault, his headquarters here in San Antonio.

"No," he told Torres. "I will not listen to reason. You will listen to me."

The one-eyed soldier wouldn't look at him. Valdez knew then that Torres didn't truly understand. For a moment, Valdez considered drawing his sidearm and shooting the man in the heart. Torres had once been a good man. The one-eyed soldier

383

had lost his wife to the Chinese, but not his courage. Yes, Torres knew how to hate. But it seemed now to the Colonel that somewhere Torres had given up his seething wish for vengeance against the insufferable foreigners.

That was the difference between him and others, Valdez knew. He kept his vengeance white-hot. He would never change. He would teach the Chinese what his vengeance meant just as he would teach the cowardly Mexican government that it shouldn't have turned on him. Soon now, he was also going to carve a lesson into Paul Kavanagh for daring to desert his daughter on the field of battle. The crime was unforgiveable. What did it matter to him, this Chinese marshal? The marshal didn't make the critical difference to the war, but the endless numbers of PAA soldiers did.

They must kill the Chinese, the Japanese and the Koreans until Mexico was a sea of blood. For that, Valdez needed dedicated men and women. They needed to know he would remember them and avenge them no matter what the cost. It was all about loyalty and utter commitment.

"I want Paul Kavanagh," Valdez said.

"Romo will bring him to us after the raid, Colonel."

"Ah, good," Valdez said, deciding this instant that Torres was to be cut out of the loop. The man was dead to him now, useless manure. "Good," he said. "You may go, my friend."

Torres gave him a troubled look, and it seemed as if the dead man was going to speak. Finally, Torres slunk away like the dog he had become.

Valdez stood and went to his radio. He would speak to the guerilla commander near the Mexican-American border. He would have to impress upon the man the extreme need to separate Kavanagh from the other commandos. It would be easy except for one thing. Why hadn't Romo already killed Kavanagh? There was a mystery here.

Could Romo have failed me? If that were true, Romo would also have to die a gruesome death.

POMONA, CALIFORNIA

Fighter Rank Zhu's stomach did a flip as his helicopter flashed upward. It was as if his helo took a gigantic leap over the defenders dug in the rubble and behind the shattered buildings below. There were several varieties of helicopters around him: more Eagle Team battle-taxis, Gunhawks and Graceful Swans with their Annihilator missiles. The helicopters flew over the blaze of enemy machine guns and launching Blowdarts.

Graceful Swan chain-guns spewed fire, the spent shells raining from their weapons, and Annihilator missiles launched from the stubby wings. Below, a Humvee Avenger blew up, a lone helmet spinning with the gory remains of a blood-dripping neck. Other Americans died in their machine gun pits.

Witnessing this destruction, Zhu clutched the handlebars on his seat of the battle-taxi. Pomona had become a sea of rubble and half-demolished buildings. Civilians huddled in the ruins while others lay bloating and rotting. Just as bad, fires raged in places. Smoke curled in long ribbons up into the black cloud over Pomona and over Greater Los Angeles. Farther away, artillery boomed with gigantic flashes from the south and to the north.

The helicopters headed toward a cluster of several prominent buildings behind the American line. The tactic of cutting off the forward enemy troops had worked brilliantly since its conception. The buildings loomed closer so scourge marks became visible in the brick walls. Many of the windows were cracked and a few were broken with jagged edges. Zhu's gut tightened and his arms tingled with anticipation.

Tian's orders growled in his headphones and Zhu lofted off his seat and ignited his thrusters. With unerring skill, the First Rank Tian guided them toward the largest structure of the cluster. Once it must have been a towering office building.

As the advanced flyers zoomed near, a terrible surprise unfolded. Americans appeared in the highest windows. The enemy must have been waiting in ambush for them. Assault guns blazed. Beside Zhu, a commando tumbled backward as his visor shattered. The soldier plummeted toward the ground. More Americans appeared; these were on the roof. They launched Blowdart missiles at the climbing Gunhawks and manhandled heavy machine guns into position.

"What do we do?" a commando shouted through the radionet.

A Gunhawk slewed to the side. A second Blowdart exploded against the tail. The helo nosedived, picking up speed, and in seconds, it crashed spectacularly into the ground.

The fight became desperate, men versus machines. A Gunhawk's machine guns began pouring fire onto the Americans. Then three Blowdarts in quick succession blasted the helo out of the sky.

Zhu yelped in terror as Graceful Swans' chain-guns whirled behind him. Ferroconcrete chunks and chips flew, along with American sprays of blood.

"There's no turning back," Tian radioed. "We are White Tigers and we never retreat."

The Americans in the windows kept firing, even as the ones on the roof died. As they died, more Eagle Team commandos dropped out the sky.

For an Eagle flyer, this was the worst possible place to be during an insertion: hanging in the air like ripe fruit.

"We must retreat!" a commando wailed.

"We can't land on the roof," another radioed. "We'll be cut down by our own Gunhawks."

"I know!" Zhu shouted. He twisted the throttle and his jets blasted so the straps dug into his shoulders. He flew at the nearest window. Twice, he heard metallic whines like angry mosquitoes—bullets passing him.

Using the crosshairs on the HUD, Zhu targeted the window and let his electromagnetic grenade launcher chug. Like fastballs two grenades hit next to the window, harmlessly exploding concrete. The third flew through the window past the American inside. It blasted the enemy soldier off his feet so he pitched out of the window. He tumbled like a flailing doll for the ground below.

"Use the windows!" Zhu shouted. "Fly into the building."

"You're crazy," a commando radioed.

"No!" Tian said. "He's right. It will take skillful flying, but it's our only chance. Once you make it into a room, get out of the way, because more commandos will follow."

Zhu's window became immense in his view. He braked hard and flew in feet first, finding himself running across the floor. An American in the room stared at him in shock. Zhu snapped off a grenade. The American flew off his feet, his chest a gaping, smoking hole. Shrapnel speckled Zhu, but his dinylon armor held. He pulled a strap and the jetpack clanked onto the floor as Zhu tore his assault rifle from it. He didn't wait, but charged through the room's door, knelt and fired a burst as Militiamen appeared down the hall.

The fight for the building had begun. Behind him more Eagle Team flyers entered. Some crashed against the building's side and fell to their deaths. Twenty-seven made it inside. They faced half a company of Militiamen.

For the next hour the battle raged, until only fourteen White Tigers survived. They captured the roof and the three upper floors. Trapped Americans held the lower levels.

"You and me, Fighter Rank," Tian panted. He lay on his back on the roof, resting for a second as they waited for reinforcements. Tian looked up at him. "The way you fight, I am asking they promote you to Soldier Rank."

Zhu beamed with pride. Before he could think of something to say, three Chinese cargo helicopters approached the roof. The nearest had open bay doors, with soldiers pointing their weapons earthward. The helos held Chinese airborne troops. An American missile sped upward and slammed into one of them, but the Blowdart failed to explode. The helicopter began to twist, but had a good pilot, and landed heavily onto the roof, disgorging the airborne soldiers.

At the run, the reinforcements filed down the stairwells. Meanwhile the Gunhawks high overhead, continued to make it a murderous sprint for any Americans trying to reinforce the building from the ground entry points.

"We're going to win this one," Tian said.

Zhu nodded as he looked into the distance. They kept occupying more of Greater Los Angeles, but there was always additional territory to take. When would it end?

"We've killed a lot of them," Zhu said.

"What's that?"

"Americans, we've killed a lot of them."

"Yes, and we're going to kill a lot more."

Zhu noticed movement below. He swung the captured American machine gun, firing at enemy soldiers sprinting for the bottom entrance to the building. *Will I make Soldier Rank? I hope so.*

COACHELLA VALLEY, CALIFORNIA

That evening, a sleek, nearly soundless UAV streaked like an owl over the nighttime surfaces of the Coachella Valley floor. Behind it in the distance were several other nearly invisible aircraft.

Inside the first ultra-stealthy insertion drone rode Paul, Romo and Donovan. There were no windows, but there was a soft blue light to show them their piled gear. Like abductees in a UFO, they had to trust an unseen operator. This one piloted them toward a lonely field in Mexico.

Paul and Romo played cards, while Donovan kept staring at the special piece of equipment Romo had chosen.

"I don't get it," Donovan finally said.

Paul and Romo looked up.

Donovan toed a bulky, two-cylinder backpack with an attached tube and special nozzle.

"What don't you get?" Paul asked. He knew Romo wasn't going to answer the man. "It's a flamethrower."

"I know what it is," Donovan said.

"Okay."

"What I can't figure out is why he wants to bring it along."

Paul glanced at Romo. "Amigo?" he asked.

The ghost of a smile played along Romo's lips. He lowered his cards and studied Donovan.

The Green Beret didn't scare. Paul hadn't thought he would.

"I have a message to give the Chinese," Romo finally said, speaking in a soft voice.

"Yeah, what's that?" Donovan asked. "Come on, baby, light my fire?"

"Si, I will light a fire," Romo said. "I will make them burn for what they did to us."

"You know we're probably going down into a bunker," Donovan said.

Romo just stared at the man.

"Fire gobbles oxygen," Donovan said. "We won't be able to breathe if you start smoking them with that thing down there."

"We will breathe fine," Romo said.

"I ain't a dragon."

Romo raised the cards to his chest, turning back to Paul.

"Am I missing something?" Donovan asked.

"Our helmets have filters," Paul said. "We'll breathe okay."

Sergeant Donovan continued to stare at the flamethrower. "It's too heavy, too cumbersome and it's not something you want to take down with you into a bunker. It's crazy."

"Si," Romo said, still studying his cards.

"You're both crazy is what I think," Donovan said.

"Is that why General Ochoa sent you with us?" Paul asked.

"No. I'm along to make sure Colonel Valdez's men understand a few realities about life and about you. You're golden, Kavanagh, at least until this mission is completed."

"Sounds good," Paul said. "I hope you've told the Chinese how golden I am."

"Nope," Donovan said. "You and me, we're going to have to show them ourselves."

MEXICO CITY, MEXICO

On his lunch break, Old Daniel Cruz with the bad knees sat on a bench in Santa Anna Park. He watched a red-colored roller strutting across the bricks.

The roller was a pigeon, but not one of the regular wild ones that infested the park near the city's main business district. Daniel used to raise pigeons as a young boy. His rollers flew in the air like homing pigeons, but they were the

389

acrobats of the bird world. As they flew, sometimes, they flipped backward. A good roller would flip backward twenty, maybe even fifty times in the air before it recovered and kept winging around. This roller here in Santa Anna Park, it must belong to a pigeon fancier, a pigeon breeder. This roller must have escaped from its loft, the name pigeon breeders called the bird cages.

"Are you free, my friend?" Daniel asked softly.

For an answer, the roller cooed and strutted a little nearer. There was a red band on the bird's left leg, with lettering on it.

Daniel liked to come to the park for lunch. He had a cheese sandwich wrapped in wax paper. It wasn't much. Donna had brought the cheese home, a gift from Colonel Peng. The man had impregnated his daughter and then he had forced her to abort the child. Donna wept at night over it, but she still went to visit the Chinese supply officer. She claimed to love him.

Daniel breathed harder. He detested the occupiers and he despised how Colonel Peng used his daughter. Now, with this forced abortion, he had yet another reason to pile hate on top of hate. Unfortunately, he could do nothing about his animosity. He was an old man trapped—

A compact man in a business suit sat down beside him on the bench. The man wore sunglasses and carried a lunch pail. He set the box on his knees, opened it and pulled out a hot corned beef sandwich. It smelled delicious and it made Daniel's mouth water.

It had been a long time since Daniel had eaten meat. Cheese—he should be grateful for what he had, not wish for something impossible like meat.

"Daniel Cruz," the man said before taking a bite of his corned beef.

Daniel froze, but he was wary enough, old and wise enough, to keep from whipping about to stare at the man.

"We have done business before," the man said softly while chewing.

Out of the corner of his eye, Daniel studied the stranger. He was white, compact, probably running to fat and looked to be a youthful forty-five.

Daniel would have loved to be forty-five again. Ah, the things he would do.

"I am from the Swiss Embassy," the man said.

Daniel's heart began to pound. And now, he could not help himself. He looked at the man. He had freckles on his cheeks. Yes, he could be Swiss but more likely, this was a CIA agent.

"You've never seen me before," the man said.

"You work for the SNP?" By that, Daniel meant the present Mexican government and the inference therefore was the secret police. They were a nasty, evil lot, who loved entrapping their own people.

"We would not be talking if I belonged to the secret police," the man said. "Instead, they would be marching you away for torture."

"Why are you here?"

"Eat your sandwich," the man said. "Watch your pigeon. It is what you always do, and you should not deviate from that."

With leaden, numb fingers, Daniel opened the wrapper and took out his sandwich. The bread was limp compared to the man's and the cheese inside a poor substitute for corned beef. A flash of hatred surged through Daniel for this well-fed American agent, but he suppressed it.

"You are CIA," Daniel said quietly.

The man stiffened slightly, but hid it well.

Secretly, Daniel smiled inside. Rich foreigners— Americans or Chinese—coming to his country and eating better than he did, it was not right.

"Do not," the man whispered. "say such things."

"What do you want?"

The man took another bite of corned beef, chewed for a time but couldn't swallow.

I have scared him. Maybe he is CIA. I don't know. He cannot help me, so what does it matter?

The man opened his suit and took out a silver-colored flask from an inner pocket. He twisted the cap and took a swallow. By the odor, it was whiskey. The man's hand didn't shake as much now as he slipped the flask back into the suit.

Finally swallowing his corned beef, the man whispered, "We need a vital piece of information. If you give it to us, it

391

might go a long way toward defeating the enemy's California thrust."

Daniel shrugged. What did he care about that?

"We have never come to you before," the man said. "That should show you how critical this is to the war effort."

Daniel could see that. He could also see that the man—the CIA—jeopardized his life by doing this. That jeopardized his daughter's life. That—ah. The man could do something for him after all.

Feeling calmer, feeling much better about the rich man with his meat sandwich, Daniel said, "You will have to pay me for this information."

"Yes. I'm prepared to do that."

"I want a gun."

"A gun?" The CIA agent actually looked at him, before turning away and blinking thoughtfully.

"I want a .38 revolver," Daniel said, "with each chamber loaded with a bullet. Can you get that for me?"

"What do you need a gun for?"

Daniel smiled. It was good to control a situation, to show the foreigner that this was his land and his country. "What do you need my information for?" he asked the agent.

The man squeezed his eyes shut as if analyzing the situation. He opened his eyes almost right away and nodded. "Done. One .38 with bullets, I can do that."

"Excellent."

"In return, you need to give me a way into Marshal Nung's Headquarters. We believe it is in San Ysidro, California."

"Ah," Daniel said, "such a small thing as that? You do not want the moon as well?"

"Can you do it?"

Daniel took a bite of his sad sandwich. The cheese would upset his stomach tonight. Donna knew that, but she fed him Colonel Peng's gift anyway. Could he do this thing for the American? He had seen the First Front Headquarters many times on the scheduled traffic routes. Pedro's computer had more detailed information. Yes, it should be possible for him to find a way. No one bothered with truck drivers bringing needed supplies.

"I believe I can do as you want," Daniel said. "I will find a special shipment order. Provided you have the needed vehicles and uniforms…"

The man nodded in a noncommittal way.

"I think with the right orders you could slip a truck, maybe two, past the first few guard shacks. I doubt such shipment orders would bring you into the guarded compound, which is where I would think a headquarters would be."

"…yes. What you suggest would be acceptable. When could you get this?"

"You need this badly, eh? Speed is foolish in these things."

"I know." The man shrugged. "I don't have a say in that."

"I might be able to get it tomorrow. I have a possible way."

"Tomorrow when?" the man asked.

"By one o'clock or it's not going to happen."

"Can you make the drop—"

"I'll drop it by two," Daniel said.

The CIA agent looked at him for a moment, then put his half-eaten sandwich on the bench. He stood, saying quietly, "My…*boss* thanks you, sir."

"The big boss?" Daniel asked. *Did the man mean the President of the United States?*

"Good luck and good-bye." The man strolled away.

Daniel sat back and he found himself holding his own limp sandwich. The roller still waited. He tore off a piece of crust and threw it to the pigeon. The roller cocked its head at him, strutted closer and pecked at the bread, eating it. Afterward, Daniel ate the rest of the American's sandwich. A .38 revolver with bullets, yes, it was exactly what he needed.

And the corned beef was very good too.

GUADALUPE'S FARM, MEXICO

The standoff came that evening at 6:32 PM in the barn on Guadalupe's Farm. Paul, Romo, Donovan and the other twelve commandos had already spent a restless night, morning and afternoon here. The ultra-stealthy UAVs had deposited them yesterday and returned to the States.

393

In the distance came the nearly constant roar of big supply trucks heading for the front. Occasionally engines sputtered or there came the loud bang of a backfiring truck. Vehicles came from Mexico City, and they came from the Baja ports. Their destinations were always California, feeding the hungry maw of the Chinese armies grinding through Los Angeles. It was one of the reasons why Chinese arms were able to push and push and push forward yet again. The Chinese artillery never seemed to stop pounding and pulverizing because more shells and supplies always reached them.

In the barn were two Chinese supply trucks and each contained large boxes of unopened Army rations. It was a testimony to the will of Valdez's guerillas that the boxes were still intact. The partisans on Guadalupe's Farm were thin with malnourishment. They reminded Paul of Maria Valdez and her soldiers.

The sixteen commandos outnumbered the seven guerillas. More Free Mexico soldiers arrived on foot, twenty-one hard-eyed killers carrying an odd assortment of weapons. That meant there were now twenty-eight Mexicans against the sixteen Americans.

The guerilla leader was a one-armed man with a large .357 holstered at his side and an even larger mustache. He reminded Paul of Pancho Villa, although instead of a sombrero the man wore a red do-rag. Romo had informed Paul that in his youth, the guerilla leader had been a Los Angeles gang member.

The twenty-eight Free Mexico guerillas marched toward the barn, with the one-armed leader in front.

"Show time," Donovan said, as he peered through a crack of the barn door.

Every commando picked up an assault rifle or grenade launcher.

"Wait," Paul said. "A gunfight isn't going to make our case."

"Sure it is," Donovan said.

"You know what I mean," Paul said. "We're here to get ourselves killed in Marshal Nung's Headquarters, not to die in a firefight with our allies. Let me speak to them outside."

394

Donovan laughed. "Sure, go ahead. They'll take you into the woods and hang you, or maybe they'll plant your ass on a sharp stick. How would you like that?"

"Paul is right," Romo said. "We must talk to them. I'll go with him."

Donovan eyed them, and he shrugged. "Yeah, you're probably right. Nice knowing you, Kavanagh."

Paul grunted. Then he opened the barn door enough and slipped outside to the approaching mob. Romo stepped out with him and closed the barn door.

The one-armed leader with the .holstered 357 and the red do-rag—his street name was Gaucho—swaggered ahead of the mob. He pointed at Paul.

"Colonel Valdez has given his orders, gringo. You must come with us."

"Look—" Paul said.

"No!" Gaucho shouted, motioning sharply with his hand. "There is no more talk. You will come with us and America can have our two trucks and our help. Otherwise, we pull out our guns, Americano, and shoot you down where you stand."

Paul's chest constricted and he had to tell himself to leave the assault rifle on his shoulder. The idea of a rope around his neck, or worse, a stake up his—

Romo stepped in front of him, and the assassin had a gun in his hand.

"What is this?" Gaucho asked. "Are you a traitor to our people?"

"I am Juan Romo."

The guerillas began talking among themselves, some of them nodding. Everyone knew about the Colonel's best killer.

"Quiet!" Gaucho told them. "The Colonel gave us his orders." He faced Romo. "It won't help if you shoot me. The rest of my men will still hang the traitorous gringo."

"You won't be here to see it happen," Romo said.

Gaucho shrugged with indifference. "Neither will you."

Romo smiled. "Good. I am tired of living in a land of fools."

Striking his chest, Gaucho took a step closer. "You can call me a fool. But you will never say such a thing about Colonel Valdez."

Romo laughed. "That is exactly what I am saying. He is a fool. We all know it and it is why we follow him to the gates of Hell."

"What does that mean?"

"It means we fight the Chinese even though they have six million soldiers in our country. Well, they did have six million. Now many have gone into America to die."

"Good," Gaucho said. "The Americans are no better than the Chinese."

"Wrong," Romo said. "They kill the Chinese, who have stepped on our country like a conqueror. I am not a slave. I refuse to bow or scrape to the Chinese."

"I don't bow either."

"Colonel Valdez has the heart of a lion," Romo said. "He fights and he devours his enemies. He lost his daughter to the Chinese. Instead of wishing a terrible vengeance on them, his grief has unhinged his reason. He wants this American killer to suffer. I have been with him now for weeks. Paul Kavanagh kills the Chinese with unrelenting savagery. Now, his country sends him to destroy one of the great military minds of China. No, now, Colonel Valdez wishes this killer dead instead. But Kavanagh is off to die in the very heart of power of the enemy. I love Colonel Valdez. I will follow him anywhere. But in this, I say, he is wrong."

Gaucho gathered saliva in his mouth and he spit on the ground. "You are a liar, Juan Romo. You—"

Romo's gun barked. Gaucho staggered backward, with a look of surprise on his face. He opened his mouth and tried to speak. His knees folded and he toppled face-first onto the ground.

"You killed him," a guerilla said.

"I saw that I could not reason with Gaucho," Romo said. "His death makes me sad. Come now. Let me know if there are more of you who refuse to reason with me."

"You killed Gaucho," the same guerilla said.

Romo swiveled so his gun pointed at the man. "Do you want to join Gaucho?"

The guerilla glanced at Gaucho and then into Romo's eyes. The guerilla looked away and shook his head, but there was stubbornness stamped on his face.

"Good," Romo said. "Then go into the barn."

The guerilla hesitated, maybe with indecision, or maybe he saw something unyielding in Romo. He took a step toward the barn door.

"Leave your gun belt here," Romo told him.

The guerilla's eyes widened angrily. He almost spoke. Perhaps he remembered how quickly Gaucho had just died. With a sharp motion, the guerilla unbuckled his gun belt and let the weapon fall in the dust.

"You may enter the barn," Romo said.

With an erect bearing, the guerilla walked through the now partly open door. As he disappeared from view, the remaining guerillas glanced at each other.

"You know who I am," Romo said.

They muttered, "Si" and nodded.

"You know I will kill whoever I must, yes?"

There were more muttered responses and nods.

"If you disagree with me, raise your hand and I will let you leave," Romo said.

Once more, a few guerillas glanced at each other. Someone in the crowd shouted, "Colonel Valdez will not like this."

"I do not like this," Romo said. "Now, I have waited long enough. Everyone will set down his weapon and file into the barn. We must wait, and I do not want to have to kill any more fine Free Mexico fighters. But I will, my friends. This raid, it is the most important of the war. Later, I will visit Colonel Valdez and explain my actions to him. If he wishes, he can kill me then."

"You swear this?" a guerilla asked.

"I swear it on the Virgin," Romo said.

"That is good enough for me," the guerilla told the others. "Juan Romo never lies."

"He never lies," another man said.

Soon, guerillas began putting their weapons on the ground and entering the barn.

Romo leaned near Paul and whispered, "It is a trick I learned a long time ago. Kill the leader and the rest will want to listen. Still, it is too bad about Gaucho. He was a good fighter. I did not enjoy that."

Paul nodded, wondering if Romo had really fixed the situation or if the guerillas were just biding their time.

BEIJING, PRC

Jian Hong stood with Marshal Kao in his underground bunker in Beijing. There were enormous framed photographs on the walls with Jian handing a leashed polar bear cub to various dignitaries. The old Chairman had brought Jian down here seven years ago. This time Jian had summoned Kao. He wanted China's top military man to explain the situation between the two of them while they were alone from prying ears.

"Leader," Marshal Kao said, pointing at the computer table, at the symbol of Los Angeles. "This is an intolerable situation. Marshal Nung can no longer cut through the enemy and slice his formations into pieces, capturing the trapped troops later at his leisure."

"I do not understand your references," Jian said. "Nung has done it again. He has broken through Pomona, through Fullerton, Anaheim, Huntington Beach and Costa Mesa. We are in Long Beach, and in some places, we have battled through to the actual city of Los Angeles. We are winning."

"We are winning if you believe acquiring a little more territory achieves victory." Kao looked up with surprise, maybe at his own boldness. "I beg your pardon, Leader. What I meant to say is that we have not yet broken *through* the defending formations, merely pushed them back."

Jian pursed his lips, nodding finally. "Army Group SoCal has been destroyed as a military formation. You told me so yourself several days ago. These are new units facing us, the last remnants of the old and the Central Californian Reserves."

"Leader, this is what I'm trying to explain. At the beginning of hostiles, with Army Group SoCal, we burst through them in places. Nung separated the various divisions and surrounded them. Those he killed or captured at his leisure. But there has always been just a little more in Los Angeles and reinforcements trickling in from the other states. Those formations have slowed us down or halted Nung from driving through Los Angeles at will."

"You've just shown me that Nung is still driving the Americans from the field of battle."

"But he no longer bursts *through* various formations. Instead, he is *squeezing* the Americans tighter. Instead of surrounding and cutting them off from supplies, he drives them closer to their bases. It means we will have to destroy all of them before we can break into the Grapevine Pass."

Jian frowned at the computer map. "Nung reports there are less than two hundred thousand enemy soldiers in Los Angeles. The Americans started the hostiles with eight hundred thousand in Southern California, didn't they?"

"Yes. That is all true," Kao said. "Yet we have taken just as staggering a proportion of losses, and we are still bottled in the southern portion of the state."

"If they have so few soldiers left, why can't we brush them aside?"

"Because their defensive area is shrinking and we're battling through one of the largest urban areas in the world. It gives them perfect terrain and it means their lines are denser than earlier, harder to break through. We are also facing the toughest and cleverest survivors, veterans now."

"A few more days and Nung says he will be through to the Grapevine Pass."

Marshal Kao straightened. "It may be as he says. If so, we could yet conquer California. There is little left in the state in terms of military power and we have reports that reinforcements to California have slowed. That is what I wish to speak about, Leader. We must begin stockpiling supplies for our Texas thrust. This..." Kao indicated Los Angeles. "This is too small. You must unleash us in Texas and New Mexico. There, with our greater numbers in open terrain and our South

American allies, we can win this war quickly. Instead, we are frittering away our strength for a worthless piece of real estate."

Jian Hong studied the computer map. "I'm unsure. We have spent so much in California and Marshal Nung assures me of victory. I do not want to stop at the goal line if it is merely a matter of a few more feet and a few more days."

It appeared that Marshal Kao would say more, but he didn't. He held his tongue.

What is the correct decision? Jian asked himself. *Who can tell me the unvarnished truth? These are hard choices. I wish there was someone I could fully trust.*

WASHINGTON, D.C.

Anna watched the President rub his face as he listened to the late night report from the briefing major.

The woman used the holo-video and an electric pointer. It was quiet tonight. The situation had turned grim again.

"We saved several Behemoth tanks," the major said. "The Chinese overran the others during the rout. Now..."

She continued to explain the Battle of Los Angeles. The Chinese had overrun too many places. They had killed thousands and made thousands more soldiers flee. The civilian death toll kept climbing higher and higher. The Chinese were merciless toward them.

"We have to hold somewhere!" Sims cried.

"Sir," General Alan said. "We're making the enemy pay for every step of the way. But it's too much to expect our soldiers to stand in place and die. Instead, they trade space for time and set up new defensive positions. They booby-trap everything."

"And the Chinese bring up their combat bulldozers," Sims said. "They plow through buildings and set off hundreds, thousands of your precious booby-traps."

"We're bleeding them," Alan said.

"It doesn't seem to matter to the Chinese," Sims said. "They're squeezing us into a ball in Los Angeles. They're taking away our maneuver room. Soon, our men will be shoulder to shoulder and the Chinese artillery will grind them into bloody pieces."

"The other side is hurting, sir. You know that."

"Do I?" Sims said, his voice nearly cracking.

"The commandos, sir," Anna said. "They will change the situation."

Sims shook his head. "We can't count on that. We have to think of something else."

Levin looked up and seemed ready to speak.

"No," Sims said. "No. I'm not ready to nuke Los Angeles. Do you realize how many civilians are still living there? ...maybe we have to start thinking about pulling back to the Sierra Nevada Mountains. Maybe it's time to let the Chinese have California."

No one spoke. Finally, General Alan motioned for the major to continue with her briefing. She cleared her throat and did just that.

SAN YSIDRO, CALIFORNIA

Paul swayed inside the big Chinese supply truck. There had been several fancy ideas about how to do this. One of them included putting each other in the big crates. Donovan had said it would be just like the Trojan Horse of legend.

Paul remembered reading that story as a kid. The Greeks had stuffed a gigantic hollow wooden horse with hoplites: soldiers with spears. The Trojans thought it was a victory honor, and had been dumb enough to accept the gift and had torn down their gates to drag it in. Afterward, with the gates partly repaired and the Trojans throwing a victory party, the Greeks had slipped out of the hollow horse and let in the rest of the Greek army, which had sneaked back to the city walls under cover of darkness. Donovan had loved the idea of their doing a similar thing to the Chinese. Romo had finally shot down the idea.

"Amigo, do you not remember your lessons? The gods helped the Greeks trick the Trojans. Who is going to help us trick the Chinese?"

"Pile the crates all the way up in the very back," Paul said. "The rest of us will stay in front of the truck-bed behind them. If our trick doesn't work, at least we can go out firing, not trapped inside the boxes like so many sardines."

They had argued about all kinds of things, including the number of trucks to take. Paul had finally told Donovan they were going to take one.

"Why just one?" Donovan wanted to know.

"Do you see how many men we have? Sixteen."

"And we have all our weapons, too," Donovan said.

"The extra weapons we put in the crates nearest us."

Now, Paul swayed in the gloom with the other commandos. He'd wrapped his arms around his bent knees and thought about better times as he stared at his wedding ring.

Two Green Berets of Chinese extraction drove the truck with the needed false papers and orders. The rest of the team was crammed tight in the body-heated space.

"We should have taken two trucks," Donovan grumbled in the darkness.

They had been on the road three hours already. Sixteen commandos out to change history—it seemed balls-up crazy.

How do people hatch schemes like this? Paul wanted to know. Desperation was the only answer.

"I got to take a piss," one man complained.

"You got a bottle," Donovan told him. "Use it."

The gears changed before he could take the suggestion. The truck slowed down.

Paul's stomach churned. They were part of a regular Chinese convoy. They knew that much, but not much more. The driver's navigator had tapped that out in code from the cab.

There were plenty of things wrong with this raid. For one thing, they hardly knew anything about the compound's present condition. An aerial photo six days old had shown a wrecked and blasted area. It would be logical to presume the Chinese had repaired the main bunker. Paul had drawn a sketch-map for the others, which everyone had studied while waiting in the barn. He'd remembered the location from when he'd guarded Colonel Norman from Washington.

Paul listened as the truck slowed even more. There would be gates, guards, check lists, who knew what else. Still, this was a supply truck bringing supplies. It would be a routine situation and the guards would likely be bored half to death.

The Blue Swan raid had been different. They'd had a plan for getting out once the mission was completed. The idea had been to use the helicopters, but those had been destroyed during the firefight getting down. There was no plan this time except to escape and evade.

In the gloom, Paul blew out his cheeks in frustration. If they could reach a location five miles away from the Chinese HQ, the insertion drones were supposed to pick them up afterward. Yeah, that was going to work.

He endured the ride and he listened to the small sounds: boots creaking, a man coughing, someone clearing his throat. Paul opened his mouth and barely kept from panting. It was too hot, too stuffy in here. Beside him, men squirmed. Someone sucked in his breath sharply, maybe in pain.

Suddenly the truck's brakes squealed as the vehicle came to a stop. Muted footsteps sounded from outside. There were Chinese voices; well, Chinese words at least.

Slowly, Paul drew his sidearm. He heard others drawing theirs.

The truck's back gate banged open.

Paul couldn't breathe. This was it, dying on a fool's errand. How had he ever let Ochoa talk him into something so stupid? After this—there wasn't going to be an afterward. He aimed his gun toward the back gate. When the final crate moved out of the way, he was going to fire until he was dead.

A crate scraped against metal. It made Paul's blood pressure soar. Wood squealed, maybe from a crowbar. Laughter rang out a moment later. Someone slapped a crate. There were more sounds, of huffing perhaps, and the tailgate slammed shut. Maybe two minutes later, the truck started up again.

Then—*one, two, three*—someone thumped three times on the back of the cab. It was a signal from the navigator that everything was okay and the plan was still on schedule.

Someone in the gloom muttered. Someone else hissed to shut the hell up.

"Phase two," Donovan whispered.

Paul expelled his pent-up breath. Were they in the compound yet? It was hard to believe. This was harebrained. Sixteen commandos to take on Marshal Nung's Headquarter guards.

Paul had read the brief. The marshal's bodyguards were tough and no-nonsense. They would have body armor and they would be ready, even if the raid surprised them.

"Soon," Romo whispered into Paul's ear. The man's breath smelled like the pumpkin seeds he been chewing.

Paul nodded. He could feel the building tension. It was as if his limbs were rubber bands and something was winding them tighter than they had ever been before.

The truck slowed again, and rolled at low speed for a time.

There came another heavy thump from the cab. It was the signal. The navigator was leaving the cab to plant a directional beacon.

General Ochoa's operational planners had come up with the idea. The commandos would never make it from wherever the truck parked all the way to the main bunker. There would simply be too many soldiers, checkpoints and guards around to fight through them. Therefore, the commandos needed those guards removed. They needed a diversion. That diversion would come as a heavy missile attack on the headquarters.

Paul knew what that meant in real terms. All the commandos did. Some of them were going to die from friendly fire—if the missiles even made it through Chinese anti-missile defenses. If missiles exploded here, it should also mean that everyone above ground would run for cover. That was the moment to strike for the bunker. The missiles would home in on the beacon and give them the needed distraction—that was a big, screw-yourself hurrah.

"Let's get ready," Paul said. He pulled out a tiny flashlight, clicking it on. Others clicked theirs on. In the wash of small beams, commandos went to work, opening the boxes nearest them, the wall of crates. Each of these was laid so the tops were aimed sideways at them.

Paul pulled out body armor. It was hard to do in their tight confines, but he donned the bulky suit and put a headband with earphones over his ears, with a small jack and microphone in front of his mouth. Over that, he secured a helmet. Lastly, he picked up a squat submachine gun made to fire exploding bullets. He had nine magazines in various pockets and five different grenades. He also had a pistol, knife and steel tomahawk. This was it—the mission of his life.

Beside him Romo strapped the flamethrower to his back. It was a brutal weapon, and burning to death was a particularly nasty way to die. One misconception about flamethrowers was that a bullet through the tank would cause it to explode. Maybe if it was an incendiary bullet. Otherwise, the fluids would simply leak out.

The truck parked, or it came to stop at least and the engine turned off. Now, they waited. If workers began unloading the crates too soon, there would be trouble. Hopefully, the driver had arranged it so that they were the last truck unloaded. Whatever the case, Paul would know soon enough.

LOS ANGELES, CALIFORNIA

Stan rubbed his scraggly chin. He had a three-day growth of beard and had far too many gray hairs. His head and shoulders were out of the top hatch. Another Behemoth followed his tank down the street.

The treads crunched rubble and flattened a discarded machine gun. Then cracks appeared in the pavement like ice. Its engine made strange sounds and the batteries were down to forty-eight percent charge.

It was a wonder the tank still worked. Four Behemoths still ran under their own power. That wouldn't last much longer, though.

These past two days, Stan had noticed a slight slacking of enemy attacks. The Chinese seemed tired, worn down after relentless weeks of combat. Even so, they still pushed through Los Angeles, using jetpack flyers, combat bulldozers, mass artillery and triple-turreted tanks. They leveled the great

405

metropolis and sent infantry teams through everything. The number of civilian dead was mind-boggling and had to be in the hundreds of thousands by now.

"Air traffic," Jose radioed from within the tank.

"What's that?" Stan asked into his microphone.

"Air traffic is coming through," Jose said. "But don't fire, this is ours."

"What are you talking about?"

Just then, Stan heard and saw them: cruise missiles. Like air-sharks, the deadly missiles streaked overhead. Hot exhaust roared out of their backs, and in the nearest, Stan could swear he saw lettering on the fuselage. The missiles hugged the ground and would do so until they reached the target.

"Is that our counter-battery fire?" Stan asked.

"I have no idea," Jose radioed, "but I don't see what else it could be."

The cruise missiles streaked away. In the distance, Chinese computer-assisted artillery knocked one down in a spectacular explosion.

Stan shook his head. That was the truth of this war. The Chinese had too much ordnance. No matter what America did, the Chinese always had three to four times as much.

Sighing, Stan wondered when the battle was going to end for him. He couldn't keep this up much longer. He was just so damn tired and sick of killing.

SAN YSIDRO, CALIFORNIA

In the gloom, Paul saw the green beep on his communicator. "This is it. The missiles are coming."

It was stifling hot now in the front of the truck bed. A restless energy filled the commandos.

"It would be our luck if a cruise missile hits our truck and kills the lot of us," Donovan said.

"I don't want to hear that," Paul said. "We're going to kick ass, Sergeant. You got that?"

Donovan shined his light on Paul's face. A second later, the beam moved away. "Are you in the zone, Kavanagh?"

"I don't want anyone stopping because he's hurt or shot in the side," Paul told the commandos. "You know what to do: follow me. Kill every officer you see and keep heading to the bunker. Once there, we go down. We're the plague. We're the Angel of Death."

The communicator beeped red.

"It's game time," Paul said. "Shove aside the crates."

With their shoulders against the wood, commandos grunted and shoved. Wood squealed and crates fell out of the truck bed. The driver was supposed to have made sure the gate was down, and he had done his job.

Light burst into the gloom as crates tumbled out of the way. Fresh air roiled in.

"Looks beautiful," Paul said.

Beside him, Romo grunted.

As Paul Kavanagh jumped to the ground, the first cruise missile slammed down into the compound and exploded with a deafening noise. Seconds later, sirens blared. Then two more cruise missiles hammered the compound. Everywhere things went into the air: parts of buildings, IFVs and Chinese soldiers.

"Perfect," Paul said. He grinned like a manic, and his eyes gleamed with murder lust. "Follow me."

He ran for the chain-link gate, the way out of the fenced-off area that was the parking lot. A guard shack stood there. A Chinese soldier stuck his head out. Paul fired a burst, hitting him in the face, exploding the man's head his bullets.

The compound was huge just as he remembered it. There were comm-shacks, new Chinese portables and shell-riddled buildings. Staff cars, jeeps, Humvees, IFVs were parked all around. Some burned. Others had flipped.

Assault rifle fire sounded behind Paul. Chinese soldiers crumpled ahead of him. Out of the corner of his eye he saw something massive in the air. It was another cruise missile. Paul crouched and ducked his head. The missile exploded, raining shrapnel and staring fires. The concussion washed against Paul and nearly knocked him off his feet. He looked up, as he got ready to stand. He saw another missile coming. It exploded closer than the first one. The blast knocked Paul tumbling, and he found himself flat on his back, gasping hot air.

Am I hurt?

With a groan, he sat up, checking his legs, his arms and finally his chest. He was good. Grunting, he stood up. One by one, armored commandos stood with him, including Romo. Four of the commandos stayed down. He would have liked to see if they were alive, but there was no time for it. This was the ball game.

He shouted, at least, he thought he did. He ran half-crouched over, heading for the bunker. Another cruise missile came down. How many had his side fired? This was too much.

"Hit the dirt!" Paul roared. He did, hugging dirt. The missile went off and he lifted, slamming back against the ground. He was slower getting up this time, and fewer commandos joined him.

Behind his visor Donovan had big staring eyes. Romo's face was like a skull. The Mexican assassin was Death's cousin, and he brought his flames with him.

This is the final lap. Oh, Cheri, you'll never know how much I loved you.

Paul gulped, too filled with emotion. It almost overwhelmed him how precious it was to live and love. What a blessing to have a wife as he did. What a great thing to leave the world a son like Mike.

I don't deserve them. They needed someone better than me, far better.

With an animal groan, Paul started for the bunker. Fires burned everywhere, including in the center of a smashed comm-shack, with wood splinters laid around it like pickup sticks. Chinese lay sprawled on the ground, some at grotesque angles. One man had his legs folded under him, meaning they had to be broken. A few stirred and groggily stood. Most of those fled once they saw the commandos. One guard picked up his rifle. From fifty feet away, Paul put a three-round burst into his chest. The soldier flopped back down, smacking the back of his head hard against the pavement. He wasn't going to get up again.

As he staggered, Paul picked up speed. He sprinted across gravel. The bunker was shut, the blast-doors secured. *All righty then, I have a little present for you.* Sliding to a halt, Paul went to one knee, unslung a LAWS rocket, armed, aimed and fired it with a whoosh. The small rocket slammed against the door and tore it open.

Behind his visor Paul's eyes narrowed to slits. The Chinese had slaughtered Greater Los Angeles. The orders to do that came from here, from Marshal Nung. It was time for this Nung to taste what he had given everyone else.

"Let's see how you like them apples," Paul muttered.

He was up. He heard thudding footfalls and flicked his head to the side. Romo ran near. Donovan was close behind. Good, good, it was good to die with your friends.

"Ready?" Paul shouted.

"Si!"

"Let's rock and roll, baby!" Donovan roared, reverting perhaps to his Viking ancestry.

Paul increased speed, reaching the blasted door first. He grabbed a grenade, armed and hurled it through. This was his private, portable artillery. It burst. Paul used his foot and bashed the door, forcing it further open. He leaped inside. A Chinese guard groaned from on the floor. Paul shot him. Another whipped around a corner. Paul shot him, too, in the face.

The handful of commandos started down the bunker, firing, tossing grenades, creating mayhem. Then four Chinese guards began firing at them from the bottom concrete stairs.

Paul was out of grenades. Donovan shrugged, suggesting they trust their body armor to see them through. Instead Romo slithered forward on his belly, the grim nozzle aimed forward. Flame spit from the nozzle in a long line. It reached down the stairs and began to burn. Chinese soldiers screamed in agony.

"It works every time," Romo said.

"Our target is down there," Paul said. He tore an empty magazine from the submachine gun and slapped in a fresh one. "Ready?"

Romo squirted another terrible line of fire. A blaze crackled down there. Smoke began to billow.

409

Picking himself off the floor, Paul charged down the stairs. The smell of cooked pork assaulted his nostrils. He knew the awful fact that humans smelled like pork when they cooked.

Kavanagh raced past the dying guards. He cut down another man and then he burst into what had to be the command chamber. It held a large computer table and more stations than he could count. Some of the personnel had backed away. Others fired at him with handguns, but they were small caliber weapons.

Paul fired back, cutting down the First Front High Command. Bullets *spanged* off his body armor, and kinetic force caused him to stagger back. One bullet smashed through and singed his cheek, creating a bloody furrow. None sank into his flesh to kill him.

A blazing line of liquid fire arched toward the enemy and Chinese officers began to burn and scream hideously. Smoke chugged and the stench was wicked. More bullets ripped into them, and mercifully they went down.

"Is he here?" Donovan shouted.

Paul flung out a spent magazine. This butchery made him sick. It felt wrong. Yet he rammed another magazine in and continued to do his duty. He was here to kill, to try to end the conflict by eliminating the mastermind behind the relentless orgy of destruction that the Chinese committed upon America.

-14-
Conference

BEIJING, PRC

Jian Hong paced restlessly in his study. The room was on the third floor of his palace in the middle of Mao Square.

He could not believe the news. Marshal Shin Nung was dead, slaughtered in his headquarters like a pig. American commandos had burst into the bunker during a particularly savage cruise missile assault. If the reports were true, Nung had burned to death beyond easy recognition. A dentist had identified the marshal through his dental records.

It was this burning to death that troubled Jian.

A knock sounded, and the door swung open. A secretary poked her head in. "Leader, Police Minister Xiao is here to see you."

"Yes, yes, let him enter."

The secretary retreated and Xiao entered. It was very late and behind his thick glasses, Xiao's eyes were puffy. The Police Minister must have already been asleep.

"Have you heard the news?" Jian asked.

Xiao nodded even as he swayed slightly.

"Sit, sit," Jian said. "You look like you're about to tumble over."

Xiao pulled out a chair and sat down.

"The Americans have apparently slain Marshal Nung."

411

"It is startling," Xiao said.

Jian laughed mirthlessly. "It is more than startling. I find it impossible."

"Leader?"

"These so-called commandos burned Nung to death beyond recognition."

Xiao blinked several times and nodded hesitantly.

"It is obvious," Jian said. "This is a staged event."

"By whom, Leader?"

"That is why I have summoned you. This piece of treachery will not stand. I want to know how such an attack against my chosen marshal could succeed in the center of a heavily guarded headquarters."

Xiao seemed awake now, and he appeared to choose his words with care. "Are we certain someone among us did this? Perhaps the Americans really—"

Jian laughed harshly. "Do not be naïve, Xiao. Treacherous and cunning enemies surround us. I suspect Deng Fong. Yet if that is true, it means his hooks have sunk into those in the Army. Marshal Kao would have to be complicit in this. Normally, I would not believe it, but I know that he loathes Marshal Nung."

"I'm sure you are right, Leader," Xiao hastened to say. "But it seems incredible Kao would help slaughter Marshal Gang."

"Ah! That was the second piece of evidence that showed me the truth of the matter. Marshal Gang survived the so-called commando raid."

"How?"

"He wasn't in the bunker, but in his quarters. He sustained injuries from the cruise missile assault, but they were minor and he is otherwise fit. And listen to this. Kao has already contacted me and suggested that Marshal Gang assume responsibility for the First Front. He was too eager, too ready in this."

The Police Minister squinted and soon began to nod. "I'm beginning to think you are right, Leader. There are too many coincidences. And you say Nung was burned to death? Why do you believe that is important?"

412

"We know the depth of Kao's hatred for him. The burning shows spite. It is Kao's fingerprint on the assassination."

Xiao stood and straightened his uniform. "Leader, this is a grave matter."

"Yes, yes, finally you're awake. My enemies—*our* enemies—are making their move against us even as we wage war."

"It is diabolical."

"I have learned a valuable lesson concerning these matters," Jian said. "One must strike first. Well, our enemies have secretly struck against us by chopping at one of the roots of our military high command. Perhaps they believed this blow would frighten me into inaction. Or maybe they thought I was too dull to see this for what it was. No! I'm neither dull-witted nor frightened. Instead, they have roused me to swift action. Tell me, Xiao. Are your flying squads ready?"

"Once you give me the code word, Leader, I can have them knocking on doors in fifteen minutes."

Clasping his hands behind him, intertwining his fingers so he could feel his knuckles, Jian began to pace. "It is a bold thing we plan. It frightens me, this step. But we cannot wait for our enemies to finish their strike against us." He whirled on Xiao. "Arrest Marshal Kao and arrest Foreign Minister Deng Fong before dawn."

"The Foreign Minister has powerful bodyguards," Xiao said.

"If you cannot do this, tell me."

The Police Minister straightened. "I can do it, Leader. May I ask one thing?"

"Speak!"

"Arresting Deng Fong might bring repercussions with the German Dominion. They trust him. This could also cause division in our Pan-Asian Alliance."

Jian laughed grimly. "So be it. I cannot wait for Deng to strike at me. Because he has political power, do I let him plot and execute his assassinations with impunity? No! They made their play. Now, I am about to make mine. Take Marshal Kao into police custody and shoot him in the deepest basement you can find."

"Yes, Leader," Xiao said.

"Once you have Deng Fong...use your best doctor. Inject the Foreign Minister with something to bring about a heart attack. We will say you learned of a death plot and hurried to his quarters to warn him. Alas, you were too late and found him beyond recovery."

"I doubt anyone will believe our story."

"Perhaps not," Jian said, "but it will give them a way to save face. People believe Marshal Kao is my man. I thought he was too, until this commando raid left his protégée in control of the First Front. The Japanese leaders and our Southeast Asian allies will not link these two deaths together. Who knows what Germans think? They are a mystery to me."

"Leader, these...deaths will damage our war effort at a critical time."

"Not necessarily," Jian said. "These undercurrents have no doubt sapped Army morale all along and we weren't even aware of it. Unity of effort is a critical component of successfully waged war. With Deng gone and Kao out of the way, we can prosecute the rest of the North American conquest with singleness of purpose."

Xiao nodded, albeit with seeming reluctance.

"You have your orders, Police Minister. Now go, eliminate these saboteurs for the good of Greater China."

"I need the code word, Leader."

Jian Hong gave it to him.

Xiao turned smartly and marched out of the study.

As the door closed, Jian felt the restlessness surge in him. Yet he sat down, as he was weary. This was a grave risk, and it could cause unforeseen political turmoil. But he had to strike. Otherwise, he would be a fool, waiting for his enemies to finish him. Once in the highest office, one was never completely secure. The death of the Old Chairman proved that.

Jian flexed his hands. He had shot the old man himself while visiting him in the deepest bunker. It had been the hardest thing he had ever done.

What should we do in California?

Jian massaged his forehead. Nung was dead and Kao soon would be. Yes, to confound his enemies, he would let them

414

have Marshal Gang in the First Front. But he would strip the marshal of power by ending the great assault. Jian smiled cruelly. He would remove one of the reserve armies, sending it back to the Second Front. Yes, he would let Marshal Gang employ the old method of heavy artillery bombardments combined with a creeping infantry assault. That would necessitate time for reorganization, which would mean an end to Nung's strategy.

Jian breathed deeply. His enemies had slaughtered poor Marshal Nung. He had been a great fighter, a worthy soldier and officer. China would mourn him. Yes, he would give Marshal Nung a splendid State funeral and would deliver the oration himself. Through Nung, China had pulverized the Americans and destroyed masses of air power. Now it was time to look elsewhere on the continent for ultimate victory.

Nung was gone. Gang could wither on the vine and therefore be taken out of play. His enemies thought they could outmaneuver him. No. He was too cunning for them, able to see through their subterfuge and more than willing to act decisively.

By first light today, Deng and Kao would be dead. He would need replacements for them on the Ruling Committee. He would have to give his enemies a place at the table. Yes, it was wise to give them a spokesman. Now he would have to redouble his Lion Guardsman, as many of his secret enemies would yearn even more to assassinate him.

Am I acting wisely? The restlessness stirred in his heart. *They burned Marshal Nung. If they hadn't burned him, I might have missed the clue.*

"Your hatred foiled you, Kao. You should have kept to your charts and battle maps."

CALIFORNIAN-MEXICAN BORDER

Paul Kavanagh helped Romo sit on a large rock. The assassin's left arm was in a sling. A bullet had torn muscle and put the man into a state of shock.

415

Neither of them wore body armor anymore, having shed it long ago. Both were battered, Romo more so.

Paul grunted as he sat on the ground, putting his back against the rock. He unclipped a canteen, unscrewed the cap and took two swallows of water. He held it out to his blood brother.

Romo gripped the canteen and drank greedily. The assassin gasped and handed the empty canteen back.

"What..." Romo licked his lips. "Where are the others?"

Paul closed his eyes. The others were dead, including Donovan. Getting out of the bunker and then the compound...Donovan had remained behind with a heavy machine gun, covering their escape. The Green Beret had been shot in the leg and he'd realized he had been as good as dead.

"I'm too old for this," Paul said.

"Si."

Paul checked his watch. They didn't have much time left. He forced himself up and gripped Romo's good arm.

"Leave me," the assassin said. "I'm too tired."

"Yeah, tell me about it." Paul dragged Romo to his feet.

They walked until nightfall, and they reached the rendezvous area. Paul clicked the communicator, and it guided him to a hidden drone.

"Do you believe that?" Paul asked, staring at the tiny aircraft.

Romo was feverish, and although he had his eyes open, he likely didn't see anything.

Paul guided Romo inside, buckled in and the portal snapped shut. Ten second later, the ultra-stealth drone buzzed into life and lifted.

"Looks like we're going home," Paul said.

Romo muttered, shaking his head.

"What did you say?" Paul asked.

"I have no home. I am a man adrift."

"You're my blood brother, amigo. I'm going to introduce you to my wife and son. You're always going to be welcome in my home."

Juan Romo let his head slump back as he closed his eyes.

Feeling his pulse—it was beating strong—Paul decided not to worry about the assassin right now. Against all odds, he was alive. He was going home and he would go AWOL if they didn't let him see his wife. Had this stunt slowed the Chinese advance? He didn't know. He'd find out soon enough.

Paul Kavanagh made himself comfortable, closed his eyes and fell asleep.

MEXICO CITY, MEXICO

Several days later it ended where it had begun, with Colonel Peng of the Fifth Transport Division. He was tired from endless weeks of work. There was a lull right now with the change of command, so he had taken the opportunity to use his special pass.

The lovely Donna Cruz had sent him a written message. It was just like her to pen this little love note. She was a romantic girl, and her ass was so delicious. Peng had been thinking about it ever since the last time they had made love.

It was true it had been a crudely written note, at least in terms of penmanship. She had also written it in Spanish. It would have been too much to expect her to write with Chinese characters. This was a land of barbarians, after all, even if very beautiful and sexual barbarians.

Peng turned the wheel of his jeep and entered the Coco Hotel parking lot. Vines snaked up the posts at the head of each parking space. A few of the vines displayed beautiful purple flowers.

She had mailed him the card-key and said she would be ready for him at 11:00 AM sharp. Smiling, Peng eased his jeep into a slot, shut off the engine and picked up his box of chocolates. Inside was a thousand pesos. He knew she still suffered from the abortion. Maybe he shouldn't have forced it on her. Guilt had driven him. If Donna had a child, Peng knew he would feel compelled to help raise it. He could barely afford Donna and continue to send his own mother enough money. If he also had to support a child—no, it would be too much.

Colonel Peng shook his head. The chocolates and money would help Donna forget. And she would help him forget the endless weeks of drudgery.

Clutching the box to his chest, Peng hurried up the stairs to Room 14. He knocked and waited, but no one answered.

Was she out somewhere?

Peng looked around at the neat little homes and tall trees. This was a suburb of Mexico City, and looked like a nice residential area. Maybe Donna was visiting a friend. He shrugged, dug out the card-key and slid it into the slot. While clutching the box with his arm, he twisted the door-handle and opened it.

"Hello," he said, in Chinese.

It was dark in here, hard to see. Ah, he heard the shower. She must be cleaning herself for him.

Grinning, Peng stepped into the room, tossed the chocolates onto the bed and heard the heavy door whomp shut behind him. He turned toward the bathroom and took two steps before stopping in surprise.

"Oh," he said in Chinese. "I'm sorry. D-Do I have the wrong room?"

An old Mexican man sat in a chair watching him. The man frowned and seemed angry.

Colonel Peng took a step back. Why hadn't the man said something when he'd first entered?

"Who are you?" the man asked in atrocious Chinese.

"I'm Colonel Peng," he said, attempting Spanish. "Do you know Donna Cruz?"

The old man nodded. "She is my daughter."

Peng blinked and then it came to him. Relief flooded his chest. "Oh, you're her father. Yes, I've sent you—"

Colonel Peng's mouth dropped open as speech failed him. The old Mexican—Mr. Cruz—aimed a gun at him. This was illegal. Mexicans weren't supposed to have guns.

"You must put that away," Peng said in Chinese.

A terrible light now shined in Mr. Cruz's eyes. He struggled upright to a standing position. It appeared as if his knees troubled him.

"Is Donna in the shower?" Peng asked.

The gun barked four loud reports, with flashes belching from the barrel each time. Bullets slammed into Peng until he found himself lying on the carpet. The world spun crazily and narrowed to a tight focus. Peng saw as from a great distance Mr. Cruz standing over him. The old man pointed the gun at his face.

"No," Peng whispered.

He didn't hear the sound, but he saw the final muzzle flash. It was the last thing Colonel Peng of the Fifth Transport Division saw before he died.

LOS ANGELES, CALIFORNIA

Three days later, near noon, Stan climbed out of his Behemoth and noticed a terrible black cloud over LA. It seemed gray now rather than black. That was something, at least. The fires were dying out, often because of a lack of fuel. Perhaps the flies would die soon too.

From the top hatch of the tank, he surveyed the enemy lines. He saw a great trench in the rubble, with coils of razor wire before it. The Chinese had put that up yesterday with huge, bulldozer-like machines. He could see machine gun emplacements. Many of those were fake, meant to draw American fire.

Frowning, Stan wondered why the Chinese hadn't bombarded them today and yesterday. That went against the Chinese methods shown these past weeks. Could the great and mighty offensive have finally halted?

It was too soon to believe that. Yet time in southern California wasn't on China's side. Every hour helped JFC SoCal stiffen the defenses. Every hour allowed more trucks to bring badly needed supplies. It meant exhausted and battle-shaken troops could rest and regain their morale. Stan snorted. It allowed the mechanics time to bring the remaining Behemoths a little closer to shipshape.

"Professor!" Jose shouted up from within the tank.

"What is it?"

419

"They're sending a jeep for you. You're to report to Battalion HQ."

"Now? The Chinese could resume their offensive at any moment."

"I'm just relaying orders, Professor."

Stan eased out of the hatch and used the rungs on the side of the tank to crawl down to the ground. The weird thing was he actually felt more tired now than he had several days ago. He'd stopped taking stims to stay awake and he almost slept normal hours. It was as if his body had used every reserve it had to keep him going, and now that things had slowed, it was letting go, collapsing from exhaustion.

He leaned against the tank and his mind shied from the endless death and destruction he'd been part of. The things he and the crew had done to stay alive were terrible. Yet what choice did they have? It was either kill or become Chinese slaves.

As Stan leaned against the tank, a jeep roared up. The driver was a Militia teenager, a skinny boy with an oversized helmet. There were too many youngsters in the Army like him, too many hastily drafted kids out of LA.

Slowing down, the kid shouted, "Captain Higgins?"

"Yep. That's me."

"I'm here to take you to HQ."

Stan climbed into the jeep. The kid glanced at the razor wire, shuddered and cranked the wheel. He drove faster, dodging shell-holes and big chunks of rubble and other debris. They passed Militia clearing this street, using their hands and wheelbarrows. A bulldozer would have been better. A lot of things would have been better.

The driver took to him Battalion HQ, a relatively intact Rite Aid store. Battered Bradley Fighting Vehicles used the parking lot, together with beat up Humvee Avengers, their Blowdart missiles aimed skyward.

Stan followed the driver, who took him to an old storeroom in back. Data net men swarmed the area with their equipment. Soon, Stan spoke with the colonel, a Militiaman and a former high school football coach. He was big and balding, and had bowed legs.

"I've spoken to the General," the ex-coach said. "We're pulling out your Behemoths."

Stan raised his eyebrows. "I thought we were stiffening the line."

"You were. But the eggheads who decide such things have changed their mind. Now the Behemoths are going to form LA's reserve."

"Because the Chinese have taken a siesta?" Stan asked.

"Did you notice all the razor wire they've put up lately?"

"That could be a trick," Stan said. "Maybe they're trying to lull us."

"Or it could indicate a change in mindset."

"There is that, too."

"Anyway," the ex-coach said, "here's the schedule for the pullout. We're going to do this by stages." The colonel handed Stan a folder.

He tucked it under his arm.

"By the way," the colonel said, as he checked his watch. "You have a call in ten minutes. It's from the Detention Center."

Stan's heart went cold. This was highly unusual. By law, there were only a few places allowed to communicate with the Detention Center facility. The middle of a battle zone wasn't one, either.

"Is it about my son?" Stan asked.

The colonel shrugged. "You can use the comm-equipment over there. Let me say it in case you don't know. I'm glad you and your tanks were here, Captain. As far as I'm concerned, you saved all our butts."

The man held out his hand. Stan shook it. The ex-football coach had a bone-crushing grip.

Soon, Stan found himself sitting at a table, staring at a computer screen. What had happened? He hoped Jake had kept his nose clean.

In time, a Detention Center officer came onscreen. The woman looked angry. She read off a list, asking a series of questions.

"What is this about?" Stan asked.

"First," she said, looking up, "I must confirm that you are Captain Stan Higgins of the U.S. Army. Until such time, I cannot answer any of your questions."

Stan kept his face neutral and told himself he couldn't afford another fight with them. He answered the many and sometimes intrusive questions. Finally, the officer gave him a perfunctory smile.

"Thank you, Captain Higgins. You are clearly Jake Higgins's father. I will now patch you through to him."

"Is Jake all right?"

"You can confirm that in..." she checked her watch. "In fifteen seconds." She faded from view.

Stan waited, and in exactly fifteen seconds, Jake appeared onscreen.

"Dad, are you okay?"

Stan found himself grinning from ear-to-ear. "It's good to see, son. Are you in trouble?"

A wary look came over Jake. "No sir, I've learned my lesson. America is the greatest country in the world and President Sims is just the man to see us through these terrible times. I made a stupid mistake in protesting against him. I see that now."

Stan nodded, but he felt saddened. Yes, America was the greatest country, but no one should have to force that idea onto his boy. It should have come naturally. Still, he couldn't fault Jake. The Detention Center surely monitored the call. The more he'd thought about it during the weeks, the more he'd liked it that his boy had stood up to them. But there was a time and place to speak up and a time to keep your mouth shut. Maybe this was a sign of Jake finally growing up: knowing when to fight his battles.

"Are you leaving the Detention Center?" Stan asked. "Are you coming home?"

"I am leaving," Jake said. "But I'm not coming home. I've signed up."

"In the Militia?" Stan asked.

"That's why I'm calling, sir. I want to thank you."

"What did I do?"

422

"You won the Medal of Honor in Alaska, and the exploits of your tanks in California have been in the news almost every day. The Detention Center Commandant has spoken to the President about me, asking for a reprieve."

Stan's face split into a huge smile. "That's wonderful!"

"Yes sir. It means I can volunteer for any service I want."

Stan blinked rapidly. "What's that? What are you talking about?"

"I'm enlisting in the Army, sir. America is under siege and she needs every patriotic citizen she has. I'm going to request armor, but I'll go wherever my country needs me."

"When do you leave for boot camp?"

"Today, sir."

Stan stared at his boy. There was something different about Jake, about how he was acting. "Is this your idea?"

"Of course it is."

"I'm—"

Jake glanced to his left, and he nodded to someone mumbling off-screen. He faced Stan again and said, "Sorry, Dad. My time is up. The train is leaving in twenty minutes and I have to be aboard. I'll call you once I'm out of boot camp."

"You can write letters during boot, can't you?"

"I don't think *I* can." Jake stared hard at him then. It almost felt to Stan as if Jake was giving him a secret message. "I'm going to make you proud of me, sir."

"I'm already proud."

"Bye, Dad."

"Good-bye, Jake. You take care of yourself, and you remember what it *really* means to be a good American."

"I understand you. Believe me, I do."

Before Jake could say more, the screen dissolved. The former Detention Center officer reappeared and congratulated Stan on the news.

"Yes," Stan said distractedly. "Thank you."

Shortly thereafter he left the Rite Aid store. His tank was ordered out of the front line. The Chinese storm had stopped for the moment. Now it sounded as if the Behemoths were going to be regrouped again. That was a good idea. What about Jake, though? What had all that been about? Stan didn't know,

423

and he wondered what branch of the service Jake would enter. At least it wasn't the Militia. They were good people, but their training and equipment were always substandard.

Stan headed for the young driver and his jeep. Jose would want to hear this. All the Behemoth tankers would, those who had survived the terrible battle.

WASHINGTON, D.C.

Several days after Stan spoke to his son, Anna Chen listened as the briefing major spoke in the underground bunker.

There had been a massive shift in Chinese behavior. It was clear the Chinese offensive in southern California had halted. Through drone-intel and other sources, they learned key formations had already left the area and were headed for the Second or Third Front.

"Are the Chinese going to attack in Texas?" the President asked.

"We're not sure if it's Texas or New Mexico," General Alan said. "What does seem clear is that the Chinese and the South Americans are planning a summer offensive somewhere there and sometime soon."

"What about the Germans?" Sims asked.

"We expect them to attack, too, yes sir."

"In Florida?"

"That would seem the likely candidate, sir, although we cannot rule out Georgia or Louisiana. If it were me, I would attack Louisiana while the PAA and the SAF assaults Texas. They could help each other."

"That would also allow us to concentrate against them in one area," Sims said. "It would help us."

"There are pros and cons for them no matter what they decide," Alan said.

"If they even do decide to attack," Sims said.

"I'm certain they will attack, sir. Every indicator points that way."

"What about California? Are they done with it for now?"

"That's an interesting question, sir. They smashed irreplaceable equipment on our side and killed and captured far too many of our soldiers. What's more, Los Angeles and the Bay Area are under a state of siege. The fight isn't over there, just the intensity has receded. Yet they could resume their offensives at any time."

"We'll be better prepared if they do," Sims said.

"In some ways, yes sir," Alan said.

The President tapped his computer stylus on the table. "What are your recommendations for the state?"

"We should shift forces to the Bay Area and drive the Chinese into the sea," Alan said. "Los Angeles can hold for now. It's excellent defensive terrain with even better defensive areas behind it. I mean the Grapevine Pass in particular."

"Can we spare the troops elsewhere to use in the Bay Area?"

"Maybe the right kind of troops, sir," Alan said. "I'm thinking about the Behemoth tanks."

"No. That's the wrong kind of terrain for them."

"Then—"

"Here's what I believe," Sims said. "I was thinking about this last night." He grinned. "You used historical evidence before, telling me about World War I. I think it was about the Battle of the Somme."

"Yes sir."

"The British and French attacked Turkey during World War I. It was called the Gallipoli Campaign."

"I've heard of it."

Sims nodded. "In all, the British sent 410,000 soldiers there and the French 70,000. They were tied down on a narrow strip of land, never able to achieve anything other than dying in ill-coordinated attacks against the Turks. Those badly needed troops could have been used elsewhere to great advantage to help hasten the defeat of Kaiser Germany. Instead, because of a number of unforeseen problems, the British and French jailed themselves on the Gallipoli Peninsula with the Turkish Army acting as their wardens. I'm wondering if we might stymie the Chinese in a similar way, at least those attempting to capture the Bay Area."

"You mean lure them into staying there, useless? That could be one way of looking at it," Alan said. "The enemy troops also tie down our men there."

"We would have to leave soldiers there anyway to guard the Bay Area from other amphibious assaults."

General Alan became thoughtful. "Your theory might work, sir, provided the Chinese don't land too many more troops. I still think we should use the Behemoths to drive them into the sea."

The President tapped the stylus. "I think one thing is clear. If we're talking about pulling the Behemoths out of Los Angeles, it means we think the great Chinese offensive into California has stopped."

"Clearly, for the moment, it has."

"It was the commandos who bought this success," Anna said. "Without Nung driving them, the enemy shifted their strategy."

The President and General Alan, along with everyone else in the chamber, regarded her.

President Sims nodded. "I concur with your analysis, Ms. Chen. It was a good idea and it worked. We're not out of the woods yet, however. There are still millions of enemy soldiers waiting to invade our country. We're going to need more ideas like that. In fact, Ms. Chen—"

Sims glanced at Director Levin. "I'm taking her away from you."

It almost seemed as if Levin was going to shrug. Instead, he said, "If you so desire, sir."

"I do desire. Ms. Chen, I would like to make you a member of my staff. Does that fit with your approval?"

"Yes, Mr. President," Anna said. This was wonderful.

"We'll speak after the meeting."

"Yes, sir," she said.

Sims glanced around the room. "We've stopped the Californian Offensive. It will likely continue as a siege, but we can deal with that for now. Now I want us to concentrate on how to meet the next Chinese thrust in other areas of the country and to look into ways of stopping any Germen Dominion offensives. We don't know much time we have,

426

days or weeks, but we'd better start thinking hard about these things."

The President clicked his stylus onto the table. "First, I would like to look into the possibility of…"

The End

Made in the USA
Lexington, KY
17 August 2014